# DARK CORNERS

MICHAEL BRAY

Copyright © 2016 Michael Bray
The moral right of Michael Bray to be identified as the author of this work has been asserted in accordance with the Copyright, Designs and Patents Act, 1988. All rights reserved. No part of this publication may be reproduced or transmitted in any form or by any means, electronic or mechanical, including photocopy, recording or any information storage and retrieval system, without permission in writing from the publisher.
A CIP catalogue record for this book is available from the British Library
All rights reserved.

"Fear cuts deeper than swords."

— George R.R. Martin, A Game of Thrones

## THE PRANK

I'm an old man now and I think I can finally pluck up the courage to talk about the day that Snoddy, Denton and me killed that kid. People say that time heals, but I don't buy into that. If anything it makes things worse. You may wonder if I'm sorry for what happened and I can't stress enough that I am. Not a day passes without me thinking of that day and wishing I could turn back the clock and change things. But I was just a kid, and at fifteen sometimes you do things just to keep up with the pack, and not to look like the sensible one. Stupid now I know, but back then it made sense. Carrying this around with me for so many years should have been burden enough, but I think I always knew deep down that it wasn't and I was right. Because now he's back and he's coming for me. I ask myself if I'm afraid and I suppose I am, although to be honest, I think I deserve what's coming to me. Ever since then, bad luck has followed me around like an invisible ball and chain tethered to my ankle. My mother and father were killed in a car accident when I was eighteen. My first wife eloped to Australia with my one-time best friend. And of course my sister Tina, Who went crazy and then made a miraculous escape from her room at the funny farm, disappearing to who knows where.

Because of this, I have done all I can to keep my family close, protected from something I guess I always knew was coming.

I can hear him scratching around behind the walls and even though I ran away from my home when he first found me I knew it was only temporary. I am writing this from a hotel room eighty miles away in Southend and he still tracked me down. I know now that there is no way to outrun it or escape it. My best guess is that they helped him to find me, the dark things. The rats and the spiders and the festering things that live in the black, wet places of the world. He's one of them now you see, or so I suspect. Kept alive by what? The desire for revenge? The pain of betrayal? Who can say for sure? All I know is that he's here and I'm too old and too tired to run anymore.

That day, the day when it happened had been hot. A

rare English summer without unseasonal wind and rain. We Brits always make the most of summers like that, but the flip side is that boredom soon sets in, especially for restless kids with no school to go to. Snoddy was hanging around at mine, the two of us wasting the day away when he asked if I had heard of the old Fisherman House. I had, of course, everyone had. It was one of those places where everyone had a ghost story to tell, usually one that came from a friend of a friend, or from somebody who knew someone who knew someone else who used to live there. That kind of deal. It was, of course, the usual schoolyard bullshit, an urban legend. I looked at Snoddy and his skinny face was taut and determined and serious. I knew that in his mind he was already concocting some scheme or other as he watched me indifferently and waited for my answer.

You wanna go break in?' he asked me, flashing his pierced lipped, crooked-toothed grin. I didn't, not really but I couldn't say that. I was already in deep shit playing hooky when I should have been at school in double English, and I was technically grounded and didn't want to push my luck anymore. But you can't say that when you are a kid, not when the pressure of expectation in heaped onto you by your friends. I wanted to say no, but how could I? So I reluctantly agreed.

We picked Denton up on the way. People didn't like Denton. The other kids said he was fat, but he was just big for his age, with a huge barrel chest and broad shoulders. He played rugby for the school team and although at a glance he did look a little chubby, he was fitter than most of the other kids in our year group. They would never say it to his face, of course, Denton had a documented mean streak and a bit of a reputation as a bully, and I think that without him driving things along that things might have been different on that day, but right from the off as the three of us walked to the old house I could tell that he was itching for a confrontation. You could sense it in the air if that makes any sense. I think Snoddy felt it too because there was a strained silence as we walked past houses ripe with the smells of fresh cut grass and the meaty charred smell of barbeques going full tilt. I hate that smell now, the smell of summer. It always makes me think of the rats. And him.

The Fisherman house had been empty for over thirty years, and depending on who you talked to had either been the site of a grisly murder of the home of a crazy old man who kidnapped local kids which he then raped, dismembered and ate. I never believed any of it, though, and although I knew it was just a building—bricks and mortar it still gave me a chill when I first set eyes on it. The grass out front was hip high and a sickly faded yellow. And the house itself was a huge ugly stain in what was otherwise a nice area. Its walls seemed to bow inwards, and the windows were covered by graffiti filled wooden boards. It certainly looked the part and despite my disbelief, I could imagine that any one of the stories made up about it could be true. Suddenly I regretted going, and I wondered if Denton and Snoddy felt the same. I thought Snoddy might have called it off given the chance, but not Denton. He had a look in his eyes that said he was going to go ahead with it no matter what. With our young boys pride on the line, and none of us prepared to speak up and state our concerns, we went on.

We saw Steven as we neared the dilapidated porch. He was sitting cross-legged in the sun, writing in an old notepad. Denton never liked Steven. The two had a history, and Denton made it his own personal mission to make Steve's life hell for the last couple of years at school. I glanced over to Denton whose eyes lit up when he saw the subject of his tireless bullying sitting there alone. Steve was brushed thin with long gangly arms and a thick greasy mop of hair. He wore thick old fashioned horn-rimmed glasses which fit him badly, and he was always pushing them back up his face when they slid down his nose. He was one of those kids that always wore the cheap brands of clothes, the ones who always turned up for school with his shirt dirty or un-ironed. You could almost smell the poverty on him, but he always did well in class.

'What are you doing out here?' Denton asked, flashing a crocodile grin.

Steve looked up and didn't answer his Adam's apple bobbing. You could see how scared he was.

'Nothing, just researching the house for my website.'

'What website?' Snoddy asked as he absently pulled the grass out in huge clumps.

'Urban exploring, I write about abandoned places like this and review them. We have a good online community.'

He flashed a hopeful grin and then realised that nobody was smiling.

'Geek. Lemmie see.' Denton said as he snatched the notebook. I could see that Steve wanted to object, but fear had long been burned into him not to fight the bullying, but to go with it and hope that it wouldn't be too bad. He looked at me then, and I gave the briefest of nods. I never had a problem with him see. I mean don't get me wrong, we were never friends, we never moved within the same circles, but I never had anything against him. My eyes flicked to Denton, who was leafing through the notebook. I could tell by the look in Steve's eyes that he didn't know what Denton intended to do. And neither did I.

'This is garbage. No mention of the good stuff like the murders, or the dude who fucked all those kids. Maybe I should tear this up and you can start again eh geek?' Panic flashed in Steve's eyes and I saw that Denton meant to do it.

'Hey Denton, leave him be. He's not harming anyone.' I said to him, giving him my best stern look. I knew he could probably take me in a fight if it came to it, but I was good at bluffing, and had somehow gathered a bit of a reputation as a tough nut to crack (although where that came from I don't know). I didn't try too hard to dispel it, though, as it made my school life easier to deal with. Either way, Denton backed down, tossing the notepad to the porch where it raised a puff of dust.

'I was just fuckin' with him. Relax.' He said, glaring at me. I was afraid of the look in his eyes but forced myself to meet his gaze.

There was an awkward silence as we stood there, nobody quite sure what to do next. It was Snoddy who made the first move. He hopped up the three porch steps to the door and tried the handle.

'Fuckers locked.' He said, pulling his cigarettes out of his pocket and offering one to Denton, who took the offering wordlessly. The pair lit up and then Denton regarded the door.

'Course it's locked. Too many crack heads and winos around. Let me try.'

Denton puffed his chest out and brushed past Steven, who I saw flinch. He rattled the door, and even tried shoving it open with his shoulder, but as old and tired as the door looked it wouldn't budge.

'What about the windows' I said, half hoping that there would be no way in and we could give up on the entire thing. I had that horrible feeling in my gut, not déjà vu, but that light, giddy feeling that sometimes comes with knowing something isn't right. Snoddy gave the windows a quick once over and tugged at the boards.

'No chance, those fuckers are solid.' he said as he

joined Denton in sitting on the porch and smoking.

'That's that then' I said, hoping that I sounded casual.

'Suppose so' said Denton, glaring at Steve as if it was his fault.

We would have left then, and none of what came later would have happened if Steve hadn't spoken up. I think maybe he was just trying to win us over, or maybe even make friends. But whatever his reasons he pushed his glasses up his sweaty face and looked at me and said he knew a way in.

'Go on then. Don't leave us hanging. Tell us.' Ordered Denton.

He did.

Ten minutes later we had squeezed our way through one of the kitchen windows at the back where the board had pulled away. Steve was with us although he hadn't wanted to come. I could see that all over his face but Denton had insisted, and reluctant to avoid a potential beating he had agreed. The four of us stood breathless in the gloomy dilapidated kitchen. The inside of the house was bare, and sunlight diffused dust motes hung heavy, making it hard to breathe. Graffiti covered the walls, some of it colourful, some vile. Hundreds of orange tipped drug needles littered the floor and the air was acrid with the stench of rot and urine.

'Watch your step' Denton said as we made our way through the kitchen.

'Fuckin' smack needles everywhere.' Snoddy muttered under his breath.

'You think there's anybody here?' Denton asked with a huge Cheshire cat grin.

'Could be. We got in easy enough.' I said, still unable to shake the horrible feeling in my stomach.

We walked into the living room. There was a huge graffiti mural on the wall of a woman being raped by a multi-headed snake, and more evidence of drug use. Several empty beer cans were stacked in a neat pyramid in the corner, and there was an old rolled up sleeping bag covered in a thin layer of black mould, which spread like spider webs across the corners of the walls.

'What now then' Snoddy asked, his face looking waxy and tired in the diffused light of the room.

Denton grinned and kicked the can stack, sending them clattering to the ground.

'Fuck's sake Denton!' Snoddy hissed as we held our breaths and waited to see if some crazed crack head would come racing down the steps or out of one of the adjoining rooms. I realised then that ghosts were the least of our problems, and the main danger was from the living. But nobody came. No crazy old man, no spirits, no crack-crazed lunatics.

'Suppose that answers the question. It's just us. Let's take a look around' Denton said as he walked off towards the stairs. So that's what we did. We split up and explored. There wasn't much to see. It was a typical old, empty house. No ghosts, no slimy things crawling around in the shadows. Just damp, and rot, and Rats.

There were a lot of rats. They were everywhere. You would walk into a room and they would scatter, squeezing through gaps in the walls or under old husks of forgotten furniture. Some of them were big ones too. I saw one that was the size of a tomcat, somehow squeezing its huge soft body between two of the broken kitchen cabinets. I could tell that Steve didn't like the rats. You could see it on his face. Whenever he saw one he would grimace and shy away, and I think I even heard him let out a small yelp when we found a nest in the corner of the bathroom, the blind newborns like plump, pink slugs as they squirmed in their nest which was burrowed into a long forgotten and filthy mattress that had at some point been dumped into the bath. I was leafing through old newspapers that dated back to the 70's that I found in an old cabinet in one of the upstairs bedrooms when Snoddy and Denton shuffled over to me. I didn't like the look on their faces. They wore matching grins of lions about to eat a mouse.

'We are gonna play a prank on Steve. We need you to help out though' Snoddy said through a grin showing too many of his not quite white teeth.

I asked them to leave me out of it and to go easy on Steve since he showed us how to get into the building in the first place, but there was no convincing them. It seemed that Denton had somehow rubbed off on Snoddy, and I knew I was fighting a losing battle in trying to talk them out of it. I asked why they needed me anyway, and why they couldn't do it alone.

They explained their plan and I began to laugh too. Despite the horrible icy feeling in my belly I laughed and went along with it because that's what I would have been expected to do. Even now I hate myself for that. But things had already gone too far for me to back out. I often ask myself why I didn't just say no, but hindsight is a wonderful thing. It's hard to explain, but I felt somehow obliged to go along with it, despite my own misgivings.

Anyway, long story short we set it up. The plan was that I would make Steve come upstairs to see some nonexistent but amazing discovery and as he came down the hall, Denton and Snoddy were going to leap out of one of the bedrooms and give him a fright. It was silly kids' stuff—but we were silly kids and that made it all right. I went downstairs to look for Steve, who was perched on the arm of a tired old sofa in the living room and scrawling into his notebook. I felt a pang of sorrow and guilt as I approached him.

'Steve, come check out what I found upstairs you have to see it to believe it.' I said, sounding as excited as I could. Part of me hoped that he would see it coming, that he might sense it was a trick and refuse, but as I said earlier, he and I had never had a problem and since he had no reason to disbelieve me, he followed. I felt sick as I climbed the stairs, knowing what was coming and that in all probability poor Steve would group me in with the large group of people who picked on or bullied him and made his life a living hell.

It makes me sad to write it down and I can feel the tears welling up in my tired old eyes. I know I need to finish, though, the sound in the walls is getting louder and I suspect I don't have long left.

I walked down the upstairs hallway, Steve just behind me. I was hoping he would see the funny side when it happened, but when it did it caught me by surprise too, because they came not out of the bedroom at the end of the hallway as we had agreed, but out of the bathroom. I remember it well. Snoddy wild eyed, Denton grinning like some kind of snarling animal. They carried a box between them and threw its contents at Steve, screaming as they did so. What happened next took seconds but I remember it in horrific, slow detail.

I remember the contents of the box landing on Steve and feeling disgusted at the sight of those fat, pink newborn rats as they hit his chest and face. I remember Steve screaming and lurching back, too far back and slamming into the old, rotten upstairs bannister rail, which broke under his weight.

I remember the look of joy at a successful prank that filled Snoddy and Denton's face start to transform into a look of sick horror as they realised what was happening. I remember reaching out to grab Steve, trying to stop his fall, but he was wild eyed and frightened, brushing his hands at his t-shirt and trying to get away from the baby rats which squealed in a freakish, high register that I have never been able to forget.

I remember Steve falling down the steps, rolling on his back and landing in a heap on the floor, and then I remember the rats.

The rats streaming from the downstairs walls like a thick, black moving carpet they streamed towards the distressed newborns in an effort to protect. I remember meeting Steve's gaze from the upper landing, or at least imagine I do, and remember his terrified, betrayed grimace as the rats covered him, biting and tearing, and smothering him until he was no more than a screaming, thrashing carpet of filthy black fur. I couldn't say how many there were. Hundreds? Thousands? It's impossible to say.

We could have saved him, could have helped but as we looked at each other there on the upstairs landing in the gloomy half-light, we ran. Down the steps two at a time and through the mass of rats, that parted to allow us to escape then closed behind us as they continued to defend the newborns. I'm sure by then that Steve had stopped screaming. I remember seeing his notebook, still perched on the arm of the sofa where just five minutes earlier Steve had been minding his own business and gathering information for his website.

I would love to say we went for help and came back to rescue Steve, who suffered only minor injuries and we all lived happily ever after, but that would be a lie, and I suspect this story will have an altogether more grim closure. We didn't go back, and we didn't tell anyone. I feel sick to think about it now and hate myself for being such a coward. The three of us never spoke much again after that day. Perhaps through shared guilt or shame, we drifted apart. Steve was reported missing a few days later. A huge deal was made of it in the news and in the local press and as the days passed I was unable to handle the guilt, so I made an anonymous call, covering the handset with a scarf to disguise my voice and advised the police to check out the old Fisherman house. They did, and I was relieved because at least it would be over and his family would be able to rest easy. But he wasn't there. They found his notebook and the broken bannister rail, but no sign of Steve or the rats by all accounts. I was tempted to go back there, to see for myself and even went so far as to make it to the porch when I was seventeen, but the rats stopped me. Not physically you understand, but I knew they were there and as I stood on the porch I was sure I could hear them, moving around in the walls, the same sound I can hear now.

That was almost seventy years ago, and in that time I don't think I have slept a full night without the nightmares or the guilt interfering. But it makes no difference. He's back. He's back and he has brought them, the rats. Like a ghastly pied piper, he has led them to me, to the walls of this cheap hotel room. The Fisherman house was demolished twenty years ago, and a multi storey car park stands where it once was. I wonder where they went from there, Steve and the rats. Where did they hide until the time was right to come for us?

He got Snoddy a couple of years ago. He had led an indistinct life, working minimum wage jobs and had developed a pretty serious alcohol addiction for his troubles. He never spoke of that day as far as I know, but I hear that when he was particularly out of it, he would mutter to himself about the sounds of the rats, and how he would never have enough traps to get them all. They found him in his bed with his eyes wide open and a look of terror on his face. They said it was a heart attack but I know better. I think Steve came for him and when Snoddy saw what he had become, how he looked now after so many years festering in the dark— well. I think it was enough to stop his clock right there and then.

I could have almost passed his death off as coincidence— at least until Denton called me out of the blue last week. His voice was familiar but strange. It wavered as he spoke and it came in a high, shrill register as he whispered down the phone to me. Of us all, he had fared the worst. His aggressive nature had led him to crime, and as the story often goes he progressed from small time car thief to drug dealer to murderer. He shot an old man in a clumsy carjacking and was jailed for twenty five years and ended up serving sixteen of them, getting out apparently reformed and fit to rejoin society. I hadn't spoken to him since school of course, but I remember seeing his picture in the paper when he was arrested, and even though he was much older than the boy I once knew, he still wore that haunted, glassy expression I remember from that day in the house. When he called me I could barely understand his manic whispers and I didn't hear much before they became screams. After that, all I could hear was the high pitched drone of hundreds, or maybe even thousands of rats. I definitely heard something speak, although it wasn't Denton. The voice was thick and wet and sounded as if it had a mouth full of fur. It said had something exciting to show me, and that I would have to see it to believe it. And I do believe it. The scratching in the walls is loud now and I fear that I'm out of time. He has come to get his own back and I deserve it. I guess it's true that you reap what you sow and it's ok because I know I deserve it.

It's time.

They're here.

## YURPLES LAST DAY

Freddy wondered what he had done to deserve such a run of bad luck. He had just turned fifty-one, and for his entire life, he had done his best to entertain people, to make them happy. It wasn't always easy, not anymore. He had arthritis in his left knee, which meant that the bumps and pratfalls that always raised such a laugh legitimately hurt him now. He sat in his dressing room and took a long drink of Jack Daniels. No glass for Freddy. He preferred it straight from the bottle these days.

Glancing at his reflection in the large mirror, Freddy wondered what the hell had happened to his life. He didn't know where the time had gone, or how the years had passed him by without him noticing. One day he was twenty with a head full of ambition and aspirations of success. In the blink of an eye, he was here. A bitter old man with nothing to look forward to but biting the big one.

Flicking his eyes to the clothes rail in the corner he scowled at the green and blue spotted shirt and red dungarees and grimaced at the thought of slipping his feet into those oversized shoes. He wanted to scream, to reach out to his reflection and shake it by the shoulders and ask it what the hell it was doing with its life but he knew it was too late for that. Much too late. As the saying went, he had made his bed and now he would have to lie in it.

Some might say he was lucky. After all, he had travelled the world and wasn't tied to a standard nine to five job. But the grass wasn't always greener on the other side. The pay was poor, and performing the same tired routine every night had long ago grown to be monotonous. Then there was the hectic travel schedule meaning he was constantly moving from place to place, city to city, and town to town. He had no friends, not real honest to god friends he could just call up and shoot the shit with. Of course, they called this an extended family, but he had never bought into that. He despised these people he worked with. He had never had a place to call his own and in the end, it had destroyed his marriage. His wife had been unable to cope with the lonely nights spent in an empty house, bringing up their two children on her own, and who could blame her?

He took another long slug of the sour whisky,

grimacing as he wiped his mouth with the back of his arm. Yes indeed. Who could blame her? What else did he expect to happen when he wasn't there to stop her falling for the affections of another man? And not a soldier or tennis player, either, not someone he might have been able to accept as better than him. Oh, no. she fell for an accountant. A Fucking accountant. He shouldn't have been surprised. She needed someone who could provide the things she needed. The things she had expected from him. Someone stable, with a good job, sociable hours and steady income. That's what she needed and when she had tired of his excuses and promises that things were about to get better that's what she went out and found. He had heard through the grapevine they had recently married, and although he knew he shouldn't hold it against her, as it was his fault, he did. The split had been amicable, if cold and distant, but he still felt a deep, simmering, hatred towards her for leaving him alone in the world. That was the problem; people didn't understand how hard this job was. His job was to be funny, to make people laugh even when he felt like screaming on the inside. Try keeping a stupid smile on your face next time you get divorced, or even better, when your entire life falls apart. The long and short of it was that he was tired. Tired of life, tired of the routine. Tired of feeling so…tired.

Even the routine, the one he used to get so much joy from performing, the comedy falls, the water shooting Lilly on his jacket, all of it had long ago lost its charm and had become something he detested, leaving him feeling devoid and empty inside. He opened the desk drawer and took out a handful of pills, and swallowed them with another shot of JD.

God, what a mess.


Pills for everything. Pills to keep him supple. Pills to keep him pain free. Pills to keep him sane. Although he had stopped taking that one. The bottle was at the back of the drawer. They made him sleepy, and in his line of work, he had to be alert. Nobody likes a woozy clown. He reached further into the drawer and pulled out the green box with the red lid that had been on the road as long as he had. Its casing was chipped and beaten, and one of the hinges was loose but it still served its purpose. He flipped open the lid, revealing the vast array of greasepaints. Bright reds, blues, and greens, yellows and purples.

How much of this shit had he plastered onto his face over the years? He couldn't even begin to guess. Taped to the upper inner lid of the box was a reference photo of himself, although this was a younger, less cynical version—one still hoping for a big showbiz break, one with a sparkle in his eye and the happy ' I can do anything' grin. He grimaced and wondered why he still kept it there. It served no purpose but as a constant reminder of his failed life. It wasn't even as if he needed the photo anyway. He could apply his makeup with his eyes closed. White base, huge red and yellow smile, oversized purple eyebrows and red nose. Easy when you have been doing it every day for the last thirty-four years.

But not today.

Today he was going to try something new. He stood and removed his shirt, trying to ignore the weight he had gained. He could try to pass it off as something coming with age, but he knew it was his dependency to drink that had caused him to develop a large overhanging gut, which gave him a flabby, ape-like appearance. No longer able to stand to look at himself, he pulled on the garish bright shirt and stepped into the dungarees. He glanced at the shoes but couldn't face them yet. He hated the way they felt on his feet and the way they made him feel like he was walking underwater. His stomach growled and he realised that he hadn't eaten again. He rarely did anymore and as a result, the alcohol had gone straight to his head. He knew he would be fine, though. He was, after all, a professional. He sat back at his dresser and looked at himself. The show had started. He could hear the muffled sound of the band strike up and the voice of the ringmaster as he made the initial introductions. Checking his watch, he calculated how long until his section of the show. Still twenty minutes yet. Plenty of time to get ready.

These big top gigs weren't too bad. Always guaranteed a decent turnout, and because tonight was sold out everyone would get paid which wasn't always the case. He could hear the muted sounds of laughing and cheering and began to feel the niggling self-doubt he couldn't seem to shake these days. He no longer cared for the crowds. The stupid adults jeering and booing whilst their even more stupid kids whooped and laughed at the fat, washed up old clown.

Well, we'll see who laughs last tonight.

As much as he hated the crowds, they were heaven compared to the private bookings he was forced to take to make ends meet. The birthday parties where it was him alone in some stranger's house acting like a performing monkey in front of a room full of snivelling fucking kids. Do a trick, monkey. Fall over again, monkey. Tell us a joke, monkey. Worse still was when the annoying little fucker's parents had grossly miscalculated the short window where kids still found clowns funny. Those were the worst of all. The kids would just sit there and watch him impassively as he went through the motions of his routine. They would invariably end with everyone involved feeling awkward and praying for a quick end to proceedings.

He began to apply the white greasepaint, his hands moving with expert precision. For as much as he hated it, at least it went some way to covering the deep lines which had become etched onto his face over the years. They were the undeniable signs of growing old. He heard an audience wide ahhhhhh in the distance and knew Stavros was up on the trapeze doing his death defying and legitimately impressive act. Not long to go now, then Showtime. Giving the white basecoat time to dry, he stood and picked up his oversized patchwork jacket and slipped it on, and, unable to put it off any longer, slipped his feet into those horrible, uncomfortable giant shoes. He saw himself in the mirror and was repulsed, and a more than a little embarrassed. He knew he was way too old for this, and felt ashamed and self-conscious He sat again, taking another great drink from the half-empty bottle then took out the red greasepaint and drew a large mouth shape across his lips and cheeks, filling it in efficiently. His next step on a routine day would be to take out the yellow to draw onto the outer edge of the red, but not today. Instead, He took out the black and filled in all of the inner parts of the oversized mouth, leaving it looking like a wide-open maw. Next, he took out the yellow paint pencil and drew in twin rows of sharp yellow teeth. Next came the black paint, which he blotted around his eyes. The left first, then the right. He was satisfied as he stared out between the twin pools of black. It looked good, better than that happy go lucky smiling crap. He looked like a grinning demon. More cheering from the crowd now, this meant that Stavros had defied the odds yet again and survived his latest feat of skill. Good for him. Not bad at all for a wife beating paedophile.

The choice of wig was next, and important to complete the overall look. He tried on the green but it didn't look right with his new makeup so he plumped for the red, a huge afro made of cheap cotton that made his skin itch.

Satisfied, he looked at himself in the mirror and at last, he could bear his reflection. He now looked on the outside how he now felt on the inside. And felt the giddy excitement that had always manifested before he went out to perform, and until today had been absent for some time. He thought it must be because he had something new for the masses tonight, something spectacular. There was just enough time to make his final preparations. He took the note out of his pocket and taped it to his dressing room mirror. It would answer most of the questions that would be asked. The ones it didn't they would have to figure out for themselves. He was almost ready, with just one more thing left to do.

He walked to the desk in the corner and filled his pockets with the props for his performance.

Extendable boxing glove.

Water squirting flower.

Handshake buzzer.

He felt the part now and was ready to perform. He

slipped the belt full of ammunition around his waist, and then the bag of hand grenades over his shoulder, making sure he could easily access them. The M16 and sawn off shotgun were already loaded, and he filled the remaining pockets of his jacket with as much extra ammo as he could carry. There was a knock on the door, then a voice, gone as quickly as it arrived.

'Yurple. Showtime.'

And so it was. The crowd was waiting now and his theme was playing. Despite it all, he managed a smile as he slipped the handgun into the waistband of his pants, and then picked up the M16 and the shotgun. One in each hand. That was the thing with clowns, he thought to himself as he walked to the centre ring. Nobody ever takes them seriously.

Perhaps today, they will.

## NO REST FOR THE WICKED

*We Serial Killers are your sons, we are your husbands, we are everywhere. And there will be more of your children dead tomorrow.*
- *Ted Bundy*

Roberts knew he was going to die. It didn't scare him; instead, he felt a liberated sense of freedom that made the long and tedious hours in his cell bearable. Huntsville prison was the oldest state penitentiary in Texas. The red brick building where Roberts was spending his last hours was known as 'The Walls' and was a three story imposing looking structure with a clock on the front. (As if time mattered in such a place) It could pass for a school, if not for the bars on the windows and the large sign outside proclaiming its purpose.

Huntsville Unit

Texas State Penitentiary

Est. 1848

Not only was Huntsville the oldest prison in the United States, it also boasted the country's most active execution chamber. Over four hundred inmates had checked in and never checked out. There were always a few who managed to slip through the cracks and would get a last minute reprieve. Anton Harris, who had protested his innocence for the murder of his sister and her friends after a drug fuelled night out had been strapped down and was about to be given the needle when the call came giving him a stay. His relief didn't last for long, as his appeal was thrown out and two weeks later he was strapped in for the second time, and this time, no call came and they gave him that little cocktail of lethal drugs that systematically shut down the organs and induced coma and death. They called it the most humane method, but Roberts thought that the idea of feeling your body shut itself down was pretty shitty no matter what kind of spin that was put on it. If it were up to him, he would choose the chair. A quick jolt and done. Your brain was turned to mush before you knew anything about it. Unfortunately, 'old sparky' had been retired year's earlier, so lethal injection it was. He had been brought to the walls earlier that morning, and with his execution scheduled at six sharp, it only left him with a few hours to live. This was the time when an inmate might beg, plead, and protest his innocence. But not Roberts. They had him bang to rights. Guilty as charged. During the first year or two spent in prison, he had to undergo a psychological evaluation. He had a series of discussions with a wiry, nervous looking doctor called Jones. Roberts didn't like the way Jones moved, the way his eyes darted and flicked from side to side as he asked his questions. He was also a nose breather. You know the type—the ones who wheeze and whistle out of their nostrils instead of the mouth. Roberts thought it was a good job he was already insane or that sound alone could have been enough to send a man over the edge.

'Why do you choose to kill?' Jones had asked as he peered over his glasses. Roberts paused to consider, and there was silence apart from Jones's maddening nasal wheeze. He considered making up some elaborate story to justify his actions but in the end, he decided to be honest and hoped that the simplicity of his answer would shock this judgmental little man.

'Because I like the way it feels.' Roberts said, adding a sneer he hoped would unsettle Jones.

'You like the power it gives you?'

'Yes.'

'And what about your victims. Do you feel anything for them?'

Another pause for consideration. More nasal wheezing.

'No.'

Jones nodded and wrote something down.

Snort wheeze. Snort wheeze.

'Tell me about your family—'

Roberts was lunging over the table before he realised he was going to do it. The guards reacted, but not fast enough to stop him. He remembered laughing at the way Jones screamed. It was high pitched like a schoolgirl. The guards pulled him off and beat him with their truncheons, but not before he had managed to get his fingers up Jones's nostrils and tear away his nose. Roberts laughed as he was dragged away and watched the screaming doctor as he tried to hold the jagged remains of his face in place. There would be no more psychological evaluations after that. He had been placed in solitary confinement and had remained there until his transfer earlier in the day.

The cell door at the end of the hallway creaked open and unhurried footsteps approached. Roberts remained where he was, stretched out on the bed—his six foot seven frame not made for standard issue prison beds. It was lucky for him he wouldn't be sleeping over. Officer Remy approached the bars. He was a flabby man who seemed to be on the verge bursting out of his uniform, which was stretched to breaking point across his immense stomach. He was short, standing a shade over five feet. His skin was freckled and he sported a carrot coloured crew cut. Every time Roberts saw him, he was sweating and had flushed cheeks. Remy watched Roberts through harsh little eyes, which, combined with his huge jowls and downturned mouth, gave him the look of a bulldog chewing on a mouthful of wasps. He looked flustered and angry, but Roberts noted that even here Remy was walking with his usual arrogant swagger, swinging his key chain and giving the thousand yard stare.

'Looks like you have friends in high places, maggot.' Remy said in his southern drawl.

Roberts smiled but didn't stand. Maggot was Remy's standard insult. It was as cheap and clichéd as the man himself, though, and for that reason alone didn't sound so ridiculous coming from him.

'Hey, motherfucker, I'm talking to you.'

'Kiss your mother with that mouth officer Remy?'

Roberts said as he swung his legs off the bed and stood, sure to stretch to his full height. Even with the bars between them, he was pleased to see Remy take a cautionary step back.

'Sit your big ass down.' Remy said, suddenly less sure of himself. Roberts didn't sit. Instead, he folded his arms and waited.

'You just made history, maggot. You have a visitor. First time in the history 'o' this fine institution that a dead man walking has been allowed a visitor on execution day.'

Roberts kept his expression neutral, but inside he wondered who it could be. Family was out of the question— those bridges had long since been burned, and he had no friends.

'Who is it?'

'How the fuck should I know, retard? All I know is that y'all must have someone way up the food chain looking out for you, cus this is unheard of. Says his name is Elgin. Don't expect no stay 'o' execution though, freak. Visitor or no visitor you're gonna die today.'

Remy smiled, showing the immense gap between his front teeth. Roberts wondered how many people that Remy had accompanied here and seen put to death. He looked the type who would get a kick out of it, like the kind of man who would get off on those last desperate moments as a prisoner accepted the inevitable. He wondered if perhaps Remy was on the wrong side of the bars. Roberts held his silence, and realising that he wasn't going to get a reaction, Remy wiped the back of his forearm against his sweaty head. 'I'll bring him a chair and he can sit right here in the corridor. You have one hour.'

Five minutes later, Remy returned with a folding chair, which he set up in the hallway. As he left he shot a few venomous glances at Roberts who had seemingly severely screwed with the mojo of his working day. Roberts paced his tiny cell. Five steps from wall to wall. It was hardly the Ritz. He waited for another five minutes then heard the door creak open and echoing footsteps approach. His mystery visitor had arrived. He had expected someone older than the man who came and stood by the folding chair with the briefcase in his hand. He looked young, perhaps early twenties and had a strong jawline and piercing blue eyes. His hair was a short buzz cut and he wore an expensive looking black suit and white shirt. Without saying a word, he placed his briefcase on the floor and sat on the chair. Unlike Remy, he showed no fear of being in such close proximity to the bars. Roberts sat on the edge of the bed, and the two strangers were face to face.

'Good day, sir. My name is Joshua Elgin.' The visitor said.

Roberts didn't answer.

'You have been a prisoner of the state for how long Mr. Roberts?

'Six years.' As he said it, he marvelled at how much time had passed. It felt like longer. Elgin opened his briefcase and began to rummage around inside. Roberts busied himself by looking at his own warped reflection in the leather of Elgin's shoe. He had never seen such well-polished footwear. Having found what he was looking for Elgin turned back to Roberts, a brown folder in his hands.

'You are awaiting execution for the murder of…' Elgin referred to his folder, leafing through a page or two as he looked for the relevant information. 'Ninety seven people.' Elgin finished.

'Yeah, but between you and me, I did a hundred and two. They just couldn't find any bodies for the rest and I can't remember where I put them.'

He had expected this to shock Elgin, but he only

nodded as he adjusted his position on the chair.

'That's a lot of blood on your hands.'

'Not enough.' Roberts fired back.

Elgin opened his mouth to speak, but Roberts cut him off.

'Mr. Elgin—I'm not interested in your psychological evaluation, and I don't care what you have to say. The last person who quizzed me found himself needing a new nose so I advise you to be careful here.'

Roberts wasn't angry— he just got a kick out of frightening people. Elgin's response was unexpected. He laughed. Slightly annoyed, Roberts waited.

'I'm sorry for laughing, Mr. Roberts, but you're wrong. I am no psychologist, and for the record, I am aware of what happened to Doctor Jones.—No. my purpose here is different.'

Roberts wasn't sure what to make of Elgin. There was a calm assurance about him that he found to be slightly unsettling. Nevertheless, if Elgin's intention was to raise Roberts's curiosity, he had succeeded.

'So why are you here? I'm sure you can appreciate that time is precious today of all days.'

'Mr. Roberts. I'm here to offer you a job.'

'A job? I got a newsflash for you, buddy. In around five

hours' time, I'm a dead man.'

Elgin smiled and leaned closer.

'I can assure you I'm quite serious Mr. Roberts. Now please let me explain.'

He was about to tell Elgin to go fuck himself but he realised he had nothing better to do, and since Elgin was already better sport than Remy, He sat.

'Thank you.'

Elgin seemed very assured as he sat on the chair in the corridor. Many lesser men would have been intimidated, but Elgin took it all in his stride.

'Mr. Roberts, I represent an organisation that is always on the lookout for someone with your unique skills.'

'What skills?'

'I think you know, but to save time I'll come right out and say it. Violent sociopaths. Remorseless, honestly brutal killers, Mr. Roberts.

Roberts shook his head.

'This is the point where I'm supposed to tell you I'm misunderstood. Or that my mother made me do it right?'

'What you tell me is up to you. My job is to assess your suitability.

Roberts laughed. It was a strange sound in a place so

associated with death. 'A fuckin' job interview? This is classic! Don't be surprised if I don't make it to work tomorrow.'

'Don't think of it as an interview. It's more a case of checking your credentials.' Elgin said, still patient and calm.

'Alright, I'll bite. What are you looking for me to do? Contract killings like some kind of off the books hit man, some shit like that?'

'No. The role we are offering is far more rewarding.'

'No offence fella, but you are one crazy motherfucker'

'Perhaps I am.' Elgin said with a thin smile 'Even so, I would appreciate it if you would indulge me and allow me to explain.'

'Hell indulge away, this is the most entertainment I've had in years.'

'Very well.' Said Elgin as he referred to his notes.

'In the brief conversation you had with Dr. Jones, you told him you kill because you enjoy it.'

'That I did. I often wonder what happened to that wheezing prick.'

'He's dead.' Elgin said without looking up from his notes.

'Yeah? I hope it was painful.'

'He suffered a stroke, and even though he recovered he couldn't handle the indignity of having to be cared for by his wife who was suffering from severe depression.'

'So what happened?'

'One morning not long after the stroke he struggled out of bed and managed with his one working hand to load the .38 pistol they kept in the house for protection. His wife hadn't heard him get up. She was in the kitchen preparing breakfast.'

'He offed her right?'

Elgin nodded.

'He shot her in the back of the head. My best guess is that he didn't want to be without her when he took his own life.'

'I'm surprised she didn't hear him wheezing all the way across the room. I guess he did her and then put a bullet in his own brain?'

'Not exactly. I have no doubt that was his intention, but the recoil of the gun knocked it out of his hand and it wedged itself in the gap between the oven and refrigerator. He tried his best but with only one working hand and being as weak as he was, he couldn't get it out, so had to resort to other methods.'

'Tough break for old wheezy. What did he do?'

'He lived about a mile from the train tracks. He had to walk through a small stream and then through rough terrain to get there, but he was determined and that sometimes counts for a lot. All he had to do then was wait until the eleven o clock express came past and step in front of it. Problem solved.'

'Not a bad way to go. Quick. Final. No fucking around. I wonder if he felt it.' Roberts said, trying to visualise the scene.

'I know that there wasn't a huge amount left to identify him by. It was quite a mess.'

'I bet it made the little nose job I gave him seem like a paper cut.'

'Indeed.' Elgin offered another thin smile and continued. 'However we are becoming sidetracked, and I am aware of the time pressure we are under so if we could please continue.'

Roberts nodded. And why not? He couldn't put his finger on the reason why but he liked this kid. And keeping his mind occupied meant that he didn't have to think about the clock which was ticking away towards the end of his life.

'Ok Kid. You go ahead and ask your questions and I'll answer them if I can.'

Elgin closed the folder that had been open on his knees. 'You said you liked to kill. Has that always been the case?'

Roberts thought about it, something in him feeling obliged to tell the truth. 'I think so. I mean, I had thought about it without knowing I was thinking about it if you know what I mean. It was always there, buried and waiting for me to find it.'

'And what happened when you found it?'

'I think it found me if that makes any sense. I mean I always suspected that there was something different about me but I didn't know what it was, not until it happened.'

'Are you talking about the first kill?'

Roberts nodded, surprised just how good it felt to get it off his chest.

'Yes. Would it surprise you to know that I was just a boy when it happened?'

Elgin shook his head. 'Most serial murderers start at an early age.'

'You can tell by my appearance I'm not native to the United States.'

'No.' replied Elgin with a small smile. 'You were raised in Southern Italy.'

'I was born in Taranto' Roberts said. 'But raised is hardly the term I would use.'

'You had a troubled childhood?'

'Actually no, more of an ignored one. I was the youngest of six siblings. Three brothers and two sisters all older than I was. You could say I was the runt of the litter. I suppose they loved me in their own way, but if its affection you are talking about then no. there wasn't any that I remember. My father was born into money and we owned a small Vineyard that saw us live comfortably. Not rich you understand, but we did well enough. My memories of him are few. I remember that he was a big man with large workers hands and a booming voice. He ruled the house with an iron fist, although as he was often away working, it was my mother who would hand out the punishments. She was unpredictable, and her moods would swing from placid calm to fierce rage in an instant. We knew not to push her, but because I wanted to test the limits or more likely because I was craving attention, I pushed. I pushed and pushed and by the time I was nine I had already become segregated from my family.'

'Did you have friends?'

'No. I never understood why people craved

companionship from others. Even now I still find it a strange concept. Not that I was unhappy. I used to wander the fields surrounding our Vineyard. I would walk for miles just thinking, trying to make sense of the world. Even then I was searching for something, looking for anything to make me feel alive.'

'Killing?'

'No. Not yet. Although I discover death. The simplicity of it, the finality. It fascinated me. The opinion I formed as a child is still the one I have today if you can believe that. See, nature has it right. The human species is concerned with doing what it deems to be the 'right thing' and as a result, most people die miserable and unfulfilled. I think they have it wrong, though.'

'In what way?'

'Well to be blunt Mr. Elgin, Nature doesn't fuck around. Take any species apart from our own and you will see it. They kill to survive, they kill to protect. And who knows, maybe they even kill because they enjoy it. I like that idea. I think us as a species, humans I mean have that inherent desire to shrug off the pressures of society and just get back to basics. To kill and maim, rape and pillage, to brutalise our fellow man as an when our desires require. Humans are savage creatures, Mr.

Elgin, and when we allow that primal instinct to take over we can be deadly.' Roberts paused for a moment, rubbing his stubble-covered cheeks. 'I first killed when I was Ten years old. The seed had been planted a year before and the only reason for the delay was that opportunity had not presented itself. That word is the only one that matters to a killer, Mr. Elgin. Opportunity. We wait for it to appear and exploit it. For me, it happened whilst I was out on one of my long, directionless walks. I was maybe a mile and a half away from the vineyard and was by the narrow creek which cut across the boundary of our land. I wasn't doing anything out there, just wandering around and trying to keep myself occupied. It was a hot day and I was enjoying the heat on my back and the peace of the water as it gurgled past me when I heard a pained whimpering noise from somewhere ahead. The creek opened up a little further downstream, and there was a small sandy bank cut away from the dirt. There were two dogs by the water. They were mangy and covered in scars both old and new. One was on its side, its tongue lolling out of its mouth as it looked blankly ahead from milky cataract eyes. The other was beside it, its jaws clamped around the throat of its companion.

It growled low as it waited for its opponent to die. I watched in fascination from the edge of the water. It was nature at its purest. Life versus death. Strong versus weak. I watched the dog with the cataracts die. I saw the light fade from its eyes and its breathing slow and then stop. You know what the best thing was? When it was over the other dog walked away. He hadn't killed for food, or for survival. It had killed for fun.'

'And that set you off on your own journey?'

'I wouldn't say that. As I mentioned, it was always within me. But it planted a seed. And over the next year that seed grew until that first opportunity presented itself and I took that first tentative step.'

'Seed?' enquired Elgin.

Roberts nodded.

'I thought a lot about that dog in the following weeks. Even as a child I knew I wanted to do the same. I deconstructed the scene, reconstructed it, and replayed it over and over in my mind. Often I would pretend the dogs had been people. I think I knew on some level then that I would make a good killer, and like that dog, I would do it for my own enjoyment. Of course, there is every chance it wouldn't have come to the fore so early in my life if my childhood hadn't been so lonely, but when those who are meant to love neglect you, it gives someone—even a boy, time to think. And I thought about a lot. I suppose it was a question of waiting for the right time.'

'For the opportunity.' Elgin said.

'Exactly.'

'And that first kill. Tell me about that.'

Roberts hesitated. 'As much as I'm enjoying getting this off my chest, Mr. Elgin, you still haven't told me anything about this company you represent. I better not be wasting my time, here.'

If Elgin was flustered, he didn't show it. He simply offered that oily smile and regarded Roberts with his cool gaze. For some reason, Roberts shuddered.

'I appreciate your concern, Mr. Roberts, and I will explain in full when the time is right.'

'Now seems like a good time to me. Tomorrow wouldn't work I can tell you that, Elgin.'

Roberts chuckled at his own joke, but Elgin's face remained impassive. He leaned forwards then, his face close to the bars. He gestured to Roberts to come closer, and as he did he could smell the expensive cologne on Elgin's skin. Elgin spoke in a whisper—his eyes fierce and serious.

'What if I said you didn't have to die here today?' Roberts chuckled and wondered why he felt so uncomfortable and even a little afraid. He took a step away from the bars. 'Pardon my French, but I would say you were out of your fucking mind, Mr. Elgin.'

If Elgin heard him he didn't react, he continued speaking, his face still wearing his lizard smile.

'Perhaps I am. But in the end, what do you have to lose?'

Roberts had no answer, and like a great salesman, Elgin went on.

'I can offer you something, Mr. Roberts. Something that not only would you excel at but would enjoy immensely. And that's just the job itself.'

Elgin tilted his head, which intensified the reptilian mask that was his face. 'There are benefits. Everyone knows the best jobs have good fringe benefits, and if you will pardon my French Mr. Roberts. The fringe benefits of this job will blow your fucking mind.'

He leaned back in his chair, and the spell was broken. Lizard face was gone. He was just plain old Elgin in his snazzy black suit and neutral look on his face. Roberts wondered why he was more afraid of Elgin than he was of his pending death. Roberts licked his lips which were suddenly dry. 'Ok Elgin. I'll play along. But you better not be fucking with me or I swear I'll add you to my tally before they stick that damn needle in me.'

Elgin nodded but appeared to be unconcerned. It didn't help with Roberts's feeling of uneasiness. He's in control. Roberts thought as he composed himself. He's in control and knows that I will do as I'm told because he's right. I have nothing to lose and everything to gain. 'Ok Elgin. I'll talk a little more if that's what it will take. But it goes both ways. I want answers too.'

'And you will get them. Please, continue.'

Roberts sighed and closed his eyes, retrieving the memories he had long since locked away. 'In the spring of nineteen eighty-three, I killed my brother, Alessio. We had been sent to the well on the border of our property to fetch some water. We had Running water in the house of course, but my father was either a traditionalist or he liked giving us jobs to do so we would be kept busy. Alessio was three years older than I was, but I was taller than him by a couple of inches, and he hated that. Alessio was always the apple of my mother's eye. He had her eyes and my father's jawline and work ethic and although he wasn't the oldest, it seemed he could do no wrong, and so for that reason alone I had a particular hate for him which was amplified by my parent's indifference towards me. The well was around a mile and a half from the house and was in a dip between two hills. Over the brow and across a short field of long grasses our land ended and became farmland belonging to the Picenzi family. They had initially claimed ownership of the well but my father was adamant it belonged to us, and after a long legal battle that cost both families a lot of money, the ruling went in our favour and the Picenzi's were furious. They had since erected a large fence around the border of their property and although they were technically our neighbours, the families would never speak directly again. The strange thing was that we didn't even need that well. I think it must have been a matter of principal but either way it was deemed as ours.

Alessio had been on my case for the entire walk to that damn hole in the ground. He was preaching about being responsible and not letting the family down as if he were the disappointed parent. I reminded him he was only thirteen himself and could keep his shitty opinions to himself. His eyes had grown wide at my profanity, and I think we would have come to blows then had we not arrived at our destination. That well frightened me; I should get that out of the way straight away. I had seen it once before when it had been uncovered (my father had installed an iron grate over it the summer after it was legally made his). And like any curious child, I peered down and was horrified that I couldn't see the bottom. It smelled of rot, earth, and moss and when I dropped a stone, it echoed back with a deep bloop which I didn't like. The walls were smooth and cold to the touch and I always thought it was like an inky eye peering up into the world from some secret place.

Alessio had the bucket and I carried the two large containers which we were to fill, then take to the barn and store them until my father needed them. The walk had been tiring, and as I set down the containers Alessio took off his shirt and started to slide the iron grate aside which covered the well. I didn't want to go near it, but he barked at me to help him as the cover was heavy, and because I didn't want him to see I was afraid, I did. The grate grumbled slowly aside, and with about half of the hole uncovered we stopped, leaving enough room to get the bucket down and do the job that had been asked of us. I had hoped that because the sun was overhead I would at least be able to see the bottom and dispel that feeling of it being some never ending hole to somewhere unspeakable, but the light barely penetrated the darkness and it still resembled an eye, although now it was one that was half closed, squinting against the sunlight.

Alessio took the bucket and began to lower it down. I watched from a respectful distance, not wanting to be any nearer to that hole than I had to be. I watched Alessio work and was overcome with jealous rage. It came down to that word again. Opportunity. I think that I had decided that I was going to do it, and even as I crept towards him I was thinking of what I would tell my parents. I would tell them he slipped as he was leaning over the edge, and although I tried to save him I couldn't get to him in time. It was plausible. I knew that the well was deep and that Alessio couldn't swim and that the outcome if I went ahead, would be his death. He was concentrating on reeling in the bucket which was taking considerable effort now it was full. I was just about to commit and had put my hands out ready to push him when he turned towards me.

'Help me with this, it's heavy.' He said between gritted

teeth. He reminded me of my father framed there against the golden afternoon sun, and I knew I had come too far to turn back. I bent as if to take some of the strain on the rope, then lunged at him and grabbed his leg. He must have seen me because he dropped the bucket and half turned towards me, but I was too quick and too strong for him despite being younger. There was a moment of stalemate and Alessio seemed suspended in midair, and then he was pinwheeling his arms as I tipped him over the edge. He screamed as he fell, the sound reverberating off the walls, then coming to a sudden end with a wet, gargled snap. Those next few seconds are as clear as any memory I have had since. The utter silence as I peered over the edge, my heart drumming as I listened and willed my eyes to see through the darkness. I half expected him to call out, or to hear him moaning and splashing in pain but the silence told me all I needed to know. I waited and watched. For how long I couldn't tell you but as time went by, I was certain he was dead. I knew that what I had done was wrong. My mother had taught me the rights and wrongs of life and death by the time I was five, which made the feelings that raced through my head even more confusing. I was euphoric.'

Elgin watched from his seat across the bars, his face still unreadable. 'Did they believe the story? Your family I mean.'

'Of course, they did. My father made me go with him to the well and rig up a harness to get him out. He thought it was a rescue of course, but I knew the truth. I remember my father lowering himself down, me and a couple of the men who worked for him on the vineyard taking the strain of the rope. It seemed like he was down there for a very long time, and only then did I consider what might happen if Alessio were somehow still alive and told my father what I had done. I began to panic and wanted to let go of the rope and leave my father down there with his precious son when I heard him scream. It was a raw, anguished sound and I knew that Alessio's days of bullying me were over. When they pulled him up his face was twisted and blue, and his head flopped around on his broken neck. I had to fight not to smile as I looked at my brother staring up at the sky with his glassy dolls eyes. I approached my father and laid a hand on his shoulder. Not because I was upset, but because that's what I would have been expected to do. He whirled on me and shoved me aside, glaring at me with red-ringed eyes containing more hate than I have ever seen. "You let him die you little bastard. Why couldn't it have been you?" he raged at me. Then he began to weep, His massive shoulders shaking with his sobs as he stroked my dead brother's wet hair.'

Roberts smiled, as he looked Elgin in the eye. He thought he might see a glimmer of humanity, but he was met with the same blank expression.

'And that Mr. Elgin is how it began. Hell of a story huh?'

'Did they ever suspect you had anything to do with it?'

'If they did they never said anything. After that day my father barely spoke to me again. He died two years after Alessio. He was never the same after that day at the well.'

Elgin looked at him with raised eyebrows, and Roberts knew what he was thinking. He snorted and offered a wry smile.

'I didn't do it if that's what you are thinking. Although I would have if I could have found a way to. I grew to hate him as much as he hated me.'

'What happened?'

'Cancer. They gave him a year but he lasted five months. That stuff doesn't fuck around Mr. Elgin. Even when he was a flesh-covered skull on his deathbed, he still couldn't look me in the eye. I think on some level he suspected what I had done to Alessio and felt responsible. I wasn't sorry when he died. It was like a weight lifting off my shoulders. I thought that by satisfying that urge to kill on my brother it would fade away and I would become the same as everyone else. But it didn't. Instead, it grew, festered, and swelled— my own cancer if you will. I fought it for a while, but things at the vineyard had taken a turn for the worst. Without my father to run things, the place fell apart. The family unit of which I was barely a part of started to crumble, and when I was thirteen My Mother sold the vineyard to the Picenzi's who finally got their well and all the lands that came with it. My oldest Brother, Marco moved away to northern Italy with his girlfriend. My two sisters stayed in Italy with my uncle and as far as I know, are still there and married with families of their own. My mother took me with her to America, where we settled in a shitty apartment in New York above a filthy dry cleaners. It was very different from the open fields and clean air of the vineyard but I didn't care. I had half hoped that with my mother to myself that she would, at last, give me the attention I felt I deserved, but with a son and husband buried and the vineyard lost she found her own comfort, but it was the southern kind and she was knocking back at least a bottle a day. The place may have changed, but the situation hadn't. I was left to my own devices. I felt like that dog Mr. Elgin, the one with its teeth around the neck of its prey. I didn't want to kill through some bizarre need or means of atoning for my shitty childhood. I wanted to kill because I knew I would enjoy it.'

Roberts felt good saying it aloud. His back had begun to ache from sitting on the edge of the bed and he stood and stretched. He watched Elgin and saw that he was smiling. Not quite the wide mouthed lizard grin from before, but more of an "I know something you don't know" kind of smile. His stomach felt bloated and without excusing himself, he crossed to the toilet and began to urinate. He couldn't see Elgin from where he was but he would bet on him having that blank but interested look on his face. He finished his business and returned to his bunk and sure enough, Elgin was waiting and as hard to read as ever. He was surprised to find that he was keen to continue, and even despite Elgin's ridiculous job offer talk, he was glad he was there. Elgin glanced at his watch.

'Just over half an hour left. We should continue.'

Roberts nodded. He suddenly wasn't so indifferent about dying as he was earlier that morning.

'What do you want to know?'

'That's up to you, just whatever feels right to talk about.'

He thought for a moment then he lowered his head and spoke to the concrete floor.

'Those first years in New York were lonely ones. I thought I had known loneliness at the Vineyard, but it was a picnic compared to this. Even though I felt isolated from my family when we lived in Italy, there was always activity in the house. My brothers or sisters arguing over the television or how they didn't like whatever was for dinner that night, or my father complaining that the grapes weren't as good as they had been the season before and how it would affect his profits. Whatever it was there was always something going on. But now things had changed, and I would come and go from that stinking apartment and my mother would either be drunk and on her way to sleep, or just waking up and readying herself to go out and get drunk. I didn't bitch about it. There was no point. Let the old fuck drink herself to her grave if that's what she wanted. I was already planning my next kill.'

'What happened to waiting for opportunity?'

Roberts smiled. It was without humour. 'That's a pretty naive question, Mr. Elgin. Opportunity is fine, but if you don't know what to do when it gets there than what is it but a wasted opportunity. And I was keen to make sure that when the time came I would know what to do.'

'I see your point. Please continue.'

'I… I invented an imaginary friend. It seems stupid and childish and I suppose it was. But to me, he seemed real. It was like…he was the real me, the one that didn't have to pretend to be normal like everyone else. It sounds strange, but I think he became a real thing. He and I would discuss best methods to kill and not be caught. That was the key thing. We were planning for the long term.'

'What was he like?'

Roberts chuckled and shook his head. 'It would sound stupid to you.'

'You don't know that. I'm a hard man to surprise.'

'I don't doubt it. You might be too young to remember who I'm talking about anyways.

'I'm older than I look.' Elgin responded as he flashed the lizard smile. Roberts felt gooseflesh prickle on his skin.

'I imagined he was this Italian gangster type guy, with slicked black hair and a smooth little moustache. Did you ever see the original Rocky movie?'

'Of course. I think everyone saw that movie.'

'There was an actor called Joe Spinell. He played a loan shark called Gazzo who gives Rocky a job collecting unpaid debts.'

'I know the actor. He also played Willi Cici in the Godfather if it's the same one I'm thinking of.'

Richards slapped his thigh and grinned. 'That's him, that's the one! That's what my guy looked like. All smooth and dark skinned, slick and confident. He was everything I ever wanted to be. I even gave him a name.'

'What was he called?'

'I called him Monde.'

'No first name?'

'Didn't see the need. I liked the snappiness of it. Just one word you could say quick and easy.'

'Did you know he wasn't real?'

Roberts looked offended. 'Of course I did. Just because

I like to kill doesn't mean I'm off my damn rocker.'

'I never said it did. I was just asking.'

'Well, the answer is no. Anyway Monde and me, we planned and schemed and hell, sometimes he did seem real. He suggested things I wouldn't have even thought of.'

'Like what?' Elgin asked as he shifted position.

'Like where to find our first victims. There were no shortages of people in New York. The early nineties had seen a population boom and there were Nineteen million potential victims to choose from, but that didn't mean we could just charge out into the streets and start waving a knife around. Monde said that we needed to be sensible. We needed to hone our craft. I wasn't sure what he meant but he spelled it out for me. The Homeless. There was around a quarter of a million of them in New York alone and they would be easy pickings. They were anonymous and nobody would care if a couple went missing or turned up dead. It was perfect. We spent weeks walking the streets and looking for the best places, seeing where they spent their nights. Eventually, we were ready.'

Roberts trailed off, and his brow furrowed.

'Is everything ok?' Elgin asked.

'Yeah, it's just that bringing everything back is sometimes not always good you know?'

'Guilt?'

'Guilt?' Roberts repeated with a short bark of a laugh. 'Don't be ridiculous. You must have read about me, you know what I said at my trial.'

'I do. You said you felt no pity or remorse for any of your victims or their families. It was a powerful statement.'

'Yeah and it wasn't just for the TV cameras either. That's how I felt then and it's how I feel now.'

'So why did you look so…Conflicted just now?'

'You know what Mr. Elgin' Roberts raged, suddenly feeling defensive. 'This has been all give and no take and I don't feel like talking to you anymore. I think you can take your job and shove it up your prissy little ass.'

Roberts was hot and sticky and–yes. A little afraid. Afraid that his life was scheduled to end in a matter of hours. Dim realisation crept up on him that he would never sleep in the bed he was now sitting on. He wondered why the cells here even had beds at all.

He had hoped to see Elgin beg and plead for him to continue, but as always, he was sitting and watching Roberts with mild amusement. Suddenly feeling stupid for his outburst, Roberts sat and without prompting continued his story.

'That first one was no fun. I was nervous, and the old fuck wouldn't die even though I choked him so hard that I couldn't flex my hands for two days. He looked at me with a glazed indifference and when he snuffed out, I was neither satisfied or elated. Monde had decided to keep quiet. He often did when things went to shit. It didn't deter me, though. I put it down to nerves or poor technique. I tried another couple of strangulations but they had the same empty feeling. I figured out then what was bothering me.'

'The anonymity. You didn't like the secrecy.'

'Exactly. I wanted people to know that I was out there and what I was doing. I wanted to smell the fear on the streets. I wanted to read about myself in the paper of watch myself on the news. I wanted to become the most famous killer in history. That was when I started to use the knife, and I christened myself with the name I would become known by.'

Elgin nodded his head and smiled. Unlike his previous reptilian versions, this one was of genuine enjoyment.

'Of course. The Demon Dismemberer. Monde is an anagram of Demon. Monde is you. Genius Mr. Roberts.

Absolute Genius.'

'It made sense to use Monde. When I was out there stalking the streets I used to pretend to be him, that swaggering Italian gangster who lived to give the middle finger to the world. As with anything the more I worked at it the better, I got. By the time I had offed my seventh hobo I was pretty damn slick. They were no sport, though. Nobody bats an eyelid when a hobo turns up dead. Monde suggested we take things up a notch, and so we did. I first saw the girl by chance. I was twenty-one and had moved out of the shitty apartment where my alcoholic shambles of a mother still lived, or more accurately, existed. She had stopped living in the true sense years before and instead wondered around with yellowed eyes and skin to match. I thought she would croak before Christmas came but the stubborn bitch is still ticking over to this day as far as I know. Anyway, I had a place of my own. It wasn't spectacular but at least it was clean and didn't smell of booze and vomit. I had taken a job working as a security guard for an all-night supermarket called Grueber's. It was easy work and because I worked nights it meant that I didn't need to mix with anyone and could keep to myself. I didn't have any friends and didn't spend much on food.

I pretty much lived on takeout and TV dinners, and so had plenty of money left each week. I saved up and bought myself a car. Again, like my apartment it was anonymous. A white Toyota. It got stuck sometimes between second and third and didn't always turn over the first time, but it got me from A to B.

I was on my one-hour break. They still called it a lunch hour, but at one a clock in the morning, it was hardly lunchtime. It was one of those hot and sticky nights where you could still feel the residual heat of the day rising off the pavement. I had walked half a block down to grab a sandwich when I saw her and knew she was the one. She was tall and slim and had long blonde hair, which seemed to shimmer with a life of its own. She looked to be around the same age as I was, but I didn't think of her sexually. I never had those feelings. It didn't do anything for me. Anyways she was just leaning there on the wall and crying. She wasn't making any sound, but I could tell she was upset. I didn't care about that of course, but Monde whispered that word in my ear and my heart began to beat a little bit faster.

Opportunity.

My mind began to race about how I could get her

somewhere quiet enough to do what I needed to. I kept my approach casual and almost backed out when she pretty much gave herself to me on a plate.

"Officer, please help me," she sobbed as she looked at me.

I was confused and thought she might have been talking to someone else then I realised what she had done. She had seen my security guard uniform and assumed I was a police officer. How I managed to suppress the smile I'll never know. I offered her the most reassuring voice I could muster, flashed my pearly whites and asked how I could help.

It was easy.

She was new to the city, and had become separated from her friends and was now lost. I nodded in all the right places and wore a smile that was no more than a mask. I was thinking you see. I was thinking about how delicious it would be to kill her, to cut her up. I had a bizarre and random flashback to one day back at the vineyard when I was a boy, and my mother was removing the legs from a chicken she was preparing for our evening meal. I remembered that crunch as the knife went through the bone and separated the joint. My stomach quivered. I wondered how it would feel to do it to this girl.

I listened politely, and with Monde guiding me and helping me when I struggled for something to say, it was easy. I loved that about Monde. He always knew what to say and make it sound good. I let him operate my mouth. He told her we would give her a ride back to her apartment and that it was no trouble. She thanked us and Monde told her he was happy to help and even chastised her for being out alone so late. She agreed, and he told her that a young girl could never be too careful and there were a lot of bad people out there. It was all I could do not to burst out laughing. She came willingly enough. It was easy to reassure her despite her questions.

'How far is your patrol car?'

'It's just down here.'

'I appreciate your help on this.'

'No problem ma'am. It's our duty to protect.'

'It's dark down here.'

'Don't worry, Miss. Nobody will harm you whilst you are with a police officer.'

'Wait, what are you doing? Officer Monde, No!'

Roberts smiled.

'Her neck felt tiny in my hands. Even though the alleyway was dark and stank wet and rotten, kind of like Alessio's well—I enjoyed every second. I tried to cut off her head but my small pocketknife was dull and try as I might, I couldn't hack through the gristle and tendons so I had to stop. It was much more satisfying than offing the hobo's though. I looked into her eyes as she died and I swear I saw the life leave her. It was exhilarating. That's when I knew that all I wanted to do with the rest of my life was to kill.'

Elgin looked up and Roberts was surprised at the look in his eye. He had expected revulsion or disgust. But what he saw was admiration.

'This is fascinating. What happened next?'

Roberts shrugged. I started to kill. As often as I could. I was smart, though. They found the girl's body the following day. It turned out she was sixteen, but she looked a lot older than that to me. I still didn't feel guilty. Someone should ask her parents why they allowed her to roam the streets in a huge city full of fucked up people like me. I was desperate to kill again but I knew that I wasn't ready to be hunted down like a dog and to do another in my own city would be risky. Monde suggested we select cities at random and drive out to look for someone to kill. I also knew that if I wanted to continue, I would have to make provision to hide the bodies. I didn't want to be caught, not when things had just begun.'

'You obviously did a great job. How long did it take for them to catch you?'

'Sixteen years. A man can do a lot of killing in that time.'

'So what happened?'

'If I had the time I could tell you in detail, but I suspect we don't have long left.'

Elgin looked at his watch and grimaced. It was the first real facial expression other than the lizard smile that Roberts had seen.

'We have around fifteen minutes.'

Roberts nodded. 'Well, the short version will have to do. I did as Monde suggested. I had a map of America pinned to my bedroom wall. What I would do is take a dart and from the opposite side of the room throw it at the map and wherever it would land, that's where Monde and I would go to find our kill. Apart from a few exceptions like the failed trip to Delaware, there was almost always an opportunity. Most serial murderers go for a specific type of victim. Ted Bundy chose middle-class white women. Jeffrey Dahmer chose only Men and young boys. All because they had a profile, a reason for choosing that particular type of victim. I didn't have limits like that. My kills weren't about repressed homosexuality or the thrill of the chase. Do you remember that business with the clown that went apeshit at the circus one day completely out of the blue?'

Elgin nodded 'Sure. It made headline news. But he was depressed, or so they say.'

'Bullshit.' Roberts said flatly. 'He wasn't depressed. He just got tired of pretending to be normal.'

'You don't know that, not for sure.'

Roberts grinned. 'His name was Freddy, he used to write to me. Sympathized with my plight or so he said.'

Elgin offered no reaction, and so Roberts went on.

'The poor guy was fucked up, tired of his life, alienated from his family. He was a lot like me. I gave him a few pointers on how to break the cycle.'

'You… encouraged him to do what he did?'

Roberts shrugged. 'I don't think so. He would have done it with or without my help. The point I'm trying to make is that sometimes there isn't always a motive. Sometimes people just lose it and want to go crazy.'

Elgin nodded but didn't pursue the point.

'I don't have a preferred type of victim. Male, female, young, old, black, white—it didn't matter to me as I chose simply based on Monde's suggestions and our favourite word—Good old opportunity. The security job got in my way so I quit and took a job as a long distance delivery driver. Not one of the big eighteen wheeled rigs Mind, but the smaller transit types. It was perfect. Not only was I left to my own devices, the company I worked for even paid my fuel expenses. I often wondered if that made them an accessory to murder. Monde came up with another great idea. Once we had selected a location via the dart and map, we would find a random address there and send an empty box weighted with bags of salt or rocks to that property via the company I worked for. All I had to do then was make sure the delivery was on my sheet and boom. I had a full expenses paid trip to my next kill.

Monde suggested we keep the dual identity game going too. That first girl had gone with me because she believed I was a police officer. People as a whole are so dumb that it's easy to fool them. It took a while, but I sourced some high quality police uniforms from a movie costume company and bought them using

Monde's name. We didn't always use the police disguise. That would have been as stupid as doing more kills in my back yard. But it was an option. Sometimes I was Monde the door-to-door salesman, or Monde the doctor. I also refined my technique, and after my eighteenth or twentieth kill, I had it down to a fine art. If my victim were a woman I would strangle them. I liked to watch that little light blink out in their eyes. If my chosen victim were a man, I would render them unconscious a different way. I favoured a lump hammer. It had a good weight and invariably did the job. In all cases, I would dismember the victim after death. I would always remove the head, but if I could I would also take the arms. I tried the legs too, but they were difficult to take off so I gave up on that early on. Depending on where I killed I would try to conceal the bodies. Monde told me that the longer I could hide them and allow the bodies to rot, the less chance of the police linking me to any of the murders, and by that time with seventy or more kills under my belt, I wasn't ready to stop. I took to dumping the body parts in weighted bags in rivers if there was one close by, or if not in woodland so that the wildlife could finish the job I started. In the winter of two thousand and two I reached my century. One hundred kills. By then, of course, despite my best efforts to hide them, many of my previous victims had been found. It didn't take long for the police to notice that the method was the same for multiple murders and as soon as word reached the press, I was in the spotlight. The press dubbed me the Decap Killer, which I hated. I had worked too hard to let them label me with such a flimsy name. Monde suggested I contact them to let them know the error of their ways, so as you probably know from the uproar it caused—I sent a severed head to the editor of the New York Times and told him they could call me the Demon Dismemberer. The public went into frenzy, and if anything I think that one moment of self-indulgence was the event that led to my downfall and capture.'

Elgin glanced at his watch. It was no more than a flicker of the eyes, but it got the message across.

'How long left?'

'Ten minutes. We better wrap this up.'

'Yeah, time flies when ya' havin' fun doesn't it Elgin?' No response. Roberts lifted his feet and crossed his legs on the bed, his long, tattooed arms dangling down past his knees.

'It was some smartass called Petrov who caught me.

Petrov. Can you believe that? A damn Russian, at least in name. Turns out he was technically an American and had become a full citizen back in the eighties. He was famous for thinking outside the box, of thinking like a killer. I don't think he was too different to me at heart apart from the fact he never had the balls to go through with committing to that first one. He was good, though. Ninety-seven percent success rate in serious crimes. Anyway, Petrov was brought in to work the case because he had caught the Green Bay rapist and was coming fresh off the back of Smashing that Female Serial killer business in Rio. I had read about him in the papers and looked at his picture and for the first time was concerned. He had these eyes Mr. Elgin and—not unlike yours—they were hungry eyes, knowing eyes. They were eyes that said he knew secret things. Monde told me not to worry about him, but I had a feeling that the game was changed. I was feeling the pressure of my notoriety then. I had become paranoid and had developed insomnia. There is nothing worse than nights spent lying awake Mr. Elgin and waiting for daylight to come. At that time, they had found fifty bodies they had attributed to me, and as they widened their search grid more and more of my handiwork was digging itself out of its shallow graves. The headlines proclaimed me as the world's most prolific serial killer. Said that I was the most feared man in history. Such a title is a lot to live up to. I was known the world over. Monde was thrilled. I was starting to feel scared. For the next few months, I didn't kill as often. It wasn't that the opportunity wasn't there. I assumed that because of my nationwide notoriety that people would be on their guard. But I soon found that people read things in the papers and watch things on television and they never think that it could come creeping up on them out of the night and tap them on the shoulder. No, Mr. Elgin. The killing was as easy as it ever was. By May of two thousand and four, my tally was at one hundred and two and unbeknownst to me there it would remain. The police had discovered eighty-seven bodies. And the public was demanding action. I was worried, but Monde smooth talked me and told me it was ok. I imagined him flashing his big Italian grin and telling me he would take care of everything. But Monde was wrong.'

'What happened?'

'I wonder if the circumstances of my capture were as random and incidental as they appeared, or if there was some higher power at work that had decided that it could no longer let me run around cutting heads off good honest citizens. It could have all been so different. Had the dart I threw at the map landed in Boston or Nebraska, you and I wouldn't be having this conversation, but instead, that dart wedged itself into good old San Antonio. Nestled right between the A and the N of Antonio. I never liked coming to Texas. I had killed here once before and it was hard work. It was too hot, too dry for me. Too much dust and not enough wind. Monde and I had driven around the streets for what felt like hours in my trusty white transit with SPEEDY TRANS written on the side in a garish orange font. The mercury was touching a hundred and four degrees and even with the windows open and the air conditioning on full, it was almost unbearable. I glanced over to Monde in the passenger seat and felt a stab of jealousy. He didn't look hot or uncomfortable. He was playing it cool with his foot up on the dashboard and his elbow hanging out of the window. He had huge reflective aviator glasses on which kept catching the sunlight and hurting my eyes. I saw a brunette with a slim waist and large hips in tattered jeans shorts walking unhurriedly down the edge of the road and glanced over to Monde for his approval to go ahead but he kept looking forward and I knew that he wouldn't speak until he had spotted the golden opportunity for us to do what we needed to do. What happened next, you couldn't even make up, Mr. Elgin. I don't believe in coincidence but if there is such a thing then that hot Friday in July was it. The first thing that happened was the blown tire. That old transit van had done well over two hundred and fifty thousand miles and had carried with it numerous packages and body parts all over the country. It happened quickly, and it took all my efforts to steer lurching, bucking van off the road without rolling it into the ditch. I Glanced over to Monde with a 'what the fuck' expression on my face but he had gone. Retreated to wherever in my mind that he lives. He had left me to deal with it alone, and so with no other option, I climbed out of the van and into the baking July heat to assess the situation. It was the Left rear that had gone. It lay against the dirt shoulder like a melted slug. There was a spare of course and I wanted to fix it as quickly as I could. I was in the process of taking the spare wheel out of the recessed panel in the back when a voice called out to me to ask if everything was all right. I turned around expecting to see some country bumpkin old timer and almost screamed outright.

It Was Petrov.

Imagine winning the lottery every week for a year. Or throwing twelve sixes in a row at the craps table. Those were the kind of odds we were talking about here. I pleaded with Monde to appear and tell me what to do, but he didn't and I stood there in the back of the van open mouthed and sweating.

'Sir is everything alright?' Petrov asked again as I stood and looked at him with open-mouthed shock. He didn't sound Russian. That was the first thing that hit me. And why should he? Even though I was born in Italy, I have no trace of an accent either. I knew I had to answer, but the ability to speak had left me and instead I managed a weak nod and went back to work freeing the tire from the well. It's funny because although I had seen his picture in the papers, I never imagined him to be real. But there he stood in his sunglasses and plaid shirt with the sleeves rolled up and his cup of Starbucks coffee in his hand. He was smaller than I thought he would be. I suppose I was guilty of the same thing I had laughed at the public for. After all, the stuff you see on TV never happens to you right?

Wrong.

My inability to speak felt as if it had lasted a lifetime, but in reality, it could only have been seconds. Words finally found their way out of my mouth

'I'm fine officer. Just a tire blowout. I'll change this up and be on my way.'

Petrov had nodded and even though I couldn't see them behind his sunglasses, I could feel his eyes crawling over me and the insides of the van. I was conscious of everything and begged Monde for some advice but I think he had smelled trouble too and had decided to stay hidden. I tried to be as calm as I could and look as casual as possible as I lifted the tire free from the well, but my hands were shaking and I dropped it.

'Here, let me give you a hand.' Petrov said then without another word he set his cup on the floor and hopped into the van. It was a very surreal moment in that small space with the man I classed as my nemesis. It still seemed unreal and I didn't like being so close to him. I could feel him glancing at me and I was sure I could hear his thoughts processing like some damn computer. I suddenly felt very afraid. We got the tire free and were wheeling it towards the open back doors when Monde made his reappearance.

You are going to have to kill him.

I wanted to laugh, or scream but wasn't sure which. Instead, I did neither and helped Petrov get the tire out onto the floor. Sweat was dripping off me but I felt better being out in the open even if it did feel like stepping into an oven. I could see his car parked across the street, its bodywork glittering in the fierce heat of the sun. I didn't know the make and noticed that the steering wheel was on the opposite side. Petrov saw me watching, and flashed a crocodile smile.

'It's European. A gift from my father. He had it sent over from Russia.'

I nodded and somehow managed to hold on to my breakfast, which churned and swirled around my gut and seemed determined to make a reappearance.

'My name is Petrov.' He took off his glasses and held out his hand. I didn't want to touch it. I forced myself to shake it. It felt solid. Workers hands as my father would have called them.

'Monde' I replied, then immediately regretted it. He watched me for a second and then blinked and turned his attention to the tire.

'Ok, Mr. Monde. Let's change this tire and get you on your way. Where are you heading?'

I couldn't think of an answer. I knew that he was reading my thoughts and could tell what I was thinking. Luckily, Monde took over.

'Just passing through. Got a delivery to make in Houston.'

Petrov nodded and I was calm. My hands had stopped shaking and I began to work on loosening the nuts on the flat tire whilst Petrov worked the jack to lift the van up. We worked in silence for a while with the heat of the day on our backs, and I had just pulled the old tire loose when he spoke again.

'You delivered here before?'

'No.'

Petrov nodded and I tried to stay calm despite a belly full of ice. We moved the spare tire into place and he looked up at me with one probing eye closed against the glare of the sun.

'You sure about that?'

'Positive. I rarely get out this far.'

He nodded and in the silence, I was sure I could hear his brain ticking over.

'It's funny.' He said, setting down the Cross wrench and standing. 'When I called to you in the van you called me officer.'

I licked my lips and tried to think. Monde was saying nothing, and I couldn't complain because I couldn't think of anything to say either. I stood and met his gaze and we faced off in the blazing sun in a backwards little San Antonio street. I tried to think of something to say that wouldn't incriminate me, but my silence gave him the time to continue putting the pieces of the puzzle together. His eyes were like vicious probes as he scanned me. Again, he reminded me of some damn computer. His next words made me feel sick.

'What do you know about the Demon Dismemberer case?'

I tried to keep my face neutral but I was certain he could see the guilt written over my face.

'Only what I have seen on the news' I heard myself say as I crouched back down to the tire. I was no longer interested in changing the wheel you understand, but my eyes devoured the abandoned wrench which lay in the dust.

'Yeah it's funny,' he said as he took a packet of cigarettes out of his pocket and lit one, blowing smoke which was dragged away by the light breeze.

'I was out here following up a lead on that particular case. There was a girl killed by him here a couple of years ago. She worked over there as it happened.'

He jabbed his thumb over his shoulder to the glass-fronted café on the other side of the street. I gave it a cursory glance as I tightened the wheel nuts by hand. I had to make it look natural when I reached for the wrench.

'Nobody remembers much about the last time she was seen alive of course. People don't tend to remember details even though we try our best to encourage them.'

I nodded, trying to look busy. I was looking for that word. The one that begins with o and ends in y but I couldn't see one. Petrov had a smile on his face now. A smug and satisfied smile as he took a cursory step back.

'I hope you get a lead soon. Terrible business if you ask me.' I said to him, both surprised and impressed at how calm I sounded. Monde would have been impressed too—if he hadn't left me to my own devices. Petrov nodded, and took a long pull on his cigarette, then dropped it to the floor and stubbed it out with his boot.

'Witnesses are funny creatures Mr. Monde. They sometimes don't even know that their information is useful, and sometimes it isn't—unless you know how to use it.'

He crouched again now and I could feel his eyes glaring

through me. My own gaze I kept fixed on the tire, even though I was no longer working on it.

'I have interviewed more than three hundred people about this particular case all over the country. Sometimes when you lay all of that information out, certain patterns present themselves.'

I looked up at him then and he reminded me of a lion. He was no longer smiling. I chose to remain silent.

'They seem like such trivial things, but sometimes they are the crumbs that lead to the cheese.'

'Like what' I heard someone say that may or may not have been me.

'Well let's say we take the three hundred interviews as a round number. Say a third of those people remember a white van near some of the murder scenes.' Petrov put his hand on my van for emphasis.

'Then of those people, say a quarter of them remember that the van had New York plates.'

I crouched there, sweating and watching him, as he seemed to grow more and more confident. I had given up on grabbing the wrench. I knew he had me and was waiting for him to deliver the knockout blow.

' Now say another hundred of those people, unrelated to the first ones who saw the van say they remember a tall man in the area on the night of any given murder—you see where I'm going with this?—and pretty soon you have a pretty good picture of who you are looking for.'

I prayed for Monde to tell me what to do. Monde always knew what to do.

'Imagine my surprise when I look out of the window of the café there to see a white van with New York plates broken down by the side of the road. That alone would be reason enough to take a closer look, but then I saw you climb out of the cab and saw that you are what? Six five?'

'Six Seven.' I replied. My calves were burning from crouching there on my haunches but I was frozen and unable to move. Petrov didn't notice my discomfort. He was on a roll.

'And that got me thinking. If I were a nationwide serial killer, how would I do it? How would I make sure I could reach all of those places? And I thought to myself. Well, I would work for a delivery firm. One where the leash was long and there was no way to track my movements—a company like Speedy Trans for example.'

I heard the approaching wail of police sirens. They were still distant, but I knew they were coming for me.

He must have called them in straight away and was just keeping me busy until they arrived. I looked up at him then and offered a smile of my own.

'Congratulations. You just caught the Demon Dismemberer.' I said simply. Petrov didn't look surprised. He had known all along.

Elgin blinked and nodded. Roberts remained silent. There was no more to say.

'You just…confessed?' Elgin asked with a note of surprise.

'I would like to say I went out in a blaze of glory but that would be a lie. We both knew that he had me. Hell, all he would have needed to do was run a blue light over the inside of that van and it would light up like a damn Christmas tree.'

Elgin nodded, then reached into his briefcase and brought out a single sheet of paper and a pen.

'I think I have heard enough Mr. Roberts.'

'Yeah? How did I do?'

'I think you will be perfect for the role.'

The sound of the outer gate being unlocked echoed down the corridor.

'Looks like visiting hours are over Elgin. Tell me what the job is.'

'How would you like the chance to have everything you ever wanted? The opportunity to be as cruel and as sadistic as you like for all eternity?'

Keys rattling now, as the second door was unlocked.

'Stop screwing around with me Elgin. You promised to get me out of here so do it!'

Roberts was suddenly desperate to be free. It was as if talking about it had made him realise that he wasn't ready to stop. Not yet.

'You must understand the terms, Mr. Roberts. Once you agree there will be no turning back.'

'Elgin just Tell me!'

'How would you like to be a Demon, Mr. Roberts?' Elgin said from behind his reptilian smile. Roberts exploded forwards and reached through the bars.

'You motherfucker! I knew you were playing me. You sorry scrawny son of a bitch!'

Elgin didn't move. He had positioned himself to be just out of Roberts's reach. Instead, he smiled and spoke calmly.

'I assure you, it's no joke. I have been sent from hell to recruit you, Mr. Roberts. You have all the qualities we are searching for.'

'You fuck, ill tear you apart!' Elgin reached up and

grabbed Roberts by the forearm. His grip was like a vice. Roberts stopped struggling and looked on wide-eyed.

'You can be all you set out to achieve. You can become Monde. Not just as a figment of your fractured imagination, but really be him. You can continue the work in death that you started in life.'

Roberts looked on as Elgin grinned and he was sure he could see a narrow forked tongue flicking around behind his teeth. The main door was now opening, the sound of its tired creaking hinges followed by the steady clip clop of footsteps on the polished floor. Elgin's eyes were now black and bottomless pools that reminded Roberts of Alessio's well.

'I need an answer, Mr. Roberts.' Elgin hissed. His breath was hot and smelled of sulphur.

'You freak. You crazy freak!' Roberts spat.

He heard Remy's lumbering footsteps and was relieved—at least until he saw him. Like Elgin, his eyes were black. His teeth were thin daggers of bone and his forked tongue probed in and out of his mouth. He stood beside Elgin and folded his arms. He looked less ridiculous than Roberts remembered. Roberts backed away, knowing the true meaning of terror for the first time since that day with Petrov. The two men—two demons stood and approached the bars. Roberts looked on in horror as the white paint on the cell bars began to peel and melt away from the heat which was emanating from them. Smoke billowed out of the neck of Elgin's shirt, and Remy's gold police badge on his chest had begun to melt and warp.

'Join us, Mr. Roberts.' Said Elgin, his own dagger teeth making his voice sound different. Deeper somehow. Roberts backed away as far as he could. He pressed himself against the cinderblock wall and kept pushing, hoping that if he pushed hard enough he would be able to push himself through the brick and come out of the other side and into freedom. He could see a thick heat haze shimmering around them now as the Demon who used to be Remy took out the keys to his cell with hands which were more like claws and unlocked the door.

'Come with usssshh Mishter Roberthhhh.' Remy Hissed as he swung the door open. Elgin entered. He was wiry and crooked as he slid towards Roberts who was still unsuccessfully trying to push himself through the wall.

'Join usth. Let usth take you away from all thsth.'

Slithered Elgin. Roberts closed his eyes and screamed.

MYSTERY DISSAPEARANCE OF
CONVICTED SERIAL KILLER

A nationwide manhunt began yesterday after the mystery disappearance of a convicted serial killer, who was scheduled for death by lethal injection at six pm yesterday evening.
Marco Roberts (35) otherwise known as the DEMON DISMEMBERER, was convicted of more than 90 killings over a sixteen year period and had been transferred to the Walls unit of Huntsville state penitentiary, Texas for death by lethal injection. Upon arriving at five p.m. To deliver Roberts his last meal, police staff were left baffled when they found his cell still securely locked, but Roberts himself was nowhere to be found. Staff Sargent Julius Remy (40), the senior officer who had been tasked with escorting the prisoner and overseeing his execution said 'Nobody came in or out of here all day, and that I can guarantee.' Security footage was retrieved for inspection but was bizarrely found to be severely damaged, melted due to an equipment malfunction and as a result un-useable. 'We

think the machine that records the surveillance overheated and destroyed the tapes' Sgt. Remy said when asked.

Although there is no evidence to suggest that Roberts escaped, authorities have advised the public to remain vigilant, keep their doors and windows locked and to not under any circumstances approach Roberts if they see him. 'If ever there was a man that was the devil on earth, then it was Roberts' Sgt. Remy warned. The search continues. If you have any information as to Roberts's whereabouts, please contact the police action helpline on 555-6342

*OBSERVATION ROOM 5*

January 14th

I've been put into isolation. The doctors still don't know what I was injected with and they're not taking any chances, but I won't give up hope that I can come through this. I'm scared, of course I am. Who wouldn't be? The good news is that I've always been a survivor and this will be no different. They gave me a pen and notepad and asked me to log everything that happens. I'm not allowed a computer as they say it's against company policy. I wonder if it's because they don't want me posting about my situation on social media and spreading panic. You can't blame them. I understand where you're coming from and so it's back to the old school way. I don't mind. It feels more real, more serious as I scrawl on paper. So where to start? How do I begin to tell this story? Maybe I should start like my favourite book as a kid, Moby Dick. My Name is Ishmael. Yeah, that works. We'll go with that only because it amuses me. So, here we go. My name is James Robinson and I work in the city for a high-end stock brokerage firm. My clients trade stock worth millions every day and rely on me to make sure they stay rich. It's a good gig and I get a decent commission every time I add a few more hundred thousand dollars to their already stuffed accounts. Although I'm not at the top yet, I'm getting there, trying to drag my way up the financial food chain. I still remember the advice of my father, the best and the only useful thing he ever told me.

'There's a lot of money out there in the world James. Just make sure you get your share of It.' he said around the hand rolled cigarette that was always wedged between his teeth. Those words stuck with me almost as much as the drunken beatings and self-confidence crushing put-downs which he shared out as and when the mood took him, but that's another story and I wouldn't want to bore you with the details. Besides, I had the last laugh. He died of liver cancer when I was fifteen and I was glad. Tough shit, old man.

I've always been attracted to the idea of success and proving my bully of a father that I was more than the worthless piece of shit he saw me as. My ex-wife (also deceased. Road accident. No love lost though) used to tell me I can come across as intimidating and pushy when I get an idea in my head and I suppose that might be true, but if it is then I don't apologise for it. I know what I want to achieve and will do whatever it takes and if you think that's wrong, then you're probably one of the high percentage of people who fail at everything they do in life. There's a huge money shaped pie out there and I want my share of it. If it means upsetting people or stepping on them on the way up, then so be it. Anyway, I'm going off track here. They want to know about what's happening now, not the past.

I don't like this room. It's too sterile, too white. I'll describe it for you from the comfort of my shitty hospital bed with its itchy sheets. It's around twelve feet square with no windows and other than the bed and small table beside it, no furniture. There is an ugly faded painting on the wall of a vineyard basking in the glow of a summer's day. Artistically it's awful, but I suppose it serves as something to look at in the absence of a real view. I have a small bathroom and have been told to bottle my piss if I need to go, as they want to test it. There is a TV, although you won't catch me watching it. No time for sitting and tuning my brain out to shitty quiz shows and the like. I'm much too busy for that. I need to keep active and not become depressed despite what happened. They keep the door locked of course (otherwise it wouldn't be called isolation) and keep an eye on me from the small security camera mounted in the corner. I can see the small red light blinking as it watches my every move. Fuck it. I won't have to put up with this for too long. They will find a way to help me and then I can get back to my life. So what else to say before I get into the story? Well, I live alone. No wife (one was enough thank you very much). No girlfriend and no kids. Rug-rats have never appealed to me, and I couldn't be bothered with the hassle of looking after one in any case. It's not as if I can't find a woman. I'm actually pretty popular with them. But I'm more of a one-night stand, no strings attached kinda guy if you know what I'm saying. I'll indulge myself a little and tell you I'm attractive. Not super chiselled like those slick guys who advertise aftershave or underwear—my look is more of a natural one. I stand a shade over six feet and have a good head of thick black hair. I also inherited my mother's Italian skin tone so I always look tanned, which is good as it means I don't have to risk getting cancer from hitting the sunbed. I always laugh at idiots who use those things. You might think I'm being harsh but think about it from my point of view. If I said to you

'Hey come over here. If you give me thirty bucks, I'll give you a long hot blast of skin cancer inducing UV Radiation! Don't worry though, you will come out of it looking bronzed and beautiful, at least until those moles appear on your skin and start growing bigger and bigger. Come on what are you waiting for, sign up now!'

You would think I was crazy and rightly so. Even though I don't tan it doesn't mean I'm lazy when it comes to my health. I always make sure I look after my body. No carbs, no saturated fats. I visit the gym three times a week and hope the work I put into keeping myself healthy pays off now as my body fights against whatever it is that rages around inside me.

Sorry, I had to stop writing for a while (why I'm apologising I don't know) as a doctor came in to visit me. He was wearing one of those white full body suits with the hood and plastic visor. I didn't like the noise it made when he walked. It reminded me of the raincoat I used to have when I was a kid and I don't like being reminded of my childhood. Besides, it all looked a bit dramatic and I don't mind telling you it caused me a little alarm. He asked how I was feeling, waiting for my response with his stupid fucking pen and clipboard. I told him I felt fine apart from the dryness in my throat, which is starting to feel like somebody installed a roll of tiny carpet inside whilst I wasn't looking. In fact, I feel pretty good all things considered. I didn't like the way that doctor had looked at me; he seemed tense and maybe even a little afraid. It was the way I imagined he looked at his patients when he was about to bear bad news. 'I'm sorry its terminal. I suggest we turn off life support. Days rather than weeks. Nothing more we can do'. Standard bread and butter of the job for a sour faced prick like him. I told him I was hungry though and as he scurried off with his answers he promised to have one of the nurses bring me some food. I hope it's not the standard hospital fare. I feel like I could use a decent meal. Maybe a steak. God, I'd kill for a nice rare steak. I skipped breakfast this morning and now it's almost three in the afternoon. It's funny how things work out, isn't it? I should be in the office. Today is Friday and most of the people on my floor leave early to extend their weekend and make a head start on feeding their habits, often a combination of booze, cocaine and or hookers, but not me. I'm no slacker. I stay until late, making sure I get my work finished to the highest standard so that the powers that be take notice. I have my eye on Ted Gordon's corner office with the private bathroom, but to get there I need to keep pushing and working as hard as I can. I suppose now would be a good time to explain what happened. I think I have been telling you so much unimportant fluff to avoid having to write it down, but there is no sense in delaying any longer. I should warn you though it's a pretty fucked up story, so, here goes.

I live in the city. My apartment is on the fifteenth floor of a huge glass and steel building that has amazing views of the harbour and suspension bridge to the left and the spires of the city to the right. I like watching the world go by from up there. The people look like ants scurrying about their business and it feels good to look down on them. My place is modern, Minimalistic. It cost me a lot of money and some would say it's self-indulgence but so what if it is? I work hard and deserve to enjoy the fruits of my labour. I'm usually up at six sharp on a workday. I like to hit the treadmill for a while before I head to the office. I read somewhere that the endorphins brought on by exercise have a positive effect on the body and I don't doubt it as it always seemed to sharpen my senses. It was a power outage that put me in this position. A fucking power outage. Some lazy minimum wage earning prick must have cut through a wire or something and put the entire building into darkness whilst I slept. For what I pay for my rent here you would expect that they have a backup generator. I'll be writing a letter of complaint to the building owners once I get out of here. I deserve better. Either way, I woke just before eight to the sight of my digital alarm clock blinking its hopelessly inaccurate display at me. I had barely enough time to shower and get ready before I set off on my way. I live six blocks from the office and most mornings I walk to work by cutting through the park. I knew that if I were to make it in time today, though (I'm obsessive about being punctual. lateness is one of my pet hates) I would have to skip the park route and take the subway which would drop me a block away. I was sure I would make it if I caught the eight thirty five train. The thought of being so close to all those people made my stomach turn. I don't like to be touched by the great unwashed. No offence, it's nothing personal; I just don't like my space to be invaded. They call it personal for a reason, you know. Besides which I knew what the subway would be like during morning rush hour. But if it meant I wouldn't be late for work then I was prepared to make the sacrifice. The subway entrance is only half a block away from where I live and as I hurried down the steps I felt a quiver of unease in my stomach. As I had feared the subway car was filling up with people. I tried to keep a neutral look on my face as I squeezed in but all I could think about was my churning guts and I had to concentrate my efforts to stop myself from being sick. You may think I'm being odd and a maybe even a little obsessive but just think about it for a minute. How many people are going to be breathing their germs on you? How many people have gripped the metal rail before you without washing their hands after taking a piss or wiping their ass? Germs. Infections. Shit like that was rife, especially with so many people crammed together sniffing and coughing. I found a relatively spacious area (no seats of course. There never were any left, even that early on a morning) but as more people streamed onto the train I found myself pushed further into the corner. If not for choosing that exact moment to look through into the car next to me, I wouldn't be here writing this now. I saw that it too was full apart from the seat nearest the door. I craned my neck to see why nobody had snatched such a rare opportunity to sit whilst they travelled to work and saw the reason. There was a hobo slouched in the corner. It was amazing how the people around him had reacted. Although that car was jammed to capacity nobody would take up the spare seat, keeping their distance as if the old fuck carried some kind of plague. (Maybe he did, but I won't think about that yet) Baffled by their stupidity, I jostled my way through the people next to me and made for the empty seat. There was plenty of distance between him and me to allow me to sit without touching him and that's what I did. You might call me a hypocrite, and that's your right. However to me, sitting next to that filthy old bastard was far more acceptable than being wedged shoulder to shoulder with those dirty, sniffling germ carrying people. The other passengers looked at me as if I was crazy but I didn't care. I was the one with the seat and not breathing in their diseases. Not that the old bastard didn't smell. There was a distinct stench of over ripe cheese and the yeasty hops drifting from his general direction. Although everyone else was doing their best to ignore him, I couldn't help but stare, fascinated and disgusted at the same time. How could a person let themselves go like that? How could they exist in the gutter and be able to live with themselves?

He was the typical homeless cliché; long hair and beard that had once been black but was now grey and matted together He had leathery, sun damaged skin from a lifetime of living on the streets. His clothes were old and tattered and the toe of one shoe was missing, revealing the stub of a filthy and overgrown toenail (he didn't appear to be wearing socks) Clutched to his chest were two things. A three quarters empty bottle of cheap red wine, and a cardboard sign. Despite my disgust I wondered what it said but whatever writing there was he had concealed by his arms. I don't know if he felt my eyes on him, or if by sitting in his space I had stirred him from his snooze but he woke up, looking at me with glassy three sheets to the wind eyes. I suppose you could feel sorry for him if he wasn't such an obvious waste of fucking space. I don't like drinkers, not heavy ones. They reminded me of my childhood and by association my dick of a father and as I said earlier, that was a time best forgotten. The old prick might have gone back to sleep, but instead his eyes lit up and he straightened in his seat, sending a fresh wave of that disgusting cheese and booze smell towards me. I glanced around and noted that now I, like him was invisible to the rest of the passengers. It was as If I had slipped into the world of the unseen hobo. You know what I mean, the ones that hassle you in the streets and ask for spare change. The same ones you do your best to ignore and keep your eyes fixed ahead as you walk past them. Anything to avoid making eye contact and having to acknowledge their existence. And that's what it was like, only now I was just as invisible as the filthy pig sitting beside me.

'Can I tell ya somethin' young fella?' he slurred, looking in my direction.

Now here is something else about me that you should know if you haven't guessed it already. I'm a prick and I don't mind saying it. You probably suspected as much but I don't care what you think. It's actually normal, the way nature intended us to be. There is no place for nice people in this world. If you want something then you go take it. Fuck everyone else. Although you, mystery reader, might have ignored him, or looked away or maybe even stood and took your chances with the other sardines crammed into the rest of the subway car, that isn't and never has been my style. I'm James fucking Robinson, and I don't get intimidated by anyone—least of all an old, stinking alcoholic bum. I told him to go ahead and talk, get it off his chest. He leaned forward and grinned, showing a mouth that was more gums than teeth.

'It's the end of times you know, sonny.'

His breath made me retch, However, I had a point to prove and forced myself not to flinch or show my disgust. Not just to him, but to the other people on the train who were now watching. I don't know if the old bastard noticed, but I did. I'm good at noticing shit like that—the little details that most people miss. I told the old guy in no uncertain terms how I felt. I told him it was people like him that were dragging down society, and that he would be better off dead and not wasting valuable resources. That one got me a few disapproving glances from the observers but I didn't care. I turned the tables, acting as if they were as invisible to me as I was to them. I always spoke my mind and if someone didn't like it, tough luck. To his credit, the old man didn't seem to mind and laughed it off.

'I used to be like you sonny, all dressed up in my suit and tie. I bet you have one of those big apartments in the city too don't ya?'

This wasn't part of the plan, and not what I had expected. This old guy was sharper than he looked and

I was more aware of the people who were watching and waiting to see what would happen. Maybe he was just finding his stride or fuelled by the attention, but he seemed bigger, somehow more powerful and I'll admit it. I felt a little bit intimidated.

'Oh I see it, boy, you live there in that big place, all decked out with luxury items but yer' alone, ain't ya? I can see how lonely you are.'

I didn't like this and was about to tell him to go fuck himself when he leaned close and whispered at me.

'We're all going to the same place.'

I thought he had meant to the same station on the subway when he flipped the cardboard sign around and showed me the words.

'This is where we're all headed, sonny. And ain't' nuthin' you can do to stop it'

What came next is still confusing, as it happened so fast. I remember glancing to the sign, reading the words scrawled on the cardboard with black marker pen.

End of the Road

Simple. To the point. I'd had enough of his shit by then and I didn't want to be caught up in some bullshit end of the world debate, so turned away from him. I heard someone shout, 'Look out' and immediately I felt it—a small sharp pain in my neck. I thought he had grabbed me and was attempting to pull me towards him, but I could tell by the faces of the other passengers that there was something more going on. They wore haunted expression that said that they had witnessed some serious event, and for the first time in years I felt afraid. Some of the other passengers grabbed at him to restrain him as I stood, not wanting to be anywhere near the crazy old bastard. It was how they were looking at me that first made me realise that there was something wrong. I saw myself in the opaque reflection of the window and realised what everyone was staring at. The fucker had stuck me in the neck with a syringe and it was still hanging out of my neck. In a panic I reached up and yanked it free, holding it in my hands and not able to believe what had happened. It's funny that as filthy and grimy as he was, the needle looked clean and sterile. The chamber was empty apart from a few drops of bluish liquid. I whirled on him then and I think I screamed, more in rage than anything else. That was the worst, hearing him cackle as they restrained him.

'End of the road, Sonny, end of the road!'

God knows what it was that he stuck me with. I came straight to the hospital, but I keep thinking of all the fucked up diseases in the world and I'm scared. Hepatitis, Ebola, HIV. The words keep spinning around my head but I'm determined to be ok. After all, as I already said, I don't feel ill which can only be a good thing. I'm tired of writing for now. I'm going to kick back and wait for the doctor to come and give me the all clear. I'm sure it will be soon.

January 15th

They kept me overnight for observation. As requested, I pissed in a cup for them which they took away for whatever tests they do. They also took more blood. That's the thing with doctors. No matter what ailment you have they always want blood and piss. I asked about going home and what they thought was wrong with me, but the prick wouldn't give me a straight answer. If it were a weekday I would have flat out refused to stay any longer. After all, I pride myself on making sure I never miss work. However, it's Saturday and I had no plans anyway so I'll stay here and let them run their tests. I'm so bored of this room. How can some people live their lives by sitting around and doing nothing? People like that in my opinion (and as you are reading this, mine is the only one that counts), should be euthanised. Put to death. They serve no purpose in society. I'm sure the doctors know something. I can see it in their faces. The way they shoot each other short, panicked glances. I hope for their sake they realise who they are fucking around with. Just let them try withholding information. I'll have them in court and take them for everything they have so fast they won't know what's hit them. I'm taking names and making records of everything they do. The man in charge is a guy called Fredericks. Earlier this morning he came in to do a routine examination. There was a look in his eyes I didn't like. He looked afraid. On the other hand, maybe it's just my overstressed brain reading too much into it.

I will beat this.

Fredericks asked me how I was feeling. I told him that other than the itching needle mark and a bit of stiffness from their shitty beds I felt fine. My own questions I noticed went, as was becoming the norm, unanswered, whilst they went on asking theirs. The best they can give me is that it's too early to tell what's wrong with me. Fucking idiots. I'll give them the rest of the day to give me some answers then there will be hell to pay.

Why am I even telling you all this? Just leave me alone. I'm tired and need some sleep. I need to let my body fight whatever poison is in me until the incompetent staff decides to help me.

January 15th (part two)

Well, it looks like my dissatisfaction was noted. It's now just after eleven o clock in the evening and I'm still here. I tried to eat earlier, pasta and meatballs but I could only manage a few bites before I was sick. I'm growing more worried now. Fredericks made a brief visit, and although he did a better job to hide it, I could still see the fear on his face. I demanded an update and he said my blood work should be back in the morning. I'll be making an official complaint about this, that's for sure. My pal Frederick's here will be out of a job, that much is certain. My neck itches. I just scratched it and when I looked I had blood on my fingers. I guess I lifted the scab a little, but I still don't like it. I think I'll try to get some sleep and hope for good news tomorrow.

Sunday.

Rough night last night. I dreamed of little soldiers in my blood fighting off whatever infection is in there. I'm resigned to the fact that because of the incompetence of the doctors here, whatever it is has infiltrated my body. I hope that the love and care I have shown to it over the years are repaid in kind and I'm able to fight this thing. I have a headache and even though I feel hungry, I still can't eat. As I glance up from this paper I can see my breakfast cereal still untouched. I looked at myself in the mirror and realise why Fredericks looked so concerned. I look like shit. My skin is pale and waxy, my eyes ringed and dark. I think the puncture wound on my neck is infected. Its edges are red and itch. I think it's starting to spread. How the fuck they didn't pick up on this is beyond me, and I'll be giving them hell when they come in and check on me. If they can't give a straight answer then I'm going home. I have to be back in the office tomorrow.

Sunday (pm)

Gave Frederick's an earful. Told him my intent to take legal action but he didn't seem concerned. I also told

him my intention to leave and he said I should reconsider as they had discovered irregularities with my blood. I didn't like that word and pressed him for more info but as always he clammed up and wouldn't tell me. Still, can't eat. No food now since Friday although the gnawing in my belly tells me I'm hungry. Also, my hair is starting to fall out. I run my hands through it and it comes away in great black clumps. I suppose the only question that matters anymore is this:
What the fuck is happening to me?


Monday.

I'm trapped here. I demanded to leave and Frederick's told me he wasn't authorised to allow it. I told him he had no right to keep me here and, for once looking flustered, he told me he would speak to his superiors. Fuck him. I hope he dies of something painful. Maybe a slow growing cancer that makes him suffer. I still feel like shit, the headache is worse and I can feel myself growing weaker. I'm so hungry but even though they brought me a decent breakfast (toast and boiled eggs), I couldn't eat it. I tried to force it down—aware that I was fighting a battle and my body needed the fuel but I couldn't swallow without being sick. The old fuck on the train has jabbed me with something potent all right. I wonder if I'm dying. I'm certain I shouldn't feel so weak. I'm tired. So tired of all of this and need to get out of here. Fredericks tells me they are going to try and get a drip into me tomorrow and feed me that way. I hate needles (especially now) but I'm also starving and so I won't complain.

Monday (p.m.)
Spoke to Frederick's boss. He came to see me and like everyone else who comes in here now, wore one of those damn hoods and biohazard suits. He told me I was—
As I was writing the entry above by the light of the small lamp by my bed, my thumbnail fell off. All of it. I'm looking at it right now. The flesh below where it once was is black and painful to the touch. What the hell is this? I touched my other nails and they also feel loose, as if I could just slide them straight off the skin if I wanted to. I'm afraid now and need help. I'm hungry, so hungry. I need to fight this. I WILL fight this. Nails or no nails it won't stop me from telling the rest of the

story. I'm a fighter and determined to win. I always do. Now where was I?

Frederick's boss is a man called Richards. He's a big man with flabby cheeks and glaring little eyes and he had a pompous air about him that I disliked from the start, but I was too tired and weak to give him the verbal dressing down as I had intended. He told me I was contagious and would not be allowed to leave. I told him he couldn't do that. I know I have rights, but he wasn't as easily intimidated as Fredericks, and quick as a flash he corrected me and told me he had all the authority he needs and that, like it or not, I was going nowhere. He claims the room is under armed guard and I believe him. Still, nobody will tell me what's wrong with me, but I can feel it getting worse. I try not to think about it but can't shake the feeling my body has given up the fight. The rash on my neck has spread onto my chest and back and shows no sign of slowing. It itches all the time and is weeping a thick liquid flecked with tiny slivers of yellow pus. I'm also mostly bald now. Can you believe that? The lovely thick Italian hair I was so proud of is gone apart from a few stubborn strands that still cling to my skull.

So hungry.

Tuesday.

Drifted in and out of sleep and lost another three fingernails during the night. They just peeled away without resistance. Still not eaten and have lost a lot of weight. I can see the shadows of ribs poking through my skin. A nurse came in to take more blood today. (What the fuck do they do with it all???) She wasn't alone and was accompanied by two doctors (all of them in those fucking white biohazard suits) who watched me even though I didn't try to resist. The needle went in easy but my blood came out in thick congealed lumps and was accompanied by a horrific stench which made me gag. The nurse screamed and hurried from the room, taking the doctors with her.
I just laughed.
Good god, I'm tired of these people. I want to be left alone. My body is failing on me. Why will no one help?

Wednesday.

Lost more nails. Toes this time. Drip wouldn't go in. blood too lumpy. I'm an Auschwitz cliché, just skin and bone and haunted eyes. Can't be bothered writing. Too hungry to care.

Thursday.

Feel a little better today. The headache has faded, but yesterday it was brutal. I can feel the bones protruding out of my skin but I still can't eat. Twice now they have tried to get a drip into me and both times the same result, the horrible congealed blood and rotten pus stench was all they got. They say my veins have collapsed and I don't doubt it. That smell has ingrained itself into me, but it's not so bad once you get used to it. My skin is turning purple at the joints and feels loose on me like it's sliding over the few muscles that haven't yet wasted away. Fredericks made a brief stop, poking his hooded head into the room just long enough to say they had results and that he would be by later to fill me in. I probed to ask if the news was good or bad but he didn't answer, and to be fair he didn't have to. His sombre look and the way I feel told me all I needed to know. So hungry. My mouth is watering as I think of eating a big juicy steak, but I know if one were to appear in front of me I wouldn't be able to even nibble at it. I wish somebody would help me.

Friday

I didn't see that coming!!!!!
HAHAHAHAHAHAHAHAHAHAHA!!!!!!!!!
That explains a lot!!!!! Hungry hungry hungry!!

Saturday.

So Frederick's tells me I'm dead and have been ever since I came in. How's that for a diagnosis? I wouldn't believe him if not for the evidence. He hooked me up to one of those heart rate monitors and sure enough, there was no response. My skin came away as he pulled the sticky pads off my chest. He screamed. I laughed. It didn't even hurt.
He looked at me as if I was some kind of monster and who can blame him? After all, I'm rotting away as I lie here in this sterile white-walled room! First the nails, and now my teeth. They are loose and two of them fell out today.
So hungry you wouldn't believe it. I dreamed of my

father last night, of eating his flesh and drinking his blood and I woke up with my mouth watering. Weeeeeee!!!!!

Sund.

hungry hungry hungry hungry hungry hungry hungry hungry hungry hungry hungry hungry hungry hungry hungry hungry hungry hungry hungry hungry hungry

Wed??

No nails. No teeth. No hair. Skin rotten. Nothing hurts anymore, though. That's good, but I'm still hungry.

Thurs.

I need meat. I crave it. My mouth waters and although I have lost a few teeth I think I could chew on a nice rare steak. What do they call it when it's barely cooked? Blue?
 Did I read somewhere that blood was blue and not red? Red

Blue

Blue

Red

Dead.

By the way, I realised that this is not a hospital room anymore. It's a zoo and I'm being watched. Observed. After all, nobody has seen a genuine living dead man before ha-ha! I'm putrid now. The rash that started on my neck now covers my chest and face, and my skin has turned a nasty shade of blue-grey. I can barely see my own eyes in the mirror, as they have sunk deep into my skull. As I peer out at my reflection, I see a stranger, a stranger who is close to giving up the fight. I think my organs have begun to settle, to liquefy inside me because my stomach is bloated (how can I be so fat when I'm so hungry Ha-Ha!). I look like one of those fucking starving African orphans. You know the type, the ones that are always shown on TV when Oxfam or some other charity is begging for donations. Don't send me money, though, just a new body, please. That and meat. Fresh juicy meat!!

Am I insane? Probably. My mind can be fixed, though. I'll pay for the very best care once I get myself well, I just have to survive. I jabbed this pen I'm writing with into my stomach to see what would happen. It felt tight, like a blister needing to burst so I decided to do it myself. The pen went straight through with no resistance and the relief was immediate. No pain, though. Just that lumpy, streaky yellow fluid and that rotten death stench. The old man was right. End of the road!! End of the road. He stuck me good that's for sure.

Hungry. So damn hungry.

I'm drooling all over the paper.

Friday??

Eaten at last. Not steak but hot and rare all the less. Fredericks only has himself to blame. He leaned too close when he was examining me and I couldn't help myself. I could smell the blood. The clean, healthy blood under his skin. God, it was divine. He didn't scream for long and I ate well even though I lost a few more teeth in the process. I already feel better and I now have his keys. I'm getting out of here. I may have eaten but I'm still hungry and now know what I need. Fresh meat. As fresh as it gets. I'll fight this. I'll beat it. But for now, all I can think about is meat.

Maybe that's what I need to reverse this waking death.

I'm leaving now. I'm so hungry and I can smell it out there, the cattle going about its business in the corridors.

Meat meat meat meat meat.

The meat is screaming, but ill (b)eat it.

Wish me luck.

## *THAT GNAWING FEELING*

Danny was dead. At least that had been his first thought as the fire in his chest exploded and sent him tumbling to the floor. He thought he had known pain, the double leg break he had suffered as a student back in 94' was bad but this was something else. He was grateful that he wasn't alone. Sarah and Jim were in the apartment that the three of them shared. He had hoped that they had heard the commotion as he fell, as he couldn't speak to call to them. Nor could he move, and could only endure the agony as the molten ball of magma that had replaced his heart continued to punish him. He heard them coming, hurried footsteps from the lounge towards the kitchen where he lay in agony on his back. It felt like a pickup truck was parked on his chest. Sarah was a nurse, Jim was a doctor and like himself was fresh out of medical school. He was lucky that they would know what to do, and thought his chances of survival were decent as long as they acted swiftly. Sarah came first, a vision of blonde hair. She crouched and grabbed the phone, which was still clutched in Danny's hand. He remembered that he had been about

to call out for pizza when it happened. She held it to her ear, then turned to Jim and nodded and placed the phone back in its cradle, where it acknowledged with a sharp beep beep. There were a tense few seconds of silence as he watched them, and they watched him.
What are you doing, call a damn ambulance!
His eyes met with Sarah's and despite the agony, her expression confused him. She was smiling.
Why is she smiling? Why aren't they doing anything?
He had heard stories of people's lives flashing before their eyes as they died, but for Danny, this was not the case. The last rational thought that he had was a simple question.
Why?

\*\*\*


White light. Awareness crept back towards him and he realised firstly and with some relief that he was no longer in pain.
Was this it? Was this death?
He thought not. His instincts told him he was still alive. He wanted to close his eyes against the harsh intensity of the light which seemed so incredibly bright, but he couldn't. As feeling came back to him he became more

convinced that indeed, for the time being, he was still a living breathing being. He felt out with his senses, probing into the unknown and yes—He was definitely alive. He could feel the floor beneath him. He wondered for a brief moment if he had been saved after all, and was now in the hospital recovering. But no. As he became more aware of his surroundings, he realised that the bright light he thought might be the great ever after was actually the ceiling lamp in the lounge. He was just about able to recognise the Maroon Lampshade which surrounded it through the glare. He thought he must have passed out and they had brought him in here to wait for the ambulance to arrive. Relief overcame him and as true as it was that he was no longer in pain, the artificial light that was burning into his eyes was maddening. He tried to lift his head or at least turn it to the side, but found that he couldn't move. He tried to close his eyes, to blink away the discomfort but even that small gesture which takes only a tenth of a second to go from brain to eyelid was beyond his ability. Terror bubbled in the pit of his stomach as he systematically tried to move any part of his body, but to his horror found that he could not manage even a tic, a flicker of the finger nor a curl of the toes. A terror in his guts churned a little more violently and he had to force himself to think rationally. He forced himself to consider the possibility he might be dead after all. Could this be it? Could this be what death is? Trapped in a body that no longer functions.

No, it couldn't be. He could still think. He could sense what was around him. He could feel the plush carpet below his body, its fibres tickling his neck and arms. He could feel the dull ache in his left knee where it hit the kitchen counter as he fell to the ground. He could even feel the light breeze coming in from the open kitchen window, which caressed and whispered against his skin. He could feel himself breathing…couldn't he?

He listened, somehow able to suppress the panic which was now a raging tsunami in his guts. He forced himself to focus, to concentrate on one task at a time. He tried to feel, to sense what his body was doing, to focus on the mundane things he took for granted. He couldn't feel his chest moving. Yet he knew he was breathing, however shallow and faint it must be.

Ok, if not death, then what. Paralysis? Some kind of incredibly vivid dream?

Whatever it was he knew for certain he wasn't ready to die yet, not at just twenty-seven and with a promising life ahead of him. A life he had taken for granted in the past but now desperately wanted to live. The next question was one that had been bothering him since he had regained consciousness, and the one he had been putting off asking because he feared the answer.

Where are Jim and Sarah?

It was a good question. They should have been here waiting with him, making sure he remained stable until help arrived.

Jim was Jim Cole, and Danny had known him for four years. They had been paired up together in medical school and found that even though they were fundamentally different as people (Jim was more of an extrovert who liked to party just as much as he liked to study) they had found that they had a similar work ethic and became friends. Jim always looked more suited for sports than medicine. He was tall and broad at the shoulders, and because he chose to unwind from the pressures of study by working out, he was put together like a Sherman tank. He was one of those friends that it would easy to be jealous of—naturally good looking and always sickeningly popular with the opposite sex. Danny had met Sarah through a mutual friend of Jim's a couple of years before, and although she wasn't the type of girl he usually went for (he preferred brunettes) they were introduced to each other and found that their conversation wasn't awkward or as forced as Danny had feared, and had started to see more and more of each other. Jim used to tease Danny, telling him to go for it.

'Why don't you make your move Danny? It's obvious that the two of you are into each other.' Jim would say over a beer, following up with the half grin that he used so effectively in his constant and invariably successful pursuit of the fairer sex. Danny would always shrug and say that he would when the time was right, but inside he didn't know when that would ever be. He was absolutely terrified. He desperately wanted to take things forward, but he was afraid to ruin the relationship they already had. He eventually plucked up the courage to approach the subject at Jim's twenty fifth-birthday party, and had approached her as she sat outside on the short wall at the edge of the driveway. It was a cool night in October, and as he looked at her in the soft glow of the lights from the house, he almost didn't go through with it. She was wearing a pink shirt with the sleeves rolled up and her hair was tucked under a beret, which she wore on the side of her head. He was intimidated by how naturally beautiful she looked in the diffused glow of the house lights and his head was screaming at him not to go through with it and risk ruining everything. The silence was awkward, which was rare and Sarah was looking at him curiously, her face difficult to read. He had taken her hands and told her he thought of her as more than a friend and wanted to take things further. He hated how it sounded even as the words stammered out of his mouth. It was clumsy and cheesy and all the things he didn't want it to be. He felt his cheeks grow hot with embarrassment. Sarah didn't answer him at first. She only looked at him, searching his eyes with her own. He was about to play it off as a joke when she kissed him. It was hard and passionate and when they pulled back, she pulled herself close and rested her head on his chest.

'What took you so long?' she asked as she wrapped her arms around him. He held her relieved and happy. As happy as he thought he could ever be. He realised as he lay there on the floor that he had a lot to live for and was determined to survive.

He pushed away thoughts of the past, knowing they would do him no good and only hinder him as he attempted to work out what was happening to him. He sat up—or at least in his mind he did. In reality, his body remained as still as when he awoke and he felt a hopeless frustration that made him want to scream out. He had read about this kind of thing before, of amputees who insisted they could feel a maddening itch on their toes days after having the entire leg removed. The human brain was a complex thing. He supposed the next obvious question was the one he had been bothering the most. It was the question that was giving him that feeling in his stomach, the gnawing churning feeling of knowing something is horribly askew and out of place. The feeling that something was badly, frighteningly wrong.

It was the reaction of his friends. The look on their face when they found him it was as if… as if they had expected to find him there. There was no look of surprise on their faces. No shock. Sarah had even smiled as she took the phone from him and held it to her ear before putting it back in its cradle.

Why would she smile? Why did she check the phone? Was she checking to see if he had managed to call an ambulance or…

His stomach churned again as he thought of the alternative.

Or was she checking to make sure that he hadn't?

And Jim. Why would Jim just stand and watch as his best friend had a heart attack? He knew what to do, what he should have done. But he had been unrushed—no. Unrushed wasn't it. He didn't react at all; all he did was stand there with his hands in his pockets and watched. None of it made sense unless…

And just like that as things sometimes do, the penny dropped.

If they weren't surprised, then perhaps…perhaps they knew it was going to happen?

He baulked at the thought as soon as it had processed. The idea was preposterous. After all, how could you plan for someone to have a heart attack? He knew you could predict the type of person more prone to have one. The obese. The heavy smokers. The couch festering, inactive slobs. They were in the high-risk category. But he wasn't. He didn't smoke. He wasn't overweight. He ate well and was still young, and yet…here he was.

The front door swung open and Danny turned his head towards the sound, or at least in his brain he did. His body stayed in situ, his unblinking eyes still fixed on the maroon lampshade. He heard voices as they came into the apartment from outside. It was them! Jim and Sarah! Of course! They had gone downstairs to let the ambulance crew in! He chastised himself for allowing his mind to run away with him they were surely just— He froze mid thought. The door closed and he heard the lock slide into place. No paramedics. No hurried conversations. No footsteps racing to his aid. He could hear hushed voices outside the adjoining door to the hallway, but there was no rescue. No attempt to help. He got that feeling again deep in his stomach. That horrible, gnawing feeling. He couldn't hear what they were saying, the closed door muffled the words but he could tell that they were in intense conversation. He tried to move, to turn his head or roll his eyeballs towards the door. Do anything. But his body was still uncooperative, ignoring his desperate requests. The door to the sitting room opened, and he could see their shadowy figures on the edge of his peripheral vision. Sarah spoke, and with the seven words that drifted unseen towards him his world and everything he knew to be normal imploded.

'My god. He really does look dead.'

There was coldness in her voice, which saddened him and filled him with anger. She came into view, leaning over him and looking at him with a neutral expression on her face. Her blonde hair hung over her narrow face as her blue eyes scanned his features. Her lips curled into a cruel smile.

'It's remarkable Jim. Are you sure he isn't dead? You didn't give him too much did you?'

Too much? What did they do? What have they done to me?

Jim then came into view, his black hair was slicked back as he always wore it, and his small eyes peered down his hooked nose. He was standing behind Sarah, Massaging her shoulders. He bent forward and kissed her neck.

'I know what I'm doing. He's alive. I gave him enough to put him out for a few hours. Plenty of time to get everything done.'

'But what if he dies?'

'Isn't that the point? You got what you wanted. Look at him. Besides, does it matter if he is dead? You still win Sarah.'

'I don't want him to get off so easy, Jimmy. I want him to suffer.'

'You're a cold bitch.'

'You still love me though don't you, Jim?' she said

with a hint of desperation. Without waiting for him to respond, she turned and kissed him, watching Danny out of the corner of her eye. The show was obviously for his benefit, and although his abject terror was still the first and foremost thing on his mind, he still found himself sickly jealous as he watched them, literally unable to avert his gaze. She broke away from her coupling with Jim and turned towards Danny, looking at him with a smug smile. There was no love, no sorrow, no remorse in that smile, just hate. Hate for him. He couldn't fathom why.

'Do you think he can hear us, or see us?' she asked without looking away.

'You know he can. Damn, Sarah, he was my best friend. This isn't as easy for me. I can't be as… cold as you can.'

Jim walked away, leaving Sarah and Danny alone.

Ah the happy couple

She knelt beside him, filling his field of vision. He could smell her perfume mingled with a slight undercurrent of sweat. She leaned closer to him, her hair tickling his face, and yet he was unable to do something as simple as reach up and itch, or push it away. Push her away. He didn't want to look at her, but under the circumstances had no choice. She whispered in his ear, her hot breath in his ear reviving memories of passionate nights spent entwined together.

'I suppose you deserve at least an explanation.' She began as she pushed her hair back and tucked it behind her ears, removing the maddening tickle. He could see as she leaned back that she was still smiling that hateful, spiteful, self-amused smile.

'I'm sorry it had to come to this Danny, but let's be honest you and I had been growing apart for a while. This is actually your own fault you know. I was going to leave you. I even had a suitcase packed on that day when you called and told me about the inheritance. The money. Of course.

'We could have had a great life, Danny. We could have gone to live overseas or travelled the world, but instead, you banked it. Who the hell banks two million in cash and keeps going to work for a living? It's a fucking joke!'

She shook her head, the smile melting away from her face as her eyes darted around the room.

'It's ok for you, you're a doctor, and you have some respect. But what about me? Did you ever think about me? I was Out there day and night working myself into the ground. It's hard on the wards, Danny. You could have taken care of me. You could have taken care of us both but you didn't. So, as usual, I had to take care of it myself.'

He wanted to tell her, to explain that he had put the money away for a rainy day, so they could get married, buy a nice house, and raise a family. But of course, he couldn't.

Her hand came into view and he thought at first she was going to hit him, and although he couldn't move, he mentally recoiled. It was then he realised that she was holding something out to him. It was a small vial containing a yellow liquid.

'I got the idea from the Discovery Channel. There was a documentary on about Zombies, about how in Haiti they believe in all that stuff. Not TV zombies, not Dawn of the Dead. I'm talking about the real deal. The Haitian Sorcerer, or Bokor as their tribes know them claimed their resurrection powers came from their ability to capture a fragment of their intended victim's Ti bon ange, or soul to you and me. The Bokor didn't have actual supernatural powers. Of course, I'm sure you already suspected that.'

She smiled at him with a dreamy vacancy that made

him wonder just when she had lost her mind. She continued.

'Instead, they used this.' She shook the liquid in front of his eyes. He watched as it swished inside its bottle. 'You have no idea what lengths we had to go to in order to get his stuff. But if you know the right people you can get just about anything. We gave you the liquid form but the traditional method of the Bokor used a powder. The Bokor would mix it together with a mixture of ground plants and animals. It comes down to neurotoxins Danny. See the powdered version was created to break and irritate the skin to allow the neurotoxin to enter the bloodstream. Of course, for this purpose that would be of no use. And so you got the more direct, and more potent liquid version. I'm sure you suspect it already, but you are in a state of complete paralysis. In Haitian folklore, the victim would be then buried and then later when the effects wore off they would rise and believe themselves to be reincarnated from the dead.'

She leaned close and whispered and he could smell the coffee laced minty smell of her breath.

'Of course, only the first part will apply to you.'

She moved the vial closer to his eyes revolving it

slowly. It reminded him of one of those late night shopping TV channels that air when nobody is awake to watch. Selling the kind of gimmicky gadgets nobody needs or wants.

GOT THAT GNAWING FEELING? THEN GET THIS EXCLUSIVE AUTHENTIC BOKOR ZOMBIE SERUM!! TIRED OF THE WELL MEANING HARD WORKING BOYFRIEND? INJECT HIM WITH THIS AND VOODOO YOUR TROUBLES AWAY! ORDER NOW AND WE WILL THROW IN THE BEST FRIEND TO HELP YOU WITH YOUR WICKED SCHEME! ORDER NOW FOR JUST TWO MILLION U.S DOLLARS!! HURRY ONLY SEVEN LEFT IN STOCK!

He was losing it, and tried desperately to regain control of his mind; it was the only thing left he had left, and he intended to at least keep himself on the right side of sanity until he could figure out a way to get out of this mess. He watched Sarah as she put the vial back in her purse.
'It causes complete paralysis and slows the heart and respiratory system to almost a complete stop.

Essentially, you're dead. But here's the best part. Tonight, Jim and I are going to a special place in the woods. I sent Jim out there this morning to dig a hole. That's where you will live out your final hours, alone and in the dark. You will eventually regain control of your body, after all, this state isn't permanent, but by then it won't matter. How calm do you think you can keep yourself? How long can you make the little air you will have last for? How will it feel to know you are down there in the dark with no way out? It's interesting, actually. I half wish I could be there to see how you will cope. I think even someone as weak and spineless as you might even surprise yourself. For a while at least.'

Buried alive.

He looked into the monstrous eyes of his former partner and wondered when the idea had begun to form in her mind, how long had she had sat on it, mulling it over. When had she realised that she would need Jim's help? He supposed the real question was what price did she put on a human life?

'I know it seems cruel and you are probably wondering why. Well, the truth is I don't have an answer that would give you the kind of reasoning you are looking for. Just believe me when I tell you it's a combination of both a need and a desire to see you suffer. Most of all it's the need to be free of you.'

The matter of fact tone in her voice astonished him, the way she was so conversational despite her plans to kill another human being.

'They will look for you I suppose. You may even make the news. I'll play the grieving girlfriend supported by the loyal best friend. We will say how it is uncharacteristic of you, and how you are usually so responsible. No, you have no enemies, nor do we know anyone that meant you harm. Soon enough there will be some other news, maybe a terrorist attack or a squabble in some backwards little country that will take centre stage and you will be forgotten. When you are declared dead the money you are holding back will come to me.'

Danny realised then she was insane. It was a combination of things. The tone of her voice, the wild-eyed stare as she rambled on at him, pointing at him all the time. And the way she was wearing that smile, that awful smile…

'I know what you must be thinking. That I have no rights to that cash if you die right? Well, think again. Jim made sure that the right papers with your signature on found the right people. I get everything. That's always been your problem. You never saw me as an equal. 'Oh, she's just a nurse, content to read her celebrity magazines and watch her soap operas.' Well, look at me now. Making a life for myself. For me and Jim and I hope you suffer a long and painful death you son of a bitch.'

'That's enough!' came Jim's voice from somewhere to Danny's right side.

Probably from his favourite chair by the window.

'Go down and check the car, make sure we have everything that we need. I want to get this over and done with before I lose my nerve.' Came Jim's commanding voice.

Jim drifted into Danny's field of view and handed the keys to Sarah, who stood and walked away. He listened as she went down the hall and the door opened and closed. Once again, his vision was filled with the maroon lampshade. Who the hell had decided on Maroon anyway? He hated that fucking lampshade. He promised himself then that he would tear that fucker down, obliterate it, destroy it, but first, he had to live. He had to survive. Jim pulled up a chair from the dining table and sat beside Danny. Unlike Sarah who appeared to be untroubled by the murder she was about to commit, he looked like hell. He was pale and looked exhausted.

Good. Fuck him.

He hadn't shaved and Danny wondered how long he had lived with the burden of what he had intended to do. Jim lit a cigarette with shaking hands, exhaling a long plume of blue smoke.

'Hey, pal. I uh... Just wanted to talk to you in private one last time.'

Forgive me if I don't answer Jimbo but I'm a little dead here, but I think you will understand. You go ahead and talk whilst I keep staring at this damn lampshade. Whose idea was it to buy that thing anyway? It's fucking horrific! Not as horrific as this little situation, though, oh no, not by a long shot.

'Look, me and Sarah I – You have to believe me that I tried to resist her ok? I tried but the three of us living together it just—well she always gets what she wants, doesn't she? I mean we have joked about it before right?'

We have Jim but there is a hell of a difference between getting control over the TV remote control and killing off your partner to get your hands on his inheritance.

'I mean I have always been there for you haven't I? In the past, I mean. I even kinda got the two of you together in the first place didn't I?'

Danny could see Jim becoming unhinged. He was starting to babble, his eyes shifting about the room. He was a man trying to convince himself of his actions.

'And hey at least you will be dead soon right? I mean I have to live with this, with this guilt for the rest of my life. So you see how it is don't you Danny? Surely you do.'

Forgive me for not being too fucking sympathetic to your plight Jim, but your feelings of guilt don't concern me too much, after all, I'm the one who's dead here Ha-ha!

Jim leaned forward and whispered, his eyes darting from the door to Danny and back again.

'You have to believe me that if I could go back in time I wouldn't do this, wouldn't do any of it. But damn that woman Danny she has a knack of manipulating people, of getting her own way. If I had another shot…I wouldn't do it I swear.'

In his head, Danny yelled out in frustration. He knew if he could do something small, even just a blink or twitch of the finger it would be enough to make Jim see sense.

He concentrated hard, willing his eyelid to move and knowing it was the most important moment of his life. He had to succeed. He willed the muscle to respond to his command but it was useless. He screamed again in his head, as he watched Jim dry his eyes.

'Look, Danny, I'm too far in this now to back out, she made sure of that. I'm implicated and we both know she wouldn't hesitate to drop me in the shit if I didn't go ahead.'

I know what you are saying Jim but think about this, no harm no foul. Help me survive this and even though you took my girlfriend, money and almost killed me, I'll put it down to a prank gone wrong. Please, Jim; I need you to help me!

'I will do something for you though Danny. For old time's sake. I still want the money or my share of it at least and I won't deny that—not to you, old pal. You could always tell when I was lying anyway but believe it when I tell you I don't want you to suffer. She might but I don't okay? So I'm going to make it easy for you.'

Stop referring to me in past tense. I'm still here you asshole!

Jim pulled out a hunting knife housed in a brown leather scabbard.

'Remember when you got me this a few years back for when I went on that safari in Africa? Well, I'm giving it back to you now. I sharpened it, and I'm going to slip it in the waistband of your jeans. When you come around from the serum, use it to slit your wrists. Nobody deserves to suffer the way Sarah intends for you to. This is my way of giving you an easy option and she will never have to know.'

Danny felt the cold of leather on his skin as Jim tucked the knife into his jeans, and he internally flinched as the metal of the hilt tip pressed into his side.

'There. I know this won't make it right, but it might make it easier for me to look myself in the mirror without feeling so fucking guilty. It might even let me sleep again. Damn it Danny I haven't slept for months. I truly am sorry. You don't deserve this.'

Months.

So that's how long this had been in the works for. He wondered how he could have been so stupid. How could he not have known? He remembered watching a Documentary about the wife of a notorious Serial Killer who over the course of twenty-two years murdered over seventy prostitutes. When he was caught, the killer's wife claimed to have never had a clue about his secret life, which Danny had always thought to be impossible. But now he could believe it. Nothing had alerted him, nothing had seemed suspect or out of place. He never had that suspicion, that gnawing feeling. He had it now all right, though. He had it bad. Jim finished his cigarette and walked out of Danny's field of vision. The door opened and he spoke again.

'Remember to slit down the vein, Danny, not across it. You should bleed out pretty fast. I know it doesn't seem like a way out but it's better than the alternative.' He left and closed the door behind him.

Although he knew it was pointless, he tried again to will himself to move, start with a finger or a toe and go from there. Perhaps Jim had made a mistake with the dosage of the serum, and he would come around in time to act, or to at least fight for his life instead of just watch as it was stolen away. In truth, he knew it was unlikely. It was obvious how meticulously they had planned, and to hope they had made such a simple error was naïve. He had to delay them somehow to give himself a fighting chance. It was then, as he was playing through scenarios in his mind that they returned. Jim had a roll of carpet over his shoulder as he stood by Danny's feet. He turned to Sarah, his eyes wide.

'Should I close his eyes? He's freaking me out.'

'No. I want him to experience every second of this.'

Jim shot her a pained look as he put the roll of carpet down and spread it out on the floor. He then moved out of Danny's line of sight. Danny felt powerful hands move him across the floor and at last, his viewpoint changed. He saw a flash of knees. The television, and then nothing as his face was mashed into the carpet. A bolt of pain fired into his skull and he began to panic, worrying he would suffocate. But then he remembered the situation and amid the horror, he laughed inside his head.

HAHA! Just relax!! It's your stupid brain getting confused! You can't suffocate when you are already dead! Some doctor you turned out to be. Anyway, it might be better to die here with your nose buried in a cheap carpet. We all know what the alternative is, and none of us want that!

The voice in his head had a point, and against all his instincts to survive he willed it to happen. In his mind, he pushed his nose further into the carpet, blocking his airways praying for true death, not this living, feeling, unable to move hell. Because the voice in his head, the one that was a little more frayed around the edges and a little closer to breaking point was right. Anything was better than the alternative. He could visualise it in horrific clarity. Slowly gaining control of his limbs in the pitch dark, knowing the freedom of control of his body would not lead to freedom itself but only the ability to take his own life. He knew how it would be. He had already lived it in his nightmares. Seconds would become hours and minutes would feel like days. And what about the end as the air in that tiny box grew heavy and thick and he had used up his limited oxygen? He wouldn't allow it. Somehow, he would fight. He had to. He found himself praying to a God that he didn't even believe in. he did it anyway, promising that if there was someone up there and they chose to spare him, he would become a believer. Hell, he would even go to church. Not just on occasion either, but every Sunday. Hell, every day if it were asked of him. All he wanted was a chance. A fighting chance.

They wrapped him in the carpet. The cheap fibres felt rough against his cheeks and the indistinct off white colour that filled his entire field of view made any sense of direction hard to judge. At least looking at the maroon lampshade he knew which way was up and down, however now he was unsure and felt queasy. Although he could still hear them speaking, their words were muffled and hard to make out. His heart jumped, although he knew, in reality, it hadn't even registered as he was lifted onto Jim's shoulder. He was moving now, out of the apartment and into the hallway, then to the left and through another door, this one creaking loudly as it was opened.

They were taking him out via the stairs.

Of course they were, he thought to himself as he was jostled along. They wouldn't risk taking him in the lift. Too much chance that someone would see them. He counted the flights as they descended. Four. Three. Two. One. And then he felt the wind ruffle the top of his hair and knew they were outside. Despite his prayers, they were not stopped. Not challenged. Probably not even seen. More muffled voices as he was bundled into the back of Jim's car, which must have been parked right outside the side door. He knew it was Jim's because Sarah drove a Firebird, big and noisy with an ugly twin white stripe painted down the middle and poor gas mileage. He had often teased her about it, and why she didn't have a car more suited to the fairer sex. She had looked at him and said with a seductive smile she 'liked the way it felt underneath her'. Even so, it was no good for this task anyway. And because Jim drove a huge SUV, which was painted jet black and had tinted windows, it was perfect for the job. He imagined Jim leaning on a bar somewhere, flirting with one of the interns.

By day, I'm a doctor, by night I ferry dead friend's bodies to the woods. Would you like another Martini? The door was closed and for a few precious seconds, there was silence, before the twin sounds of the front driver and passenger doors opened and closed. He heard Jim speak, and even without seeing could sense the uncertainty in his voice.

'Are you sure that this is what you want? This is the last chance to back out.'

'I already told you this is what I want, this is what we wanted Jim. Don't pussy out on me now. Don't be like him.'

'Look you know I'm in deep on this and that's fine, but you can't expect me to be happy about it. Danny and I have been friends for years... I just think we could have done this some other way.'

'Well, I'm sorry if this offends your morals Jim but you will just have to learn to live with it. Believe me, I bet a couple of million in the bank will go a long way towards healing your conscience.'

'Look all I'm saying is that we could stand to lose a lot here if we get caught.'

'Well, it's up to us to make sure that doesn't happen. Did you dig the grave where I told you to?'

'Done. It's not perfect but will do the job.'

Until that point, he had held out some hope, however small that he could somehow escape. But as he listened to his girlfriend and best friend in a casual discussion about the plans to kill him as he lay there still unable to do anything about it, he realised that this was really going to happen. They intended to bury him alive and it was happening now. Even the survivalist in him was silent, reflecting on this revelation.

'Good. Come on, let's get this over with, I want to be back in time for American Idol.'

Choosing not to respond, Jim started the car and put it into gear. They were on their way.

Time lost any sense of meaning for Danny. He wasn't sure how long they had been driving for. To him, it felt like hours, days even but he suspected it was less than an hour. After a while, the smooth ride of the road surface changed to the suspension-jolting ride of a dirt road. He tried to think where he might be but realised that not only could he be anywhere, he didn't know the area enough to even hazard a guess. He tried to coax survivalist Danny out from wherever he was hiding but it was fruitless. He had already slinked away deep into some dark corner of the mind perhaps looking after himself and leaving frightened Danny to his own devices. The car stopped.

'Is this it?' asked Sarah.

'Yeah, just a little way into the woods. Right where we planned.'

'And you sure everything is ready?'

'Checked and double checked.'

'Ok, let's go then. Grab the head, I'll get the feet.'

That was all he was to her now. Not a him, not a name, just an object. He was nothing to her. An obstacle between her and the money she so craved.

He was pulled out of the car and then they were on the move again, this time on foot and probably for the last time in his life. It seemed that he might have been right about the length of the journey here after all. It was definitely full daylight just before he was wrapped in the carpet back at the apartment but now he could see the ground as Jim hoisted him over his shoulder and could tell that it was dusk, with full darkness less than an hour away.

Despite knowing what was coming, a strange sense of calm overcame him. He watched the dirt track veer off from his line of sight, replaced by yellowed, tired looking grass and branches. He felt the limbs of trees tugging at the carpet and was strangely happy to have its protection from their gnarled grasp. Suddenly they stopped and he found himself lowered to the ground. He could see the sky through the trees, a deep and ugly slate grey colour as the sunlight faded away.

'Is this it?' Sarah asked with a note of irritation in her voice.

'You know that it is for Christ's sake. The damn coffin is right in front of you.'

'Relax Jim. Nobody is going to stop us.'

'Don't tell me to relax. Let's just get this done. The sooner the better.'

'You sound like you might be having second thoughts.'

'Jesus Sarah, he was my friend. Surely the time you spent together counts for something?'

'Actually, it doesn't. I just need to know that you aren't about to go limp on my like that son of a bitch would.'

'I'm here aren't I? Let's just get it done before he

wakes up. I don't know about you but I can do without any Dawn of the dead shit.'

*This is no time for jokes Jimbo. You are minutes away from becoming a murderer. Think about that why don't you?*

'Is that going to be deep enough? I told you to dig six feet down.'

His grave. He wished he could see it, but somehow not being able to was worse. He could still only see the ugly skies in his tiny world that for now consisted of itchy, synthetic fibres.

'Hey, I'm a surgeon, not a damn grave digger. Relax; this is what you wanted after all.'

'We Jim. It's what we wanted.'

'If you say so.'

Danny prayed for an argument, for Jim to realise that she was the one in control. That she was pulling the strings, and the second the police grew suspicious, she would cut him loose and let them have him. But Jim reacted like Danny himself had in the past too many times to remember. He backed down.

'Look I'm sorry Sarah; it's just that now we're here I'm a little freaked out.'

'All the more reason to get it over with. Come on, I'll

help you to get the coffin in the hole.'

He could hear the scraping of wood against soil, and then the dull thud as his final resting place was prepared. Footsteps approached and he knew it was time. He was out of options. He was about to die.

'Should we take the carpet off him?' Sarah asked.

'Yeah, it's covered in his D.N.A anyway; I say we put it in the box with him. Want me to grab it?'

'No ill get it.'

He felt himself jerked to the side, his face smashing into the ground as he was rolled from the carpet and slammed into the ground

'Damn it, Sarah! Why did you have to do that?'

He could feel a dull pain in his temple and his right arm was twisted under him. He could smell the earthy rot of the ground and realised that his hope for some kind of miracle was only that. A hope of a desperate man.

'What does it matter, it's not like we have to be nice to him. So what if he gets a little roughed up on his way.'

'Don't you think we are putting him through enough? Now cut that shit out or I swear I'll drive away and leave you here alone.'

Silence.

She had let him win this one because she needed him

and he knew it.

'Ok, whatever. Look let's just do this already, it's almost eight.'

He was rolled over onto his back, his open eyes now looking into the face of his best friend. He looked even worse than before as if the last couple of hours had drained away his life force.

'Sorry buddy, you deserve more respect than that. Come on, let's get you in there and seal you up.'

There was a vagueness in which he said this; perhaps he was just as crazy as she was. Or maybe the real Jim, uncorrupted by this monster had locked himself away somewhere deep in his mind where he couldn't be found just like survivalist Danny. Maybe it was the mental strain and months without sleep had broken him. Either way speculating about it didn't make any difference. Because the result was going to be the same.

He was grabbed under the armpits and dragged across the leafy forest floor. His legs trailed out behind him and he watched as one of his Nike pumps pulled loose and was left behind. I think I'll stay up here if it's all the same to you, Danny. Shoes like me work better above ground. No offence. He was lowered to the ground, his view now of the sky and the wiry tree tops which danced and swayed in the breeze.

'Ok' said Jim breathlessly. 'Here's how we are going to do this. I'll get down there in the box and take the weight of his upper half; you lower his legs over the side when I tell you to.'

'Got it. Just make sure his eyes are open and he can see it all happen.'

You bitch. You fucking bitch.

He heard the dull thud of boots on wood and then he was moving, being lowered just as Jim had said it would be. He saw the ground begin to grow around him and it was exactly like his nightmares. He was laid flat, the rough edges of the grave filling his field of vision and framed in stark contrast against the thunderheads above, which were now growing like an ugly bruise. He felt his body come to rest as Jim hoisted his leg over the grave edge and pulled himself up to solid ground with a grunt, speaking to Sarah as he did so.

'Grab the carpet. Come on hurry up'

Jim was in a panic, his eyes darting from side to side as Danny screamed in his head, terror in its purest form had now consumed him. He couldn't be here, not with the dark things. Not in this tiny hole.

'Give me the lid. And grab that shoe.' he said breathlessly as Sarah did as she was told.
It looks like my poor escapee Nike is joining me after all, Danny thought to himself as he felt his sanity begin to fragment. Jim looked into the hole. Danny thought he was crying but the light was bad and it was hard to tell.

The escapee shoe and re-rolled carpet were tossed into the makeshift coffin, landing on Danny's lower half. If this were a movie this would be the point where he would be rescued from the jaws of death by an armed police squad led by a cigar chewing lead detective, or an inquisitive dog walker alerted by the voices out here in the woods would stumble on their fiendish plot and call the police. But there was to be no rescue. He understood that now. He could feel the blood pounding in his temples as he willed himself to live, for his body to overcome the poison which coursed through its veins and fight back. Sarah came back into view with the lid of the coffin and then he felt it, horror so pure that it felt like a solid thing that filled his veins with ice. Seeing that makeshift lid made it real.
 This is my grave.
The thought stayed with him as he looked at the remaining daylight shining through the gaps in the

wood. What if the soil came through the holes? What if it filled his ears, mouth, and eyes before he regained control of his body? He imagined the worms, touching his skin with their cold and wet bodies, or the maggots, burrowing into his eyes, nesting in his mouth, feeding on his tongue.

Oh, god please let it be quick...

Jim moved the lid into position and then hesitated. The gloom was heavy now and Danny felt the occasional wet splash of rain on his skin. For a moment, it looked like Jim was a child. His eyes were wide and showing too much of the whites and his grimy face was streaked with tears. A huge mucus bubble expanded and contracted in his left nostril as he breathed in ragged gasps. Perhaps now at the end, he had realised what was happening, understood what he was doing. But there was the fear that stopped him from doing anything about it. The fear of her. His puppet master. And the knowledge that it was now too late to go back.

'God forgive me,' he whispered as he lowered the lid of the coffin, shutting out the light of the day and plunging Danny into suffocating darkness. In his head, Danny Screamed.

He didn't stop even when the hole was filled and he

was plunged into silence.

*Rio, Brazil.*

The man sipped his gin and tonic as he looked out over the glorious panorama of the Rio coastline. The sun was just beginning to set and the sky was a beautiful red orange hue. The ocean was dabbled with golden reflections from the fading light of what had been a glorious day. As the sodium streetlamps began to fizzle on in unison, the man smiled, for he had seen another day come and go. His hand, the palms rough and calloused, went to the large crucifix he wore around his neck, and he let his fingers glide over its contours. He would often let his mind wander to a different time. The sixteen hours between Danny Harding's burial, revival and escape are ones he prefers not to think about. However, on this day, the anniversary of it happening he always did. It had been seven years now and although he still had to sleep with the lights on and most nights woke screaming and clawing at his sheets until he realised that he was safe, he didn't mind, because he was alive. Never a religious man, not back then, Danny had changed his outlook.

It had, after all, been a bizarre set of circumstances which had come together to allow him to escape from his intended grave. Of course, Jim and Sarah had planned well, meticulously in fact but they didn't account for the variables of the situation. Even now, he still liked that word.

Variables.

Things such as the homemade coffin being much larger than a regular one, allowing Danny to roll onto his side then on his knees once he regained control of his body. Then there was the knife Jim had left Danny with which to kill himself. How he was able to use it to cut away the cheap wood around the nails holding the lid in place. Even these fortuitous circumstances could have been for nothing, if not for Jim.

Jim with his surgeon's hands. Jim who never liked nor had the dexterity for manual labour. The six-foot grave that Sarah had demanded was, in reality, a little more than three and combined with the flimsy coffin made from cheap timber and the heavy rain that followed, made digging through the softened earth possible.

He had wanted to give up. Of that, there should be no mistake. As he lay there in the blackest darkness imaginable, listening to the soil land on the wooden lid, so deafeningly loud from inside but slowly fading to silence as he the hole was filled. Those hours after in absolute blackness and silence so heavy and oppressive were the worst. As he began to regain control, first of his toes and fingertips that came alive with pins and needles as he first moved a finger, and then made a fist. It was the survivalist within him, the voice so quiet for so long that had finally resurfaced and made him try. He had known the chances were slim, but when there was nothing left to lose, so why not try it? He told himself that he would just to see how far he could go. One-step at a time.

First the knife. Check along the edges of the lid to find the nails, cut them free, after that let's just see how far we get. It was still a living hell, clawing through the darkness with the heavy earth pressing against his body, the feeling of total claustrophobia as he sobbed and struggled for breath was almost unbearable. Worst still was not knowing if he were about to die, or if he might just survive long enough to claw his way to freedom with his bare hands.

He finished his drink and pulled out two things from his wallet. The first was a photograph. The years had seen it become dog-eared and there was an ugly crease down its middle. He wasn't even sure why he still carried it. He tried to tell himself that it served as a reminder that life was there to be lived not wasted. But the reality was that he liked to look at it. And why not? He had survived against all odds and had every right to remind himself of it. The photograph was of Jim and Sarah. She was right about one thing. If you knew the right people you could get your hands on just about anything. He just happened to know a certain overweight Italian mob boss who gladly took his fifty thousand and acquired him the things he needed, and made sure they were also untraceable. In the photograph the pair were in the same hole as they had dug for him, only they were in a much smaller coffin. He had trouble fitting them in and they were pressed face to face, nose to nose. Their eyes seemed lifeless, already dead in fact but of course, he knew better. He knew they could see and feel everything that was happening. He had measured the dimensions to make sure that once the lid was on that they would have no more than an inch of space on any one side. It was…Snug.

He often wondered if they had had a survivor type within them if they had at least made a try to escape. He supposed they would have, although he couldn't fathom how. He remembered sitting on the edge of the grave, his feet on the edge of the coffin still without its lid and looking down at his two friends. It didn't seem as scary from up there.

'I'm going to give the two of you the almost the same chance that I had. It won't be as easy because frankly it looks a bit cramped in there and I doubt you would get the leverage, but if it's meant to be, it's meant to be. The hole is the same depth too, just less than three feet so escapable if you can get out of the coffin.'

He had looked at them, watching the waxy dead eyed faces of his friends who looked about to engage in a bizarre open-eyed kiss.

'Because of your disadvantage I gave you a watered down version of the zombie serum, you injected me with. You should know I didn't go to the police about what you did. I thought a more personal method of retribution would be more suitable.'

He had checked his watch then and swung his legs out onto the ground. 'You should come around in say... two hours from now, which means I better get to work. If you do manage to escape then consider us even. I'm leaving the country. Now in fact, so don't come looking for me.' They were still motionless of course, but in his mind he imagined them screaming and pleading for their lives. It made him smile. He took out his phone and selected the camera, and took the photograph, which had since resided in his wallet behind his driver's license and photograph of his parents. He had then put the lid in place and hammered in exactly six nails, which was the same amount as was in his own coffin. He then went to work and filled the hole as the sun poured down on his back.

His lasting image of the two just as he closed the lid was of them nose-to-nose, eye to eye. He liked that image. It seemed fitting, it seemed right.

He smiled and wondered not for the first time if God would forgive him when his time to pass on did come. He could have gone to the police and had them arrested, trialled and convicted, but for what? A few years in a comfortable prison then free again in a world where they had no right to exist.

No.

There had been no other way, and he hoped that God would take that into account when his judgment came. He left some money for his drink and stood, stretching as he watched the sun begin to fade below the horizon line. The photograph he slipped into his pocket. As he looked at the second item, a small piece of paper folded into four, he wondered if something inside him had been broken that day. Something in his mind certainly had never been the same, and in some respects, the man he used to be did die that day in the shallow grave dug by his friends. The man he was now was different. Even though he lived a relatively normal life, his mind felt somehow…fractured. He imagined it like a pane of glass with a crack in the middle, and as the cracks splintered ever outward, it became less and less possible to repair. He supposed that one day it would shatter all together, and what would happen then he couldn't even begin to guess. Still, that was all in the future. He would enjoy this day and every other from then on as if it were his last.

He supposed in a way he should thank them, Jim and Sarah for showing him the value of life. For years, he had taken something so precious for granted and since his ordeal had learned to appreciate it. To treasure it. It was something that perhaps you couldn't understand unless you had looked death in the eye and lived to tell the tale. His eyes drifted over the list on the folded paper, even though he had long ago memorised it.

List of items.

Zombie serum??
Rope
Car keys (Jim)
Good wood for coffin
Tape measure
Hammer
Nails
Shovel
Gloves
2 x bags of ready mix concrete (for hole)

He folded the paper up and put it in his pocket with the photograph. He had told them what to expect. He said he would give them almost the same chance to escape. Even without the concrete, he doubted they would have been able to get out of the coffin anyway. He glanced over at the ocean, the sun almost invisible now apart from a golden sliver, which still hung above the horizon. He didn't like the night, not anymore and always made sure he was indoors before the sun fully set, and would make sure that every light in the house was switched on. It would stay that way until the morning. Too many shadows in the dark. Too many cold, wet things that could be dragging themselves around unseen. They couldn't come into the light, though. That's not how it went. Those were the rules. He smiled to himself as he began to walk, and he quickly became another anonymous figure lost in the crowded Rio streets.

It was good to be alive.

## TINA

Thomas Rhodes had worked as a detective for almost fifteen years and had seen pretty much everything there was to see. But even he could not believe that the young girl sitting in the interview room could be guilty of anything other than denying herself a decent meal or two. He always had a good instinct for sniffing out the truth and he was rarely wrong, but from the moment she was arrested covered in blood and walking in a daze, something had not felt right to him. He looked at her now as she sipped from her polystyrene cup and wasn't sure what to think. Her skin was smooth and pale and she had a narrow oval face which seemed both guilt and trouble free. She hadn't given any personal information when she had been arrested but he guessed that she was young, perhaps very early twenties. Her frame was thin—borderline undernourished and the bones in her shoulders stood out and cast ugly shadows in the harsh light of the interview room. Her hair was long and black with a red streak at the fringe, and she wore it parted down the centre, which brought out the brilliance of her piercing blue eyes. Rhodes searched her features looking for any evidence of guilt but saw none. She could have just as easily have been sipping coffee in the park with friends rather than in under arrest and wearing a white paper forensics suit.

He set down his own cup and stretched, trying to ignore the dull ache in his arthritic knee. He was only forty-two but was starting to feel the unstoppable onset of old age creeping up on him. The hair that hadn't gone grey was thinning, and the dimples in his cheeks that had given him a chiselled look as a young officer had deepened into worry lines. He hadn't shaved for two days and found that even his stubble had lost its once natural blonde colour, and had started to take on a salt and pepper tone. He made a reluctant mental note to see the doctor about the pain in his knees, even though he knew that as usual he would be given the same advice that he had ignored for the last few years. Lose a few pounds, cut out the saturated fats, stop smoking, and exercise more. He would usually grudgingly agree if only to speed things up and get out of the doctor's office. Although he could benefit from losing a few pounds, he didn't think it was as doom and gloom as they loved to imply.

'Ok,' he said, folding his hands on the table. 'Let's start

with the basics. How about a name?'

She looked at him and smiled. It was a warm and friendly smile—not the twisted smile of a killer or a maniac. Her voice was soft and calm and although it was just a single word, it gave him an inexplicable chill.

'Tina.'

'Thank you. I'm Detective Rhodes. I need to ask you a few questions. Ok?'

She nodded and put her cup on the table.

'Now I need you to tell me what happened, why you were covered in blood when we picked you up.'

She frowned, and for a moment, there was a look of uncertainty on her face.

'Oh, I forgot about the blood.' She said, lowering her gaze and staring at the wooden table top.

His mouth felt dry and he had to force himself to stay focused.

'When our officers picked you up you were covered in it. You were walking down the middle of the road and singing. Do you remember Tina?'

'Of course, I remember. I always sing when I'm out walking. It's an old habit.' She said with a shrug.

'What about the blood. Tell me about the blood. Where did it come from?'

'From Lexi of course. Where else?' she said as if he had asked the most obvious question in the world. She was looking at her hands now as if they held the answers to his questions. Even though he had shared rooms like this with some of the vilest and dangerous criminals that had ever roamed the country, he had never been as unsettled as he felt in the presence of this young girl.

'And where is Lexi now?'

She didn't answer, and wouldn't meet his gaze.

'Tina, I want to help you but you have to talk to me. What did you do to Lexi?'

She threw her head back and laughed. Again he was troubled, for it wasn't the cackle of a psychopath or a deranged maniac, but a natural sound that somehow made it even worse.

'Me? I didn't do anything. I could never do anything like that.'

'Then who did it, Tina. Talk to me.' Rhodes pressed.

She stopped laughing and looked him in the eye her gaze unwavering.

'It was Monde.'

Rhodes took out his pen and held it over the notepad.

'Ok, spell that for me, please. M-o...'

'n-d-e.' she finished as he scrawled the name and double underlined it.

'And where is he now, this Monde?'

She shrugged. 'He comes and goes.'

'Is he a friend? Boyfriend?'

'Sometimes.'

'Sometimes a friend or sometimes a boyfriend?'

'Both.' She replied with a small smile.

'And what did Monde do, to Lexi I mean.'

'Only what he had to. I tried to warn her but she wouldn't back off.'

Finally feeling that he was getting somewhere, Rhodes added the name Lexi to his pad and set the pen down on the table.

'So you and Lexi are friends?'

'She and I had been friends for years, but she kept pushing and pushing, and Monde didn't like that. He hates it when people don't do what he says.'

Rhodes didn't like the way Tina was speaking about her friend in past tense. He pressed on.

'Tina this is very important. What happened to Lexi?

'I don't want to talk about it.'

'Look I'm trying to help you here but you have to talk to me.'

She looked up at him and her eyes were hot with defiance.

'You won't find him, you probably won't find her either. He will make sure of that.'

'Let me worry about that. Just talk to me, tell me what happened. You realise that you could be in a lot of trouble unless you give me something?'

She smiled at him again, showing her perfect white teeth.

'I'm not afraid. Monde said he would come for me and take me away from here.'

'Look, Tina, I'm going to be honest with you. It's not looking too good for you right now. I want to help you but you have to tell me what happened. Do you realise you are going to go to prison for a long time unless you start talking to me?'

She shrugged, and looked unconcerned.

'I haven't done anything. I told you. Monde did it.'

'So you keep saying, but it was you we picked up covered in blood. Now unless I get some answers you are only a matter of hours away from being charged.'

'Monde said it didn't matter. He said he would take care of things.'

'Tina, don't be fooled by the stuff you see on CSI. The

fact is that the bloody clothes you were picked up in are now with forensics. All they need to do is determine if it's human blood and we would have enough to charge you.'

For the first time, she seemed to be flustered and chewed her lower lip.

'That's not right. I didn't do anything.'

'Look I suggest you forget what Monde told you and tell me what happened. All of it from the beginning.'

She leaned on the desk and sighed. He sipped his coffee and watched her, waiting until she was ready to continue. After a few minutes, she leaned back and looked him in the eye. She looked tired and waxy under the harsh strip lights of the interview room.

'It doesn't matter anyway but if you want to know what happened I'll tell you.'

Thomas picked up his pen.

'Tell me everything, starting with how you met Monde.'

Two

Quint's bar was the only place to go in the small town of Oakwell. During the day, they served hot lunches and the place had a mellow easy going feel. Tina didn't work the day shift. Her clientele were a different breed, the factory workers and hillbillies who were looking to unwind after a hard day's work. The nights were noisy and smoky, and she had lost count of the number of times she had been groped or had her ass grabbed by some too drunk to remember local. She saw the man watching her from the end of the bar when she first arrived for her shift. She noticed him because he looked so out of place that it was impossible not to. It was just after eleven and even though the place was almost full and getting rowdy he still hadn't moved. He simply sat and sipped his drink. He was very tall and thin with broad shoulders and dressed in an expensive looking crème suit. As he toyed with his vodka, she could feel his eyes crawling over her. His skin was tanned and he had a small thin moustache and slicked-back jet-black hair. He looked familiar, maybe like an actor, but she couldn't place who or which movie. She didn't normally like men with facial hair but it looked right on him.

She glanced up from the glasses she was collecting and found his brown eyes still locked on to her. She looked away, embarrassed, then gathered the rest of the bottles and headed behind the bar and into the kitchen area, enjoying the brief respite from the country music that was being played with gusto by the house band. Lexi was there, leaning on the stainless steel counter and sipping a beer.

'Here she is, the object of affection,' she said with a smirk.

'What do you mean?'

'Come on Tina, you know what I'm talking about. The guy in the suit. He hasn't been able to take his eyes off you since he came in.'

'Cut it out Lexi, he isn't watching me.'

'Oh come on, you must have noticed, he doesn't even try to hide it. You should go talk to him.'

Tina had known Lexi for the three years she had worked at Quint's, and although they initially hadn't liked each other, over time they had become friends. Lexi was more confident than Tina was and was unafraid to respond to the drunken approaches and gropes of their customers with fire and verbal abuse of her own, somehow knowing just how far to push without going over the line. She was two years older than Tina was at twenty-three and she dressed like a punk rocker from the Eighties. Skinny jeans and vest tops were her thing, and she had that maddening knack of looking stylish in everything she wore. She was naturally pretty, with smooth skin, Green eyes and full lips that made her popular with the men. However, she considered herself a free spirit and wasn't the type to get bogged down in a relationship. Lexi tucked a stray lock of blonde hair behind her ear and took another swig of beer.

'I'd lose my job; you know how Stokes feels about us getting too involved with the customers.'

'Fuck Stokes.' Said Lexi with a chuckle. 'He's a fuckin' prick with an attitude problem. Besides, he's holed up in his office and probably won't show his fat little face tonight anyway.'

'That's easy for you to say, you always get away with whatever you want.'

Lexi offered her beer, which Tina took and sipped.

'It's no secret. I just know how to push his buttons just enough so he doesn't fire my ass. People like him stalk around angry and self-important but it's always just front.'

'I need this job Lexi. I don't wanna rock the boat that's all.'

'Are you kidding me?' Lexi responded, taking the

offered beer back and taking a drink. 'It's not like you have your hands in the fuckin' cash register or anything. Even a dick like Stokes can't fire you for talking to a customer.'

She chewed her lip and turned back to Lexi.

'It's not just that Lexi. It's just after all the business with Paul, I don't need the hassle of men; I'm going through a lot right now.'

'Oh come on T. you need to get out there and stop moping around on your own. Besides, old crème suit out there looks rich. Hell, I would go for it myself if he didn't have such obvious eyes for you.' She said with a small smile on her black painted lips.

'I'll give it some thought. Look, could you watch my tables for five minutes for me? I need to go use the bathroom.'

'Yeah, no problem, you go right ahead. I'll pass Mr Smooth your best' said Lexi with a wink, and then disappeared through the swing doors and into the bar. Tina went through to the back, heading for the employee's bathroom. She glanced into Stokes' office as she did so, but he was enthralled in his paperwork, the top of his bald head moving from side to side as he worked through the books. She was glad. The last thing she needed was any more crap about unauthorised breaks or whatever else he decided to complain about. She watched him, his small fat hands working quickly as he counted his money. Even from the doorway of his office, she could smell his cheap aftershave mingled with sweat and felt her stomach roll. He was a nasty piece of work all right and seemed determined to make up for his physical and social shortfalls by pressing his authority on the staff. Even the gold plaque on his desk stank of self-indulgence.

Henry T. Stokes
Manager

She wondered why he even had that sign. It was unnecessary, and she assumed it was more for his own benefit. She glanced to the family photograph on the wall, the one that said more about the real Henry Stokes than any amount of bullying or nastiness could ever hide. It was awkward, to say the least. The five foot four Stokes smiling beside his mountain of a wife who towered over him by a good seven or eight inches, and there was no way of sugar coating the fact she was dog ugly at best. Their daughter stood in front of the mismatched pair, and looked to Tina like a twelve-year-old Jabba the Hutt from the Star Wars movies, with her chinless face melting into her neck and the unfortunate inheritance of her father's large bug eyes, which sat almost on the side of her head. Tina suppressed a smile and walked past the office entrance before she was spotted. She reached the small bathroom and went inside, locking the door behind her and basking in the silence. She shot a repulsed glance at her mirror image and realised that she hated what she had become, what her life had become. Three years in the same dead end job and nothing to show for it. Her stomach vaulted, and she knew she needed to do it now before things got worse. Besides, she always felt better after.

She removed the small zipper bag from her purse and opened it. Inside were her most prized possessions, the only thing in the world that made her happy. Her drugs. She took inventory. Checking them off one at a time. Heroin. Needles. Cocaine.

She had tried to tell herself that she was a recreational user but knew deep down that she was gradually becoming the dreaded 'A' word. The one that people like her always insisted they would never become. She had a need for it now. It took her to a warm fuzzy place and allowed her to at least tolerate the mess that her life was. The heroin was for later, for when she was back in her damp, cold flat with the door locked where she could drop the act that she was as happy and content as everyone else was. She could barely contain herself and greedily eyed her favourite drug but knew she would have to restrain herself. She couldn't afford to use it and drift away into her secret warm place here. She was on thin ice as far as her employment went as it was and as much as she detested the job, she had to keep it. It paid for her home, and more importantly it paid for her drugs. She opened the small wrap of cocaine and arranged it into two neat lines on the counter top, then holding one nostril closed with her finger she snorted it up, blinking at the warm feeling that overcame her. She immediately felt better. More able to cope. It was a lesser quantity than she normally had when she wasn't at work but it would be enough to see her until her shift finished at three. Only then she could get back and ready herself for the main event. The bliss of her beloved Heroin. It was the one constant thing in her life that never let her down. Straightening her hair and making sure she hadn't left any evidence behind she headed back to work, feeling better and more confident for the shift ahead, even though the need for more was already tugging at her guts.

Back in the bar, the band was just finishing their cover of Roy Orbison's 'Pretty Woman' and Tina thought they were doing a decent job at it. She watched the locals dancing as the band surged towards the song's finale and felt embarrassed for them. They looked ridiculous enough at the best of times, but add alcohol and bad, jerky dance moves into the mix and you had a recipe for either disaster or comedy gold depending on your viewpoint. She was in the latter bracket but fortunately for her customers had long ago mastered the art of keeping a straight face.

She found her eyes drifting to the strange man at the bar and unsurprisingly he was looking right back at her. She couldn't read his expression. It was completely neutral, but she couldn't deny she was attracted to him. It may have been because he was by far the pick of the bunch in here in Oakwell—the land where mullets and beer bellies were king. She looked around it was as if the eighties had never ended. As she crossed the room towards the bar, she could feel them leering at her with half drunken glassy eyed stares which made her uncomfortable. The room was too hot, the air too thick and as she reached the bar and exhaled, she couldn't help casting a quick glance towards her admirer as she waited for the bartender to prepare the next round of drinks for her to deliver. She watched the band finish their set to drunken and sweaty whoops and applause from the crowd, then finally the room was quiet. Already she felt better.

'You look like you could use a drink,' came the voice from behind her. It was smooth, deep and confident and she knew it belonged to him. To the man in the Crème suit. He was looking at her, and she felt her heart skip with giddy excitement. There was something in his eyes, an animalistic intensity that either scared her or aroused her. She wasn't sure which. Trying to recover her composure she threw back a reply she hoped was as witty as it sounded in her head.

'I could, but I don't think my boss would approve of me drinking on the job.'

She would have half expected a clumsy line or response here, but the man only nodded, still watching her as he swirled the dregs of his vodka around in its glass. She looked at his hands, his fingers long and thin, his nails manicured and imagined him touching her with them, running them over her body—she blinked, pushing the thoughts aside.

'I haven't seen you in here before.' She said.

'Yes, you have.' He replied as he drained his glass and set it down. 'You have seen me watching you.'

She smiled at him, but his face remained neutral, his eyes intense and locked on to hers.

'You don't mince your words, do you?' she said, flashing a smile at him.

'When I see something I want I take it. It is the only way. Tell me your name.'

She felt herself blush with embarrassment as she looked at him. It wasn't a request. It was a demand.

'Tina. My name is Tina.' She said softly, trying to keep the tremble out of her voice.

'I am Monde. Why do you work in a place like this?'

'It's not by choice believe me, but the bills won't pay themselves.'

'You are much too beautiful to work in a shithole like this.'

'I don't know about that.' She replied, feeling the hot flush bristle on her skin.

'I can take you away from all this. I can show you a world you have never seen before.'

'You don't even know me.,' she said, this time, unable

to keep the tremble out of her voice. He reached over and took her hands; his skin was hot to the touch. All the time he kept solid eye contact. She thought they were eyes she could look into forever. He leaned close and whispered into her ear.

'I can give you everything.'

He smelled of soap and expensive aftershave and as he pulled back, still watching her with that intense stare. She wished it were that easy and that she could just walk out with him and leave everything behind.

'As good as that sounds, I can't.'

Monde didn't seem at all put out by this, instead, he offered his perfectly white smile and released his grip on her hands.

'Tomorrow I will take you to dinner. Be ready at eight.'

She laughed and she saw something in his face, a millisecond of rage that was enough to make her stop and explain herself.

'Look, you don't know how appealing that sounds, but I'm working tomorrow. In fact, I work every night. Comes with the job.'

She meant it as a joke, but she regretted saying it. Monde didn't respond, instead, he reached into his pocket and took out a business card. It was white and his name and number were printed on it in gold. She didn't think anyone actually carried business cards anymore and smiled as she took it.

'You are persistent, I'll give you that.'

'If you change your mind, call me.'

'Look, don't get me wrong here, I'm interested in seeing you again, I don't want you to see this as a brush off but I don't know when I'll be able to see you.'

He smiled, and then drained his glass and stood. For the first time, she realised how tall he was. Jimmy who worked behind the bar was around six feet tall, but Monde had at least six or seven inches on him. He straightened his jacket and turned that deep brown-eyed gaze onto her again.

'One thing you will learn about me Tina is that I get everything I want.'

'Well, don't be disappointed if you don't hear from me. I can't just leave my job. You understand that right?'

He flashed her that smile again and her heart skipped.

'I'll see you tomorrow.' He said, and made his way towards the exit. She watched him go, waiting to see if he would turn around and look back at her from the door. He didn't and she felt deflated. With a sigh, and encouraged by the Heroin need gnawing at her guts, she picked up her tray and went back to work.

Her shift had finished at three am, and exhausted she had gone home, eager to satisfy the heroin induced craving in her stomach, which by now demanded her full attention. She locked herself away in her dingy apartment, at last able to drop the mask and be herself she felt more alone than ever. As she cooked up the shot that would take her through the night, she looked at the business card he had been given to her. It resembled the man that had given it to her. Clean, straightforward. To the point.

Monde
555-2624

She syphoned the heroin into the needle and readied to inject herself, wishing there was another way to take away the pain. Rolling down her long elbow length fingerless gloves she looked at her arms, which were marked with scars from the self-inflicted cuts. She did it less now she had her heroin, but on those occasions when she couldn't afford it, she would take out the razor blades and use them, enjoying the stinging of the pain as she hurt herself. She selected a vein, the skin

around it bruised from the months of injections into the same place. She knew she needed to stop, but at the same time, she was a slave to its power. She decided she would cut it out of her life, but first, she would do it just one more time then start fresh in the morning.
She inserted the needle and pushed the plunger, the immediate rush of warmth overcoming her as she slumped over onto her bed. She felt warm and safe, cocooned from the world with which she felt no connection. Tina drifted away.

Three

She woke to the maddening vibration of her phone on the bedside table. She had been dreaming of Monde, of him making love to her, caressing her as she looked into his deep brown eyes, and whispering into her ear about how he could give her everything she ever wanted. Now roused from her dream she grabbed at the handset and fumbled for the answer key.
'Hello?'
'Tina? It's me.'
'Hey Lexi, what's going on?' Tina stifled a yawn as she glanced at her alarm clock. It was just after nine am.

'Are you fucking kidding me? There was a fire last night at the bar.'

She sat up in bed. 'Holy shit what happened?'

'Nobody knows yet. Could be an electrical fault.'

'Was anybody hurt?'

'Nah, the place was empty but you should see what's left of it. I'm down there right now.'

'How bad is it?'

'It's gone. Burned to the fuckin' ground. Looks like we just got the night off. Hell, what am I saying; it will be months before they get this place fixed up again. I was saying to Sasha that…'

Tina wasn't listening anymore. She was thinking of Monde. Of how he had been so sure she wouldn't be at work the following night. Surely he couldn't have had anything to do with the fire; nobody would go to that extreme just for a date, but on the other hand, maybe some people would. She knew she should be both repulsed and scared, but was surprised to find that she was neither. She though it was no more than coincidence anyway, and the tall, handsome Monde had just lucked his way into her freeing her schedule for the foreseeable future. She saw his card tossed on the bedside table and picked it up, wondering if she should call or make him wait a while. She already knew the answer. She was desperate to see him again, and her dream of being with him had not faded away as dreams often did. Lexi was still talking, although Tina wasn't sure what about, as she had been too lost in her own thoughts to pay much attention. Tina waited for a pause in babble.

'Hey Lexi, do you want to meet up this afternoon for a bite to eat? I could do with some advice.'

'Yeah sure, where do you wanna meet?'

'You know that bar down on the corner by the park?'

'Yeah, I know the one. Down by that Italian place right?'

'That's the one. How about we meet there at around twelve?'

'Sure thing, I'll be there. Is everything ok Tina?'

'I'm fine I just need a friendly ear that's all.'

'Is it about Mr Crème suit?'

She hesitated and felt an irrational stab of anger and jealousy at Lexi's teasing tone.

'Yeah, it's about him. I'll fill you in when I see you.'

'Ooh sounds exciting. Ok T. I'll see you in a few hours.'

'Thanks, Lexi. See you soon.'

Tina hung up the phone and thought about the implications of having no job. Then, remembering she had a little heroin left decided she would do that and drift off for a while, and think about it later. 'Tina you stupid bitch' she muttered to herself as she cooked up the last of the potentially deadly drug and injected it into the same vein as the previous night. She promised herself that would be it. No more now it was gone. She felt that familiar warm blanket envelop her, and she drifted into a dreamless sleep.

Tina was running late and when she arrived at the bar, Lexi was already waiting for her. Tina felt a pang of jealousy at how relaxed and worry free her friend looked. She was reading a magazine and was dressed in an oversized Ramones t-shirt that hung off one shoulder revealing a singular pink bra strap. As Tina approached, revelling in the smell of fresh coffee and cooked bacon Lexi looked up and smiled. For the next hour, Tina told Lexi all about Monde and her suspicions that he might have had something to do with the fire at the bar. Lexi listened intently barely speaking and allowing Tina to tell the story in full. When she had finished, Lexi took a second to consider, then gave her verdict.

'I think you should stop worrying about coincidental

shit and go out with him.'

'I don't know Lexi, there's something about him, and I'm not sure what it is.'

'Can I be honest with you T?'

'Always.'

'I think you're scared to commit to this and are looking for an excuse not to. Give him a call. Meet up with him. See how it goes. It can't be any worse than spending your nights alone.'

Or fucked up on drugs she thought to herself but didn't say it, as that was one little nugget of information she wanted to keep to herself. Instead, she sipped her coffee. It was hot and bitter and tasted good. For a while, Tina made idle small talk with Lexi but it felt somehow distant. She was desperate to get away and call Monde as soon as she could. Although she could tell that Lexi was worried about her, and despite reassuring her friend she was fine, she wasn't sure it was true. There was a restlessness that had overcome her, an uneasy feeling of something being off balance, Or more off balance than normal at least. She finished her drink and made her excuses to leave, telling Lexi she would call and update her with any new developments. Tina hugged her friend and left, and almost immediately she took out her pink Samsung and punched in Monde's number from the card he had given her. She half convinced herself he wouldn't answer anyway, or if he did that he wouldn't even remember who she was.

Four

Rhodes looked up from his notepad, ignoring the pain in his wrist from writing for so long. Their conversation was being recorded of course. All interviews were as per standard police procedure, but he always made his own notes to refer to later when he was home and able to think more clearly.

'You think Monde started the fire at the bar?' he asked, watching for her reaction.

She shook her head. 'I don't think so. I had considered it at the time but knowing him as I do now it doesn't seem his style.'

'I don't know about that, I have seen some pretty crazy things over the years. You would be surprised what some people can be capable of.'

She nodded in response, and he couldn't shake away his own uneasiness.

'You said you didn't think he was capable of starting the fire. Has that changed now Tina?'

'I didn't say that. I said I didn't think it was his style.' She said, offering a slight smile.

'Did you ever ask him?'

'Eventually I did, but he didn't want to talk about it and Monde isn't the kind of man who you would ever want to make angry. His temper is… bad,'

'Look let's not get too far ahead of ourselves here. What happened after you tried to call Monde on the phone?'

'He answered on the second ring. He wasn't even surprised to hear my voice. It was as if he had been waiting with his phone in hand for me to call and maybe he was. I was nervous of course, but he took over as he does with everything and guided me through the conversation. He wanted to pick me up from my place but I was embarrassed about how it looked, so I convinced him to meet me at the restaurant he had booked. That was the night when I first began to suspect there was more to him, not as a person, but…spiritually…I don't know.' She trailed off and shrugged.

'Tina please, I need you to focus. What happened

next?'

'Well I went out and I met him. I thought I would be more in control of myself the second time around but as soon as I saw him and our eyes met I fell under his spell again, and that's exactly what it was. It was a spell. An enchantment. Something he does with his eyes that makes you lose free will. It sounds crazy but you had to be there. It wasn't just me either. Everyone seemed to be in awe of him. Now, of course, I know why, but I'll get to that eventually if you don't mind, as it would just derail things and I'm feeling better talking about it.'

'That's good. Please continue.'

'So the meal was fine. Actually, that's an understatement. It was amazing and unlike anything I had ever experienced. High class, rich snob stuff. Way more expensive than anything I would ever be able to afford. I wouldn't have been surprised if the meal cost more than a month's rent for my apartment. But Lexi was right. Monde had money. He picked me up in a Limousine for god's sake! He even had his own driver. It was crazy! I thought at first that it might have been awkward; you know how it is sometimes when nobody can think of anything to say to plug the silences, but I needn't have worried. The conversation came easily. I couldn't stop looking into his eyes. God those eyes are beautiful. I could have looked into them forever.

Five

She had never eaten so well. When they had arrived she had felt awkward and underdressed, but Monde had relaxed her, taking the lead, and oozing with the confidence she lacked. They had been making small talk during the course of the meal, mostly about her and her life. She found that whenever she tried to ask a question about him, he would evade it and divert the attention back to her.

She normally wasn't the type to talk about her childhood, but she found that whatever question Monde had asked her she felt compelled to answer. He took her hands across the table, and she gasped at the heat that seemed to radiate from his skin.

'Let me take you away from all of this. Let me give you the life you deserve.'

'Away from what?' she said, feeling the heaviness of her own voice. It felt distant. Faraway. All she could think about were those eyes, and how easy it was to lose herself in them.

'I can give you everything, Tina. More than you could ever imagine. All you need to do is give yourself to me.'

'She could barely breathe and her pulse pounded thick in her temples. The chatter of the restaurant seemed muted and distant and she knew then that she would do anything he ever asked her without question. She recalled her dream of making love to him and stirred in her seat.

'I'm yours.' She wanted to say, but the words wouldn't come, and she just looked at him in breathless need.

He smiled at her, acknowledging the unspoken agreement.

'Then we should go.'

'Where?'

'To my apartment. Come.'

Heart racing she allowed him to lead her out and into his car, which was waiting with the engine running and Monde's driver holding the door open for them. It was as if he knew the exact time that they would arrive. She couldn't think about that now, though. All she could think about was how it would feel to be with him. They climbed into the car and fell upon each other.

When she awoke in the morning, she could barely

move. Being with Monde had been very different from her dreams, and instead of the gentle lovemaking she had imagined, it had instead been a frenzied and violent affair. She had been afraid at first as he ravaged her, his hands clutched around her throat as he glared at her with a terrifying intensity. Unable to breathe, she had feared for her life but it served to intensify the pleasure and six more times that night they had engaged in their violent coupling. Scratching, biting, and tearing at each other in an animalistic savagery, which she didn't even know existed within her.

She stirred under the tangled mass of sheets on the huge bed and looked around, her bruised and beaten body throbbing in agony. She looked at her skinny reflection in the mirrored ceiling and winced at the ugly purple finger marks around her throat and the bite marks on her breasts and stomach. Monde was nowhere to be seen. She climbed gingerly from the bed and slipped on her pants and vest, hissing in agony but completely satisfied. This was her first real look at his apartment, and she thought it suited him well. It was on the seventeenth floor of a large newly built building deep within the city. The building was modern—all steel and glass, with deep red carpets with gold trim in the hallways. Monde's apartment was the penthouse of the building and was sparsely but tastefully decorated with clean lines and plush furnishings. Apart from the bathroom, which housed a huge and ornate marble bathtub with gold taps and a lion's head faucet, it was a large open space with expensive white carpets and lavish furnishings in gold.

She walked to the window and looked out over the city, which looked beautiful in the blue and purple hues of the early morning. It was wonderfully picturesque and for the first time in a while, she felt at peace. She closed her eyes and leaned her forehead on the cool glass of the window.

The harsh vibration of her mobile phone broke the silence and demanded her attention. She couldn't locate it at first, eventually finding it in the pocket of her jeans which were still discarded on the floor, one leg turned inside out where Monde had clawed them from her hips the night before. She retrieved the phone, and answered the call, expecting it to be Lexi.

'Hello?'

'Tina it's me.'

Shit.

It was Paul. She cursed herself for not checking the

caller I.D before she had answered. 'I told you not to call me anymore.'

'I heard about the fire. I wanted to check you were o.k.'

'I told you to leave me alone. Stop calling me.'

'I want us to be together again. We were good together.'

Monde walked into the room from the bathroom. He was wearing a towel around his waist and the sight of him standing there dripping wet made Tina ache with desire despite her ravaged body. He looked at her as she spoke but said nothing, instead sitting on the bed and watching the conversation unfold. She turned to the window but could still feel his dark eyes crawling over her.

'No Paul we weren't. Jesus just stop bothering me. I'm trying to get on with my life.'

Tina felt awkward conducting this conversation with her ex-boyfriend in front of Monde. Paul had that sarcastic mocking tone in his voice she hated.

'Look you can't blame everything on me all the time Tina. You had a part to play too.'

'Fuck you. I'm not going through this again. Just stop calling me.'

'You don't control me you little bitch. I'll call if I want

to you got that?'

She was upset now and old memories surfaced and brought fear with them. She had learned the hard way that Paul had a temper. At first, he blamed the drink for the times he had beaten her, and over time as the drinking intensified, he stopped even trying to make excuses, grunting reasons for his actions between gritted teeth. She remembered them all. She looked at another man. She was flirting with his friends. She made him do it. That was the best one. He had introduced her to the drugs, and because she was afraid to say no, she had started to do them with him—anything to keep his fists from connecting with her body. The end came when he tried to force her into prostitution. He had called it something else, accompaniment…no—escorting. That's what he had called it. He said he had good friends that would look after her and they would make a ton of money. She told him she wouldn't do it. His response was to punch her in the face and throw her down the steps of his apartment where she had been living at the time.

All of this was conducted in secrecy of course. Lexi had told Tina that she was lucky to have found such a good-looking guy, and wanted to know if he had a brother to introduce her to. And that was the problem. In public, he treated her well. Hugging her close, holding her hand, but she could always sense it. The anger simmering below the surface of his skin. Fearing that her next beating might be one she wouldn't wake up from and desperate to avoid becoming his personal whore to his circle of friends, she plucked up the courage to leave him, doing it whilst he was out at work. She was scared; terrified he would find her so she left a letter and warned him that if he didn't leave her alone she would go to the police about some of his less than savoury dealings. That had worked for a while but recently he had started calling her when he was drunk and would slur abuse at her which frightened her even though she knew he didn't know where she lived. If she had been alone when he had called she would have been terrified to stand up to him, but she felt strong with Monde in the room with her.

'Look, Paul, I won't let you do this to me again. Just leave me alone.' Her voice was shaking but she managed to blink back the tears, which threatened to spill over onto her cheeks.

'You better watch yourself, Tina. You had better remember who you are fuckin talking to you little cunt.

I might just drop by to your place one day and remind you,' He spat down the phone before disconnecting the line.

'Problem?' Monde asked her.

Apart from being absolutely fucking terrified of my psycho ex? Nope, not a thing. 'No, no problem.' She said as she tried to still her heart, which pounded in her chest.

Something in his expression changed. Maybe it was no more than a trick of the light but his eyes seemed to darken.

'Tina I will not let anyone ever hurt you again. You have my word.'

For the next few weeks, the routine was the same. Tina and Monde's nights would consist of several bouts of frenzied and violent sex, then in the mornings Monde would dress and leave to conduct his "business". She had asked him what he did for a living, but he would always evade the question, telling her that he owned an import and export business and he worked long hours in the city. Her obsession with Monde grew, and the less he revealed about himself the more she wanted to know. He had given her a key to his apartment and a credit card and lavished her with expensive gifts and clothes.

Also curious was her drug addiction. She no longer craved the Heroin that had been such a huge part of her life in recent months, and as she spent more time in Monde's world, she found that she no longer desired it. There was no painful drying out or sickness whilst the drug flushed itself out of her system like the last time she had tried to get herself clean. This time, there was no such drama. This time stopping was as easy as breathing. Her need for the drug had been replaced by her obsession with Monde. It was one addiction in place of another. He had become her life, her existence. She forgot the Tina of old and devoted everything to him.

It was a Friday afternoon when she received the voicemail from Lexi. The usual bubbly exuberance in her voice was absent and had been replaced by a tension Tina had never heard before. The message asked Tina to call her back to arrange to meet up, as there was something Lexi wanted to talk to her about. The thought of being away from Monde filled her with dread. She had begrudgingly called back and arranged to meet her at the same coffee house as before.

It had been the first time since their last meeting that Tina had seen Lexi. In what seemed to Tina to be something of an irony, there had been a role reversal since that day. Now it was Lexi who appeared distracted and carrying a world full of worries on her shoulders, and Tina, in contrast, felt good, ecstatic with happiness even despite the painful bites and bruises, which she wore on her body like trophies.

'Hey there, stranger.'

Tina detected a bitter tone to Lexi's voice, which she tried her best to ignore. She was already missing Monde and wanted to get back to him.

'Hey, Lexi. How are you? You sounded strange on the phone. Is everything alright?'

Lexi swallowed as if trying to select the right words. Tina noticed that her friend couldn't look her in the eye.

'Look Tina I need to tell you something, and I don't think you are gonna like it.'

Her stomach vaulted. She masked it by sipping her drink.

'What is it?'

'It's about that guy you are seeing.'

Panic. Rage. Jealousy.

She smiled and sipped her drink. 'What about him?'

'He's not what you think Tina. He's bad. Really bad.'

'How would you know?'

Tina got the impression that there was some kind of bombshell coming, a revelation, a plot twist.

Stay in your seats folks, here we are in the third act and you won't BELIEVE what's about to happen.

She waited for it, whatever punch line was to come.

'He… He went to see Paul.'

'Don't be ridiculous. He doesn't even know Paul.' She argued, but she knew inside that knowing him didn't matter. He had overheard her argument on the phone and had gone to see him. She knew it as much as she knew the sky was blue and that she hated the taste of mushrooms. What was it Monde had said about not letting anyone hurt her again?

'Look Tina you know me ok? You know I wouldn't just say shit for the sake of it. But this guy is bad.'

'How can you know? You haven't even met him,' she said between gritted teeth. She knew it was stupid, but she was angry and jealous, and even though she was doing a fine job of burying her head in the sand, somewhere deep down she knew there was more to Monde than she would ever know.

'I know because I was there with Paul when your man knocked on the door.'

There it was. She imagined it playing out as a movie

script: plot twist enters stage left.

'What do you mean you were there?' Tina asked.

But Lexi didn't need to answer. The look in her eye said it for her.

'You were sleeping with him?' she asked, unsure if she was more jealous, betrayed or angry. She decided she was a little of all three.

'I know I shouldn't have after what he did to you but you know me, Tina. I'm attracted to men like him. You know… I always go for the wrong kind of man.'

'Wrong doesn't even cover it. You don't even know half of the things that that bastard did to me. You think you know everything Lexi but you don't. How could you do this? Why him?'

'Hey, you're the one who just disappeared off the face of the earth with this new man of yours. Think about that before you judge me.'

People were looking at them now, casting disapproving looks at the two women who were spoiling their quiet mid-morning brunches.

'That's it isn't it, you are jealous. Well fine, you have him. I don't care. Just don't come running to me when he gets loose with those fists of his.'

'He would never hit me'

'I thought that too once'

'Yeah but I'm not as—'Lexi trailed off.

'Go ahead and say it Lexi. You aren't as weak as I am. Was that what you were about to say?'

There was a tense silence between them. Lexi shuffled awkwardly and continued.

'Look, T, that's not the real issue here. That man Monde…He Hurt Paul.'

Tina opened her mouth to speak but her brain refused to give her any words. It was interested to hear what else Lexi had to say and was holding back on releasing a reply until she had finished. Tina closed her mouth and waited. After all, silence means consent. Although with Paul, sometimes screaming no and begging to be left alone also counted as consent, so that little argument meant nothing. She listened.

'We were at his place, you know, just fooling around when there was a knock at the door. We had ordered in pizza so assumed that's what it was. Paul was drunk, or at least on his way so I opened the door and there he was. Your man Monde.'

Tina searched her friends face for a lie, hoping to find one. She was horrified to see nothing but truth and felt sick.

'Go on.' She said with a voice that didn't even sound like her own.

'So I asked him what he wanted. I mean why would he be there right? He didn't get mad or anything he just calmly asked to speak to Paul who by that time had heard the commotion and come to the door. Well, you know how he is when he's drunk T.'

She did. He became a violent and unpredictable rapist—but both she and her brain agreed that it best to keep quiet about that one.

'So Paul starts getting in Monde's face or more his chest because that guy of yours is big, I mean holy fuck is he tall. Anyway, so Paul was ranting and raving and Monde just stood there with a crazy look in his eyes and an amused smile on his face. Now I'm trying to calm things down right because I figure these two are about to get into it right there on the doorstep so I'm in the middle and then he…'

Lexi swallowed and Tina noticed that she could no longer look her in the eye.

'He—He moved so fast T, that I didn't see him move, you know? One minute Paul was pointing and shouting and the next he was sitting on the floor and holding his face, and there was blood, good god there was a lot of blood.'

Lexi had grown pale and Tina thought she had aged at least ten years in the last few minutes.

'I wasn't sure what happened until after, but Monde had leaned in and whispered something to Paul as he sat on the floor. And I heard him, I swear I heard him as clear as day.'

'What did he say?' Tina asked, trying to ignore her somersaulting stomach. Lexi looked Tina in the eye and Tina knew then that any friendship they once had was gone forever.

'He said 'she's mine now.' And he was calm, so calm even though he had it in his hand and it was still moving….'

'What happened Lexi? TELL ME!' Tina demanded. Tears began to roll down Lexi's cheeks but there was no accompanying sobbing or wailing, just a lost and neutral look on her face. Tina wondered if something in Lexi's mind had broken.

'He pulled out Pauls' tongue. I don't know how he did it, or how he could move so fast but…he yanked it out with one fucking hand. Oh god T. he looked at me then and his eyes were black…I swear they were black as night.'

Tina felt repulsed but also a sense of pride that both surprised and sickened her. Nobody had ever gone to such extremes on her behalf before.

'And the thing I will never forget, the thing I can't get out of my mind is that Pauls' tongue was still moving. It was as if it were still trying to talk or something, I don't know but surely, now you see why you have to leave him. Leave and get as far away as you can.'

Lexi was in borderline Hysterics, but Tina wasn't listening. She was imagining Monde deep inside her, both of them covered in fresh hot blood. She saw it vividly in her mind; her tied naked to the bed, and Monde licking her breasts and her belly, moving down, down down—not using his own mouth, but Paul's severed tongue which he held in his right hand like some bizarre phallus, still twisting and licking. She found herself becoming aroused and wished she were with him now. Lexi was looking at her, crying. Tina could only think of that severed tongue exploring her. She smiled.

Lexi's face screwed up into an expression of disgust and anger.

'Why are you smiling? What has happened to you!' she sobbed, the pair now had the full attention of the neighbouring patrons who had received a free show with their Lunches.

'Did you tell him to do it?'

Tina blinked in shock, and her depraved thoughts were gone from her mind as if they were a balloon jabbed with a large pin.

'Of course I didn't! I don't know anything about it! How can you even ask me that?'

'Then leave him. Get away from him whilst you still can. You aren't safe with him.'

'He looks after me Lexi. Just because I'm happy doesn't give you the right to try and wreck things for me!'

'I'm trying to help you, Tina!'

'No, that's not it. You want him for yourself, don't you? You want Monde.'

'Of course not, what the hell are you talking about?

'Poor little depressed Tina finally gets a man. Well it's no joke now, is it? Now I'm doing well and he's looking after me.'

'He's changed you, you aren't yourself!'

'And how would you know? You were never there when I was crying myself to sleep on a night when I was wondering where my next meal might come from.

When that animal you are sleeping with was fucking raping me! Monde is the only one who cares about me, and I love him and none of your lies will change a fucking thing!' Tina was shaking now and gripping the edges of the table so hard that her knuckles had turned white. Lexi shook her head, wiping her hand across her nose in a subconsciously childlike gesture.

'He's brainwashed you. Don't you get it yet Tina? He's wrong for you. Why can't you see it?'

'Look' said Tina as she stood quickly, tipping her chair backwards onto the floor. Even the staff had joined the rest of the customers in watching the show. Tina pointed at Lexi and spoke through gritted teeth.

'You and I are through. Don't contact me again. I love Monde and that's all there is to it. He's no monster. You keep away from me and you keep away from him or I swear to god I'll kill you.'

Not one to back down, Lexi also stood and put on her leather jacket, which had been hanging off the back of her chair.

'You know what that's fine. I tried to warn you and help you but you don't want to listen and that's fine. But if our friendship ever meant anything to you Tina then think about what I said. How well do you know this guy?'

'I know enough to know that he is no monster.'

Lexi smiled and Tina went cold. It looked oddly false and reminded Tina of the grinning rictus of a Halloween mask.

'Try re-arranging the letters of his name. Then you will see what I think he is.'

Tina gave Lexi a disgusted sneer and left, sweeping out of the coffee shop and away from the watching and judgemental eyes of the customers.

Six

Rhodes looked up at Tina but he still couldn't read her expression. He returned to his notepad casting his eyes over the scrawled arrangements of Monde's name.

*Do men.*
*Mod en.*
*Em don.*
*Demon.*

*Demon.*

Rhodes snorted an uneasy bark of laughter, and then looked back at Tina. 'Demon? Lexi thought Monde was a Demon?'

He was anxious to hear Tina's response but she sat and watched him with half a smile on her face. Rhodes's mind buzzed with the bounty of information he had taken on board.

'Tina, are you still with me?'

'Yes. I'm just resting my voice. I'm tired of talking now.'

'I understand but we have to continue. Would you like another drink?'

'You got any Vodka?' she asked with a teasing smile. He felt a quiver in his groin at the flirtatious way in which she had said it, and he wondered if she were deliberately trying to tease him. He pushed aside the images of being with her that began to form in his mind and pushed on with his questions.

'What happened to Paul?'

'He couldn't handle what had happened to him. I guess he didn't like being on the receiving end for a change.'

'What do you mean?' pressed Rhodes.

'He's dead. Suicide apparently. I heard the rumours the same as everyone else, but by all accounts, Paul went and bought himself a big old dirt sandwich. And good riddance too if you ask me.'

She was so nonchalant, so matter of fact that it made Goosebumps pop up on Rhodes's arms. He pressed for more info.

'What happened?'

'What do you mean what happened? He died.' She said with a chuckle.

'Come on Tina, you know what I mean.'

'Sorry Tom. I was just messing with you. I don't know exactly. I heard he filled the bath, took a bunch of sleeping pills, put a plastic bag over his head tied it around the neck with duct tape and then slit his wrists.'

'Jesus.'

'You could tell he wasn't fucking around. You can bet that this was no cry for help, no sympathy seeking. He wanted to make sure. I hear he left a note that said 'god forgive me'.' she shrugged and leaned forward and he could smell the clean and soapy smell of her skin.

'If you ask me, Tom, even God wouldn't have enough compassion in him to forgive that fucking pig. But I admire the style of his note. Simple. To the point. A shame that that's the best thing he ever achieved in his wasteful existence. But of course, as I said it's all rumour. I'm sure you could dig up more than me with all of these 'police resources' at your disposal.

She was still smiling at him and began to pick away at the edge of her polystyrene cup. She was right of course, and he felt slightly annoyed at the way she had taken control of the conversation. He took a deep breath and tried to get things back on track.

'I'd like to hear more about Monde.' Rhodes chose his next words carefully, knowing that Tina's reaction could spell the end of their conversation. 'Tina…Do you think Monde was a demon?'

She laughed again and shook her head.

'I'm not mentally disturbed detective Rhodes.'

'You still haven't answered the question.'

She considered for a moment, flicking her top lip with her tongue, which didn't help Rhodes's efforts to push aside his attraction towards her. He looked at her neckline and sure enough, he could see the ghosts of bruises shaped like fingers on her neckline. At last, she responded.

'I think it's best if you save questions like that until the end.'

'That's fair enough, but I'm almost out of paper here. How much more is there to tell?'

'Not much. We have almost reached the end of the road.'

The way she said it sent a chill through him.

'Then please, continue.'

She smiled at him, and again there was a seductive element to the way she looked across the table. Baby's growing up he thought to himself, although he had no idea why or where the quote even came from, or why it came to him. He thought that it might have been a long forgotten movie or book.

'You don't quite know what to make of me do you Tom?'

It was becoming more and more difficult for him to ignore the physical attraction to her. It was the way she kept calling him by his first name, the way she kept looking at him, even in the seductive secrecy of her smile. There was an innocence there, that much was true but there was also an explosive sexuality to her which he was struggling to ignore. He could still smell her soapy, clean smell and to his horror felt himself stiffening under the table. He saw stabs of images; of her coming close, those full red painted lips slightly open as she repeated his name.

Tom, I know what you want to do to me….so just do it

And he wanted to. He really did even though he was a happily married man of twenty-three years and had four wonderful children, right then he would have given it all up for just one night with this mysterious girl in his interview room.

He forced himself to clear his head and concentrate on his job but the question was a good one. Did he really know what to make of her?

'Honestly? No. I don't. But that's why we are here isn't it?' his turn to smile now, and he was pleased with how well he had managed to hide his growing uneasiness.

She faltered, just a slight frown, but nonetheless a chink in the armour. He decided to press on.

'Please, tell me what happened next.' Rhodes said as he picked up his pen.

'Well, after I calmed down I started to feel guilty. As bad as it sounds to say it to you aloud, I think we both got a little defensive and said things in the heat of the moment. I hadn't wanted to fall out with her—it's just that Monde has this way of driving me crazy you know? I mean obsession doesn't even scratch the surface. I dwelled on it and decided to ask him about it outright. We had words, and things got heated but when it was all done we understood each other, and he sat me down and told me everything. It was a lot to take in, and I had to go out and get some air. I don't know if it was just subconsciously or a deliberate action, but I found myself outside Lexi's.'

## Seven

Lexi lived in a small ground floor apartment. The walls were whitewashed and beside each white panelled door, there was a mailbox and gold painted number. Lexi lived at number six, and as Tina knocked, she hoped that it wasn't too late to put things right. She waited and was about to leave when she heard the chain rattle on the other side of the door. It swung open, allowing the acrid smell of cannabis to drift out. There was no welcome, and no excited hello, just an awkward silence as the two friends looked at each other awkwardly.
'Lexi...we need to talk.'
'I'm listening.' She replied, watching Tina with glassy half-baked eyes.
'I spoke to Monde about the things you told me...I need someone to talk to.' She barely finished the words before breaking down, and in an instant, the argument was forgotten as Lexi draped her arm around her friend and ushered her inside.
'Hey come on in.'

Tina allowed herself to be led as Lexi kicked the door closed behind her. She was wearing black leggings and an oversized Iron Maiden vest. The apartment was cluttered but cosy, one wall devoted to a large shelving unit filled with records and her extensive CD collection. Tina sat in the chair beside the wall, and Lexi perched on the sofa opposite, putting out her large oddly shaped joint in the overflowing ashtray on the table.

'Sorry about that, I was feeling down in the dumps.' Lexi said with a shrug as she wafted away the smoke.

'So what happened?'

'I confronted Monde. I asked him about Paul. He didn't deny it. Lexi I'm so sorry for doubting you.'

'Forget about that hon.' she said with a dismissive wave of her hand. 'I'm just glad you saw sense. Look, here's the thing, I have been doing some research on your friend Monde.'

'Lexi…'

'Look I'm sorry, but I needed to know. I was worried about you, hell I still am worried about you.'

Although she felt the prickle of anger stir within her, Tina let it slide. She didn't want to get into another argument. Besides which her curiosity was piqued

'So what did you find out?'

'Nothing that will put your mind at ease. I made a few calls. Did some independent research of my own. Tina, he doesn't exist. No social security, no traceable history. It's like he popped up out of thin fuckin' air.'
Tina said nothing. She felt sick with nerves.
'And then there's the other stuff that doesn't add up. The night at the bar when he was sure he was going to meet you and the place conveniently burned down, then Paul….'
She trailed off but Tina was still thinking about it, about Monde licking her with her ex-boyfriend's severed tongue.
'And to cap it off, the fucking name! Did you get it when you rearrange his name it spells...?'
'Demon.' Tina said. It felt good to say it aloud. It rolled easily of the tongue. De-mon. she watched Lexi as the look of realisation formed on her petite features.
'You already know don't you?'
Tina nodded.
'When?' asked Lexi. Her face looked grey and waxy.
'I think I suspected something right from the start. I knew there was something; I just wasn't sure what it was.'
Lexi looked like she wanted to say something but

instead she sat and looked at Tina, her revulsion barely hidden.

'But you argued with me, I mean you defended him…'

'I didn't know what he was then, not right away at least. But I suspected something. I decided to outright ask him, and you know what the funny thing is? He didn't deny it. He praised my perception.'

'Tina, have you considered that this guy could be some psycho using a clever false name to manipulate you?'

'I did at first, stranger things have happened after all. But it was the little things that add up Lexi. The way his skin is always hot to the touch, the way he can make anyone bend to his will. And the way he is in bed… well, I won't go into detail but the way he does it… the way he snarls and bites and hurts me…'

'You're sick,' Lexi whispered, her eyes flicking towards the door. She wanted to run. Tina could sense it; it hung in the air like an unseen presence.

'When I asked him about what he was, and he admitted to me. I asked him to show me his true self. How he looked behind the human mask.'

Tina smiled, sitting back and crossing her legs as if she were discussing the news or the movie she watched the night before.

'He didn't want to but I insisted and when he did I was glad. You would have screamed, of course, screamed and run away because you don't understand. But when I looked at him, I could still see how beautiful he was. I let him take me then. Not as Monde but as the thing that lives underneath. His skin was so hot I had burns on my belly, and his nails tore at my flesh. Here, look at this.'

She lifted up her shirt to show her ribcage, which was lined with scratches and just below her navel there was a deep bite mark that was still weeping blood.

'He has branded me Lexi. I'm his. You know what he told me? He said he chose me because he could see I was just as lost and as dark a soul as he was.'

Lexi leaned across the table and took Tina's hands in hers.

'Tina you need help, you're delusional.'

'I'm pregnant Lexi. He told me. Our baby will be half of our world and half of his.'

Lexi let go of Tina's hands and half rose.

'This is sick. I won't listen to it anymore.' Lexi marched to the door on rubber legs that felt as if they were going to give up on her.

'I want you to leave,' she said as she opened the door. Monde was standing outside. Lexi shrieked and backed away. Her eyes darted from Monde to Tina then back to Monde as she back-pedalled away from the door.

'What is he doing here, why did you bring him here?' Lexi shrieked.

'Lexi come on, just relax. I wanted to explain, to make sure you understand that this is what I want.'

'Tina snap out of it! Think about what the fuck you are saying!'

Monde smiled at Lexi then, and his teeth were needle like daggers, his eyes black pools of hate. He walked into the apartment and closed the door behind him.

'I want to go with him Lexi, back down there.'

Tina pointed to the floor, and Lexi knew that she didn't mean the maintenance basement, but somewhere much, deeper and hotter. Lexi licked her lips nervously, her eyes bugging out of her head as she backed away from Monde who was standing there with his arms folded. Lexi thought she could see the tip of a forked tongue flickering between his partly open lips.

'Tina don't do this; tell him to leave me alone. I know you are a good person. Please!'

'I'm not a good person Lexi. I pretend to be, but I'm not.' Said Tina with a shake of her head.

Lexi was now backed into the corner with nowhere to

run as Monde's six foot seven frame loomed over her.
'I asked him to do it quick Lexi. That's the least I can do.'
'Tina please.'
'Goodbye Lexi.'
Tina watched as Monde went to work. The violence and frenzy excited her. She tried to hold back for as long as she could but the wet ripping and tearing sounds and the copper smell of blood overcame her ability to hold back, and she set about him, pushing her tongue into his mouth, pulling the heat of his body towards her. They rolled in what was left of Lexi, smearing it on each other, lost in the primal act. Tina knew somewhere deep down she should feel some sense of guilt or remorse, but she found that there was none. All she could think about was Monde. They finished, climaxing together as she held lexis severed hand in her own, their fingers interlocked.

Rhodes felt the nausea roll around his guts as he looked at Tina in a new light. When he first saw her, he thought it was an innocence he had seen, but realised now it was nothing more than an utter lack of remorse or guilt. Unlike him, she would sleep tonight. Rhodes wasn't sure if he would ever sleep again. She was insane of course, of that there was no longer any doubt. Rhodes thought it was a shame; such a young and pretty girl could have achieved so much in life. It also illustrated just how thin the line between sanity and batshit crazy was. The silence was heavy, and he tried to organise his thoughts. There were questions that still needed to be answered, but even with a lifetime to talk to Tina, he didn't think that it would be enough to peel back the layers to see what really made the girl tick.

'So what happens now?' she asked.

'We check your story. But you need to give me Monde. Where is he?'

'Gone.'

'Tina come on. Gone where?'

She flicked her eyes to the floor.'

'Back there. He said he would come back for me once the baby was ready to be born.'

Rhodes leaned forwards, looking her in the eye.

'Can I tell you what I think Tina?'

'I'm hardly in a position to stop you.'

'I don't think there is or ever was a Monde. I think you invented him as a clever means to try and get away with murder.'

Even as he said it, he glanced at the bruises on her neck. The ones that looked like hand prints even as he said the words, their presence destroyed his thesis.

'No, that's not it.'

'I think you found that Lexi was sleeping with Paul and you killed them both, then you tried to cover it up by creating Monde hoping to claim temporary insanity.'

He had expected this to rattle her, but she smiled at him. He had grown to hate that smile.

'Well I suppose that's for you to prove isn't it detective Rhodes.'

No more Tom. No more seductive flirting. She had clammed up, and he felt guilty for even feeling attracted to her.

'Tina, you are going to be put away for this, you must know that don't you?'

'I suppose I will, but only for a while. He'll come back for me. He promised.'

She believed it. As Rhodes looked into her eyes, he could see she absolutely believed everything that she had said. He realised that there was no helping her. She was broken mentally, and even though he would push for a criminal conviction, he was sure she would be institutionalised. Taking his notes he stood, and stretched. He wanted to say something profound, something thought provoking. He felt as if something should be said, and Tina seemed to be expecting something too as she watched him with her icy blue gaze. But try as he might he couldn't think of anything. Without a word, he walked out of the interview room and closed the door.

Eight

The subsequent trial of Tina Rose Delatros was a whirlwind of media attention and speculation. As Rhodes had feared, Tina was deemed unfit to stand Trial for the murder of Alexis Greene whose remains were only identifiable from her dental records. (Although Rhodes had speculated that she had been involved with Paul's death, it was indeed a suicide as Tina had said) Those who attended the trial had commented on the way Tina had carried herself during the proceedings, showing neither remorse nor shame, which echoed how she behaved during the interviews with Rhodes. Despite an exhausting and frustrating search, no evidence of Monde's existence was ever found. His apartment was never located, and when pressed Tina claimed she didn't remember where it was.

Some argued that it would have been impossible for Tina to do the damage that was inflicted on Lexi by herself, and that the scene looked more reminiscent of an animal attack rather than anything a human could be capable of. The defence also pointed to the bruises and bite marks which seemed to corroborate Tina's story, however, experts classed the bite as that of an animal, perhaps a large dog.

Three months after her discussion with Rhodes, Tina stood for sentencing, the bump of her stomach now impossible to hide. (The fact that she was pregnant also seemed to confirm Tina's version of events.) The judge described her as a mentally disturbed monster, who was unsafe to roam the streets. As had been the case during the entirety of the trial, opinion had been divided and although there were a few cheers from Lexi's mother and uncle, there were also jeers and cries of injustice from those who believed Tina to be innocent. Tina accepted her sentence with the same indifference as she had displayed since she was arrested. Rhodes had talked to her several times following her incarceration, and after corroborating with the psychologists and staff at the Wren State Mental health institute, they verified the same findings as he did. Her story never changed, never wavered. Those who spoke to her were in unanimous agreement. She was either telling the truth or was so deeply invested in her story that she believed it to be true.

In late September with the baby only weeks away, Rhodes arrived to visit Tina, wanting to follow up on some potential sightings of Monde from customers at Quint's bar the night before it had burned down. (The case was now closed, but he wanted to know more due to his own personal interest in the story) What he saw when he arrived would haunt him forever. There had been no alarms triggered, no breach of security, and no break in the twenty-minute hall patrols. However when Rhodes was let into her room which was still locked from the outside he saw it all in vivid detail.

The white walls and wire covered double bar windows. The bunk style beds, the bottom one, which was Tina's had the covers tossed aside as if she had got up in a hurry. He could still see the wet patch where her waters had broken, and a thin trail of liquid leading to the wall. It looked like this is where she had sat down, and her cellmate, a young woman named Melissa who had severe schizophrenia had tried to help her to deliver the baby. Blood stained the floor and Rhodes could still see the imprinted shape of her body where she had come to rest.

Alerted by the excited screams and cries, the staff had hurried to the room and unlocked the door. Melissa was under the bed. She was trembling and her face was lined with four deep scratches. The staff had tried to get some sense out of her but could make no sense of her terrified babbling. They saw the blood and only then realised that Tina was missing. Rhodes spoke to Melissa once in the days after the incident, but her words were ones that would haunt him forever.

'What happened here, what happened to Tina?' he had asked, already suspecting that he knew the answer. Melissa looked at him, the scars on her face still healing. Rhodes thought they could almost look like claw marks if one believed in such things as ghosts and ghouls and slimy things that lived under the bed. He had coaxed Melissa, asking her again what had happened. Then, bottom lip trembling, she looked Rhodes in the eye, her own gaze clear and unclouded by her mental illness.

'He took her. He came out of the floor and took her.'

Rhodes wanted to ask Melissa more but he didn't have to. He wasn't a betting man but he knew that if he were, then he would bet his life on the description she would give. She would say it was a tall man with olive skin and a crème suit, with black eyes and pointed teeth that climbed out of the fiery hole in the floor to take Tina and their newborn child away. Rhodes shook his head in wonder and felt the gnawing need to light up a cigarette even though he had quit more than ten years before. He thought about the world, and what a crazy place it was. But it seemed that even in a world built on lies and deceit, where people seemed to live only to fuck each other over at any given opportunity, that even demons sometimes told the truth.

## NO.5 SYCAMORE STREET

Alex looked in the rear-view mirror, smoothed a stubborn lock of his hair into place and checked that his tie was straight. He saw it was askew and made a slight adjustment. Satisfied He picked up the stack of pamphlets from the passenger seat, stacked them neatly, then shut off the engine, and climbed from the car. It was a beautiful day. The sky was a pale and cloudless blue, and birds were in full song the length of Sycamore Street. It was a perfect example of Middle American suburbia. Tasteful, neat homes with trimmed lawns and white picket fences. He paused by the car, enjoying the beauty of it all. Somewhere in the distance, he could hear the jolly jingle of an ice cream truck making its rounds and whipping the local children into a frenzy of pumping arms and legs as they ran to their parents for change for an ice cool treat. And why not? Alex thought to himself. Any ice cream truck with even the smallest iota of common sense would make sure to stop on Sycamore Street. He thought this was the kind of place he would like to live when he retired. Somewhere quiet where he could sit in a rocker by his front door and watch the world go by, perhaps sipping a beer or freshly made sweet lemonade as children played hopscotch or ball games in the street. But all of that came later. Right now, he had a job to do.

He inhaled, allowing himself a contented smile. He loved this job. At first, the idea of spreading the word of God grated with him. He was never religious, at least until the last few years. But sometimes things happen in a man's life to make him change his outlook. Yes, sir. Now he lived to spread the word of his church. He felt alive there, and his parish loved him. They praised his enthusiasm and his drive, but they didn't know it hadn't always been this way. Indeed, there was a time when Alex Childs only ever saw the inside of a church for Funerals, Weddings and occasionally at Christmas if his wife had managed to bully him into going to a carol service.

That was when he used to work for a man called Victor. Victor was a nasty piece of shit. He was a drug runner, up to his neck in all sorts of activities, and none of them legal. He was a large flabby man with small eyes and a long cruel mouth. Every time Alex would be summoned to him in the back room of the Restaurant Victor owned in downtown New York, there were always two things he could guarantee. That Victor would be eating and sweating, both in massive amounts. He would also always be surrounded by his bodyguards who were never far away if trouble should arise. Sometimes his Brother, Salvatore would be there, but he was different to Victor. He didn't give off the same oozing sense of slimy insincerity and seemed like a decent guy as far as criminal mob families went. Of course, he would never say that to Victor in person. He didn't want to end up missing a finger or taking the express line to the bottom of the ocean with his pockets full of rocks for company.

Alex was the man who Victor would call in to do the jobs that required his own brand of special attention. He did the jobs that required a hands on but clinical touch. Alex was very good at his job.

He was moving up the ladder in Victor's organisation. He had developed quite the reputation of his own as a nasty and volatile piece of work.

'Aleeeex,' Victor would drawl in his thick Italian accent as he slurped down his meatballs.

'Nobody gets a jooob done like you dooo my frieeeend. Stick with me and you wiiil go farrrr.'

Alex never liked Victor. But he had seen enough to

know never to question him. He knew what happened to people who got on victors bad side. In fact, it was often someone like Alex that would be sent out to deal with those people.

As he looked around now at the lush green lawns that lined Sycamore Street and the beautiful pale morning sky, he thanked God for the intervention. For without it, he too by now might be an overweight mass of flesh surrounded by frightened tough guys waiting on his every whim. No sir, he wouldn't go back there. Not even for all the tea in china or all the money in victor's deep pockets. Even so, he still had a lot of blood on his hands, and although he wasn't there yet he was working on redeeming himself.

He remembered the day that everything in his life changed. He had been sent to do one of his special jobs for Victor. He was ordered to pay a visit to a guy in Queens who was late on his loan repayments and had started to drag his heels and make excuses. He remembered well Victor's instructions.

"Either briiiing me my money or bring me soooome body parts." he had said from behind his private table in the back of his restaurant where he had somehow been able to wedge his massive frame.

The man had owed fifty grand but only had four when Alex had called. Later as he made his way back to Victor, his right inside pocket contained the four grand. His left contained a bag with three fingers, seven teeth and half an ear.

Lesson learned.

You don't fuck with Victor.

Although he didn't know it at the time, the divine intervention that steered him onto the right path had already begun. Alex drove a big Pontiac Firebird. It was painted black and had a gold eagle painted on the hood. Some would say it looked sporty. Alex always thought it looked mean. He liked the sound of it when he fired the engine, the aggressive way it growled, spat and grunted as if it came from hell itself. He hadn't paid attention to the no parking signs as he pulled up outside Tony Montana's apartment block. If he had he would have moved a little way down the street first, but he was keen to get on with the job. When he returned twenty minutes later with his knuckles still sore, he found his beloved Firebird clamped and ticketed. He was furious. More at his own stupidity, but he had been left with no option but to return to his pasta slurping employer on foot. It was an amateur mistake and one which embarrassed him immensely. His hands and shirt had been spattered with blood, which made the journey incredibly risky. He pulled his jacket around his neck and thrust his hands into his pockets, which did an adequate if not perfect job of hiding the mess. Realising there was no way to fix the problem, he set off walking, hoping to flag down a Taxi further down the street. He was starting to think everything would be ok when he heard the unmistakable wail of a police cruiser. It rocketed around the corner, tires squealing in protest and casting its harsh blue and red lights onto the darkened streets. He was certain that Tony Montana hadn't called them—at least not if he valued his life, but Alex was known to the NYPD and would have a hard time explaining his bloody appearance and pockets full of cash and body parts if they should become curious enough to stop him. Deciding that discretion was the best course of action, Alex ducked into an alleyway, pushing himself into a recessed archway as far as he could as the car raced past him almost as fast as his heart raced in his chest. He felt a strange tingling in his left arm as alarm bells began to ring in his head. Please, not now.

He willed himself to remain calm, thinking not for

himself but the bag in his pocket and the blood on his clothes. A heart attack was something he could not afford to happen. He was sweating profusely, holding onto the wall with gritted teeth willing the feeling to pass. He felt the grip on his chest begin to loosen, and thought he might be ok when he was overcome by incapacitating agony. He couldn't breathe, and could only manage a weak gasp as he staggered into the street, stumbling forwards, his face smashing into the pavement as the vice holding his heart increased the pressure. He began to drift in and out of consciousness and was vaguely aware of the crowd of people that were gathering around him, ghostly faces swimming in and out of focus. He tried to talk, but even the smallest of movements caused a searing bolt of pain to fire through his body.

Twenty-nine.

That's how old he was when it happened. His next memory was waking dazed and groggy in a hospital bed with his ashen faced wife beside him. Her eyes relieved and pleading for answers. She knew he worked for Victor, but not in the capacity he did. She thought he was a manager of one of Victors export businesses, and that arrangement had suited him fine as it gave him the freedom to do the real job that Victor paid him to do. Every part of him hurt. He tried to talk but he couldn't muster the strength. All at once, his memory returned and he remembered the bag. The bag containing the non-essential (but incredibly incriminating) parts of Tony Montana that he had removed. Surely they would have found it; perhaps as a nurse removed his clothes as they tried to save his life. He could imagine her screaming and dropping the bag on the floor, the other doctors working on him recoiling in horror and wondering what his man had been doing before his heart gave up on him. It would transpire that on this occasion luck would be on his side.

Two things had happened which managed to get him off the hook. First was the heart attack itself. When he fell, he had smashed his nose and face on the kerb, which would explain away the blood on his shirt. (He had lost three teeth himself in the fall, which he thought later was a bitter irony)

Then there was the bag.

The bag that contained Tony Montana's missing body parts. That one he could not explain. Each day he waited for the police to arrive and question him, and each day passed with nothing. It was made clear a week later.

He received a visit from one of Victors Men. Alex had seen him before, lurking around the restaurant that was the base of Victor's operations, but he couldn't remember his name. He thought it might have been either Gino of Giuseppe, but wasn't certain. He remained quiet and wondered if he was about to be snuffed despite surviving his near fatal heart attack. Gino or Giuseppe sat beside the bed, watching carefully with his shifty rat like eyes. He leaned close to Alex, so close that he could smell the mint on his breath from the gum he was chewing.

'Boss sent me to tell you not to worry about the bag. We took care of it.'

It was as simple as that.

Victor had come through for him. He almost felt guilty for thinking him a slob. And was more than relieved to know he might get the double whammy of both surviving and getting away clean. It seemed that his visitor had more to say

'He also said that with that ticker of yours, he can't keep you on the payroll. Here.'

Rat eyed Gino-Seppe pushed a sealed envelope into the pocket of Alex's trousers, which were folded over the stand by his bed.

'Five G's for the job as agreed, plus an extra hundred grand for not spilling your guts.'

Alex nodded and almost wanted to tell rat face he wasn't sure if he had spilled his guts or not. He couldn't remember a thing since the accident and was still woozy from the medication. However, he took the decision not to push his incredible run of luck and said nothing.

'Take it easy pal. You had a close call.' said rat features as he stood and walked away without looking back.

Just like that, Alex was unemployed, and in the space of five minutes had made more money than in the last year and a half. Something in him told him to heed it as a warning and told him that perhaps he was meant for greater things that the life of a thug.

He looked at the pamphlets in his hands as he crossed the street and prepared to start work. The sun was warm and the breeze cool. It was perfect conditions for working outdoors spreading the good word of God. It was difficult at times. Most people were unwilling to listen, and he had noticed the world had become a cynical place desensitised to the value of a true miracle. But still there was hope, as scattered amongst the dark that lived in many were a few bright souls who were waiting to be given something to believe in. This was his third street of the day, and already he had found a few people interested enough to come to one of the sermons at his church the following Sunday. He had high hopes for this street, there was a wealthy vibe to it, and the rich in Alex's experience were often more tolerant than the rude lower classes. As he prepared to begin, his mind drifted once more to his former life and the change which made him the man he was today.

The hospital discharged him three weeks later. He had been luckier than he thought. They told him he had died three times on the operating table, and they were about to give up on the resuscitation when they managed to get a faint pulse. The instructions were clear.

No stress. Less salt. Less fatty foods. More exercise, but not too much at first. He listened. Death had made him appreciate life even more. Even without the payoff from Victor, he had decided to change his ways. God had given him another chance to live, and he intended to use it by spreading the word and hoping one day he will be forgiven for his former life's sins. They had even managed to save his teeth, and following several painful surgeries once again found his perfect smile restored. His wife, Lori had been sceptical at first of his change in career, but understood why it meant so much to him and once she had seen the passion which he had attacked his new faith, she got behind him and supported him. She was his rock, and he wished he could tell her the truth about his former life, but knew to do so would destroy their marriage and so he kept that part of him buried away deep.

As the months progressed into years, his old life had faded away and his tireless hard work with the church was rewarded as he was made a minister. Lori had told him she was so proud of him for working so hard at what he believed in, and suddenly his old life seemed like a distant memory as if it had never belonged to him. He had already been thinking of starting his own church, doing things his own way. Although he liked Father Mitchell, he felt he was a lazy old man set in his ways, and Alex could see that there was so much more scope for the word of God to be spread. He was no preacher, but he believed there was someone out there looking out for him and he wanted to tell people about the miracle that had saved him.

The first two houses he visited had been busts – a disinterested middle aged man at number one who seemed to Alex as if he was on his way to being drunk (even though it was only just after ten a.m. on a Wednesday morning) and the woman who lived at number three was just leaving the house as Alex had approached with his pamphlets, and didn't have time to speak to him. There was no point in getting frustrated; it was the nature of the game.

He approached the third house on the street, number five and looked it up and down. Well-kept gardens. Neat and tidy driveway. Clean windows and curtains. He had learned that the outside of someone's house was often a good representation of their character, and Alex thought the occupier of number five might well be willing to open the door and who knows, perhaps even listen. He opened the gate, whistling as he walked up the neat pathway to the door. He took a moment to compose himself then put on his best smile and knocked, waiting for the occupier to answer. He was about to leave when the door was opened just a little. He could see a floating female eye peering through the crack watching him.

'Yes?' said the faceless eye, looking him up and down. Here we go, Alex. Showtime.

'Good morning ma'am my name is Alex and I wonder

if I could talk to you a little about our lord and saviour Jesus Christ?'

He smiled at the floating blue eye, which continued to look at him mistrustfully.

'You're not trying to sell me anything are you? Came the shrill voice from the other side of the door.

'Oh no, of course not ma'am. I merely wish to speak with you, that's all.'

Silence.

'You had better come in then.' came the voice from within, before the door closed and Alex heard the chain slide free.

Ten minutes later Alex was sipping his cup of tea in Mrs. Bendtner's sitting room as she fussed in the kitchen. He looked about the room, noting that it was the typical dwelling of a lonely old woman. High backed chairs with gaudy floral patterns out of fashion since the seventies, mantle place full of photographs of what Alex presumed were her grandchildren and on the small table by her chair (he could tell it was hers as it looked far more 'lived in' than the one in which he was seated) was an old black and white photograph of a much younger Mrs. Bendtner alongside a man who Alex presumed was Mr. Bendtner, who was holding a chubby baby in his arms

She shuffled back into the room carrying a tray of cakes and sandwiches, her slippers making a swish swoosh sound as they padded on the carpet. He looked at the old lady and smiled. He was sure that if he were to pick up a dictionary and look up the word 'Grandma' he would find a picture of Mrs. Bendtner, standing there with her tray of cakes. She was a small woman, her skin lined with the scars of age. Her cheeks sagged below her jaw into heavy looking jowls. Her hair was a white permed mass on her head, and her tired brown eyes looked out with semi-glazed indifference. Age had not been too kind for poor Mrs. Bendtner, thought Alex as he compared her now to the picture by her seat. She could be anything between sixty and three hundred years old. It was hard to tell. She set the sandwiches on the coffee table and shuffled slowly to her own chair, sitting with some effort.

'Please, help yourself to a sandwich.' she said as she wrung her hands together.

'Thank you,' said Alex, noting a slight European flavour to the old woman's voice. Russian perhaps? Maybe polish. Definitely Eastern European. Alex selected a Cheese and cucumber which was cut into a neat triangle and took a small bite. It was good, and he finished the rest before helping himself to another.

'Those are delicious, Mrs. Bendtner.'

'I don't have much cause to make a fuss these days, my family are grown up and don't visit.'

Bingo.

Here was an old lady looking for something to fill her life. 'It must be lonely,' he said as he took another bite of his second sandwich, this one egg and cress.

'It is. I miss my William dearly' she said, glancing at the picture beside her.

'I'm sure God is looking after him Mrs. Bendtner, in fact, that's why I have come to you today, to talk of the great lord himself.'

She looked at him then, a flicker of cold in her eyes which was gone as soon as it arrived.

'I'm not sure if I believe in God anymore, young man.' she said with a shake of her head, the European twang to her voice more evident this time.

'Please, call me Alex.'

She failed to respond, instead taking a sip of her tea. He thought he could lose this one if he didn't move fast.

'May I ask why you don't believe in our lord Mrs. Bendtner?'

'I know God, and let me tell you he is no Savior.'

Alex nodded, perplexed at this response. Perhaps the old woman was senile or on her way at least.

'I once felt as you do, Mrs. Bendtner. I was a man without faith or direction. Yet I was saved, and I am thankful every day for God's intervention.'

'Intervention?' she laughed, causing Alex to shuffle in his seat.

'He is no more interested in you than you are interested in the feelings of a common Ant. God is cruel and enjoys watching us live out our miserable lives in desperation and pain.'

The venom in her words took him aback. Recovering quickly he set down his plate and handed over one of his pamphlets. She took it from him and read it as he spoke to her.

'We at The Church of The Devine would love to show you the way in which our Lord loves us. If you were able to join us a week from Sunday we would love to introduce you to his love.'

She looked up at him with a smile that held no humour. 'Love? What does he know of love? As much as you I suspect.' She said firmly, the strange twang of her dialect coming through ever more strongly.

Somewhere in his mind, a long forgotten alarm bell began to ring. The alarm bell of self-preservation. He used to rely on it when he worked for Victor, and now this old lady was making it ring. He pushed it away and continued.

'I must disagree Mrs. Bendtner, I have been fortunate to find solace in his love.'

She chuckled.

'No. You survived a near fatal heart attack that should have killed you and think God was responsible. But we know different, don't we? Do you think it was God who got rid of Tony Montana's teeth and fingers for you?' she said with a long, ugly smile that seemed to stretch too far across her face. He couldn't speak. A chill surged through him as he looked at this old woman sitting opposite him and realised that he had never felt as afraid as he did at that exact moment. How did she know? Nobody knew. His tongue felt like dead weight as it sat on the floor of his mouth, unwilling to cooperate. He willed it to move

'I'm sorry... I don't know what you are talking about ma'am.'

She smiled then, a ghastly, wide smile showing her teeth, which were crooked and yellow. Her eyes burned with contempt.

'Oh yes, you do. I know all about you and your kind...murdering Dog!'

His alarm bell had served him well. It was time to go.

'I'm afraid I'm going to have to leave, Mrs. Bendtner. I'm starting to feel unwell.'

It was true, nausea was driving through him in waves and he was suddenly hot. He lifted a hand to wipe the sweat from his forehead, but it felt heavy and disconnected from him. Mrs. Bendtner smiled and licked her lips.

'That will be the muscle relaxants I slipped into the sandwiches. I'm afraid you won't be able to move for some time. The nausea will pass in a few moments.'

Terror. He tried to lurch to his feet, his legs buckling as he fell forwards, crashing into the glass table which gave out under his weight, sending shimmering diamonds of glass exploding outwards. Fleshy remains of the sandwiches were scattered around him along with the shards of the broken table. He heard the scuffle of the old woman's slippers as she stood and walked close to him, causing him to panic.

'Where is your God now?' she asked.

'Please... why have you done this to me?'

'Because you and I have something to discuss.'

'You are a crazy old bitch!' he spat, claustrophobia overcoming him as his nose pushed into the deep pile carpet.

'Why don't you pray to him, for forgiveness? Your God. The great almighty.'

'What do you want?' he asked, wishing he could see her rather than just hear her voice floating behind him.

'I want to talk to you about your sins.'

'What sins? I have no idea what you are talking about!'

'Tell me about Victor.'

Silence.

He tried to untangle the jumble of thoughts, which raced through his mind but could not. This woman, old and decrepit as she appeared to be was so much more.

'I think you are mistaken ma'am, I don't know anyone called Victor.'

'Really,' she said as she stood and approached the fireplace. She picked up her walking stick in gnarled and liver spotted hands. Alex craned his neck and noticed that it was one of the old-fashioned kind—a thick length of dark polished oak with a black rubber stopper on the end.

'I'm going to ask you again. Tell me about Victor'

He could hear that European twang again in her voice, the V of victor sounding more like a 'W' it was no longer the voice of a sweet old woman, but that of an interrogator. He was scared now, and unable to move his arms or legs.

'I don't know who you think I am, but I don't know any Victor; I'm here to spread the word of...'

Agony.

She had jammed the end of the walking stick into the back of his hand, leaning all of her weight on it and twisting it back and forth. He felt one of the small bones snap as he yelled out in pain. She lifted the stick and took away the source of the pain, although his hand still throbbed. Returning to her chair and sitting calmly Mrs. Bendtner set the stick across her knees and watched him with cold, cruel eyes.

'Young man, do not make the mistake of underestimating me. You have no idea what I'm capable of.'

He believed her; despite the complete absurdity of the situation, he believed that this old woman was dangerous. He looked at his hand, an ugly round purple and red bruise already forming.

'Look, just tell me what you want, I'm sure god can

help you to find the way…'

She laughed at him, again showing those ugly, crooked yellow teeth.

'Save your prayers, young man. Your God is not welcome in this house. Now I'll ask you again. Tell me about Victor.'

It was hopeless. She knew. He didn't know how but she knew. Despite the care he had taken to construct a new life, she knew about Victor. Perhaps knew about him. He had to get out. Out of this house. It was too hot, and his hand screamed at him in pain. From somewhere Deep inside him, he found a little of his old self, a nugget of the long forgotten self-preservation instinct that had served him so well. It told him to start talking.

'Ok, Look, I used to work for Victor, but it was a long time ago.' Alex blurted around a mouth full of carpet fibres.

She stood again and shuffled towards him. He could smell her, like mints and mothballs and dry rot. She was holding the walking stick by her side swinging it with intent. He realised that it was for his benefit. She wanted him to see it. It was obvious enough she didn't need it to walk. Perhaps it had belonged to her husband when he was still alive. But now it served a different purpose. It was making a very good torture device. He knew well enough himself that often pain was secondary to the idea that pain was coming. And Mrs. Bendtner was using that technique expertly.

'Very good. Now tell me where he is.'

'I don't know.'

'Do you intend to test me, young man?'

'Please, I swear to you I don't know. I haven't worked for him for a long time I—'

She hit him in the face with the walking stick, the wood smashing into his nose and teeth. He let out a surprised urk and lowered his head to the carpet. His vision swam in and out of focus, as he spat out a great red gout of blood along with two broken teeth. Not again he thought as he tried to clear the cobwebs. His eyes fell on the jagged slice of Tooth where it lay nestled in its own pool of bright mouth blood. It reminded him of Tony Montana and he felt a dizzy giggle flash up to his throat. He could feel the warmth flowing down his lips and chin as he struggled to compose himself.

'Ok I'll tell you what I know,' he spat as he touched his tongue to the jagged remains of his front teeth.

Despite the rich and heavy sense of fear that had consumed him, he still thought he might have a chance to escape. Already he could feel his fingers and toes beginning to come back to life. He wondered if the muscle relaxants she had used were old. Perhaps they had been sitting in the back of a cupboard unused for years until he was stupid enough to knock on the door. Do muscle relaxants have a use by date? He wasn't sure but it was a chance, and the one advantage he may have over this crazy old bitch. He would talk. Talk until he was blue in the face and strong enough to make a break for it. He watched now as she returned to her chair. She sat with an arthritic groan and then opened the brown wooden box on the table by her chair, the one Alex had thought may have contained old photographs or reading glasses or a half-eaten packet of mints, the general Daily clutter used by old ladies worldwide. But he should have known. Because he was quickly realising that this was no ordinary old woman. This was some kind of monster. He watched as she pulled out a syringe and a vial of clear liquid. Terror, pure and honest raced through his body.

'What the hell are you doing? I said I'd talk. Please!'
She filled the syringe, watching him as she did so.
'Relax, Preacher. This is just so we might talk in more comfort.'

He began to panic as she approached him, her slippers padding along the deep pile carpet as she came.

'What are you doing? What are you doing to me?'

She crouched and jabbed him in the neck and he began to feel woozy. His vision danced, and as it faded, he saw one of his pamphlets, now strewn across the floor. The question on the front printed in bold black text seemed as relevant now as ever.

DOES GOD REALLY LOVE US?

It was a good question, intended to stimulate conversation, to allow him to ease into his sales spiel. After all wasn't that what he was? A salesman of God? The question resonated within him. If he did, he had a funny way of showing it, especially to someone who had tried so hard to make amends for his past. He would have liked to give it some more thoughts, but his eyelids were now lead weights and he couldn't keep them open anymore. He passed out.

TWO

He awoke slowly, and in the hazy bliss of those early

seconds could not remember the terror of what had been. It was as he became lucid that the fear found him again and he forced himself to swallow the scream that so desperately wanted to escape.

He was still in the old ladies sitting room, although the light had now shifted, turning the shadows into long, gnarled talons reaching up and grasping across the walls. He was no longer on the floor but was instead sat on a sturdy wooden chair. He tried to move but found that not only were his muscles uncooperative, but he was also securely tied to the chair. Arms behind his back, feet to the chair legs. He was hot, and his face was in agony. He was unable to breathe through his nose, which was clogged with dried blood. He suspected that it could well be broken. He swallowed dryly, wincing at the copper taste, then looked around the room, which was mostly unchanged; although he could see it had been tidied. The broken remains of the glass table were gone apart from a few missed tiny shards of glass which glinted like tiny diamonds when caught by the late afternoon sun, which had cast the room in a hellish orange hue. He could still see the red stain on the crème carpet where he had bled, although his broken teeth had been disposed of. Absently he ran his tongue across the sharp stumps in his mouth, moaning at the pain. His thoughts felt cloudy, as they were being forced to wade through a thick fog in order to present themselves. He wondered where she was. His insane captor. Holding his breath, he listened intently, past the irritating tick tock of the huge grandfather clock against the far wall. He thought he could hear voices. No, not voices. It was the radio. He could hear the steady drawl of the DJ as he pronounced what a beautiful day it had been.

Not for all of us pal. He thought to himself as he tried to formulate some kind of plan. He looked up and could see the fireplace, and above it the rows of old photographs which stood on the mantle. From his seated position he could see himself in the mirror. He thought he felt bad but he looked even worse. His face was swollen, and his nose which when he arrived was straight and true, now had an ugly bend around halfway down. His lips and chin were covered in dried blood like some kind of horror movie zombie. He looked into his own eyes he could see reflected fear looking back at him. A Bloody, Terrified, Thirty seven year old man who had set out that morning with the sole intention of spreading a message of love and happiness, and was now held captive by a crazy old woman with a grudge against Victor.

He heard her coming, the unmistakable shuffling of slippers on carpet as she approached. He instinctively tried to free himself. He wanted nothing to do with her, this crazy old woman who pronounced her 'V's as W's, who kept syringes of tranquillizers and muscle relaxants in the house and thought nothing of breaking the teeth and nose of her houseguests? The rest of his thought process froze. She came into the room.

He was still amazed at how harmless she looked. She was carrying a tray containing a cup of tea and a plate of digestive biscuits. The tray also contained several things that had no sane reason to be there. Things that made his stomach knot. A scalpel. A pair of old red handled pliers. A small hammer. He watched her frail form as she shuffled across the room, glaring at him with emotionless eyes. She set the tray on the table beside her chair and lowered herself into her seat. He watched her as she looked at him. For now, they were both happy to be silent. He swallowed his fear as she again opened the wooden box. This time, it was the type of items that he would have expected in the first instance. A small notepad and pen, some thick-rimmed reading glasses and an old pack of cigarettes and lime green lighter. Still, she said nothing, her deeply lined face watching his bloated and bloody one. Slowly—deliberately so, Alex thought, she took out a cigarette and lit it, exhaling as she sat back in her high backed chair with the garish floral pattern. Alex watched her and thought that she had snakes eyes, alien and lifeless. He glanced at the grandfather clock in the corner and saw it was just after four in the afternoon. Still, she was silent. She finished her cigarette and took up the notepad, and, turning to a clean page, she spoke.

'Tell me about Victor.'

That same line. No pleasantries, just straight down to business. This was his chance to keep her talking. He had regained control of his fingers and was exploring the knots of the ropes, looking for an opportunity to untie them.

'That's a broad question, it depends on what you want to know.'

'You work for Victor, no?'

'Actually no, not anymore. I used to do…errands for him a long time ago.'

She smiled then, but there was no humour in the gesture.

'You speak of errands like you speak of your God, lapdog!' She barked as she scribbled something in the notebook.

'I must tell you it would be unwise to lie to me because you see me as a shrivelled up old fool. I am capable of more than you perhaps give me credit for. Now I have no desire to hurt you and am perfectly happy for you to walk free from here as soon as I have the information I require. However, you must tell me the truth or there will be…repercussions.'

Alex knew this patter, he had used a similar one himself. It was the classic reassure the victim talk, but he knew as well as she did that his chances of leaving that room ever again were slim, in reality probably less than that, but they were both playing the game now and there was no turning back.

'Look, I'll be honest with you. I have no loyalty to Victor. Not anymore. And I have no interest in whatever squabble you have with him. I'll answer your questions if you will set me free.'

Game on. Cat and mouse. Tit for tat.

'I appreciate your willingness to assist. Let us do this quickly then, so we can put this unfortunate incident behind us.'

Bullshit. They both knew it. One of them was going to die in this room, and Alex was determined that it wouldn't be him.

'That's all I want.' He said, adding a tremble to his voice. He was proud. It was a nice touch. Let the old bitch think she had rattled him.

'Very good. Now tell me. When did you last work for Victor?' She waited, pen poised.

'I don't remember the exact date, but it was over seven years ago.'

She wrote it down, and then those vulture like eyes were upon him again.

'When did you last speak to him?'

'The day of that last job. I never spoke to him again in person after that morning.'

'I see, and this job you refer to would be the serious assault of a...' she referred to her notes, leafing back a few pages.

'A Tony Montana, is that correct?'

He had to be careful here, had to keep playing the game. He had to appear weaker than he was.

'I can't remember it's been a long time.' he lied. He remembered all too well. He wondered where she had got her information.

'And during your time working for Victor, you had training yes? Specialist training?'

'No.'

She closed her book.

'I thought we had an agreement preacher. Now I will ask again. Did you have training?'

He wondered why she kept calling him preacher. It irritated him.

'I don't know what else to tell you. I had no training.'

Another lie. He had received lots of training. Victor liked his staff to be good at their jobs. Hand to hand combat, explosives making, torture techniques, firearms handling. He could give the average army commando a run for his money—or at least he could have back in what felt like another lifetime. The bottom line was that he knew how to look after himself, but this crazy old bag didn't know the odds of survival went more in his favour.

She pursed her lips and glared at him shaking her head.

'I told you not to underestimate me and yet you lie through your broken teeth.'

'I'm not lying, I haven't received any training!'

The fear was easy to put into his voice this time, as it was real. It was real because she had stood and was now walking towards him. He wished that along with his military style training, he had also learned the art of resisting interrogation.

'I'm afraid Preacher that until you begin to appreciate the severity of this situation, that you and I will be quite unable to engage in any kind of fruitful conversation eh lapdog?'

He could feel the crazy coming off her in waves. He was trying to appear unafraid but it was a losing battle. She flicked her yellowed eyes towards the tray beside her chair and considered. She decided on the pliers and approached him; the maddening sounds of her slippers on the carpet were now secondary to the terror. All he could see were those silver teeth as she neared.

'Mrs. Bendtner, please....'

'I think you and I are not too dissimilar lapdog. Many years ago, I too used to work for a powerful man who demanded results, and it was I that would get those results for him. Tell that to your Master eh. Woolph!'

She was behind him now, gibbering and insane and armed with steel-toothed pain. Ha, that almost rhymed he thought to himself in some distant corner of his mind. He wasn't even sure if he were still playing the game of cat and mouse anymore. He flinched as she leaned close, her foul breath hot in his ear.

'You stupid Americans are all the same. Overconfident fools. Let me tell you something Mr. Preacher man. You think you know of pain and how to inflict it, yet you know nothing. I have extracted secrets from better men than you, puppet of Victor! Now tell me what I want to know.

She sounded like one of those clichéd war Movie Russian actors, trying too hard to sound authentic, but this was real. He knew he had to tell her the truth, at least keep her talking in the hope he could regain control of his limbs.

'Yes.' Alex said with a sigh. This time, the tremble in his voice was not an act.

'In what fields?'

'Weapons, explosives. Hand to hand combat.'

'And torture yes?'

She was still behind him, and although he couldn't see her, he could feel her smile as she spoke.

'Yes.' He said with a sigh, lowering his head. He knew then he couldn't win this; somehow, the world had gone crazy and he was massively out of depth with this frail old woman. He waited for the sting of pain, for the cold feeling of steel on flesh, but nothing came. She seemed to be satisfied and returned to her chair, setting the pliers down and picking up her cup of tea, which she slurped loudly.

'Who the hell are you lady?' he croaked as she continued to drink.

'The questions about things are mine to ask eh?'

He didn't understand and was about to speak again when she twitched and blinked, the said again more calmly.

'I will ask the questions. You will answer.'

Back to playing the game. He needed to buy time.

'I understand that, but at least be fair. I mean it's obvious that you aren't just an average old lady. What are you? Russian intelligence? KGB?'

'She chuckled then and shook her head. 'Nothing so dramatic I'm afraid. I worked for an agency who extract secrets from traitors, enemies careless enough to be caught on our lands. They would be sent to me and I make them talk.'

'And if they didn't?'

'They would talk or die. Something you may wish to heed Preacher.'

'My name is Alex.'

'Does it matter?'

He broke her gaze and lowered his head. He needed to keep her busy, keep her mind off her questions. His hands were now fully under his control, as he did his best to read the knots binding them, probing them with his fingers in the hope of being able to untie them. For now, though, he reminded himself to keep the old nutcase talking.

'How did you plan of this? I mean how did you know I would come here?'

She smiled, taking another long sip of her tea and lighting another cigarette. He saw with dismay that her hands were rock steady. His wouldn't stop shaking.

'It was a chance encounter. I saw you at your church.'

She nodded towards the pamphlets, now stacked by the telephone.

'I wasn't sure it was you at first. You have lost weight since you last worked for Victor.'

It was true. Without the need for the bulk on his body which had helped him to intimidate those unfortunate enough to get on Victor's bad side, He had cut out the steroids and three times a week visits to the gym and trimmed down. He was now thirty-five pounds lighter.

'Of course, I still have a few contacts, people who owe me favours. I made a few calls. Of course, I had already been following Victor and his affairs for some time, so finding you by chance was something of an unexpected bonus. I'm sure you of all people understand that preacher man.'

He tried to process the information, but as she spoke, more questions were raised.

'I still don't understand. How did you know I would come here?'

'Oh, it was educated guesswork. This is a nice street and within the catchment area of your church. I knew from my research that you were doing a drive to recruit new members for your parish; it was just a matter of time and waiting for you to knock on my door. And what else does an old woman like me have but time to wait?'

'But why? What do you want with me? I haven't had dealings with Victor for years; you should know that if you've researched me, I have nothing to tell you that you probably don't already know.'

He was frightened and angry and had let his guard slip. The old woman smiled, knowing she had the upper hand. She continued as if he hadn't even spoken.

'The strange thing is, Preacher that even when you knocked on my door I still wasn't sure it was even you.

You have changed in appearance. And in your defence, it seems that you love the work you do for the church. It wasn't until I let you in this morning and I saw the look of recognition on your face when you looked at the photograph of William that I knew I had the right person.'

He was confused and tried to recall earlier that day. It already felt like a lifetime ago. It was true that he had seen the old black and white picture on the fireplace as he walked in, the man and woman on their wedding day, both smiling proudly, the small child in the woman's arms not quite looking into the camera. A small pang of recognition had come over him but he dismissed it as a false memory, perhaps confused with an old family photograph that was similar in content. One thing was for certain, he didn't know the man in the photo. He had never seen him before.

'I don't know any William, you have the wrong person.' He pleaded. In response, she sneered, stood, and moved to him quickly. He tried to recoil, but she moved with the skitter quickness of a spider. He was wondering how she could move so quickly when he was rocked by a fresh wave of pain. He didn't realise at first what she had done, and then a tight sickness in his gut overcame him as he glanced at his horrified reflection in the mirror above the mantle. She had cut off his left earlobe.

'Do not lie to me again dog! You killed my William on Victor's say so. Well, let's see how brave you are now, Preacher. Whoreson!

He was breathing heavily now and began to squirm in his seat, trying to ignore the wild-eyed way she was staring at him.

'Ahh, I wondered how long you would keep up the pretence that your limbs were still paralysed.' She said as she sat back in her chair. He glanced again at himself in the mirror, and barely recognised the man who looked back at him. The sweating, puffy eyed, bloody nosed stranger. And yes—he could see it. The flap of skin that belonged to his ear was sitting on his shoulder of his blue suit.

'Look, I swear to you, I don't know anything, you have the wrong man!'

It was no longer a game. The loyalty to Victor that was no more than a token gesture for the assistance with the Tony Montana situation was gone. The loyalty to himself and his self-preservation had taken over. He had decided that he would tell this woman whatever she wanted to know. Not only because he wanted to live, but because he could see it in her eyes that she was not only prepared to kill him for something he hadn't done, she looked like she would enjoy it.

'Look, no bullshit ok? I'll tell you whatever you want to know!'

She had picked up the screwdriver now and was walking back towards him.

'I know you will.'

She jabbed him in the arm, and although it still hurt, his suit jacket cushioned most of the impact. She realised immediately, and without hesitation reared back and drove the metal shaft into his thigh. Searing white-hot agony surged through him as he screamed, then clenched his remaining teeth together, breaking off more of the damaged ones in the process.

'Tell me why Victor ordered you to kill my William.'

Despite the horror, she was calm. Her voice flat and toneless. This was nothing unusual to her, an ordinary day. He wondered how many she had killed. Tens. Hundreds? Thousands? He began to writhe, but the knots were holding firm.

' I don't know him, I didn't do anything!' he was sobbing, a bloody mucus bubble forming in the left nostril of his crushed nose as he tried to force air through it.

'You had him drowned. You took his money. His pride. You took everything lapdog eeeee!!'

'I didn't have anyone drowned! I was just a heavy, hands on, it was never my style!!' he pleaded, trying to ignore her gibbering.

'Then give me Victor, tell me where he is!'

'I don't know you crazy bitch!'

She wriggled the handle of the screwdriver back and forth where it still lay nestled in his leg and he could feel it scrape against the bone as a wave of nausea overcame him. He thought he was about to faint.

'It was you. You and Victor together. For two weeks they didn't find him, bloated and fat.'

'It wasn't me!!! You have the wrong man!'

She was no longer making sense. Her eyes were wide, and her chin lined with slick spittle. She was leering at him, her face inches from his. He couldn't stand to be near her and lunged backwards, pushing off the floor with all of the force he could muster. He had read about the strength that people could find in the most extreme situations when their lives depended on it. He thought this was one of those instances. The chair pitched backwards and tipped over, his knees connecting with her chin as he tumbled to the floor. She twisted away, grunting as she landed on her side. The impact had hurt him. Jarring his shoulder and crushing his lower arms, which were pinned below him. Horror overcame him as he twisted his body to see where the old hag was. He didn't like not being able to see her. It was as he did this that the old chair gave up under the punishment of his struggles, the legs popping free and leaving him in a heap on the floor.

He came to his knees and managed to free his hands. Trying his best to ignore the pain in his face and thigh, he looked to his left and saw that she was already up, coming at him with the screwdriver. She lunged towards him, slashing at his face. Instinctively he rolled to the right, his shoulder clattering against the armchair. Her eyes were wild now; he could feel the fury as she stalked towards him. He tried to scramble to his feet, but his legs were still too weak, and he stumbled back to the floor with a grunt. He knew she was on him now. He could smell the mothball stench and could hear her shuffling slippers. Looking over his shoulder, he saw the screwdriver coming towards his face. He managed to flinch away, but the metal shaft gouged into his cheek and tore a large wound into his skin. Fueled by adrenaline and the fire that burned his face, he turned and shoved her hard with both hands, catching her flush in the stomach. She staggered backwards and he saw the screwdriver skitter across the floor as she lost her grip on it. Unable to walk, he crawled towards the sitting room door, hoping that he could make it to the front door and the freedom of the lush gardens and picket fences of Sycamore Street.

He pulled himself up at the door and felt pain again, this time in his side as she stabbed him again with the screwdriver. He instinctively threw an elbow behind him, rejoicing at the feeling of bone on flesh. He heard her utter a surprised grunt, and then he was on his way, door open and into the hallway. His face and side burned with pain, and as he looked down at his side, he could see an ugly maroon stain forming on his shirt. But adrenaline was helping him to keep going. He focused and took in his surroundings as he wheezed and snatched for breath. Staircase directly ahead. Two doors to the right, front door to the left. He prayed that she hadn't locked it. He thought that if she had, he would probably die.

He crawled on all fours to the door and grabbed at the

handle. He knew it would be locked. He just knew deep inside. He pulled and rejoiced as it turned in his grip. He opened the door, his freedom so close when he felt pain, worse than all the others he had endured. An inferno of agony in his left leg caused him to lurch forwards and slam the door closed again, and shutting out his freedom.

Blood pooled around the long slash in his trouser leg, and he knew what she had done. She had cut something back there, a tendon or perhaps his hamstring. Something vitally important to his ability to walk. She hadn't cut it through full, he could still flex, but it felt loose and rubbery. He turned and glared at her as she walked towards him, scalpel blade shining ominously. She swung the blade at him again and he snapped his head back, wincing at the sickening swish sound as it missed his throat by inches. Alex grabbed her ankle and drove his shoulder as hard as he could into her knee. She wailed, and he felt a flash of satisfaction as he heard something break and she crashed to the floor banging her head on the wall as she went.

He hoped that it would keep her down long enough for him to escape as he tried to drag himself upright, but whatever she had cut back on his leg had incapacitated him, and he could only just get to his knees, holding one arm against his bleeding side. He looked on in dismay as she grabbed the dropped scalpel and tried to stand but then rejoiced as she shrieked as she tried to put pressure on the leg he had damaged and stumbled back on all fours.

Battle of the cripples he thought to himself as she shuffled towards him.

'Tell me about Victor!' she cackled as she lunged at him again with the blade, narrowly missing his throat for the second time. Instinctively he grabbed her wrist, and without pausing to think balled his fist and hit her as hard as he could in the face. Guilt immediately overcame him as she crumbled to the floor. The guilt was replaced by searing agony, as he felt the tendon or hamstring or whatever it was back there that she had cut snap away as he rolled onto his side and clutched at his leg. As he lay there, he could see the doorknob, tantalisingly close and yet out of reach. His entire body was in pain, and only his willingness to survive and belief in God allowed him to continue. He crawled past her, trying to ignore the pain and eying the steps then immediately dismissing them. Perhaps a back door then. He dragged himself along, His left leg limp and useless as it trailed behind him, his right still functional but in agony from the screwdriver wound. He made for the kitchen, and barged into the swing door, falling onto the cool black and white tiled floor.

He could see clean white tiles and lemon coloured painted walls. He could see the kitchen work surface which edged the room. He could see the back door, open and inviting. Outside the door, he could make out the tall wooden fence and a flash of green from the oak tree in the next-door neighbours small neat back yard. He could also see the huge Rottweiler, which was lying in the doorway and looking at him, growling aggressively.

He froze, and tried to remember if the rule was that you should or shouldn't break eye contact with an aggressive dog. He couldn't remember and decided to take his chances. He inched forwards and suddenly it was up, leaning towards him and drooling, daring him to come closer. He didn't like dogs, never had, but now cursed this one for blocking his escape. He wondered if he could take it on, disable it somehow but knew it would be stupid to try. He would bet his life that the crazy old bitch had trained it to kill at her command. He backed out of the kitchen, grateful that it wasn't a swing door and closed it. He turned back around as best his crippled body would allow. She was there waiting for him, kneeling at the bottom of the staircase, her mouth and nose bloody where he had struck her. She had the scalpel in her right hand, waving it back and forth.

'Don't think you can get out of here, I have been waiting for you for too long!'

She slashed at him, and he ducked away, yet already he could feel his reactions becoming sluggish. He had lost a lot of blood and was exhausted. He grimaced at her as she gibbered and grinned.

'Come on Victor; let's see those pearly whites hmmm.'

'I'm not Victor, you have the wrong man!'

She was mad. Not senile, but mad. Crazy. Her eyes shone wildly as she licked her lips, bloody drool hanging from her chin. He wondered if perhaps when he struck her he snapped the last thread of sanity that she had been holding on to. Whatever had happened, she had lost her mind.

'Do you know how many nights I have listened to you eating that slop Victor?'

He had no idea what she was talking about and that in itself made her even more terrifying. She licked her bloody lips and rocked from side to side as she glared at him.

'Look at me and take it easy. I'm not Victor, I'm Alex.'

'Victor's dog you are! My dog is better. Ha!'

She slashed at him again, lightning quick. He couldn't avoid it in time and threw his hands up, the blade slicing across his palm. He reared back and slammed against the closed kitchen door. The Rottweiler had heard enough and began to bark and growl as it scratched at the door, trying to get out.

'See lapdog, not so funny with the red blood anymore is it?'

Her eyes were vacant pools of insanity, and he wondered who she saw kneeling in front of her. He felt faint, the world beginning to ebb and flow as he tried to focus. His life depended on it.

'I can tell you where Victor is, I can get close to him, he trusts me!' he pleaded, aware more than ever that he was cornered.

'Not the puppet, but the puppet master. His strings I will cut like I will cut you, yes!'

She sounded like a bizarre psychopathic Yoda as she hovered there, just out of arms reach waiting for him to make a move. He saw in horror that she had urinated where she knelt, the carpet below her dark and yellow and pungent. The foul smell reached his broken nose and he felt bile rise into his throat. She was psyching herself up to lunge at him, he could see it in her eyes and knew he had to act or he would die. He watched, waiting for her to strike, knowing that this would likely be his last chance before he passed out due to blood loss. She slashed at him, and this time, he was ready. He twisted away from the blade and leaned towards her, grabbing her wrist and biting down hard, ignoring the agony of the shattered remains of his teeth. She screamed, the sound was impossibly high pitched and she dropped the scalpel. He reached down and picked it up, almost losing his grip on the handle due to the hot, slick blood on his hands. With everything he could muster, he jammed the blade into her shoulder and twisted, glaring at her and smiling his broken crimson smile. Like the flick of a switch, he was the Alex of old, the violent, remorseless beast of a man he had worked so hard to bury away. He felt euphoric. With a defiant grunt, he shuffled forwards and lifted her frail body by the arms, slamming her into the side of the doorframe. He heard her head smash against the wood, and she went limp. Shoving her aside, he made for the steps;

something so simple suddenly looked impossibly high, especially with legs that didn't work. He began to drag himself up on his elbows, keeping his eyes fixed firmly ahead and not thinking about her, the crazy old lady with the Yoda voice.

His left leg was quite useless, but his right still partially worked and he was able to get some purchase as he climbed. He focused on ignoring the pain, ignoring the wet squelch of blood with every bend of his damaged limb, to ignore the bloody handprints he left as he dragged himself ever up, so bright against the pale crème carpet.

He was halfway up when the world began to shift under him. He felt sick, and black spots began to dance in front of his eyes. He thought he was going to fall, and tottered on the edge of balance for what felt like an eternity before the world came back into focus. He could hear her, stirring below him and he screamed at himself in his head. Why did you try for the stairs, you fucking idiot! It was the groan inducing, slap the forehead stuff of bad horror films. Nobody in their right mind would head upstairs, and it was true. But he wasn't entirely sure he was in his right mind anymore and when it was a matter of real life and death, common sense didn't always prevail. Breathless and dizzy, he made the small square landing area before the steps took a left. Just three more then he would be on the upstairs hallway and could plan his next move. Down the hall that there were three doors, the bathroom being furthest away. He could see the edge of the bath, white and draped with a black towel. He looked back down the stairs, past the bloody trail he had left and saw her approaching on her knees, the scalpel still embedded in her shoulder. He chastised himself for not bringing it with him and then groaned in when he saw what she had in her hand.

Where did she get that?

It was a large butcher's knife. Black handled, long and sharp. He had one himself, in a wooden block beside his toaster.

'Bad puppet Victor, you should control this pet of yours!' she gibbered.

She was glaring at him, eyes wild and defiant, face bloodied and frightening. She got to her knees and then stood shakily, brushing her hands at the wet patches on her blue skirt.

'I'll clip you, puppet, then his puppet master. Organ grinder, not the monkey eh?

He lunged for the hallway, ignoring the agony as he banged his wounded leg on the top step. She was coming; he could hear her babbling as she followed him up the stairs. He wished she would stop. It was somehow worse than the pain.

'I told him about you, my dear, I told him his puppet was a bad one, but he didn't listen, he never listens.'

He began to crawl, boosted by fear and the surge of adrenaline. He tried the first door, but it was shut and he could not reach the handle.

'Those meatballs don't taste so good now do they puppet?'

She was close, and stealing a quick glance over his shoulder could see her at the top of the steps, glaring at him. He turned and shuffled to the next room, knowing he would never reach the bathroom in time. He could see that the door was open and dragged himself in, closing the door behind him as she screamed again, hurrying after him

'Come out of there puppet, eeeee eeeee!'

He leaned against the door, propping his good (or less damaged) leg against the chimney wall and holding it closed. She tried the handle but didn't have the strength to get in. he could hear her stabbing at the door with the knife, but the wood was strong and thick, and he suspected that she would be unable to penetrate it. He could hear her out there babbling and weeping as she paced the hall. He turned his attention to the room, hoping to find something to defend himself with, or even better a telephone so he could call for help. He had never been a fan of the police, and would normally refrain from having anything to do with them but he was after all in distress, and more importantly innocent. He paid his taxes after all and—

His thoughts were interrupted as he looked around the room. It was at first glance ordinary. Pale green wallpaper, single bed pushed against the far wall. Clean and tidy. All was as you might expect, apart from the shrine that dominated the wall by the window. Set upon a large table, it was covered in photographs and candles and sprinkled with pink and yellow flower petals. The centrepiece was a large colour photograph of a smiling man, perhaps twenty with blonde hair and a crooked toothed smile.

Recognition.

That horrible sinking feeling of recognition. He knew this face. He had seen it before. When he last saw this face, it was terrified, its owner begging for his life. He searched his memories, trying to put a name to the face, and then he had it. Billy. Not William, but Billy. Billy Somers. He recalled the picture downstairs, the one that the crazy old bitch insisted that he had recognised even though he was adamant that he hadn't, but he thought he understood now. Of course, he didn't recognise Billy from the photograph. After all, Billy was just a baby, held by his loving mother and father. A mother and father who had no idea that one day, Billy would grow up to be in the wrong place at the wrong time, and thinking that he could get himself out a hole, he would one day turn to a man called Victor for help. And when he couldn't pay his debts, when he couldn't pay Victor back the money he had loaned plus the huge interest that had accrued, Victor had sent Alex to pay him a visit. Alex recalled in horror as the memories flooded back to him with sickening clarity. Rough handling Billy into the Firebird, ignoring his pleas, ignoring the desperate tears.

He remembered meeting Victor by the docks at dusk, the air crisp and salty with the taste of the sea. He remembered thinking to himself how ridiculous Victor looked in his white suit, like some out of place safari explorer. Victor was sweating, and even though it was near dark was wearing sunglasses. He remembered stopping the car and dragging young Billy, who had saucer eyes and a trembling bottom lip to Victor who stood and waited by the end of the dock, smiling his lion's grin.

'Aleeeex,' he had said as they approached. 'This is why they say you are the best. I ask you to bring the trash, and you do as I ask.'

He had shoved Billy towards Victor, enjoying the stench of fear, enjoying his own feeling of power and self-importance.

'Tell meee,' Victor had said to Billy. 'Why do you fuck with me? Why don't you pay back what you owe?'

Billy had begged, pleading for more time.

'You make a fool out of Victor Mallone, and then have the balls to ask for more time? You must be made an example of.'

Victor nodded, and that was all it took. Alex tied Billy's hands and feet. Not with rope like the one he had been tied with earlier in the day, but with heavy-duty cable ties. It was Quick, efficient. Hands bound in front of him, feet together. Secure. Inescapable. Victor had watched this appreciatively, enjoying Alex's work almost as much as he himself had.

'Now Biiiily you understand that you give me no choice here? How can I expect to run a business if people think they can fuck around with me eh?' Another nod to Alex, who shuffle stepped Billy to the edge of the dock, the black water below frothing and crashing against the wooden struts of the pier. Alex knew the procedure. He reached into Billy's pocket, taking out his wallet and removing the cash and credit cards and handing them to Victor, and yes, that was where he remembered the photograph from. A much smaller wallet sized version he had dismissed and thumbed past to take out the MasterCard.

'Take this as a lesson Billy. Nobody screws with Victor Malone.' Victor had said around his cigar which he lit with an expensive gold Zippo lighter

A barely perceptible nod from Victor and Alex shoved Billy hard in the back, watching him plummet into the icy cold waters. He waited and watched until the air bubbles subsided. Ever the professional. Making sure that the job was done.

He blinked and was back in the present, the shrine looming ahead of him, a symbol of his guilt. He shuffled forward on his knees and prayed to god for forgiveness. Sure enough, Billy wasn't innocent—he had debts he should have paid, that was true, but not at the cost of his life. For the first time, he felt a sense sympathy and kinship towards the gibbering and crazy old woman out in the hallway. He had never understood until that exact moment the damage he had caused over the years. He had moved on and changed his lifestyle, and thought it would be enough to bury the man he used to be and pretend it had never happened. But what about them? The people that he had affected. The Billy Bendtner's and the Tony Montana's of the world? He felt sick and ashamed and was about to call out to Mrs. Bendtner in the hallway to try to explain when the doorframe exploded in a shower of splinters behind him. Even as he shielded his face from the deafening roar of the gunshot, he saw her standing in the doorway. She was still crying, the Russian issue pistol clutched in her right hand.

'This is William's room, puppet.' she cackled at him as she stepped closer. There was nowhere left to run, nowhere to go. It was over.

'What a cost for this life eh?'

It was babble, and he was fairly sure that even she didn't know what she was saying, but this seemed a good question. What a cost for this life? What would he pay? How could he atone for his sins? She came towards him then, licking her horrible blood red lips.

'Does the puppet remember now, my William?'

He did remember, and he had made a decision on what to do.

'I remember, and I'm sorry…I truly am.'

He lowered his head and wept, as she inched closer.

'Cry now eh? I know how that feels puppet. Many lonely nights I have wept!'

He knew now what he had to do. He lunged, tackling her to the ground. The gun knocked out of her hand and across the floor. He was on her, hands around her wiry throat, crushing down with what remained of his strength. She didn't fight, she just glared at him defiantly.

'I'm so sorry,' he said as he watched her, and pleaded for her to die. He thought at the end she understood, the insane glimmer in her eyes seemed to clear, if only for a second. Then she faded.

It was over. She was gone.

It took him most of the afternoon and into the evening to finish cleaning himself up. The tendon and cut on his cheek would need hospital attention but he had managed to remain mobile by using the old walking stick retrieved from the front room, and the face wound was bad but not life threatening. He would deal with it later. The rest of his injuries he had managed to patch up using the first aid box from the bathroom. The dog in the kitchen had been dispatched with a single shot from the old woman's service revolver. He had tried to get into the kitchen to set it free into the yard, but it was violent and as he suspected had been trained to attack on sight. In the end, he had been left with no choice but to put it out of its misery. He had cleaned up the house as best he could but knew that his fingerprints, his blood were in too many areas to really do an adequate job. He had laid Mrs. Bendtner in her late son's bed in the shrine room, along with the wedding photograph. It seemed fitting to him that they all, at last, be together. He had used the time in the stillness of the house to think about his future. He knew he could no longer live in the fragile belief that he was free of his sins just because he believed in God. He knew he had much to atone for and passing out leaflets and spreading the word was never going to be enough. He had limped his way around the house, checking through the old woman's records. It seems she had quite the research folder on Victor; some of the depth of information even surprised him. It seemed Victors reach went further than anyone could have ever known. He found a half can of gasoline in the garage and paying particular attention to the bloodied areas and the shrine room. Had poured it through the house, leaving a trail to the front door. Pausing by the open door, he hesitated, listening to the house. He thought he could hear that swish swish sound of slippers on carpet, but knew it was his exhausted mind playing tricks on him. He took the matches he found in the kitchen drawer and lit one, touching it to the rest of the pack and dropping to on the carpet, where it ignited the petrol with a satisfying whump. He quietly closed the door and made his way down the ornate path, past the neatly trimmed lawn and out into Sycamore Street. He was careful to close the gate behind him. Yes, this was a lovely street. Although he no longer thought he would live somewhere like this. This was a place for the sin free. For the happy people looking to retire after a good life of hard work. No. his work was just about to begin.

He got into his car and watched the dull orange glow coming from the windows of the Bendtner house. It had dawned on him as he had read through the wealth of files that in order to truly earn his chance at forgiveness, he would have to cut off the head of the snake. The snake that made him. The snake that was Victor Mallone. He was under no illusions. He knew it would be difficult—some might say impossible. But he would find a way. He would use his skills, the ones he had buried away so successfully over the years and turn them against their creator. He would find his forgiveness and avenge the Mrs Bendtner's of the world. He slipped the car into gear and rolled down the street. He glanced into the rearview mirror as the flames took full hold of No. 5 Sycamore Street.

## A STRANGE AFFAIR

So much blood.

Harry blinked as his brain tried to process the violence in front of him. His wife's eyes stared blankly, devoid of any semblance of life as the eight inch serrated knife fell to the ground. It was at that point, as it came to rest on a pile of soggy slick entrails that he felt something in his mind break. He tried to speak but instead only smacked his lips, a strange gurgling sound welling up from inside. He was sure he could have controlled it had she not chosen that moment to speak. Her tone was both an accusation and a question, pleading and angry. It was that one word that sent him over the edge.
'Harry?'
It was then that the true impact of the situation hit him. As he turned and vomited noisily, He wondered how this could have happened, how his life could come to this.

Earlier.

Flicking through the news channels, Harry hoped for something to catch his interest. Anything to take him away from the horrible sticky humidity that seemed to hang in the room like a blanket. Wiping his arm across his forehead, he wondered to himself what was happening to the world. The news channels were as bleak as always. CBS. NBC. CNN. All rehashing the same stories of the latest atrocities in the world. Militants had killed two hundred civilians in some country Harry had never heard of.
An earthquake in Japan had flattened a village; they say a school is the priority for rescue.
A suspected Serial killer was still at large in Ohio, police have no leads.
'Fucking world gone crazy,' he mumbled to himself, as he gave up on the news and switched over to catch the end of Wheel of Fortune. He shuffled as the chair creaked under his weight His shirt was ringed under the arms with sweat, and he made a mental note to call Daniels and chew him out about still not fixing the air conditioning. The apartment felt like an oven and Harry's mood was not helped by the headache which

lingered ominously, just waiting for the right time to strike. He had not washed for a week now and didn't particularly care. Ever since losing his job he had found himself to be in a great cycle of depression. Initially headhunted by a slimy piece of work called Daniels to run his company's export division, he had been offered a rock solid job with great benefits and an apartment just off the expansive beach. The downside was that Harry would have to move from the family home in Atlanta, and relocate to Rio. The decision had strained his and Maggie's relationship as she had been reluctant to leave her job as a part time nurse. The battle had been long but she had eventually agreed. Harry had talked her into the move in a way that would make even the best suit and tie salesman proud. They had sold the house and embarked on their new life in Brazil.

It became apparent that it was not at all as they had been led to believe. The factory itself was ramshackle at best and staffed with locals who couldn't speak a word of English. Their unrushed and relaxed work ethic was a frustration for Harry from the start and on top of that, the beachfront house he had been promised was actually a tiny two-bedroom apartment located right in the center of the tourist heavy area of town. It was boisterous on an evening and by early morning, the streets were filled with empty bottles and half-eaten cartons of takeout food. Although the beach was within walking distance as advertised, it was also within close proximity to the Favela's — ramshackle shanty towns stacked on top of each other which covered the Rio hillsides. Instead of the dream job talking him to retirement, Harry was confronted with humid, sticky evenings and intense arguments with Maggie all set against the backdrop of gunfire and police sirens that were uncomfortably close. All of it was just about bearable until without warning Harry's job was gone. Unable to adjust to Harry's new regime of hard work and long hours spent being productive instead of playing cards and smoking the day away the local staff had threatened a boycott unless things reverted back to the way they were. Faced with losing either one man or a hundred, the company made Harry the scapegoat and he was released from his position after just three months in charge. Maggie was furious and had demanded they go back to Atlanta, but Harry being as stubborn as he was had refused to return with his tail between his legs. He told her in no uncertain terms they were staying where they were. He had tried to find work but many local businesses were reluctant to employ a foreigner and as the rejections increased, his confidence plummeted. With a grunt, he tossed the remote onto the small coffee table, dragged himself with some effort out of his chair and moved to the window. Peering out into the near dusk gloom, he glanced at his watch. Almost seven thirty. It was time for them. The city's night people. The pushers, the pimps, and the whores to seep out onto the streets to go about their business. It was a world away from the picture painted for him by Eng. Tec when they had approached him. They had promised him clean streets, a peaceful environment in which to live and work. They called it the perfect place to grow old. Perhaps he should have done more research of his own, but the truth was that he had been dazzled by the sales patter and accepted without question everything that was said to him. With an irritable sigh, he yanked open the window, praying for a cool breeze to refresh him. Instead, sticky, humid warmth attacked as he leaned out. He hated that the heat even at dusk was so oppressive.

'Hottest damn summer in years.' he muttered as he squinted off into the distance.

He was only just able to see a blue grey smudge of ocean on the horizon between the labyrinth of buildings and hotels that dominated his immediate view. He let out a deep sigh and surveyed the landscape, wondering if other people out there were as miserable as he was. He certainly hoped so. As dusk gave way to darkness he could see the sickly neon glow of the main town parade that was depressingly close to his apartment block. He realised that Rio was a place split right down the middle. The days were for the respectable tourists—young families looking to see the sights or buy souvenirs for friends back home. Maybe a postcard showing a crescent of white beach set against a perfect and cloudless blue sky.

He could see it now. 'Welcome to sunny Brazil, enjoy your stay.'

It was this image that had been sold by Daniels. Harry hated him, but to his credit, Daniels was good. Really good. Harry suspected that he could sell sand to the Arabs; snow to the Eskimo's or even Rio to Harry Harris. Daniels aside, as soon as the sky began to grow dark and those sickly neon lights cast their harsh red and blue hues onto the streets, the other half of the city crawled out of the shadows. The pimps, the pushers, the gangs. And of course the prostitutes. Many were old and broken, their bodies ravaged by life on the streets or addiction to crack cocaine which was as easy to get here as groceries from the local supermarket. Many of the prostitutes were painfully young. Thin waifs of girls with desperation and fear in their eyes as they touted for business—usually watched from nearby by the gangs or their pimps who lingered in the shadows. It was clear that the night was theirs. In those early days he had ventured out to see for himself, to convince himself that he wasn't afraid. He realized soon enough that the world had changed into one he no longer understood. As he walked, he would see them watching him with eyes that said

'Hey old man, you better get the fuck out of here cos I've been sleeping off my hangover all day and now I'm ready to fight, fuck, drink, and maybe do some coke. This is no place for the likes of you.'

They were right, and after that, he rarely ventured out after dark. He had seen enough and ducked back into the room, slamming the window closed.

'Motherfucker!' he barked, overcome with rage as he snatched up the phone and punched in Daniels's number. The air conditioning was meant to have been fixed the week before but the little shit had slinked away citing some lame excuse about a family emergency. Harry blamed him for this whole mess. He was the one that had talked him into the move, sugar coated the shit as it were. Daniels was a small, insect like man, who harry thought oozed insincerity. At first, he couldn't do enough to help.

'Whatever you need, and I do mean anything, call me anytime night or day and I'll make it happen. We at Eng.-Tec look after our own,' he had said, flashing his veneered salesman's grin. Since Harry had been fired it seemed that Daniels was gradually phasing them out. Taking the wireless handset with him, he stalked through to the small kitchen slamming open the fridge as he yelled over his shoulder.

'Damn it, Maggie, The air conditioning is still not working and Daniels isn't answering the fucking phone!

A disembodied voice drifted back from the bedroom.

'He's not home Harry, his mother died last Friday.'

Harry shook his head, squeezing the handset so hard his knuckles turned white. Even though he knew anyone who was home would have answered by now, still he let it ring.

'I don't give a damn about his dead mother, its a hundred degrees in here!'

She came out of the bedroom giving him a disapproving glance as she swept past him, the smell of her perfume causing him to wrinkle his nose.

'Maggie, how much of that shit do you have to plaster yourself with? I can hardly god-damn breathe as it is!'

She didn't rise to the bait, pausing instead to look at herself in the mirror over the fireplace

'Don't start Harry, I'm not in the mood.' her irritation was undisguised as she glared at him. He snapped open a beer, tossing the lid into the sink rather than the bin.

'You aren't in the mood? Fuck Maggie, neither am I. Family emergency my ass. The son of a bitch is avoiding me, I know it.'

She swept past him again, a vortex of perfume and hairspray as she grabbed her purse from the worktop.

'Come on Harry, give the guy a break, I imagine our air conditioning is the last of his worries.'

He grunted and threw the handset on the worktop, took a great chug of beer, almost draining the entire can.

'I don't give a fuck about his mother or him, I just want my damn air conditioning fixed, and it's like a GOD DAMN FURNACE IN HERE!'

Ignoring Harry's rage Maggie checked the contents of her purse before spraying yet more perfume onto her wrists and rubbing them together. She carried her age well. She was a slim build, a regular at the local gym she carried an air of confidence in her posture he was both proud and somewhat envious of. Usually, she wore her hair down to the shoulder but tonight Harry noticed that she had restyled it and coloured it blonde, a radical departure from its usual auburn shade. She wore it swept back and tied into a ponytail. He felt a stirring in his groin which he quickly dismissed. He knew that getting lucky was no longer on the cards, and hadn't been for some time. Although she was only six years younger than he was at thirty nine, she could pass for late twenties. He had always known he had struck lucky with her. Under ordinary circumstances he would have classed her as well out of his league; however, they shared a certain spark, an intensity that had died somewhat since the move here. She appeared distracted and as time went by, he found affection harder and harder to give.

He watched her now as she found what she was looking for—the earrings he had bought her for Christmas. She watched him looking at her as she clipped them in.

'Go easy on Daniels; he's having a tough time right now Harry.'

'Maggie he's been promising to have someone come and fix the damn air conditioning for two weeks now. It's hotter than hell in here. He needs to get his priorities straight.'

'He has got his priorities straight, that's why he is with his family.'

Before he could stop himself, He jabbed a finger at her, eyes bulging from the sockets.

'It's ok for you,' he snarled 'you're never here, always somewhere with those damn friends of yours.'

She took a step towards him opening her mouth as if to speak then changed her mind, instead letting out a deep sigh. He was filled with fury and although he had never laid a hand on her, he had to restrain himself from lashing out.

'Whatever Harry I don't have time for this crap. I'm going to be late.'

'You and those damn women. I don't like them, Maggie. You've changed since they started whispering in your ear, telling you how to think.'

Maggie didn't look at him; she was at the mirror toying with her hair.

'Harry, they're my friends. You could go out too you know, get out of this room for a while.'

'I shouldn't have to leave my own damn house because some lazy shit won't do his damn job!' he bellowed, face flushed red with anger.

'Besides, you know I have no friends here. Do you expect me to go out on my own?'

'Betty's husband is a nice guy, the two of you could go out for a beer or something. Just stop making me feel guilty for having a life.'

'Betty? The bitch with the buck teeth? Her husband is a fucking prick. No thanks.'

He saw her reflection glare at him in the mirror.

'Do what you like Harry, I'm sick of this shit.'

She turned and swept past him, her anger at him obvious. He grabbed her arm and spun her around and was unable to ignore the flicker of hate and revulsion in her eyes. He let go of her arm and lowered his gaze.

'Look, Maggie, I'm sorry. I just worry about you. I know things haven't worked out since we moved out here. I'll put it right ok?'

She looked at him and nodded but he could see it was a token gesture. He felt a pang of sorrow deep inside which hurt more than he expected. Maggie smiled, leaning forward and kissing him on the cheek.

'Harry please don't worry. There are a whole bunch of us and I will be getting a taxi back. I'll be fine. But I meant what I said. You need to start getting out of here. It's not good for you staying home all the time.'

He looked at the floor, scuffing his feet on the cheap carpet.

'Look, Maggie, I'm sorry. I have been in a god-awful mood all day and this business with the air conditioning just set me over the edge. I think I'll get an early night and wake up in a better mood tomorrow. You go have fun.'

She kissed him on the cheek flashing him that smile that always won him over.

'No need to wait up Harry, I have a key. Get some rest. You look tired.'

He sank into his chair and stared at the TV as she swept towards the door. She opened it and looked back.

'I love you, Harry.'

'Love you too.' he responded, keeping his eyes fixed on the television screen. She waited for a few seconds as if she were thinking of something else to say, then left closing the door behind her and leaving the smell of her perfume in the sticky heat of the room. He waited for a full count of thirty before he switched off the TV and crossed back to the window. He watched the street below and waited for her to appear. She left, walking away from their building and towards the centre of the town which he so despised. He pulled on his jacket as a fresh wave of anger flowed through him.

He was certain she was having an affair.

As a man who had learned to live his life based on his instincts, Harry had for a while ignored the knots in his stomach. He had also ignored the voice in his head which so often was right. It was only when he had started to pay attention to it that he found himself able to act.

Something isn't right Harry.

'No shit chief,' he mumbled to himself in response to his inner voice.

You had better find out what's happening before she has a chance to cover her tracks.

'Yeah, I know.'

Besides, at least it will get you out of this heat.

Harry moved to the door, pausing with his hand on the doorknob. 'Say again?' he mumbled to the empty room

I said don't forget the knife.

'Knife?'

Just in case you need it. For protection.

Harry grunted and went to the kitchen. He couldn't find the largest knife that normally sat in the wooden block on the counter top, and didn't have time to sift through all the overflowing dirty dishes in the sink to find it. Instead, he selected a medium sized steak knife. He wrapped it in kitchen paper and slipped it into his pocket; making a mental note to be sure he set the blade away from him. The last thing he wanted was to accidentally castrate himself. The voice inside spoke up again.

Ready? Now let's go

Harry opened the door and set off after his wife.

TWO

It didn't take long for him to think his suspicions may have been more than the paranoid delusions of a depressed husband. For the last half hour, he had followed her at a distance. As he pushed his way through the crowded streets, his heart sank. His initial curiosity and anger had now given way to an overwhelming sense of sadness. They would probably divorce and he supposed that she would go live with her sister for a while and he would be painted as the bad guy. For the first time in years, he craved a cigarette. Just wait it out harry old pal. Let's wait and see what happens.

'Shut up.' he barked, drawing a few puzzled glances from the people around him. Embarrassed, He pulled his collar tight around his neck even though it was still hot and humid. He walked on in a daze feeling like a passenger in his own body. The thought of confronting her made him feel sick. There was a fluttery giddiness within him about finally resolving the situation. He had barely slept since he began to suspect, spending his nights wide awake and listening to Maggie breathe in her untroubled sleep. There had been some nights when she hadn't come home until four or five in the morning. Harry had lay there pretending to be asleep—watching her through half closed eyes as she undressed from clothes that were different to the ones she had gone out in. She always smelled freshly showered and it didn't take Harry long to put all of the pieces of the puzzle together. Knowing she was lying made him more determined to find out what she was up to. Shoving his way through the humid streets, head aching and drenched with sweat he felt a rage boiling up within him. In a sudden shift, the anger melted away to sadness when he thought about what would happen once he confronted her.

He had met her by chance in a bar back in Atlanta. It was a busy night and the room was bustling and full. He noticed that the seat next to her was free and had approached to ask if he could sit. She nodded, her head buried in a notebook in which she was writing. He was mesmerised by her natural beauty. The way her nose tilted upwards slightly at the tip and the way her mouth moved as she wrote. He saw her glass was empty and asked if she would like another. She smiled at him, and Harry sat and plucked up the courage to engage conversation. Harry had told bad jokes at his own expense and Maggie had laughed at him and gradually opened up. When discussions turned to her notebook, she told Harry that she was a nurse by day but also an aspiring novelist, and was working on her first book, which she hoped to have published. She had even allowed him to read a few pages. Harry fell in love with her writing style. Her copy was punchy, the characters vivid and full of life. His praise was met with shyness and over the next few weeks as they continued to see each other their relationship grew. The following summer they married. Their friends had raised their eyebrows and thought it was way too soon but Harry and Maggie had no doubts. They wanted to be together. For a while, life was perfect for them. Maggie's book was coming on in leaps and bounds and Harry continued to work hard and bring in good money so that Maggie could leave her job and stay at home to concentrate on her writing. It seemed to them like the world was theirs for the taking. Things got even better in the spring of 87' when Maggie fell pregnant. Harry was over the moon, and couldn't believe the lucky hand that life had dealt him. It was around this time that things began to spiral out of control.

He snapped back to the present, pushing his way through the throng of people walking the streets. The faces were a blur, insignificant obstacles between him and his pending confrontation with his wife. The only thing that was clear to him was the back of Maggie's head as she walked towards the seedier area of the town. The bars and nightclubs were just as numerous; however, the lights didn't shine so brightly or penetrate as far into the recesses and darkened corners of the street. This was where the locals spent their nights. Away from the tourists and within spitting distance of the Favelas which Harry could now see stretching across the landscape, an ugly maze of passages, doorways, and switchbacks. Here the locals weren't interested in being tourist friendly. They sat on doorsteps or in groups on street corners smoking huge acrid smelling cannabis joints which made Harry's nose wrinkle. He tried his best to ignore the icy stares of the locals as they watched him. He knew he looked out of place and felt the glare of hateful eyes on him as he passed them. He wondered if he would survive long enough to confront Maggie after all. Here everyone was an alpha male, and Harry was on their turf. Every fibre of his being told him to run. To go back to the relative safety of his shitty overpriced sweatbox apartment and forget about this, and just go on living the lie. After all what good would come out of confronting her? He would only end up alone and at least if he went along with it, she would stay with him. At least he would still have company. Besides, he may have even got it wrong. There could be a reasonable explanation and he had put two and two together and come up with five.

Come on pal, you know the score here as well as I do. Just take a look. She isn't out with her friends, so she has already lied to you. Who knows what else is on tonight's agenda?

'Shut up.' he muttered again, this time under his breath so as not to draw any more needless attention. The voice inside responded with patience, as someone would if explaining a simple fact to a child.

I just don't want you to hold out hope, that's all buddy. Let's see where she goes from here.

He froze on the spot, his heart leaping into his mouth as it skipped a beat. He hadn't noticed that she had stopped ahead of him to talk to two locals. To Harry's horror, they seemed to know her, the three of them laughing and joking as Maggie handed them a roll of cash and was given a small plastic bag containing a white powder which she slipped into her pocket. Harry was in shock. Drugs? He couldn't believe what he was seeing. Although they had both smoked a little pot when they were younger, they had been anti-drugs for years.

Not anymore Harry old pal. Looks like drugs are back on the menu. Aren't you glad you didn't pussy out now old buddy?

Harry ignored his inner voice and instead mentally kicked himself for getting too lost in his thoughts and not concentrating on the job in hand. As a result, he had

almost walked into the back of her. She was so close he could smell her perfume. If she looked up she would see him–of that there was no doubt and he didn't want that. He had come far enough now to want to see this out, to let it play to the conclusion whatever it may be. He looked around for somewhere to hide and ducked into a ramshackle news stand, turning his back to her as he pretended to browse the magazines. He kept a careful but watchful eye on her as she spoke with the locals before saying her goodbyes and setting off walking again. Harry relaxed, glancing at the wiry old man behind the counter who was looking back with a bemused and somewhat distrustful look on his face.
'Can I help you sir?' the storekeeper asked, his English sketchy and rolling uncomfortably from his tongue.
'No, no thanks.' Harry went to leave, then reconsidered. 'Actually, I'll take a pack of Marlboro's.
He thought for a horrifying moment he had lost her when he saw her go into a bar a little way down the street. Even from a distance, he could see how seedy it was. Its windows were grimy and covered with posters.

COCKTAILS 2-4-1! FREE SHOT OF VODKA B4 11PM!

Proclaimed the hand drawn poster board outside. A tired neon Budweiser sign hung in the window flickering intermittently as Harry slowed, licking his lips with a tongue that felt too dry. This had been the most exercise he had undertaken in recent memory, and he felt tired. He fumbled with his fresh pack of cigarettes, placing one in his mouth then remembered that he had no means to light it. He shoved the pack into his overcoat pocket, careful to make sure he didn't catch his hand on the knife which was still sitting snug against his body. He then took the useless cigarette that hung from his lip and wedged behind his right ear, an old habit which had ended with the smoking – until tonight that was.

Just like riding a bike.

Harry tried his best to peer through the grimy window, scanning the vague humps and forms within the dark recesses for his wife. Although difficult to see, he found that if he cupped his hands around the glass he could get a reasonable idea of the layout. Although he knew she was in here, he still hoped against hope it was merely a pit stop. Perhaps to use the restroom or the phone. The voice in his head, the one he had become accustomed to listening to, remained silent, content to let Harry figure this one out for himself. He continued to peer through the grime, looking and at the same time hoping not to see. His heart skipped as he saw her, the body language unmistakable. She was at the bar, legs crossed towards the man beside her. She was watching him speak, a half smile on her lips as she ran her index finger around the rim of her wine glass. A succession of emotions overcame Harry. Anger, Sorrow, Rage then once again that overwhelming sadness which hit him all at once. His eyes scanned the man with her, his instinctive human nature assessing the threat of the challenge from this stranger. He watched him speak, his unheard words holding her full attention. Although he couldn't see perfectly, Harry could tell that the man was young. Maybe only twenty-five, certainly no more than thirty. He was wearing a pristine charcoal suit which even from outside the window Harry could tell wasn't bought from a clothes rack in a department store, this was tailor made to fit. Harry watched him flash his perfect smile at her, before stealing a quick glance at her chest, which threatened to spill from her dress every time she moved. He tried to think back and recall if she was wearing that dress when she left the apartment.

Surely he would have said something if he had seen her dressed so provocatively. Had he even looked at her at all? Or was he so preoccupied with the air conditioning and the plan to follow her that he hadn't paid any attention?

A wave of nausea hit him as he turned away from the window. He thought he was going to throw up and he began to feel dizzy. He couldn't decide what had upset him the most, the fact that his suspicions had been correct, or that sat there in that bar she looked happier than at any time during their marriage. Unable to hold back any longer he put his hands on his knees and vomited noisily, his vision dancing with bright white spots as he tried to keep himself from passing out. People walked around him, eying him cautiously but keeping to themselves.

I don't want to say I told you so, but... I told you so.

Harry didn't answer. He stared at the yellow brown puddle of liquid which had just ejected.

So, what are you going to do now?

He stood upright and reached into his pocket, feeling the wrapped handle of the knife still nestled there. The voice inside was silent, but Harry knew it was smiling.

# THREE

For almost an hour, he waited across the street on a bench beside a bus stop that was partially secluded by trees. From his vantage point, he could see the entrance to the bar, but he himself could not so easily be seen. As he sat amongst the filth and stench, he grew more and more furious. He was acutely aware that he smelled bad—a heady combination of stale sweat and vomit and perhaps sadness. Does sadness have a smell? He wondered to himself.

If it does, it smells like puke and wino piss, chief. Ignoring his inner voice, he wondered how he might look to the strangers walking by. He had noticed more than one throw a wayward glance in his direction before averting their gaze and hurrying along. He suspected that he no longer looked quite so out of place anymore. He felt tired. Not physically so much now that he had rested, but mentally. His brain had been working overtime, trying in vain to rationalise events as they unfolded. He let his thoughts drift again to the past. To a time before humid nights spent spying on his adulterous wife, to a happier time long before all of this happened. He let his mind roll back through the years;

back to the day she had told him that she was pregnant. He tried to recall the utter joy of that moment but over time, it had been lost within the misery that followed. The baby was a boy. He had Maggie's eyes and Harry's nose. Maggie took a break from writing to try her hand at being a mother and excelled at it. Harry was also keen on helping out and doing his share of the work. Despite his initial struggles with changing nappies and getting used to the joys of broken sleep, Harry had loved every minute of being a father.

The baby died at seven months old.

He could still remember that day in every detail. The way Maggie was still sleeping beside him even though he had woken early, his body clock telling him that a feed was overdue. He could recall the way the sun warmed his face as he woke. The way the dust swirled around the room, caught in the golden rays of the early morning. The way he had checked his watch and smiled at first that baby Harry had slept late, giving him and Maggie a much-needed full nights night's sleep. He remembered going into the bedroom to wake him, warm bottle of milk in hand as he peered into the crib. The horror and fear of being unable to move, unable to do anything. He remembered his son—blue and lifeless and staring into oblivion. He remembered screaming. The cause of death was determined as natural causes. Something not uncommon with babies although they were told later that it typically happens within the first five months. There was a funeral, and Harry carried his son's small white coffin by himself. For everyone else, life went on. For him and Maggie, it seemed to stop. They didn't speak about it, but it was always there. Harry came home one day to find that Maggie had redecorated the baby's room which had remained untouched since the funeral. Harry was furious and the ensuing argument was highly charged, both of them crying as they took out their frustration and sadness on each other. They had been told time heals, but Harry knew it wouldn't. Over the course of the next few months, the pain did ease and although it would never go away, it became tolerable enough to allow life to continue. He went back to work. After all, even with a death of a child, rent and bills must be paid, and the bank would only show so much sympathy for their plight. Maggie was a different story. She was a mess and even though Harry suggested counselling to help her, she refused. She would spend days staring into space and weeping silently. Work was out of the question. The novel remained unfinished, even with harry pushing her to at least try to write, that it might do her some good. It was as if something within her had broken, something, which Harry realised now, had never come back.

Hey, Harry. Heads up.

He glanced up at the entrance to the bar. Right there outside was the man that his wife had gone to meet. He was talking to someone on his mobile phone and pacing back and forth. Harry could tell by his body language that the intrusion had been unwelcome and for that reason alone Harry wished nothing but good fortune to whoever was on the other end of the line. He watched as his wife's date ended the call and shoved the phone into his jacket pocket. He headed back inside but instead of turning right to return to the bar, turned left and went into the restroom.

Looks like he's going for a piss Harry.

'Yeah.' Harry muttered to himself.

He didn't remember crossing the street, or even entering the bar but now found himself outside the door to the restroom. His hand drifted to his pocket containing the kitchen knife. He glanced around, checking that Maggie couldn't see him.

Remember, you can't give it away yet. You have to see for yourself. You have to catch her in the act.

Harry took a deep breath and opened the door. He blinked as his eyes adjusted to the harsh lighting. The smell of pine filled his nostrils as he looked around the long L-shaped bathroom. Harry was surprised to see Maggie's date standing in the centre of the room, once again on his mobile phone. The two made eye contact, Maggie's mystery date tipping a nod in Harry's direction as he continued to listen to whoever was on the other end of the line. Ignoring the gesture, Harry went into one of the stalls and closed the door behind him. He had a headache, but still he strained to hear as he listened to the whispered conversation from the other side of the door. It sounded like the mystery man had a wife or girlfriend who was grilling him as to his whereabouts.

'I'm sorry baby, but I have to look after these clients...'

'This could be a big case for me; it will be worth it in the end if Mr. Mashima hires me...'

'I don't know when I'll be home. I may stay in a hotel and head home tomorrow morning...'

Ok baby... ok Love you. Bye.'

Although Harry found his stuttering attempt to lie

flimsy at best, he had apparently convinced his wife or girlfriend that he was indeed with Mr. Mashima, who was a very important client, and that he was not in a seedy Rio bar trying to screw Harry's wife.

Let's bleed this motherfucker and get out of here!

His shock at the directness of the thought turned to horror as he glanced down to see the knife already in his hand. He couldn't remember taking it from his pocket. His reflection was haggard and warped as he looked at himself in the blade, his features twisted into that of a stranger.

'Oh god I'm losing my mind,' he whispered to himself as he tried to regain control. His stomach tightened and he let out a stale burp that tasted of the Cheese sandwich he had for lunch.

You ok there big guy? Don't you go losing it now. Just relax and take it easy.

'What do you care'? Harry mumbled to himself under his breath. He couldn't take his eyes from the blade. He turned it slowly, his reflection twisting and pulsing under the harsh strip light above. Harry thought that twisting and pulsing was a good approximation of how he felt inside right now. He smiled at the thought but the gesture felt alien. Uncomfortable on his skin, which felt loose against his skull. His reflected self appeared to be making an anguished grimace, mouth twisted somehow up and down at the same time. It should have alarmed him, but he didn't mind. In fact, he thought twisted, melt faced Harry was a better fit for how he felt.

Hello? Anyone home? I'm starting to worry about you pal. You ain't looking so good and I want you to think about this before you go off half-cocked as usual. Besides, we agreed. Catch her in the act. That was the plan. I agree that this guy seems to be a slimy fuck but come on, let's not do anything stupid here. It's my ass on the line too!

'Fuck you.' he said as he put the knife back into his coat pocket. He felt strange like he was coming apart at the seams. It was imperative he held himself together and regain control of the situation. Closing his eyes he counted backwards from ten in his head, a technique taught to him in therapy to combat his anger issues. It didn't always work, but he had to try.

Ten

Nine.

Eight.

Seven.

He slowed his breathing and ignored the crescendo pounding in his head. He always hated the headaches, but this was a particularly bad one.

Six.

Five.

He was starting to feel more in control. More like old Harry. Not old Harry from Atlanta, the one who had an easy smile and a huge circle of friends, The Harry who was always the one at the party to raise the laughs, the one who took life in his stride, who believed in working hard to get what he wanted.

Four.

Three.

No. Because that Harry was gone. He was buried somewhere deep, decomposing and festering with maggots. But even the Harry of a few hours ago, the one he had thought to be the lowest he could be. The angry, frustrated, estranged, lonely man who had only ever tried to do his best in a world that had chewed him up and spat him out into Rio De fucking Janeiro. Home of the scum of the earth. Home of the pimps. Dwelling place of the teenage prostitutes and murderers, gang bangers and drug dealers. Welcome to your new life here in sunny Brazil! Murder capital of the world!

Two.

One.

Sure enough, that Harry was a prick, and had spent too long feeling sorry for himself and letting the bitterness grow. But make no mistake. He is nowhere near as bad as this new Harry—the twisted, melt faced Harry with his rage bubbling under the surface. The Harry that feels no connection to humanity anymore. No empathy towards society. No. That Harry is one to keep well away from because that one has no limits and no intention of resolving anything unless it means bloodshed. So come on Harry, pull yourself together and let's do something positive.

He opened his eyes. For now, his thoughts were clear and concise, and although the other Harry was still there, waiting in some dark corner of the mind with his twisted up and down smile. He knew that sitting here wasn't going to achieve anything, and decided he had nothing to lose by seeing this through. Perhaps there would even be reconciliation. An hour ago he would have baulked at the idea, but he knew once all the bullshit was cut away he still loved Maggie and although he had lost sight of it along the way, was hoping that somehow the two of them could pull through this and move on. Could he ever forgive her? In truth, he thought probably not. However, he thought could do the next best thing, which is learn to live with it. But all that came later. For now, he had to find out the extent of the situation. Harry opened the door. At first, he thought he was alone and that Maggie's date had left but then saw him in the mirrors that ran the full length of the wall. After the hard work of convincing his better half of his reasons for not coming home that night, Maggie's date was now taking care of the business at hand, and urinating noisily. Harry went to the sink and started to wash his hands.

He looked in the mirror but couldn't make eye contact with his reflection. He didn't know if he would see melt face Harry, still bent and twisted, grimacing and grinning, sneering and snarling—Or if it would be his usual self. Overweight, tired, depressed and lonely, Wondering why him? Why had God decided to make his life hell? Thinking of such things, he set his gaze on the other person reflected in the glass. The man who had ruined his life and was now pissing without a care in the world.

He could feel the rage welling up inside him like a volcano. His temples pounded thick with blood. He had the power to put everything right. He was sure this man didn't know Maggie was married. And Harry was pretty sure that if he did he would definitely make his excuses and leave. He wouldn't want the hassle. He looked to be the 'no strings attached' type. But that was hardly the point, was it? Even if this guy disappeared back to wherever he came from Harry was sure there would be another. Then another. And what about before? She was too well practised for Harry to believe this guy was the first. How many others? How long had she been doing this, picking up men in bars? Maggie was the catalyst here. She was the instigator. Harry realised that even after so many years of marriage he didn't know her at all. He wondered if this was what Alzheimer's was like. You have the familiarity of someone you should know intimately, but can't recall anything that makes sense about them. Maggie's date came over to the sink and began to wash his hands.

'Hot as hell today.'

Harry grunted, unable to muster any words as he continued washing his own hands. The water was hot. Too hot, but Harry didn't care. He felt detached from himself like the hazy first few minutes after waking from a vivid dream. He was vaguely aware of the burning sensation on his skin, but he didn't feel anything.

'Hey buddy, are you ok? You don't look so good.'

He was turned towards Harry now, looking at him with genuine concern. Harry nodded.

'I'm fine. Tough day that's all.' He was surprised to find that now he had found the will to speak, his voice was perfectly normal. The man laughed, and continued to wash his hands.

'I heard that. Did you see the news tonight? Police found another body. That's seven in the last three weeks now. Someone out there is on a spree. Damn city is going to hell. Fuckin' gangs if you ask me.'

Harry shook his head. 'I haven't seen the news today' Harry lied, not wanting to share polite small talk with this man.

'Let me tell you pal, this last one was nasty. Some kid got his fuckin head cut off and displayed in the street for all to see. I hear they found his dick in his mouth.'

Harry glanced up at the man, then back at his burnt hands. The pain was good; it kept melt face Harry occupied.

'It's kind of been the day from hell.' Said Harry.

Maggie's date nodded. 'I've had a day like that myself. Hell, I'd buy you a beer, but I'm with someone tonight.'

He flashed a half smile, one that said more than words ever could. It was a predatory smile. Harry nodded in response, as he felt the seams of his mind fray a little more. On autopilot, Harry heard himself reply. It was a little like hearing a TV playing in the next room. He wasn't quite sure what was being said, but he could hear his own voice responding in conversation.

'Understood. Three's a crowd. I get it.'

Harry felt a chill as the man smiled, showing a mouth full of perfect white teeth. Not for the first time, a streak of jealous hatred coursed through his body.

'You understand right? See I work away from home a lot. I don't see my girlfriend too often, and I have needs you know. Are you married?'

Harry swallowed his rage, mustering all of his willpower in forcing a smile of his own. It felt like a mask, hanging loose over his face and hiding his real emotions. He could now only faintly register the burning of the hot water on his hands as he continued to wash them.

'Fifteen years. I found out today I'm divorcing. Like

said, today has been a pretty shitty day.'

Maggie's date nodded, flashing a sympathetic look which made Harry want to tear his eyes from his skull. He spoke with mock sincerity, which only served to further agitate the situation.

'Damn sorry to hear that, buddy. Really.'

Harry said nothing, shutting off the hot water and drying his throbbing and sore hands.

'What reason for the divorce, if you don't mind me asking?

Harry sneered, somehow managing to keep his anger in check.

'Adultery. Turns out my wife has been fucking around behind my back.' Harry looked him dead in the eye as he said this, pleased to see Maggie's date squirm a little then lower his gaze.

'That's pretty shitty. I'm sorry to hear it. It's different for me; don't get me wrong, I love my girl. I would do anything for her but you know how it is right buddy?'

'I hear ya. So your date tonight... you just met?'

Harry couldn't help himself. He had to ask

'Not exactly. A buddy of mine set me up. A few of the guys I know have had the pleasure of her company. She's a sure thing.' He grinned and began to dry his hands. Harry glared at him, numb with shock as he chewed the words over in his head. He tried to swallow them but they wouldn't go down. He continued to chew. Maggie's date continued, grinning as he finished drying.

'I mean I'm a busy man, I don't have time to waste on someone who isn't going to deliver the goods. This way, I know I'm on for some action I –'

He stopped speaking, the smile fading from his face.

'Hey pal, are you alright?'

Harry knew he was going to do it. He was going to kill this man right here in this bathroom.

You do this and you do it without me, once you do it, there is no coming back.

He reached towards his pocket, glaring at the man who had now registered the danger. His eyes were fearful and Harry liked it. He took a step back, sensing the change in atmosphere. Harry sensed it too; it was heavy and palpable, charged with static. He would have done it if at that moment someone hadn't decided to walk into the bathroom. Harry blinked and broke eye contact. Maggie's date swallowed hard. Harry was pleased to see he was ruffled and uncomfortable. It didn't suit him.

'Look I gotta go. I don't want to keep my date waiting.'
He went to leave and then paused at the door.
'Hey look. I may be able to help.' He reached into his suit pocket and pulled out a business card, which he handed over to Harry.
'I'm a lawyer, I specialise in divorce cases. Give me a call if you need any representation. I'll make sure you get everything you deserve from the separation.'
Not if I give you what you deserve first you sick fuck.
Harry looked at the card, at last linking a name to the face. Mark Fife.
'Thanks, Mark. I'll keep it in mind.'
Fife grinned. It was a lawyer's grin and once again Harry felt the urge to tear this man's head from his shoulders.
'No sweat. I better go; my date will wonder where I am.'
Well, that went well, didn't it? You should listen to me more often, and shit like this wouldn't happen.
'Shut up.' harry muttered. 'I need to think.'
He made his way outside and into the cooler night air. It was then it dawned on him that he had nothing left. Nothing to lose. Everything in his world was a sham, an illusion. The only thing he had was revenge. He would

take it. First on Fife, then on her. He would make sure she knew how much she had hurt him, that she knew what she had driven him to. For sure Fife wasn't to blame, not really. His girlfriend was in the same situation that Harry himself was in, only she didn't know it yet, and nobody deserves that. He would do this for her, a woman he had never met and whose name he did not know. And Maggie. After he had given her everything he could, she had reduced him to this. He was sick of giving. It was time he started to take. And revenge was top of the list.

FOUR

Fife was a fast worker. Harry had returned to his original vantage point and had been waiting across the street for no more than half an hour when the pair left the bar arm in arm. They lingered outside, just another couple heading home after a quiet drink or two. At least that is how it would look to anyone who passed them in the street. Maggie was leaning on Fife. She appeared to be drunk, although Harry knowing her as he did noted that she wasn't as inebriated as she was letting on. He reflected again back to a time when they first met, trying to mask the horror of the situation with memories of better times. He tried to recall when things had changed, when they had started to grow apart. He kicked himself for not trying harder, for not fighting for what they had, but then reminded himself that he had done nothing wrong. He had never been unfaithful. He had never lied to her or raised a hand to her. He had tried to lead a good life, and he hoped that if there was a God, he would take that into account rather than the actions which were about to follow. His heart sank as he watched them. Fife whispered something in her ear, and she responded with a laugh, kissing him on the lips before the pair began to walk down the street.

This is it, Harry. Showtime.

'Yeah, Showtime.' Harry mumbled, not caring who could hear him. He took a deep breath before crossing the street and following at a distance. They walked for a while, away from the busy centre of town. Harry needed to piss and kicked himself for not going back at the bar. He wondered where Fife was taking her and considered in the back of his mind what he intended to do about it. He knew he would have to confront her but the exact means of doing so was still uncertain. Harry stopped, ducking into a doorway as the pair came to a halt up ahead. He watched as Maggie leaned towards Fife and whispered something to him, and then pulled away, holding his gaze. Fife grinned, that predator's smile that Harry had witnessed earlier. Maggie grabbed his hands and pulled him towards the alleyway they had stopped in front of. Harry's heart raced. He could feel the blood surging in his temples as he licked his lips. Ok Harry, let's put an end this.

He inched his way towards the entrance to the alleyway, his senses acute, aware of everything going on around him. He peeked around the corner expecting to see them but there was nothing. The alley extended for around thirty feet and then turned to the left. He was about to proceed when he heard a noise ahead, a grunt from around the corner. He walked down the alley on legs that felt like they were made of rubber, careful to stay in the shadows. He took the knife from his pocket holding it with his right hand as he inched across the wall. He was at the edge of the turn. He could hear them, grunting and fumbling in the shadows. His heart pounded as he closed his eyes, a single tear rolling down his cheek. He took a deep breath and turned the corner.

So much blood.

Harry blinked as his brain tried to process the violence in front of him. His wife's eyes stared blankly; devoid of any semblance of life as the eight inch serrated knife fell to the ground. It was at that point as he watched it come to rest on a pile of soggy slick entrails that he felt something in his mind break. He tried to speak, but instead only smacked his lips, a strange gurgling sound welling up from inside. He was sure he could have controlled it had she not chosen that moment to speak. Her tone was both an accusation and a question, pleading and angry. It was that one word that sent him over the edge.

'Harry?'

It was then that the true impact of the situation hit him, and as he turned and vomited noisily, he wondered how this could have happened, how his life could come to this.

Fife was sitting on the ground, his legs splayed apart. His stomach and internal organs pooled on the floor around him. Harry registered the copper smell of blood, causing his stomach to vault. Fife's eyes stared lifelessly at the floor, his chin resting on his chest as Maggie crouched beside him, her own knife – the large one that Harry couldn't find earlier - still wedged in his throat.

Maggie stood, pulling the knife free with a wet crunch

as she stared at Harry. He searched her eyes for any semblance of the woman he had loved but saw only darkness which terrified him. She walked towards him smiling without humour. Harry was frozen, unable to move.

'Close your eyes Harry.' she said to him as she approached. Too shocked to do anything but cooperate, Harry did as he was told. Finally, he understood. Fife's words echoed back to him from their conversation earlier.

'Did you see the news tonight? Police found another body. That's seven now. Someone out there is on a spree.'

'Yes, they are.' Harry muttered under his breath 'You and I will be eight and nine by the morning.'

He could smell her now—the expensive perfume mingled with the wet copper smell of blood. He felt his bladder let go and prayed it would be quick.

## EVERY LITTLE HELPS

Steven Grimes had known the Joneses, Alice and Frank for fifteen years and they had always been the perfect neighbours. Yet he was certain as he watched the two of them from the edge of his bedroom window that the large black bag which the pair struggled to carry to the back of their garden contained a dead body. He had only been there at the house on Sycamore Street by chance to pick up a few more of his belongings and take care of a few outstanding bills, a task which left a sour, bitter taste in his mouth since the house was his—bought and paid for in full and yet he had still been the one forced to leave. Such mundane things were forgotten as He looked into the garden of no. 9. Frank was sweating under the tattered red baseball cap he always wore, the tufts of his white hair poking out from the back as he strained with the weight of the bag. And of course Alice, her liver spotted arms straining with what looked to be the feet of the body as they shuffle-stepped their way towards the large compost heap which Steven knew sat in a secluded corner of the garden.

He knew because a couple of years before he and his now ex-wife Jane had been invited to a barbeque to celebrate Frank's retirement. Forty-one years for the same company, who had thanked him with a golden handshake and imitation watch and then sent Frank on his way. Word was that he didn't want to leave but the company insisted. They had found a younger, more efficient replacement, and so with no real choice, Frank was retired. The barbeque also signified another milestone. It would be the last social engagement for Steven and Jane as Mr and Mrs Grimes. Of course, they had long ago become adept at putting on a show of being a happy and in love couple. The cracks in their marriage at that point were too large to mask over, but they did it anyway. He turned his mind back to that day, his stomach feeling now like a tight ball as he remembered a conversation he had with Frank which at the time seemed so trivial that he wasn't even sure why he recalled it with such clarity.

It was a blazing hot day in July and perfect weather for cooking outdoors. The heat was dry and uncomfortable, the sky blue and cloudless, and the dozen or so guests were doing all they could to keep cool. He remembered that he was speaking to Frank about his garden, which was perfectly maintained. The grass was always trimmed, the soil always turned and he had a small pond with two rosy-cheeked gnomes they called Fred and Betty. As the two men stood by the grill (as men tend to do at these types of events) Frank had rubbed his forearm against his head as he looked Steven in the eye

'You know Steve I'm not sure what the hell I'll do with myself now.'

The old man's eyes glinted in the sunlight, and in hindsight, Steven should have seen something then, but at the time his attention was on Jane who was doing a fine job of drinking her way through the bounty of alcohol that the Joneses had been kind enough to provide. He looked on in pained embarrassment as she tottered around the garden with a half-eaten cheeseburger in one hand and a glass of wine in the other. Cringing inside, he decided that feigning ignorance would be better than causing a scene. He turned back to Frank, noting just how old he looked. His face was thin and leathery, lined from years of working outdoors. His nose was a bulbous lump and he peered from below bushy white eyebrows with eyes so pale blue they could almost be grey.

'I'm sure something will come up Frank. Take some time to relax, hell, after all the years you put in, you've earned it.'

Frank had smiled then, just a curl of the lip but his eyes told a different story. Glassy. Reflective. Ponderous.

'You know me Steve; I'm not one to sit around waiting for something to happen. I think that's why people die sometimes when they don't have anything left to live for.'

Steven nodded, sipping his beer as Frank flipped the burgers, sending the delicious aroma of the grilled meat billowing towards Steven's nose.

'You have worked all your life, Frank. Maybe now you and Alice can spend some quality time together.'

'Quality time,' he chuckled. 'If I can tear her away from her damn bingo then maybe we would. We don't talk much these days Steve. But we are too old and too afraid to be alone, so we stay together.'

Steven felt his heart pinch a little. This old man had said exactly what he thought about his and Jane's relationship. For a time, he had loved her but as he got to know her, really know her the way people who spend a significant amount of time together always do, he had started to notice the cracks, the flaws in her character.

There was darkness in her that over time was gradually pushing its way to the surface. Before they married she was slim and athletic, and always looked her best. Over the last ten years, however, she had let herself go, both physically and socially. She had started to drink and was fond of voicing her opinion on anything and everything with cynicism and bitterness; particularly if it were a subject which Steve himself was interested in. He wasn't entirely blame free. He was guilty of not standing up to her constant put downs and abuse, but as time went by he had developed a weary resistance to her brand of cynicism, and as the love died, so grew the indifference, which in turn gave way to hate. He shot her another quick glance. She had gained weight and now saw the world through small, piggish eyes, which glared at everything she chose to set them upon. It was as if the sweet, loving woman that he had fallen in love with had, over time, been consumed by some horrible and malicious imposter. Frank had said something to Steve which he didn't catch.

'Sorry Frank, I was in a world of my own. Say again?'
'I said at least I have my garden. My pride and joy this place is Steve. My solitude from a world I don't understand anymore. Worked my ass off to make it

look good.'

Steve looked around at the pristine surroundings.

'You certainly did that, it looks amazing. It makes me more aware of how my own could use a little TLC.' Steve said with a sheepish grin.

The two men shared a laugh as Frank continued to work the grill, earning them a disapproving glare from old Mrs Bendtner from no. 5 who was standing by herself over in the corner, picking at a bowl of salad.

'It's all about recycling these days Steve, everyone is going green. Did I tell you we had a circular come through the door a while back telling us that if we don't change our ways then the planet will be beyond saving in just a few years' time?'

'Yeah, we got the same letter, although I must admit I didn't read it. Too much damn junk mail. We threw it out.' shrugged Steve, again glancing towards Jean who had found some poor unfortunate guest to talk at for a few minutes. Steve didn't recognise him but felt sorry for him nonetheless.

'I read it,' said Frank, manipulating the chicken legs on the grill with his metal tongs. 'Everyone on the planet leaves a kind of impression based on how much energy they waste, like an imprint.'

'Oh, a carbon footprint?'

'Yeah, that's it, a carbon footprint—anyway they say everyone in the world leaves one, and if we don't reduce it then the planet will be uninhabitable for our future generations.'

Steve nodded, not interested in the save the planet talk. He was sure that his own carbon footprint would be pretty huge. He didn't recycle; he didn't try to save energy by turning off lights or reducing his aerosol use. He was too set in his ways to change, yet it seemed to be important to the old man so he would go along with it for the sake of being polite.

'That's pretty interesting Frank. I haven't thought too much about it.'

Frank nodded. 'I did. I like being outside, see? And the last thing I want is to be forced indoors or underground by some damn acid rain or air so poisoned that you can't breathe. If a man can't enjoy his own garden in peace Steve, then the man has no real life at all.'

'Thing is Frank not everyone takes it too seriously, and unless the law changes, well... nothing is going to change.' Steven said with a gentle shrug.

'Ahh but every little helps. Every little helps. For me, it didn't mean too much of a change. We started off by recycling. Just plastic and glass from our groceries and we put those new energy saving light bulbs all through the house. Hell, I even started out here. I got myself a good sized compost pile down the back of the garden there past the decking.'

Frank jabbed a charcoal smudged thumb over his shoulder. Beyond the wooden deck and chairs covered by a gazebo, there was a small stone path that wound out of sight behind the large pruned bushes.

'I keep it back there as it's unsightly and doesn't smell too good but it's pretty remarkable. Everything returns to the earth, Steve. It takes us all back eventually.'

There was coldness in his eyes which Steve had noticed but dismissed. He didn't want to spend his Saturday afternoon talking about saving the environment and began to think about changing the subject.

'Did you catch the game last night Frank?' he asked.

Frank either did not hear or failed to acknowledge his question.

'Too many people, that's the problem. The planet is overpopulated by people fucking. Fucking and then having kids they don't want and can't afford to look after so they go ahead and feed off the money of the taxpayer.'

Bitterness had crept into Frank's voice which shocked Steve. He had never even heard the old man raise his voice, never mind drop the F-Bomb. He listened on, content, for now, to hear him out.

'Back when I was young we didn't have all these electronics. Laptop computers, games consoles, big screen TV's. People have become lazy and are wasting space, wasting resources. We have to compensate for that Steve, so even if it's not a world changer, it all helps. Every little bit of it helps.'

'Maybe I should look into it.' Steven muttered.

Frank nodded 'maybe you should. It's worthwhile.'

As Steve watched now from the upper bedroom window as Frank and Alice put the bag down by the decking to catch their breath, he wondered just how far Frank had taken his recycling. Of course he would often see him heading out in his blue Nissan every Saturday morning to take his bottles to the recycling plant, often waving and smiling as they passed if Steve had happened to be in the front garden washing the car, or sitting on the bench to read his morning paper away from the prying and piggish eyes of his wife. He also sometimes heard the car go out in the middle of the night.

He tried to think how many times he had heard it, and for the first time asked himself why the old man would be heading out at such unusual hours, and more to the point what he was doing. He thought he knew, but couldn't bring himself to believe it yet. He watched on, careful to ensure that he was out of sight as he peered around the corner of the bedroom curtains. He watched as the pair lifted the bag up again with some effort, then Frank lost his grip. He snatched at the heavy duty plastic, but he couldn't maintain his hold and the bag tore free as the object they were carrying fell back to the floor by the stone path.

Steve recognised the girl. He had seen her on the T.V and on the front cover of most of the newspapers. She had been reported missing a few days earlier after disappearing on her way home from a night out with friends. He tried to remember the name given for her on the news report. He thought it might have been Lucy but it escaped him. She looked quite different to the happy and smiling photograph used in the news appealing for her safe return. Now her skin was almost grey and her blonde hair was matted with dried blood from the ugly, jagged wound in her throat. Her eyes looked lifelessly into oblivion, perhaps asking why her.

Why someone so young could have found herself here, rather than tucked up in her own bed, or snuggled up to a boyfriend somewhere. Steve looked on as Frank covered her, tucking the plastic underneath the body and getting a firmer grip before they two shuffled down that small path beside the decking. If this were a movie, thought Steve, this would be the point where Frank would look up and see his nosey neighbour, and so would begin a game of deadly cat and mouse. But Frank didn't look up; he was more than occupied enough to worry about the next-door neighbour who as far as Frank knew was at work. With a mind that was trying to process a thousand thoughts, Steve sat on the edge of the bed.

'What have you done?'

He wasn't sure if he had meant Frank or himself, or in fact, if he had even said it out loud at all. It's possible it could have just been a thought, a snatch of sane questioning within a mind already fighting to keep control. He cast his mind to all of the missing person's reports on the local news in the last few years that suddenly made sense. It seemed that Frank had found something to do in his retirement.

And at what point did Lucy find out?

Was she too afraid to leave him, or just too afraid of him to seek help from the authorities? Perhaps it started off just as using a different kind of light bulb here or turning off the plug sockets at the wall before turning in for the night, but at some point for Frank, it had all changed. He had taken it to the next level, but Steve was sure that in Frank's mind it still all boiled down to one thing.

Recycling.

A chill coursed through his body as the word floated into his mind, then melted away as he recalled the conversation about the compost heap.

'I keep it back there as it's unsightly, and doesn't smell too good but it's pretty remarkable. Everything returns to the earth, Steve. It takes us all back eventually.'

And of course Frank was right. It did.

Steven wondered how large that compost heap was now. What would be found if the topsoil were pulled away, how many—

An idea struck him, one which horrified him and thrilled him at the same time. She would be home soon, and wouldn't expect to find him here. And why would she? She had thrown him out of his own house after all and seemed to be enjoying making his life a misery despite his best efforts to keep things amicable. Maybe it was time he stood up for himself and took a stand. He thought he could do it and—more importantly, get away with it. He would be doing the world a favour.

After all, every little helps.

## VICTOR

Mallone's restaurant was located in the centre of New York's Mulberry Street. Known as Little Italy, it was once a thriving neighbourhood of authentic Italian restaurants and local stores, but since the influx of Chinese immigrants, the neighbouring Chinatown district had begun to grow and over time had absorbed much of the district. Now, just Mulberry Street remained as part of a single row of fine Italian restaurants determined to keep their tradition alive. Mallone's was quaint with warm red brick walls and large plate glass windows across its front. Their menu boasted the finest Italian meals in the city, and to those who dined there its reputation was entirely justified. A red white and green awning fluttered above the door, and the hand painted sign in large red writing above the door, had been the same since the fifties and only added to the places charm. On any given evening, the restaurant was a hive of activity, with tourists and locals alike keen to sample their excellent menu of traditional dishes. The daylight hours were quiet, and it was during this time that Victor Mallone ran his other business.

He sat at the private table at the back of the room flanked by his personal bodyguards. Even though the only other people in the restaurant were the waiting staff who were already preparing for the evening rush of customers, he had learned not to take any chances. As the staff polished silverware and changed the red and white patchwork tablecloths, Victor ate his lunch, slobbering and grunting as he shovelled the Cannelloni down his immense gullet.

At three hundred and seventy pounds, he was the largest of the Mallone family and also considered himself the smartest. The oldest of three brothers, his siblings had fared worse than he had. Joey, who was the youngest was serving a twenty-year stretch for armed robbery and murder when the gun he was carrying during the botched bank job accidentally went off and shot an old woman behind the counter in the face. His other brother, Salvatore was never cut out to be a leader, and worked as head of Victor's security Victor glanced at himself in the mirror that ran down the side of the restaurant and smiled at the reach of his power. He was large and flabby with greasy black hair which although thinning he wore swept back and down to his shoulders. His eyes were small and piggish but incredibly cruel and he had the hooked nose inherited from his father, Tino.

Tino had introduced Victor to the world of organised crime when he was a wet behind the ears teenager. At first, it was just simple entry-level stuff. Money laundering, protection rackets and the like, but Victor had taken to it like a duck to water. Although he appreciated the introduction to a world he had known nothing about, he saw the potential to do so much more. From those humble beginning, he began to position himself to take over the Mallone Empire, and whilst his brothers were out chasing women and drinking, he was working with his father and getting his hands dirty, proving that he was cut out for the job. He had aspirations of his own of ways to grow the business, but they would have to wait until the old man decided to die or retire.

Victor eventually got sick of waiting, and in the spring of 94', he smothered his frail old mentor as he slept. Nobody questioned the circumstances of his death, and it was classed as a tragic case of natural causes. The end result was that Victor had what he wanted. He was in control. Over the last seventeen years, he had expanded the family business from the small roots where it began to a sprawling and feared empire. Not content with protection rackets and money laundering, Victor had added drug smuggling, prostitution rings, extortion, kidnapping and contract killings to his Repertoire. The business that initially turned over eight hundred grand a year now turned over five times that amount, and there was no shortage of customers. Over the years, Victor had dealt with all manner of people from all walks of life who needed that little something. Be it the woman who came to him looking to buy an American baby no questions asked, or the lovers who wanted to rid the world of their respective spouses, or the old recycling crazy couple who wanted help with getting away with the perfect murder. To Victor they were all the same and as long as they had the cash, he asked no questions. Everyone knew that Victor was a man without a conscience, without morals and without the capacity to forgive. And although he had homes in Madrid, Sicily and Southern France, he chose to stay in New York, close to the roots of his businesses. It was a tactic designed to show he had no fear of living on street level with minimal protection (or to at least let it appear so) but the flipside was that it made him a target. Several attempts had been made on his life and apart from a narrow escape in the early part of two thousand and two, Victor was always one-step ahead and always managed to escape unscathed.

He finished his meatballs and let out a huge tomato flavoured belch as Salvatore hurried out of the kitchen, wringing his hands. He was stick thin with tight, drawn in features and prominent cheekbones. Like Victor, he had inherited his father's thin hair and was bald apart from a stubborn and persistent ring of black hair around the back of his head.

'Victor I need to talk to you.'

Victor motioned for Salvatore to sit as he wiped his mouth with a napkin.

'What is it, Sal?'

'More trouble with the Chinaman. He got Crespo.'

Victor tossed his napkin down in disgust. The Chinaman was Wang Li and he had been a thorn in Victor's side for the past seven years. Their paths had crossed many times, as they often found themselves with their fingers in the same lucrative business pies. Like Victor, Wang Li was willing to do whatever it takes to make his business successful. Whereas Victor was very much a public figure, Wang Li was something of a recluse and was rarely seen outside of his fortress like home above the Chinese restaurant he owned in the middle of Chinatown. People feared Wang Li as much as they feared Victor, and realising that leaving such a rival alive would be unwise, Victor had put a bounty on the Chinaman's head of fifty grand.

The first to try to claim the bounty was a Russian contract killer called Valuev. He came recommended to Victor as a man who would get the job done. Three days later Victor received a package in the mail containing Valuev's severed head. Others had tried, but had either turned up in pieces or just disappeared altogether. The bounty on the Chinaman was now at an even two million dollars, but there had been no takers for two years. Word had spread of the fate of those who went before.

'Crespo? Ah, he was a nobody anyway. No loss.' He said with a dismissive wave of his hand. Inside, however, he was furious. Crespo was a major player in the weapon smuggling arm of Victor's business and would be a terrible blow to that particular revenue stream.

'That's not all. The Chinaman wants to meet you.' Victor felt a rare flash of fear, which he masked with a smile.

'I bet he does. Then what? An ambush? Does he think I was born yesterday?'

'Word on the street is that he's sick, and wants out. I hear he's planning to retire and end his days back in his homeland.'

'In my experience, Sal, word on the street isn't always right. People tend to make shit up to feel important.'

'I thought so too, but he sent this.'

Salvatore reached into the pocket of his jacket and took out a DVD.

'It's from him.'

This was intriguing. Despite their on-going dispute, Victor had never actually seen the Chinaman. He turned the DVD case in his pudgy hands and considered his options as Salvatore looked on.

'What are you thinking, Vic?'

'Let's watch it and see what the old bastard has to say. Be in my office in an hour. And keep this quiet Sal.'

'No problem. I'll see you up at the house.'

The two brothers shook hands and Salvatore left. Victor wondered just what the Chinaman was up to. In his experience, people always had an angle and rarely did anything unless they stood to gain something. He checked his watch and right on cue the door to the restaurant opened and the man walked in for his appointment. He was one of Victor's best. A real hard-ass with a thirst for pain and a vicious mean streak. He reminded Victor of the Americana version of himself. The man nodded to Victor and sat at the table opposite, hands folded on the tabletop.

'Alex, it's good to see you.'

'Mr Mallone.'

Cold. To the point. Victor could see that he was in the zone and ready to work. He wished more of his staff were the same. He briefly considered giving his assignment to someone else and bringing him in for the Chinaman situation, but Tony Montana had been ducking out on his loan repayments for too long, and Victor needed someone who would take decisive action.

'I want you to do something for me, Alex. I want you to go visit Tony Montana and get me my money. Whatever he doesn't have in cash, I want you to bring back in body parts.'

'How far would you like me to go Mr Mallone?'

'Oh don't kill him. Just do enough to scare him or anyone else who thinks they can pull one over on me.'

'Understood. Where does he live?'

Victor handed over a folded slip of paper with the address scrawled on it.

'You are an asset to this business, Alex. And I'll make sure you're well looked after.'

'Thank you, Mr Mallone.'

Victor nodded and was grateful to have someone so good at his job on his side. As Alex left, Victor turned his attention back to the DVD, which was beside his empty plate. This Chinaman business bothered him, but he was curious to see how it would play out. He didn't lose and wasn't about to start now. He slid, with some effort out of his chair, and snatched up the DVD.

'Take me to the house,' he barked at the two men flanking the table who hurried on ahead of him. One opened the door as the other rushed out and got into the driver's side of the bottle green nineteen sixty-three Rolls Royce. Victor waddled out of the restaurant and clambered into the back of the car. He thought he might take a vacation soon, he was feeling drained and could do with a break. Stifling a yawn, he closed his eyes and dozed for the twenty-minute journey to the house. Surrounded by twelve-foot high walls and situated on five acres of lush land, Victor's home was more of an armoured bunker than a living space. Boasting eight bedrooms and two swimming pools, it was a visual expression of the fruits of his labour. He employed a full time staff of cooks and cleaners as well as a twelve-man rapid response security team to patrol and protect the outer perimeter of the property. As an extra precaution, all of the windows were constructed of the same bulletproof glass used in presidential limousines. Victor's office was on the upper floor. It was panelled in oak and the large wall length window looked out over the panorama of grass and large waterfall which dominated the courtyard. The carpet was Persian and deep red, offset by the antique furniture. His desk was large and clean and as he sank into his oversized leather chair, he nodded to Salvatore to play the DVD. The pair then watched as the fifty-inch television that hung on the wall came to life.

The screen faded in on a darkened room and a simple wooden desk. A black suited figure walked slowly into view and sat, looking directly into the camera. He looked to be anywhere between sixty and eighty. His white hair was thin and straggled and his features were gaunt. His aged skin stretched over his skull, and although he had obviously attempted cosmetic surgery to mask the signs of age, the folds in his gizzard like neck were still visible. His eyes had the expected oriental slant, but at the same time, they were hard and cruel, somewhat like Victors own. They appeared to look through the screen directly at Victor and Salvatore. He folded his bony hands on the desk and managed a weak smile. He began to speak, his English vaguely tinted with his Cantonese dialect.

'Mr Mallone. I'm sure this message has come as a surprise to you, and I would not have sent it to you unless I had something of interest to say.'

'It's really him,' said Salvatore as Victor silenced him with a wave of his hand.

'I'm growing old, Mr Mallone. Too old for this constant battle between our respective organisations. I grow weary of the bloodshed and as you can see, my health doesn't allow me the luxury of the time or energy required to continue the battle. I long to return home and die in the peace of my homeland and as I have no siblings to hand over my empire to I have decided that if you desire it, I will hand over control of my territory to you.'

Victor and Sal shared a quick glance. Then looked back to the screen.

'I know you are wondering why I would hand over my

life's work to you, Victor and I wouldn't blame you. The fact is that despite everything that has gone between our organisations, I respect you. I respect your work ethic and I respect the ruthlessness with which you conduct your business.'

'Un fuckin' believable.' whispered Salvatore under his breath. Victor watched on.

'I have one condition, Mr Mallone, and that is that you retain my staff. My immediate family will be returning to China with me but the rest of my men are hard working with families to feed. You will need them as it is, as my territory is far larger than your own.'

The old man smiled but his eyes remained focused and sharp

'If this is something you find agreeable, I would suggest a meeting between you and I in a secret location. To dispel any thoughts of deception on my behalf, I will allow you to choose the place and date of the meeting. You may bring up to three of your most trusted advisors, as will I, but I must stress the importance of keeping this arrangement confidential. There are certain parties that would be interested in knowing we are together and would benefit from one or both of our deaths. Of course, you are under no obligation to accept this offer. If you do not, there are other parties who would be more than willing to take such a large share of both territory and business interests. If you would like to proceed, send one of your men to my family's store with the details of the date and location of the meeting. Tell him to ask for Lei Ling. She can be trusted with any information.' The old man leaned forward, his face now out of the shadowy half-light looked even older and more tired.

'Let us put an end to this war Victor. I have had enough of the bloodshed and wish to retire peacefully. You have three days to respond after which I will assume you have declined my offer.'

The screen faded to black, as Sal looked to Victor. 'Did that just happen, Vic? Did the old bastard just give up the fight?'

Victor smiled. He wasn't convinced. Granted the old man looked like hell but his eyes were still sharp, the body might be failing but the old man still had it upstairs.

'Don't get too excited, Sal. This could be a ruse to draw us out.'

'I'm not so sure Vic, did you see him? He looked sick.'

'Sick or not, it's his mind that concerns me, Sal. It

seems out of character for anyone to give up on everything they have worked to build. I don't buy this retirement crap either.'

'What about if we use the situation to our advantage?'

'What do you mean?' Victor said.

'Well, he said we can choose the place right? So let's choose somewhere we can hide a few people, just in case things get outta hand. I know it's a risk, but think of the gains.'

He nodded. He was already thinking of the gains. Undisputed control over little Italy and Chinatown, bragging rights. It was the power of fear, and he could enhance it massively. If the worst happened and it turned into a bloodbath then that was ok too. He wasn't afraid to get his hands dirty if he needed to. This was too good an opportunity to miss.

'You know what Sal, you're right. Maybe the old fuck has dementia, but that's not my problem. We need to organise this, do it properly and discreetly. The fewer people who know about this the better. Bring in Joey and Franco.'

'What about Alex?'

'Nah, he's working something else for me.'

'Marco?'

'I thought he was still banged up?'

'Paroled last month. He's reliable and a hard ass when it's needed.'

'Ok, sounds good. Make the arrangements.'

Sal nodded. 'Understood. Any ideas where you wanna set up the meeting?'

'I doubt he's senile enough to come here for it, so we need to find a place where it's still private but gives us the advantage if things go to shit.'

'What about the waterfront?'

Victor considered for a moment and then nodded. 'That's not bad, Sal. We can use one of our boats. It will eliminate the possibility of ambush.'

'Are you legit gonna meet him, Vic? No funny business?'

'The way I see it, Sal, is that worst case, the old man tries something and we let fate decide what happens. On the other side, if he's not pulling our chain we get our hands on a huge slice of his businesses.'

'You know Vic you shouldn't discount him. There's nothing to say he won't try to put a bullet in you anyway, retirement or not.'

Victor thought about that. He had learned to live by his instincts and they had never failed him so far, and they were telling him to go with this one and see how it played out.

## TWO

The Docks were situated just off Broadway. Split into three distinct sections used for not only commercial import and export purposes but also as a naval shipyard. Millions of dollars' worth of goods were imported and exported here, going to and from all corners of the world. The ninety-foot vessel 'Lady of the sea' was tied to the dock and blended in perfectly with the other boats around it. Its white hull painted with red shimmered in the mid afternoon sun as the waves gently rocked it back and forth in its berth. Initially used for deep-sea fishing, Victor had purchased the boat five years earlier to make it easier for him to smuggle weapons and drugs. It had also been used on two occasions to traffic people, although due to overcrowding the below deck compartments, some had died in the journey, costing Victor a lot of money.
The boat had been refurbished to Victor's specifications. The maze of corridors typically found on boat interiors had been done away with. The lower

decks had been converted into compartments (or cells when they needed to be used for that purpose) with which to store the various goods that were being transported. Above this were the crew's quarters, which retained some of the ships initial design and were a labyrinth of low ceilings and narrow walls with several cabins branching off. The upper deck had been opened up and was split into three areas. There were Victor's private bedroom and bathroom, next to which was the large living space with the huge projector TV hanging on the wall. Towards the stern of the boat was a long, windowless meeting room, which was to be the location of Victors meeting with Wang Li. Although he had never used it for meetings (usually preferring the comfort of his restaurant), It had been arranged in such a way to enhance his superiority. The large elongated table had room for twelve to sit around it and Victor's high backed leather chair sat at the head. Natural light streamed in from large rectangular bulletproof windows set in the roof which could be opened if required onto the deck of the boat.

Nervous and not wanting to show it, Victor sat and sipped his double scotch whilst he waited for Wang Li to arrive. His people had already arrived and checked the ship, and now satisfied with the arrangements had given the all clear. As agreed, each had left armed guards in the outer room. Three each to deter any chance of things getting out of control. On the dock itself, discreetly hidden were more men from each faction watching each other and waiting for any sign of trouble. Never one to leave himself without an advantage Victor had also positioned a sniper on the crane directly across the dock in the event of things going wrong. Although there would be no line of sight to this room, he was under instructions to kill Wang Li at Victor's signal, which would be sent via the panic button under the table. He sipped his drink thoughtfully, as Salvatore ducked his head into the room.

'He's here.'

Victor nodded and drained his glass.

'Show him in.'

He looked even older in the flesh than in the video as he shuffled into the room. He was walking with a cane and his hand shook with the effort of supporting himself. Victor suppressed a small smile as he was assisted to his seat by one of his aides who then left, closing the door behind them. They, along with Victor's men, would wait in the next room whilst the discussions took place. Victor looked Wang Li in the eye and was met with an equally icy stare that made him uncomfortable. He was used to people breaking eye contact, too intimidated by Victor's reputation. Wang Li folded his hands on the table, and Victor fought the urge to grimace at how thin and wiry they were.

'Mr Li. Welcome.'

'I am happy that you agreed to this meeting, Mr Mallone. As you can see, I am quite unwell and desire a quick end to proceedings.'

'If what you said in your message is true, then I'm sure we can come to an arrangement.'

Wang Li smiled and Victor couldn't imagine him having very many years left. He looked frail, weathered. He looked to Victor like a man beaten. Subconsciously he sat up further in his seat and puffed his own sizeable chest out. He thought this would be an easy negotiation.

'Mr Mallone, I know you are no fool, and nor am I. I desire an end to this pointless battle. For many years, we have fought over territory, over business dealings. Both of us have lost people we care about. I no longer desire these things Mr Mallone. I am too old, too tired.'

Victor nodded, indeed the old fuck looked like he was

ready to drop dead at any second, but he wouldn't say that. Not when it looked like he was about to inherit a huge stake of territory without lifting a finger. He lived for days like this.

'Mr Li. I don't believe in extended negotiations or wasting people's time, so I will tell you where I stand and we can make this deal happen. I'm sure you are aware of the dangers to us both of meeting in this way. Now the terms you mentioned about retaining your staff I am prepared to accept. My concern is their loyalty.'

Li looked offended, but only for a second.

'Mr Mallone, the loyalty of my men is unquestioned. They will do as I instruct them.'

'I appreciate the sentiment, but how can I be certain that when you have retired they will remain loyal... and do as I tell them.'

Li smiled and sat back in his chair.

'If I command it, they will do it. Let me give you an example of their unquestioned loyalty. Two years ago, I needed a transplant. Liver failure. Of all of my men, only one was suitable. He was in excellent health, a young man of just twenty-two. He gave me his life Mr Mallone. He committed suicide and demanded that his liver be given to me. That is loyalty you cannot buy.'

'Loyalty to you, Mr Li. Not to me.'

Wang Li leaned forward and appeared angry, and then smiled. His grin was too clean, too white. Victor suppressed another internal smile. Of course. Dentures. Obvious ones too.

'Mr Mallone, there is no question that they will do as you ask, or they will answer to me.'

Victor decided to let the point go. Bottom line was that if they didn't do things his way, they would disappear, deal or no deal. It was crunch time. Victor wanted to see if the old man was genuine. It was time to put the cards on the table.

'Ok Mr Li, then I think we can do a deal here.'

'Very good. You will assume full control of my assets and my territory upon transfer of three hundred million united states dollars into my account.'

Victor chuckled and then saw the old man was deadly serious. He licked his lips, cursing at the monumental misunderstanding.

'Mr Li, I was under the impression that no money would be changing hands on this deal. I assumed you were looking for someone to take over for you. A successor.'

'Indeed I am, Mr Mallone, but give away everything I

have worked for? Oh, that won't do.'

'Then we have nothing further to discuss.' Victor said and stood.

The old man laughed.

'Victor my friend, sit your fat ass down and listen to what I have to say.'

It was like someone flicking a switch. Gone was the frail appearance, the shaking hand. He still looked like hell, after all, some things can't be faked, but even looking like a ghoul he had an air of supreme authority about him that made Victor's confidence falter. Shocked, he sat back in his chair as Li leaned close, spitting his words venomously.

'I have something to show you, Mr Mallone.'

Li shouted over his shoulder in Chinese and the meeting room door opened. Victor could see his men, or what was left of them smeared over the walls. He wondered how they had managed to be so quiet. They were dead apart from Salvatore, who was on his knees, hands behind his head and mouth gagged. Their eyes met for a split second and then the door was closed. Lei Ling, the courier brought in the laptop and set it in front of Mallone, then opened the video on the screen. Victor glanced over to Wang Li, who watched on expressionlessly.

The video was shot in Victor's house but it wasn't the pristine and clutter free space he would have expected to see. The walls were riddled with bullet holes and a thin haze of smoke drifted across the screen. There were three chairs lined up in the centre of the frame, and tied to them were Victor's wife and two children. Victor glared at Wang Li who was now smiling.

'I must applaud you Mr Mallone; your home is well protected. My men had some trouble gaining access.'

Victor felt sick but kept his expression neutral. He knew if he had any hope of escaping this boat alive, he would have to be at his best. He discreetly reached under the table and pressed the panic button.

'Mr Mallone, the sniper has already been taken care of. It is now just you and I, so please, relax.'

Victor slumped back in his chair and glared at Li. He was hot and the air felt thick and heavy. His eyes drifted back to the jittery video of his family. He could see his cousin Francisco lying face down on the crème rug, his throat cut and pooling blood.

'I must say, I'm surprised that you fell for such an obvious ploy Mr Mallone. When you agreed to this meeting I almost felt sorry for you.'

'You never intended to make any deal.' spat Victor, finally losing control.

Wang Li smiled. 'Actually, you are wrong. The deal stands, Mr Mallone. I'm retiring and will be leaving once you pay me for my territory.'

'I don't have that kind of money you fucking idiot!' roared Victor.

'Again, you lie, Mr Mallone. I know the Mallone bank account in your name contains two hundred and ninety seven million dollars which you will transfer to my account using the computer in front of you.'

'Are you insane? That would wipe me out, leave us with nothing.'

'I wouldn't worry about that Victor,' said Wang Li with a cruel smile. 'I would worry about where you intend to find the remaining three million dollars to complete the transaction.'

'Are you insane you old fuck? There is no deal!'

'You have already agreed. To change your mind now would be disrespectful. I urge you to think carefully about the next words you say.'

Victor bit his tongue. It was clear he was dealing with a crazy man, and that made it even more dangerous as crazy people in Victor's experience had no self-restraint. Victor licked his lips and folded his hands on the table.

'Fine, then let us negotiate. But I ask you to let my family go Mr Li. I have acted with good faith and come here unarmed and prepared to talk.'

'Apart from the sniper, of course.'

'Yes…but still...'

He trailed off and tried to think of a way out. For him, it was all about self-preservation.

'Here is my suggestion to you Mr Mallone. For the outstanding balance of three million, I will allow you to pay by other means.'

'What do you mean?'

'I want your family. More specifically your wife and two daughters.'

Victor could no longer hide his terror as he glared at his nemesis, then back to the grainy video of his wife and children.

'There is no way. Surely you understand that. More than anything in this world, family means everything to me.'

Li continued, acting as if he hadn't heard Victor's protests.

'I think it's a fair price, Mr Mallone. Three million for

three human beings. Indeed, is it not a higher price on life than you yourself typically value it?'

'Fair price? I'm supposed to sell you my fucking family?'

Wang Li chuckled and shook his head. 'Don't preach to me about family, Mallone. You have no concept of family values. You have no honour. No respect, and this time it's going to cost you.'

'How about we renegotiate, come to some arrangement?'

'No. The time for that has passed and the offer is non-negotiable.'

'Then there is no deal. You will have to kill me.'

'I don't want to kill you, Mr Mallone. What would I want with a fat, greasy shit of a corpse like you?'

Victor lurched to his feet. 'You fucking prick!'

Wang Li didn't move as the door to the meeting room opened, and three armed guards burst through, training their guns on Victor.

'Sit down, Mr Mallone before you get yourself shot. You are, after all, a large enough target to make sure they don't miss.'

'Why my family? What do you want with them?'

Victor flopped into his seat, wiping his arm across his

sweaty brow. His eyes darted around the room, scanning for a way out. He noticed with dismay that his attention to security meant that he had inadvertently trapped himself. Wang Li motioned to Lei Ling and whispered something in her ear, then turned back to Victor. She left the room and closed the door, leaving two armed guards flanking Wang Li's seat.

'In my culture Mr Mallone there is a legend. A story that my family has told for generations. I want to share this with you now, and please listen, for you are the first person outside of the Li family to hear it.'

Victor remained silent. In his head, he remembered an old jingle from somewhere in the past. Perhaps a TV or radio programme. Silence gives consent. Wang Li continued.

Sometime in the early sixteenth century, my ancestors found a way to enrich their lives by the drinking of human blood.'

A chill brushed Victor's spine as he watched the old man. He tried as best he could to ignore the intensity of the fire in his stare.

'It is much like the basis of the vampire legend, although nothing so supernatural I'm afraid. The legend says he who sacrifices and drinks from the body of another will earn the years they themselves would never live.'

Wang Li leaned forward, watching Victor.

'It has been practised and its effects are real, Mr Mallone. It is said normal civilian blood is good, but the blood of a rival's family, his immediate family is the most valuable of all. And you Mallone are my greatest rival.'

Victor was furious and had to force himself not to glance at the computer screen at the grainy image it contained. He knew he had to act, to call the old man's bluff. He wasn't even sure that he was bluffing, but had no option but to go all in and see if the situation was as dire as he thought.

'I'll tell you what I think, Mr Li.'

Victor stood, and although Wang Li's guards sprang into action, he held them off with a wave of his hand as Victor continued, now leaning on the desk on his knuckles.

'I think this is all bullshit. More to the point, I think you are full of shit. You think I was born yesterday, Chinaman? Well, let me tell you this right now. All this old wives tale bullshit doesn't sway with me. Now I am going to leave this room, get my brother and get off my boat. I'm then going to come down on you and every single slant eyed gook in this damn city.'

Although he had intended to walk around the table and leave, he knew his legs wouldn't allow him to. They felt like jelly and it was taking all of his effort to keep upright. He had hoped to see Wang Li falter or at least his confidence waver but he just continued to smile his knowing smile.

'A fine speech, Victor, but pointless all the same.'

He barked a command over his shoulder in his native tongue and Salvatore was bundled into the room by Lei Ling. His nose was bloody and Victor could see defiance and fear in equal measure on his face.

'It is unfortunate that you have chosen to respond to my offer with your typical narrow minded arrogance. And now it will cost your brother his life.'

Wang Li stood and Victor noticed that the frail and slow moving man on the video was no more. Victor applauded the old man's acting skills. He watched as Salvatore was forced to his knees and Wang Li stood beside him, placing a bony hand on his bald head.

'Out of respect for you as a rival, Mr Mallone, I give you one last chance to agree to my proposal and save your brother's life.'

Victor forced himself to meet Wang Li's gaze, but couldn't help but flick his eyes towards Salvatore who was watching him with a pleading look in his eyes. Victor was sweating now and his heart was thumping in his chest so hard that he thought everyone in the room must surely be able to hear it. He licked his lips and then smiled, showing his slightly yellowed teeth to Wang Li.

'Fuck you Chinaman.'

'Very well' Wang Li reached up to his mouth and removed his teeth, the dentures that were so obvious to Victor earlier. Victor felt a scream leap into his throat that he somehow managed to swallow.

Wang Li's teeth, his natural teeth that is, were sharpened into points. Victor thought he looked like a great white shark, a Chinese Jaws – but there was no Roy Scheider or Richard Dreyfuss on hand. you're gonna need a bigger boat he thought to himself and this time instead of a scream he had to force back a cackle which he knew would make him sound insane. Wang Li was grinning now and showing as many of those horrific pointed daggers as he could. He licked his lips, and Victor marvelled at how his tongue looked incredibly bright and vivid as he began to salivate and dribble down his chin. Salvatore tried to push himself away from danger, but he was held in place as Wang Li crouched and grabbed Salvatore by the face, trying to push his head back to get at his neck. Victor knew it was now or never. Willing his legs into action, he launched himself across the table, smashing into the guards and Salvatore and knocking them to the ground. Victor began to wrestle the guard nearest to him for control of his weapon. Acting just as swiftly as Victor, Salvatore was doing the same. Wang Li looked on his eyes wide.

'Get them, control them!'

Victor slammed his elbow into the young Japanese guard's throat, enjoying the resounding crack as he wrestled the gun free. With an enraged roar, Victor rolled onto his back and sprayed gunfire towards Wang Li, peppering the walls with bullet holes as his intended target threw himself to the ground, avoiding the storm of bullets. Lei Ling wasn't so lucky, and her delicate face was obliterated in a shower of blood and brain fragments. Only a second or two had passed, and the guard on the floor although wheezing from his damaged throat was again wrestling for control of the weapon, trying to pry Victor's fingers away. There was a deafening gunshot from the left, and Victor heard a wet splattering noise and was showered with warm wet liquid.

Oh god, please not Sal.

Sal and his guard had been wrestling for the weapon and had managed to fire it. The single bullet had penetrated Sal's shoulder and then angled up into the guard's neck as the wrestled with the gun. Both men slumped to the floor, Sal bleeding and moaning, his guard dead, his neck sheared away to the bone.

Victor rolled onto his knees and was now on top of the guard. He managed to turn the gun towards the guard's face. Victor realised that the guard was frightened. He was only a young boy of no more than twenty. Nevertheless, he was the enemy, and Victor felt no remorse. The barrel of the gun was pressed into the boy's cheek now and Victor could see the terror in his eyes. Victor managed a smile.

'Fuck you, gook!' he roared as he squeezed the trigger. An explosion of blood and bone erupted as the boy's face was disintegrated. Victor's triumph was short lived, however, as he felt a searing pain in his shoulder and hands around his throat as Wang Li leapt onto his back. Throwing himself back, he smashed his body against Wang Li and the table, but like a rabid dog, Wang Li wouldn't release his grip, shaking his head from side to side as he sunk his teeth deeper into Victor's shoulder. Victor yelled out in pain and tried to reach behind him to get the old man off him, but he couldn't reach. His ears were still ringing and his nostrils were filled with the stench of blood and smoke. He slammed his head back in blind hope and felt it connect with Wang Li, who let out a surprised grunt and released his grip, allowing Victor to roll free. His shoulder was burning in agony, and he whirled around to see the Chinaman crouching on the floor, his lower face now covered with Victor's blood. Wang Li was babbling in his own language and glaring at Victor, but Victor wasn't looking back. His eyes were on the discarded semi-automatic machine gun lying on the floor. Victor lunged for it and a split second later Wang Li did the same. Victor's hands momentarily touched the metal casing and then more pain as Wang Li sank his fangs into Victors' forearm and tore away a huge flap of skin. Victor screamed out in agony and instinctively batted away at Wang Li, catching the old man on the shoulder. He went for the gun again, his instincts screaming at him that Wang Li was upon him.

He tucked his shoulder and rolled to the left whirling and firing blindly towards where he though the Chinaman would be, but he missed the target. Wang Li leaped over the table to the other side. As Victor emptied the magazine.

So much for being a frail old man Victor thought to himself with a grimace as he tossed the empty gun on the floor. He struggled to his feet and staggered to the door, glancing at the ugly tear in his arm. He could see the yellow flaps of fat and gristle under the skin and felt a wave of nausea. He could hear Wang Li, scurrying unseen around the underside of the table, but Victor's main concern was for himself, and making sure he survived. He was almost at the door when he tripped, sprawling over the leg of Sal, who was still incapacitated and on his back, moaning softly. Victor felt his ankle twist under the full weight of his three hundred plus pounds. He crunched to the floor, smashing his head into the polished wood floor and almost knocking himself unconscious. Exhausted, he rolled onto his side and could see Sal looking at him. Afraid. Pleading. Victor could see that Salvatore had severe damage to his shoulder area, but he suspected that he would live. In theory at least. As much as he wanted to help his brother, Victor knew he needed to survive. He froze as Wang Li spoke Victor craned his neck but was unable to spot him from his prone position.

'You know this is pointless, Victor.' came the soft voice. It sounded different somehow, perhaps the shape of the natural form of his teeth had changed his voice somehow, or maybe this was the environment the thrived in. Rooms full of blood, smoke, and fear. Victor knew he was vulnerable and exposed, and his shoulder and arm were in agony. He wiped the sweat from his brow and saw that his hand was covered in fresh blood from where he had banged his face on the floor. A horrified scream welled up inside as he saw Wang Li approach. He had stripped naked and was crawling on all fours around the bottom of the table, his wrinkled old body had the leathery appearance of a mummified corpse as he snaked his way towards Victor, grinning his horrific red dagger smile.

'I'll give you credit Victor, you put up a good fight.' He was by Salvatore now, and rested on his haunches, arms in front of him and fingers splayed out on the floor. Victor could not help but feel repulsed by his horrible, naked old man's body as he glared at Victor with eyes that seemed more alive than ever. Victor realised that Wang Li was completely at home in this situation.

'You know it's too late don't you Victor? For your family I mean. They are already dead; I was just offering you the chance to get some value for money.'

Victor said nothing. Deep down he knew it to be true. After all, if the positions had been reversed it's what he would have done. Victor struggled up to his elbows, panting and staring at Wang Li with a defiant look. He spat on the floor, and despite trying his best to hide his fear, there was a definite tremble in his voice as he spoke.

'It was always going to come down to this. It was always going to come down to the two of us. And one of us was always going to die.'

'Yes, a pity it has to be you, Mr Mallone.'

Victor laughed and flipped Wang Li the middle finger. 'Fuck you.'

Wang Li grew serious and bit into Salvatore's throat, and tore it away with a great wet ripping sound that Victor almost instantly blotted out with his anguished scream of terror. Wang Li gorged on the fleshy mass in his mouth, rubbing the blood all over his body as Sal kicked his legs and gurgled as he tried to fight off the coming death.

Victor struggled to his knees and began to crawl, desperate to get away from Wang Li and the sight of his dead brother. He pushed through the door into the main room of his quarters, trying to ignore the dead bodies of his men. Loyal men who had worked for him for years. He struggled to his feet, hobbling and trying not to put too much weight on his ankle, which was swelling and painful. The doors swung open behind him and Victor looked over his shoulder to see Wang Li standing there, naked and streaked with blood and fleshy lumps of body matter.

'Leaving so soon Victor? I don't think so. We have business to attend to.'

Wang Li scrambled forwards, upright yet partially on all fours as he closed the distance between himself and Victor in seconds and knocked him to the floor, a searing bolt of agony shooting through Victor's ankle as he tumbled to the ground. He was now on his back and scrambling backwards, trying to put as much distance as he could between himself and Wang Li. He was afraid and felt his bladder let go, a dark patch spreading out from his crotch as he watched his tormentor approach. Wang Li sniffed the air and then pointed to the spreading wet patch on Victor's trousers. 'Such a wonderful smell that is Victor!'

Victor felt the back of his head touch the wall and he knew he was out of options. Nowhere else to run, nothing left to fight with. Wang Li came towards him in his half crouched chimpanzee way, and now Victor could smell the blood on him.

'I'll make this quick Victor, out of respect. For you, it will be over.'

He grinned, and Victor tried to push himself into the wall, anything to get away from that mouth, those teeth that were still stained with shards of jagged flesh.

'And then,' Wang Li added with a smile 'ill fuck your dead wife, eat your children and send them all to join you in hell.'

Victor sobbed as Wang Li came towards him, opening his mouth wide. Their eyes met and Wang Li had a split second to register that Victor was smiling. Victor grabbed the back of Wang Li's head with one hand and pulled it towards him, at the same time shoving his free hand into Wang Li's open mouth. Wang Li tried to bite down, but Victors' arm was too big. Victor ignored the agony of the teeth scraping at his skin, at the frenzied tearing and scratching as Wang Li tried to free himself.

Victor gritted his teeth and pushed as hard as he could, his arm sliding past Wang Li's teeth and down his gullet into his throat. Wang Li's eyes bugged out as he began to suffocate, his airway blocked. Victor lurched forward and now had Wang Li on his back. He tried to ignore the horrible, leathery feel of his skin on the outside, and the hot, wet, slick feel of his innards. Instead, he concentrated on pushing his arm deeper, ever deeper into the old Chinaman's mouth, watching as his throat expanded to accommodate Victors' arm. Eventually, Wang Li stopped moving and Victor slumped forward, completely exhausted. His arm buried almost up to the elbow in Wang Li's mouth. For some time he lay there in the silence and wept.

Epilogue

Two weeks had passed since that day on the boat. The death toll for Victor's organisation had been severe, with over thirty losses including his brother Sal and wife and two children who were beheaded in the sitting room just after the video made by Wang Li had been shot. Despite the rumour mill from the locals working overtime, Victor had managed to contain most of the truth from leaking out and had put the word was out that anyone who talked about or mentioned the incident would be dealt with severely.

As with most Fridays, that night in Mallone's was busy and the tables were filled with customers who were eating, drinking and enjoying themselves. Those closest to him had noticed a change in Victor. Something in his eyes was different. His demeanour was more intense, and although nobody knew what had happened that day on the boat, they knew enough to understand that it must have been serious. It was a hot day and as Victor walked into the restaurant, his eyes hidden behind his Armani sunglasses he smiled. He always loved the sounds and smells of his restaurant when it was running at capacity. There was a certain comfort about it and Victor thought if he had been a regular person with a regular life, he would still probably find himself in the restaurant business. He strolled towards his table at the back, pausing to say hello to his regulars or to take praise for the excellent service. This was one of his main pleasures, hearing the praise of satisfied customers.

'Hey Victor,' came the voice from a table nearest the window.

Victor approached and smiled, shaking hands with the retired police chief and acknowledging his wife with a courteous nod. Former Chief Wigelow had been on Victor's payroll right up until his retirement, and even though they no longer maintained a professional relationship, the chief and his wife still dined there at least once a month.

'Chief Wigelow, Mrs Wigelow. I hope you are enjoying your evening.'

'As always Victor. Those boys in the kitchen outdid themselves.'

'I'll be sure to pass on your regards. Was the meal to your satisfaction?'

'Yes sir, we tried the special. It was delicious! What was it?'

Victor smiled and rubbed his left arm, still bandaged up the elbow, then leaned close in mock whisper.

'Special imported steak, from China. You won't find it anywhere else,' he said with a wink.

'I must say it was astoundingly good. Perhaps the best I have ever tasted.'

Victor smiled and nodded.

'Thank you chief, I appreciate the compliment.'

Victor excused himself and headed to his private table

at the back of the room. He liked to sit there. It offered him an unobstructed view of his customers as they enjoyed their food. He sat in his usual place and let out a deep sigh, thinking he might well take a holiday. Somewhere hot and quiet where he could heal and unwind. The waiter approached to take his order and after some consideration, he thought he would have the special too. The Chinese steak, extra rare. After all, it would be a shame to waste it. The waiter scurried away as Victor set his napkin on his knee, took a sip of his water and waited for his meal to arrive.

## THE BOX

The box was outside her door. As she looked at it, she wondered why the delivery driver hadn't knocked or left a note to say they had tried to call. She had just been about to head out to meet Jane when she had almost fallen over it. Her irritation was soon replaced my curiosity as she looked closer. It looked innocent enough. It was wrapped in brown paper and had her name, Terri Browning hand written on the top of the package. There was no return address and no postmark. She wasn't expecting a delivery. It had been months since she had given in to the urge to browse the web to buy more books or clothes. She wondered if it might be from Mark, another desperate effort to make up for the affair that had shattered her life. She had no intention of taking him back, and as much as the loneliness of living alone was something she still couldn't get used to, she knew that she had been hurt too badly to ever let anyone get close to her again. The box was maybe fifteen inches across and the same high, and yet for as innocent as it looked she still hadn't picked it up. Shifting her weight, and still holding her front door open with one hand she glanced down the hallway to the apartment building, hoping to catch a glimpse of who might have delivered it, but the hallway was empty. Perhaps one of her neighbours might have heard something. She was sure Mrs Molde from down the hall would know who left it. She was a one-woman neighbourhood watch, and knew everybody's business equally as well as her own, if not better. Terri briefly considered knocking on her door to ask is she had heard anything, but she couldn't stomach having to listen to the nosy old trout ramble on about the Gout in her leg, or the Noisy students who lived upstairs in number Thirty-Two. No, she wouldn't put herself through that when simply opening the package would probably answer her questions anyway. With a final look down the hallway, she picked up the box, went back inside and closed the door.

The apartment still looked empty now that it was devoid of Mark's belongings. All that remained of them was a box of books, some old T-Shirts and a bottle of cheap aftershave he always insisted on wearing on the few rare occasions they went out. She had told him they were here and that he should come and pick them up, but through either stubbornness or unwillingness to accept that it was over between them, Mark had been putting it off for weeks now—saying that there was no point collecting them as he was sure they would soon be back together anyway. They had argued frequently, the affair festering like an open wound. She wanted him out of her life so she could attempt to rebuild, and he was full of excuses; reasons why they needed to stay together and not let something 'silly' like him cheating on her keep them from being together. Although she knew she would never allow him back into her life, she still loved him, and she feared that his persistence would one day break her fragile defences.

She set the box on the dining table and then went to the kitchen to make a fresh pot of coffee. As she waited for the kettle to come to the boil, she sent a text message to Jane, explaining that she was running late but would meet her at the coffee house at ten thirty instead of ten. Setting her blackberry aside, she leaned on the work surface and eyed the package sitting on the dining table. The apartment was open plan, and now it was devoid of Male clutter, it had a definite feminine (if minimal) look. Early morning sunlight streamed through the large balcony windows that ran across the far wall of the apartment. She sometimes sat out there late at night, crying and hating herself for the rut her life was in. She cast a guilty glance towards her computer, Silent and unused. It's black screen seemed to glare at her.

Hey Terri, what did I ever do to you? Remember when we used to spend time together? When you used to write? Write all day, write all night. What happened? You haven't written a word since Mark left. Come on, show me some love at least.

It was true. Her latest novel was supposed to have been handed over to the publishers two months ago, and not only was she nowhere near finished, she still hadn't written an ending. It seemed that every time she sat down to work, her mind would go blank and she would simply stare at the screen, fingers poised over the keys. The couple of times she had managed to string a few paragraphs together, the results had been disastrous, the copy poor. The stuff she liked to call cookie cutter ghost writer stuff. Now with her deadline long dead, her editor was giving her hell and had taken to calling her daily for a progress updates, which had resulted in a frostiness between them as time rolled by with nothing to report. The kettle clicked off and as she poured her coffee, she realised that her life was a complete mess. At twenty-nine, she should have a handle on her situation but the fact was that she was struggling to cope, and her stubbornness forced her to pretend to her friends she was fine. Her eyes drifted to the mystery box on the table. The more she thought about it, the surer she was that it was from Mark and perhaps that was why she was so reluctant to open it. She didn't want his gifts to soften her and allow him to worm his way back into her life. She suspected that the box might contain a new snow globe. He knew she had been collecting them since she was a child, and had over three hundred in her collection, some of which were extremely rare. It was a hobby that she was slightly embarrassed about, and as a result was one she kept secret from her small circle of friends. Mark knew well enough, though, and it would be just his style to try and win her over with a glass dome filled with water and fake snow.

She took a sip of her coffee, set her 'Little Miss Perfect' cup down on the counter and approached the table. The box looked innocent enough sitting beside the fruit bowl and her half-finished John Grisham novel (unread since Marks departure). She saw that it was packaged differently to how she would have expected. It was tied with string and wrapped in brown paper. It was how she imagined that packages were sent in the fifties, before the days of UPS and DHL. She looked again at her name written in block capitals on top of the package and had a strange and inexplicable feeling of dread. Deciding that she was being ridiculous and that if she couldn't even open a box then getting her life in order would be impossibility, she pulled the knot on the string and peeled away the wrapping.

Beneath the brown paper was another box. This one was red and had that horrible velvet outer material which was designed to say 'luxury' but to her said 'cheap.' It looked like some incredibly tacky, garish late Christmas present. Now she had opened it, she wasn't so sure that Mark had sent it. He hated tacky stuff like this, and more to the point knew that she hated it too. He was a dirty cheating lowlife bastard but he wasn't stupid. He wouldn't send something to win her back that he thought she might despise. She was contemplating this when the phone rang. Her heart leapt into her mouth and she cursed herself for letting this stupid package get her so jittery. She made it to the handset before the answering machine kicked in.

'Hello?'

'Terri? It's Bob.'

Shit. Bob was Bob Greenwood, and he was her agent. She wished that she had let the machine pick up the call.

'Hi Bob, how are you?' she said, forcing herself to sound cheery and happy.

'Fine, Fine, Just had some time to kill and thought I would check in.'

Unlikely. They both knew the reason for his call. Her book should be long finished and in the advanced stages of the copy editing process by now, not three chapters from an end she hadn't even thought of yet. He wanted a progress report. Bob was a funny character. A large man with a deep booming voice, he was the definition of stress. Her last novel hadn't sold well, not as well as her first at any rate which had been something of a sleeper hit. The agency that Bob worked for wanted to cut the dead weight from their client list and they had included her in that category. Bob had been put under immense pressure to cut her loose and take on some fresh, new, undamaged and deadline meeting blood. In Bob's defence, he had declined their request and stuck with her, which by all accounts had raised some speculative eyebrows within the company. Now both of them were relying on this most recent and as yet unfinished book to justify their mutual faith, and Bob, in particular, was keen to vindicate himself. She could imagine him sitting in his office, chewing his nails or running his hands through his thinning hair. Bob had a reputation of being a hard act to please, but she had always found him professional and more importantly unafraid to share his opinions on her work, which as a writer she valued a hell of a lot more than people who stroked her ego and told her that every word she wrote was amazing. Bob had a small nose and deeply set eyes which were topped by large bushy eyebrows. She could see him now in her mind's eye, frowning in his brown office chair, scratching his carroty beard as he considered the best way to approach the unfinished novel sized elephant in the room.

'Hello? Terri are you there?'

He had been talking and she had drifted away.

'I'm here. Sorry, Bob, you caught me at an awkward time.'

'I'm sorry; I didn't disturb you working did I?'

She had to give it to him. As far as approaching a sensitive subject goes, he had done it well.

'Not exactly. I was just heading out.'

'I'm sorry; I wouldn't have called at all it's just—'

He trailed off, hoping that she would pick up the bait.

'You want to know about the book?'

'You know I wouldn't ask if it wasn't important, it's just that the powers that be are breathing down my neck and I need to tell them something. Can you send me at least a few pages so I can shut the damn pricks up?'

She felt sorry for Bob and would have done as he asked without question if she had something to send him.

'Look, Bob, you know I have been going through a tough time lately. I just haven't been able to concentrate on my work as fully as I would like. I'm sure it's only a matter of time.'

'I understand, really I do but I need something from you, Terri. I hate to do it, but it's my duty to tell you that there are serious discussions about cancelling your contract.'

She was stunned.

'Can they even do that?' she blurted, hating how whiny she sounded.

'They can and they will. I'm doing all I can to fight your corner Terri, but I can only do so much without evidence that you can get this thing finished.'

'Bob, I'll finish the book, I swear to you I will but you have to see it from my point of view; I can't just pull it out of my ass. I gave them two books already in the last year; surely they can give me a little leeway?'

'Hey, I'm on your side here Terri truly I am. I know that you and Mark Breaking up has put you under serious strain, but they are already forty grand in the hole with the marketing campaign which has had to be pushed back twice now. As well as that it's…'

'What?'

'Well, the fact is that although the first book sold well, Moonlight Shadows barely scraped enough to cover the distribution costs.'

'They put me head to head with J.K Rowling. It was a bad release date.'

'You and I know that but they don't see it that way. They paid you an advance for three books and only have two. And are already losing money on the third. They want this one finished and in print whilst they can still make money off your name.'

'That makes me feel loved.'

'Forget love. This is business and like it or not it's the nature of the game. I just want to help you to get back on track here ok?'

'You think I don't?' she barked, cheeks flushed with anger. She instantly regretted her outburst. If he was offended, Bob didn't show it.

'Hey look, I'm on your side here. I told them you would turn the book in, and they would have nothing to worry about but they kept pressuring me for a deadline.'

She didn't like the way this conversation was going. She sensed that she was about to hear something she wouldn't like.

'I know my damn deadline, Bob. You told me. Three weeks.'

There was an awkward silence whilst Bob chose his words.

'That was the old deadline. I had to act Terri, believe me, I did my best for you.'

'Spit it out Bob.'

You have until Monday to turn it in; otherwise, they are terminating your contract and will start legal proceedings against you for loss of earnings.'

Fear and anger erupted within her. She was squeezing the handset so hard that her knuckles had turned white.

'How the hell could you let this happen? I thought you were on my side!'

'I am on your side Terri, and if you had any idea what I had to go through to delay this then you would be a little more grateful.'

'Grateful? Grateful? You don't get it do you, Bob? It's not that I won't write, I can't write right now, my fucking head is in pieces!'

Silence apart from the steady sound of Bob's breathing on the other end of the phone. He spoke calmly, trying to reassure her.

'I understand that but it's not just your ass on the line anymore here Terri. Do you have any idea what I have had to sacrifice for you? It's not for the pay check; let me make that clear from the start. And it certainly isn't for the stress it puts me under.'

'Then why do it, Bob. Why not cut me loose like everyone says you should?' she was desperately trying to keep her voice from wavering.

'I do it because I have faith in you. I'm doing the best I can for you, and that's regardless of my twenty per cent fee.'

Her anger dispersed, and she realised that it wasn't Bob's fault. The blame fell at the feet of that sham of a woman in the mirror, the twenty nine year old, red haired, green-eyed girl from upstate New York who dreamed of making a living as a writer and living a happy life with the man she loved, and yet here she was. Unable to write, on the verge of being dropped by her publisher and completely alone in the world. She closed her eyes.

What a mess.

'Hey Terri, are you going to be ok?' Bob asked.

She was crying now, unable to help herself

'I'll be fine; it's just... a lot to take in right now.'

'I understand, believe me, I do. I'd come over and see you in person, but I'm out of town right now meeting with another client.'

'That's ok Bob. I understand. I don't know where I'd be without you.'

'Look I told you before, you are a great writer. You just need to push everything aside and churn out the words. Now bullshit aside, how much do you have left to write?'

'The last three chapters.' She said with a sigh.

'Ok, that's doable. You have until Monday. Today is Tuesday. You have plenty of time.'

'It's not the time I'm worried about, it's the writing itself. I don't know what to do.'

'Look, let's just get it done. Wing it, re-hash it, make it

up. Hell plagiarise it if you have to, just hand something in on Monday and we can get this one behind us. After that, take a break and recharge your batteries. Maybe take a vacation.'

'I can't do that, it wouldn't be right.'

Bob laughed then, a hearty sound that made her smile despite her woes.

'I was only half serious anyway. Look I have to go. I have a damn meeting that's due to start in twenty minutes and traffic will be hell. Seriously, though, do yourself a favour. Lock the door, take the phone off the hook, sit in front of the computer and write. I know you have it in you.'

'I'll do my best Bob. You have my word. Thanks for calling. And sorry for being such a bitch.'

He chuckled again and she felt better.

'Don't worry about it. I'll drop by on Monday and pick up the pages ok?'

'I can just as easily email them to you. It's not the dark ages.'

'I know that, but I'm passing through anyway and want to check in on you. We agents aren't all the devil's spawn you know.'

Now it was her turn to laugh, it was a sound she hadn't

made for some time and it made her feel good.

'Ok, point taken. I'll see you Monday when you pick up your rehashed, plagiarised pages.'

'I look forward to it. Take care Terri.'

She smiled again as he hung up the phone, and thought about how she was going to finish her book. One thing was for sure, she would have to cancel her meeting with Jane. She had a lot to do and would need to get started straight away. She grabbed her phone and sent another text to Jane skimming over the details of her conversation with Bob. Then she Switched off the phone, walked to her computer and powered it on, watching as the screen illuminated.

'Now then my old friend. It's time you and I did some work.' she said to her empty apartment. Despite the dramas of the morning, she felt strangely optimistic. Perhaps his wake up call was what she needed to kick start her on the road to normality. She forgot all about the red velvet box on the table and delved into her work.

TWO

Steve Reynolds had worked as a delivery driver for

CASHCO for over seventeen years. He was considered amongst his colleagues as one of the most experienced men in the fleet, and although he didn't make much of a fuss about it, he secretly liked the attention. He drove the huge, snarling cherry red eighteen-wheeler down Grove Street, one tattooed arm leaning casually out of the window. He turned left and changed gear, heading up the steep hill at Grove Lane, remembering the previous winter when the hill was covered in sheet ice and said to be impossible to climb. He had made it, though, coaxing his truck, which he had nicknamed Stella after his Second wife up, over the crest, and on to his destination. As the truck ascended in low gear, it briefly protested with a throaty growl of its Ford Engine. He stifled back a yawn and began to fiddle with the radio tuner, looking for something other than the stream of modern Pop music that seemed to fill the airwaves these days. He missed the days of Real music, rockabilly or country, something with a real groove. He glanced into his rear-view mirror, wincing at his reflection. The young twenty-something year old who first sat in this cab was long gone, and the grizzled grey haired man with the scar on his lip and heavily lined skin had at some point snuck in and replaced him.

Finally, his scanning of the radio frequencies was complete, and he settled on KWLM East, who always played the good stuff. Johnny Cash was on now, crooning about spending time in Folsom Prison. Steve had to admit, he thought many of today's modern musicians could learn a lot from the man in black. As he crested the hill, the road was straight for a few yards, and then rolled steeply down and to the right, at the bottom of which he would turn left at the McDonalds on the corner, and then take a right and pull into the loading Bay of Emmett's Wholesalers, where he would deliver his full load of cane sugar and canned tomatoes. After that, it would be a quick drive back the depot and the start of his two-week vacation.

He set off down the hill, allowing the vehicle to coast as he always did, saving a little fuel in the process. This was one of his regular runs, at least twice a month he would drive the same route and was somewhat on autopilot when the accident happened. Later, there was speculation he lost control, or that he was drunk at the wheel, but Steven had been alcohol free for over seven years. His colleagues wouldn't even entertain the notion of him losing control. They knew how good he was.

It would be later, during the inquest that Steven would

be cleared of any wrongdoing. The fault had been with the truck itself, Steve's pride and joy, Stella. The same truck he had been driving since he got the job, the truck that on numerous occasions he had refused to trade in for a more modern model. Perhaps if he had done so the brake line wouldn't have sheared loose as Steve had tried to slow his descent in order to make the turn off onto Cabal Lane.

With no means to slow down, the eighteen-wheeler was a thirty-five ton missile. Even at the end, it was his supreme driving skill that had saved many lives, even though his own and that of Jean Steen would be lost. He had wrestled with the Truck, narrowly missing a class full of school children out on a day trip, and somehow avoiding the customers eating lunch outside Sam's, one of his favourite burger joints. The truck ploughed into the brick wall between the Good cup Coffeehouse and the town library at over sixty miles an hour. Not wearing a seatbelt, something that was an old habit from the eighties, Steve was thrown through the windscreen and later had to be identified by his fingerprints. The unfortunate pedestrian just happened to be in the wrong place at the wrong time, and having just received a Text message from her good friend Terri

Browning cancelling their planned meeting for coffee, was on her way home. She might have even heard it coming, but as was her habit when she was walking, she was listening to her iPod and had it turned up loud as the truck crushed her against the wall. She never heard the warnings or the desperate honking of the trucks horn as he tried to signal to her to move. Killed instantly, Jane would never Hear about the Mystery box Left on Terri's Doorstep. Nor would she see her daughter, Mia, who was at school, expecting to be picked up later that day. By a bizarre twist of fate brought on by the arrival of a strange hand delivered Box, Terri's best friend of Twenty-two years was dead.

3.

She was unsure if it were Bob's words or the fact she was on the verge of losing her career, but for the last six hours Terri had been sitting at her computer, and for the first time in weeks was writing. On a roll, she had reached that magical place where the story was writing itself, and she was no more than a passenger, hurriedly trying to keep up with the ideas as they formed in her head. This was the feeling she loved—the joy of pure creation. She had breezed through two chapters and was well into the third and final one to meet her deadline when there was a knock at the door.

Blinking away the tiredness, she checked her watch and was shocked to see it was just after five. Now, with the spell of writing broken she was aware of her body. She was hungry and needed to pee. She wasn't expecting any visitors and was crossing to the door when she froze at the muffled voice as it shouted through the letterbox.

'Terri, it's me, are you there?'

It was Mark.

She couldn't face him, not now when she had finally been able to get some work done. She debated staying silent and hoping that he would go away, but she knew him. He was persistent and although the last thing she needed was to deal with him now, she would rather speak to him and get it over with than have to explain the commotion to Mrs Molde, who she suspected would already be shuffling her way towards the hallway and hoping for a show. With a sigh of resignation, she opened the door, hating herself for the way her heart raced as she saw him.

Mark Fife was coping with the separation better than she was. He looked to have come straight from the office and was dressed in the grey suit she had bought him for Christmas. He was tanned, and she noticed that he had cut his hair, his previous long fringed style replaced for a buzz cut, which she saw with dismay, only emphasised his chiselled features. His eyes were blue, and he flashed her that winning smile, the one that was always able to make her forgive him.

'I hoped you would be home, I wanted to drop by. Can I come in?'

'Now isn't a good time Mark.'

'Look, I have something I need to discuss with you, and I'd rather not do it out here in the hallway.' He motioned to his left with his eyes, and as Terri looked out of the door, she could see Mrs Molde, standing and stroking her ginger cat as she watched with a prune-sucking look of disapproval etched onto her old hag face.

'You have two minutes,' she said, before heading back inside. Mark followed, closing the door behind him and denying Mrs Molde the opportunity of gaining some new gossip to share with the rest of her coven. Terri stood by the window, arms folded as Mark looked about the room as if he were seeing it for the first time. She knew she would need to be careful. She was determined not to allow him back into her life.

'The place looks…Barren.' He said as he flicked his gaze towards her and sat on the couch, putting his foot on the coffee table.

'I like the minimalistic look. What do you want?'

'How have you been?'

She felt anger rising and quashed it. She wouldn't give him the satisfaction.

'I'm fine; I was working when you disturbed me.'

'Good, I'm happy for you.'

Here it comes she thought to herself as he looked at her. She broke eye contact, trying to ignore the flutter caused by his stare.

'I want to come back, Terri. We were good together.'

'Jesus Mark, not this again.'

'Look I know what I did was stupid, and you know I'm sorry. We both know you need me.'

'I don't need you Mark, and I don't want you. If this is all you wanted to talk about, you have wasted your time.'

He stood and approached her, trying to grab her by the shoulders.

'Get your fucking hands off me!' Spat Terri, shoving him away from her.

'Hey take it easy.' He said flashing her his best puppy dog eyes.

'Just get out of here Mark. This is my place. My life. It doesn't involve you anymore, not since you fucked that whore!'

'Hey come on, I told you I'm sorry! Alicia meant nothing to me. I was confused. How many times do I have to say it?'

'Just get out of here. I don't have time for this.'

He grinned and sat on the couch.

'No.'

'What do you mean no?'

'I mean no. this is my apartment, Terri. I gave you time to get over what happened, but if you won't take me back then it's you that is going to have to leave.'

'I can't believe you have the nerve. This all happened because of you.' she said.

'Look, I'm not trying to be a dick here, Terri, it's just that you know you need me, and it doesn't make sense for us to live apart like this.'

She strode across to the door, opening it so forcefully that its handle dented the plaster as it slammed into the wall.

'Just go, get out of here!'

He stood, brushing the creases out of his suit.

'You had your chance Terri, and I did my best to make you see sense.'

'Out!' she raged.

'Hey relax, I'm going' replied Mark, holding his hands up as he sidestepped her.

'Don't forget that box of your crap either. I don't want you coming here again.'

She kicked the box by her feet, watching as he picked it up and backed out of the door.

'This isn't over Terri. I want you out of my place. Don't make me take things further. You know what I can do.'

She did know. Mark was a lawyer and had many slimy friends in the legal profession. Lawyers she could never hope to be able to afford. He even knew a few less than straight judges who would ensure that he didn't lose if he decided to take things further.

'That's right, kick me when I'm down you son of a bitch. You know I have nowhere to go.'

'Then forgive me and we can put this behind us. You know it makes sense.'

'I wouldn't have you back if you were the last man on earth. Even if it means I have to sleep on the damn streets. I hate you.'

He flashed that winning grin again and shrugged his shoulders.

'Your loss Terri. I want you out by the end of the month.'

She wanted to scream a barrage of abuse at him but restrained herself. She was unwilling to give him the satisfaction. Instead, she slammed the door closed, not caring if Mrs Molde heard. She leaned on the door and was doing all she could to hold back the flood of tears that were threatening to overspill when she saw the box on the table. Fuelled by a fresh wave of rage, she stormed across the room, snatched the box of the table and then opened the door, stepping out into the hallway. He was still there, waiting for the elevator.

'And you can top sending this shit to me too!' She raged and was about to throw it when she saw the bemused look on his face.

'I didn't send you anything. That's not from me.'

Feeling foolish, she held onto the box and watched as the elevator chimed to herald its arrival. Mark stepped in, and then poked his head out of the door.

'I meant what I said, Terri. End of the month.'

The elevator chimed and the doors closed leaving Terri standing alone in the hallway.

FOUR

Back in her sanctuary, her anger and upset were replaced by curiosity at the red velvet covered box. She sat on the couch and set the box on the coffee table. She didn't like the feel of the velvet on her fingertips. It felt fleshy and slick and somehow alive. Without realising, she wiped her hands on her jeans. She didn't like the box and had the strange sensation it was watching her just as she was watching it. She knew it was ridiculous of course. It was no more than her writers over active imagination, making the most of being stirred back to life. She didn't believe in the odd. Of Wet things that go bump in the night or unseen beasts crawling in the darkness. But something about this situation concerned her. She knew she was never going to find out what was inside without opening it and seeing for herself. And told herself that the doom mongering was both silly and inefficient. She reached out, lifted off the velvet lid, and looked inside.

Inside was another box. This one made of wood with a hinged lid. She removed it, reminded of Russian Matryoshka stacking dolls.

Box in a box in a box.

She set this new smaller box down. It looked to be made of birch or pine and the faint odour of old polish reached her nostrils. Other than the hinged lid, it had no other significant markings. She realised that she had been holding her breath, and as she let it out, wondered why her heart was beating so fast and why she still couldn't shake that horrible, anxious feeling of doom which was still wriggling around in her stomach. Chewing her lip, she reached out to the box and opened it, half expecting something to leap out and grab her. It took a moment for her brain to process what she saw.

The box contained a button.

It was surrounded in the same red velvet as the outer box and was circular with a red top. Below, printed in red on a white background was an instruction of sorts. It comprised of just two simple words.

Erase All.

She leaned forward to take a closer look and saw a small folded piece of paper tucked into the underside of the lid. She fished it out, anxious not to touch the button itself. The note had been hand typed. She could see the imperfections where the ink hadn't printed onto the paper. She read the four lines and then read them again.

Terri.
This button does exactly as it says.
When you feel like you have had enough,
Simply press it and everything will go away.

She turned the box on the table. There were no wires, no battery compartments and no visible means of powering it. She shook her head, wondering if she were the victim of a very elaborate practical joke. She tried to think which of her friends would do something like this to try and raise her spirits. The more she considered it, the more names she was able to tick off the list until it was empty. She decided that she would call Jane and ask her advice, as well as apologise for standing her up earlier.

Why not just press it?

She paused as the thought popped into her head and hovered there, waiting for a response. It was a good question. Of course, she didn't believe that anything would happen and yet there was the great 'what if' factor, which her writer's imagination had already twisted into spectacular scenarios of what might happen if she pressed the innocent looking red button. Without taking her eyes from the box, she took her phone out of her pocket. She had switched it off earlier in the day as per Bob's suggestion, and now as she powered it back up. She glanced at the Blackberry's display. Her stomach vaulted as she saw the twelve missed calls and six voicemails that had been left. She glanced at the box, and the box looked back.

FIVE

She hadn't slept. As she stood in front of the bathroom mirror a little after five in the morning, at the time when the dark of the night and coming of the new day are balanced perfectly, she forced herself to look past the dark rings under her bloodshot eyes, and to ignore the pale blue-white hue of her complexion. She tried to look within herself and find a way to pull herself together.
If I were a man, I would be starting a pretty good beard by now.
The thought made no sense, and its randomness

frightened her. She felt as if she were clinging onto her sanity only by her fingertips. She closed her eyes, trying to rid her brain of the memory of the anguished voicemails left by Jane's mother informing Terri of her death. They were words she thought would haunt her forever, as would the guilt and the huge void that would be left behind in her life. Unable to stand to look at herself any longer, she walked to the balcony, unlocking and sliding the door open in the hope that the air would clear her head. It was wonderfully quiet, and as she watched a contrail of an airliner arcing across the sky, she wished that she were on board, heading anywhere as long as it was far away. Looking at the streets below, she marvelled at how peaceful it was. Traffic was sparse, and aside from a few individuals heading off to start the working day early, it was graveyard quiet. She wondered for a split second if the world would miss her if she climbed over the balcony and jumped. Would it hurt? Would she feel pain in the instant of death? She shivered at the chill breeze and tried to shake off the morbid train of thought.

Heading back inside, Terri was surprised to see the answering machine blinking, signalling a new message. She hadn't heard the phone ring and wondered if she might have dozed off during the night without realising. She crossed to the machine and played back the message.

'Terri, its Bob. I uh, I'm not sure what time it is there, damn time zones always confuse me. Anyway, just letting you know that this meeting was a damn waste of time, and I'm heading back early. I'll swing by your place in around six hours, which will be somewhere between eleven and one your time, so if you could have me those new pages ready I'll take them with me and try to buy us more time. I'll see you soon, bye.'

She managed a small smile and switched on her computer. As it whirred and clicked into life, she made herself a fresh pot of coffee and decided that she would at least try to appear human despite everything that had happened. Once the coffee was ready, she returned to the computer, opening the latest draft of her novel, selected the new pages, and sent them to print. As the printer began to churn out her pages, she scrolled to the bottom of the document, and the half-complete Chapter fifteen. She looked at the blank page and because she knew sleep would not come to her again that night, she might as well at least try to do some work if only to forget the horrors of the real world for a while. First, though she had to make herself at least appear human. She couldn't allow Bob to see her in her current state. It was bad enough that there was a concern for her wellbeing without anyone seeing her current ghoul like appearance and adding more fuel to the fire. Knowing she would get no work done until the printer silenced and that there were still over seventy pages still to be churned out, she decided to shower and get dressed, then settle down to try and finish the final chapter. Thirty minutes later and feeling better, Terri went to the now silent Hewlett Packard and picked up the pages, skimming through them to make sure they were in good order. Often she was unsure about the quality of her work, but on rare occasions, when she knew she had been in the zone the results were better. These pages fell into that category. She placed her work into a brown envelope and set it on the table for when Bob arrived. Her eyes drifted to the wooden box, and that awful cold simmering feeling churned deep within her. With a frown, she returned attention to her computer, grimacing at the screensaver and making a mental note to change it. It was a slideshow of photographs of her and Mark during happier times. Laughing together, holding hands on the beach in Hawaii during their holiday. Various other snapshots of a dead relationship. She realised that she no longer had anything in common with the happy and smiling woman on the screensaver images. She couldn't stand to look at it anymore and moved the mouse, breaking the cycle of images

Her brain didn't at first register what she was looking at.

The page had been blank when she headed off to shower but that was no longer the case. Now there were words written on the page. Words she had not put there. Until that point, she hadn't experienced fear, not real, raw fear anyway. But as she looked at the pixels on the screen and felt her flesh crawl and her stomach flutter. She knew this was the terror that writers like her tried to convey to their readers, but knew now she had never even come close to accurately describing the feeling. Her mouth began to water and for a second she thought she was going to vomit, but somehow she managed to keep control of her gorge. She let her eyes drift across the words, so innocent in their composition, yet at the same time horrifically sinister.

Terri.
Don't let the world get you down.

You know what to do to make it all go away.

She reached to the outlet with a hand she couldn't stop from shaking and pulled the plug on the computer, plunging the phantom words on the screen into darkness. She couldn't breathe and imagined that the walls were closing in on her. Her skin was cold with gooseflesh and she had the sick sensation she was being watched. She turned on her seat and looked at the Box on the table, and in her mind, she imagined it was looking right back at her with a sick, sharp-toothed smile. Unable to hold it back anymore, she vomited onto the carpet.

SIX

The park was bathed in mid-afternoon sunshine as Terri fidgeted on the wooden bench. Still shaken, she couldn't stand to be in the apartment anymore. She felt as if it had secret, hidden eyes and was watching her every move. She had convinced herself that it was the smell of her ejecta, which still lingered despite opening every window and spraying a full can of air freshener that had caused her to vacate, yet knew deep down it was none of these things. It was the box. She didn't want to be near it. It seemed to her to have a very real presence. It was as if the atmosphere around it was heavy and thick and charged with some kind of unseen power. She had called Bob and asked him to meet her here instead of the apartment and informed him she had his pages ready to pick up.

Minus a few extra words I didn't write.

She thought to herself as she sipped her Starbucks. She was watching a young couple tossing a Frisbee for their enthusiastic Alsatian who chased it with determination. She enjoyed coming here. It was her haven against the harsh brutality of the city. The park itself was two acres of lush green, ringed by a path which was often populated by early morning joggers in their garish shades of luminescent spandex. Large birch and oak trees lined the outer side of the park, offering cool shade from the heat of the day. Bees hurried about their pollination duties, and the numerous species of birds seemed to be joined in endless song. Terri had always liked it here. She conceived and roughly formed the entirety of her first novel on the very bench where she now sat. She remembered the pure joy of that day, of knowing she had stumbled onto a good idea and furiously fleshing out the scenes on her notepad, developing the characters, refining the plot. By the time she had finished writing, her wrist had ached and her eyes were tired, but she had an outline which would remain mostly unchanged from the final manuscript save for a couple of small edits at Bob's suggestion. She didn't like to come here during public holidays, as it was crammed with bodies fighting for picnic space on the grass. Days like this, though, midweek days when most people were out doing their nine to five jobs, she was grateful that she had the freedom to choose her own working hours. She looked up and saw Bob striding down the pathway towards her. He had removed his jacket and was carrying over his shoulder, three fingers hooked into the collar. He was covered in a light sweat as he sat beside her.

'Damn hot today,' he remarked, wiping his brow with his handkerchief.

'Tell me about it.'

She handed him the coffee she had brought him, and waited until he had added sugar and placed the plastic lid back on the cup. She was debating whether to tell Bob about the box and decided that under the present circumstances, it was a bad idea. There was a comfortable silence as they both sipped their drinks and watched the Frisbee loving Alsatian run back and forth with its owners. It was Bob who was first to speak.

'How are you holding up Terri?'

*Not bad, apart from the psychological torture I'm being subjected to*

'Not bad.' she said, neglecting to add the rest of her thought. 'How about you?'

She had said it only because it was protocol when someone asked after your health. She didn't expect the answer she received.

'I'm not great if I'm honest.'

She looked at him and saw that like her, he had tried to hide his fragile state with a show of normality. Terri's heart sank a little for Bob.

'Why, what's wrong?'

'It's Marge. She. She's not doing too well right now.'

He fingered his wedding band nervously, then realising he was doing so, folded his hands into fists and set them on his knees.

'Is she sick?'

He looked at her, no longer able to hide the sadness in his eyes.

'She's dying, Terri.'

She wasn't sure how to react and was fumbling for the right words to say when he continued.

'Damn Alzheimer's. She hardly even knows who I am anymore.'

'Bob, I had no idea. You never mentioned it.'

'It wasn't something we wanted to make public knowledge. I always hoped she would recover, that maybe she would be different but…well over the last six months she has deteriorated.'

'Bob I'm so sorry' she said, placing a reassuring hand on his shoulder. She could see he was fighting back tears as he opened up to her, this being one of the few conversations between them that didn't revolve around business.

'I thought I could cope with it, I mean she's only fifty one for God's sake, I thought she might have the strength to pull through. It—It's the blank stares that are the worst. The way she looks at me sometimes and doesn't even know who I am. Let me tell you, Terri, there is nothing more heartbreaking than that.' He said with a dejected shrug of the shoulders.

'Why didn't you ask someone for help?'

'I'm not sure. Stubbornness maybe? It was my problem

to deal with. I sometimes wonder if someone up there hates Me.' he said, rolling his eyes skyward.

'Twenty seven years we have been married. Can you imagine someone you have shared so much with suddenly not knowing who you are? She called me Martin the other day. Martin was my brother; he died when he was a boy. I… I don't think I can take this anymore.'

I wonder Bob if you had an Erase button, would you push it right now? And— here is the million-dollar question— if you did what would happen?

'Look, Bob, I don't know what to tell you. Marge has always been kind to me, and I'm sure you have done your best to look after her, but maybe it's time to get some help?'

'I know I should, but to tell you the truth, I'm a little embarrassed. I couldn't cope if I lost her Terri. I can't be alone.'

'Look, why don't you take the advice you gave me. Have some time off work, recharge the batteries. You look like you need it.'

He snorted, shaking his head. 'Unlikely. I'm up to my neck and I'm struggling to keep up. I have always prided myself on being able to do more, push harder than everyone else in my field, but I don't know if I can do it anymore.'

Unable to hold them back any longer; his tears broke free, rolling down his round cheeks and collecting in his beard. Terri felt deep sorrow for Bob and helplessness that there was nothing she could do to make him feel better.

'Look, Bob, I didn't mean to contribute to your stress, I am doing my best to finish the book I really am.'

'No no no no,' he said, managing a smile as he wiped his eyes.

'Really, you are one of the few writers I'm proud to have on my books, and I really do mean that. I know you haven't had a great time of it yourself Terri, and no amount of makeup and hairspray can hide the exhaustion in your face. Something is troubling you isn't it?'

She almost told him then, about the box, about the writing appearing on her computer screen but didn't want to burden him.

'Not really,' she lied. 'It's just that on top of everything else with the book and Mark, one of my friends was killed in a traffic accident yesterday.'

'I'm sorry. Were you close?'

'Really close, it's kinda hit me for six if I'm honest.'
'Life has a strange sense of humour sometimes doesn't it?'
It did. She didn't doubt it. She decided to change the mood, perhaps give Bob something a little more positive to think about. She picked up the envelope containing the manuscript pages and handed it to Bob.
'Here you go. Two chapters finished and ready for the ruthless editor's pen.' She said, and even managed a smile.
'Thanks, Terri. I knew you could do it...' he already seemed more in control as he opened the envelope and leafed through the pages.
'This is good... really good. It should get those pricks in the office off our backs, at least for a while.'
'I should have the final chapter for you in a day or two. In truth, I can't wait to finish it.'
'That great Terri, I appreciate you coming through for me with this.'
The relief was as evident on his face as it was in his voice.
'Same applies Bob. You just make sure you take care of yourself, and please see someone about some help with Marge.'

'I'd say I will just to please you, but you know me too well. I think she is beyond help, and I don't want her to spend her last months in some sterile hospital bed. I appreciate the concern, though, I really do.'

She hugged him then, and he awkwardly returned the gesture.

'Look, Bob, I have to go, I have some errands to run before I knuckle down and do some work.'

Unless somebody has done some for you whilst you were away

She ignored her inner monologue as she stood, Bob following suit.

'I have to be on my way too. I have to get back to the office and send these pages across, and traffic will be hell soon. I'll be in touch in a few days. You take care of yourself, Terri.'

She nodded and smiled, then tossed her empty coffee cup in the wire waste bin by the bench.

'You too, I'm sure things will pick up soon. They say bad luck goes in cycles.'

'You know what I was thinking Terri?' asked Bob with a haunted and reflective expression on his face.

'What?'

'I was thinking that if there was a way to go back in

time and start things from scratch, I would take it in a heartbeat.'

It was an innocent sentence, the words meant reflectively, but inside Terri screamed. Her reply was automatic, and her split second of horror didn't appear to have registered with Bob.

'I think we all wish that sometimes. You take care, and give my best to Marge.'

She turned and left, fearing that if she stayed he would see through her and know there was something wrong. Fighting back tears of her own, she glanced over her shoulder to see Bob standing by the park bench, finishing his coffee. She hoped that if there were a greater power; that they would spare Bob from his misery. He was one of the good ones and deserved a break.

SEVEN

The I55 highway stretched out in front of the Silver Mercedes as it made its way towards Seattle. Bob had the window cranked open, and was enjoying the cooling breeze as he made good time through traffic. Although still upset, he was happy to have met with

Terri, and because he had no children of his own, already thought of her in some way like a Daughter. He was pleased to see that the road was surprisingly clear, and accelerating to a steady sixty-two miles an hour, he activated the cruise control and took his foot off the pedal, allowing the car to do the work. Sunlight glinted off the traffic in the oncoming lane, which was far more congested than the relative clear run that Bob was enjoying.

Glancing over to the envelope containing Terri's manuscript pages on the passenger seat, he picked them up and began to scan through them, making sure to check the road ahead every few seconds for potential problems. He was happy for her that she had managed to get herself together and get some work done. He would never tell her, but he saw she had great potential. He had over the years, read some great work by some fantastic authors, but she was definitely up there with the very best.  The idea of presenting a fourth book to her had been manifesting away for some time, and yet he couldn't find the right way to approach the subject, especially as she was going through a tough time herself at the moment.

He felt a migraine sluggishly begin to form, a thick

heaviness behind his eyes, which made him feel nauseous. His last rational thought was that he hoped to get back to the office in time before the headache got worse when an agonising pain surged through him, causing him to spasm and kick out his feet and depress the accelerator as the car veered over the reservation and into the oncoming traffic, where it met head-on with a school bus travelling in the opposite direction. The impact was violent, the crumpled Mercedes rolling several times across the highway. The traffic behind the bus began to swerve to avoid the devastating knock on effects of the accident, but the closing speed was too great, and two other cars ploughed into Bob's car, which erupted in flames as it came to a twisted stop on its side. Bob was already dead when the impact happened; killed by the Brain Aneurysm which he had carried with him for the last seven years without knowing it was there. As the flames took a hold of the car, and Bob's body began to burn, his dead hand released its grip on the envelope containing the manuscript pages, which fell and was engulfed in flames.

# EIGHT

The bottle of Smirnoff was already three quarters empty, and yet Terri still didn't feel like she was drunk enough. She was slouched on the couch, watching the news with glassy, half-closed eyes. They had been circulating reports of Bob's accident all evening. She swigged from the bottle and looked at the T.V images of the twisted and blackened wreckage of the crash site shot from overhead by a helicopter. Every time Bob's picture came up on the screen fresh floods of tears would fall from her sore and tired eyes, and she would take another drink to numb the pain. She had never been much of a drinker and didn't have the tolerance for it. On the occasions when she and Mark would go out together, she often felt tipsy after just a couple of glasses of wine.

She glared at the box, still sitting on the coffee table and she still imagined that it was a living thing. She thought if it were able, it would be smiling smugly right now.

Don't be stupid Terri. It's just a box.

The thought process felt detached and alien, and even despite the fuzzy alcohol induced state, she was aware enough to feel a flash of concern for her sanity.

'This is all your fault,' she whispered under her breath as she took another long drink, unsure if she were referring to the box, herself or Mark. She turned her attention back to the television, concentrating hard to bring it into focus. Now her picture was on screen, the horrible publicity shot from her first book. Even though she was watching without sound, she knew what the report was saying. It had been the same for the last few hours, repeating and re-repeating the same information as they awaited fresh morsels of knowledge to trickle through.

'Free advertising. Thanks, Bob.' She slurred, taking another swig of the vodka. She was tired now but knew she wouldn't sleep. It was as if the instant her head touched the pillow she became awake, dwelling on her thoughts, running through scenarios in her mind. She couldn't remember the last time she slept. She was tired of stalking around the house in the dark, wondering from place to place, not knowing what to do with herself. She had lost the two people closest to her in consecutive days and knew she couldn't handle much more.

Push the damn button then.

She was in the habit of dismissing her ever-bolder inner monologue, but on this occasion, she hesitated. What harm could it do? It probably wouldn't do anything anyway and she would have spent the last few days stressing over nothing. But something in her wouldn't let her go through with it. The box didn't feel like a cheap trick or a hoax. Although she still wasn't sure why she felt that there was a genuine sense of some kind of power attached to it. She decided that pushing the button should be a decision best saved for when she was sober.

'There I go again,' she whispered to the television screen as she saw her smiling promo photo. She felt herself sliding into the comforting arms of her drink-induced state as she fell asleep.

She dreamed.

Dreamed of the end of the world. Of cities burning, the earth becoming wiped clean. Buildings flattened, billions simply... erased from existence. The oceans were drained. In the end, all that remained was a barren globe of brown rock, and of course her. Terri Browning standing alone on a barren plateau, the box in her hand, button depressed between her thumbs. She could see faces. Faces of the dead. Jane, with her face misshapen and stitched together like a macabre Jigsaw. She saw her cancer-ridden mother, no more than a hollow skin covered skull. And she saw Bob, now no more than a shapeless thing, blackened and scorched. They were not alone. Countless other shadowy beings she couldn't make out lingered in the background. They were all chanting to her.

Push the button, push the button, push the button…

She awoke with a jolt, a short yelp escaping her lips as she knocked the almost empty vodka bottle to the floor, where it spilt onto the rug. She was aware of the searing headache and dry feeling in her throat. Checking her watch, she saw it was just after four in the morning. The room was illuminated by the flickering of the television, which had, for now, tired of showing Bob's accident coverage and was instead showing the weather for the coming day. She had hoped that her dream would fade away like nightmares often do but this one stayed fresh in her mind, the vividness even worse now she was awake. Her first hangover since college was the last thing she needed. Later that day was Jane's funeral, and although she couldn't bear to face it, she would never forgive herself if she didn't go. Ignoring the Smirnoff induced dizziness and headache, she dragged herself to her feet, flashing the box a quick glare as she staggered to the bathroom, then to her bed where she collapsed into the welcoming covers and fell into a deep sleep, this time thankfully dreamless.

## NINE

Awoken by the steady pounding which she thought was her headache, she realised that there was someone at the door. Sunlight streamed through the windows now, which only served to increase the intensity of the pain which vibrated in her skull, and which even with a decent sleep was vicious. Every time she moved, a fresh wave of nausea swept over her and as she dragged herself out of bed, she wondered what life would throw at her today. She unlocked the door with clumsy hands which didn't feel like they belonged to her and swung it open, silencing the persistent knocking. It was Mark. He had opened his mouth to speak and then saw how dishevelled she looked.

'Jesus Terri, what the hell happened to you?'

She had no strength left to fight him and motioned for him to come in. He had his suitcase, the one on wheels she had bought him to replace the tired old sports bag he used to carry. Striding into the room and dragging the case behind him he turned to look at her, a look of genuine concern on his face.

'Talk to me, tell me what's wrong?'

As much as she hated to show him weakness, she couldn't help herself and began to sob. He held her in her arms and although she initially tried to fight, she gave in, enjoying the safe and familiar feeling of being in his arms.

'I just saw the news about Bob and came right over.'

He was stroking her hair, and she hated herself for allowing herself to be so weak. In the end, it had come down to need. He was all she had left, her cheating lowlife boyfriend.

'Let's stop this nonsense, Terri. Let me come back and ill help you through this, we can do it together.'

She was starting to believe his soothing words, and realised that she couldn't last on her own; she had tried and failed miserably. Burying herself deeper into his chest she allowed him to keep up the sweet talk, for the first time in what seemed like forever she felt warm. She felt safe.

'We don't need to be like this with each other baby. Come on; let's put this behind us.'

She looked up at him then, and before she could stop herself, she was kissing him. He responded, and before she realised what was happening they were in the bedroom, joined in frenzied lovemaking. Later as she watched him dress, she realised that she had made a huge mistake and hated herself for it. She felt ashamed, and a sense of failure that despite her best efforts to be strong, he had won. She couldn't entirely blame him of course. It was an act of need for her as much as anything, a longing to be loved by anyone, even if she did still hate him.

'I have to run baby, or I'm going to miss my flight.'

'Where are you going, I thought you said you were staying with me?' she said, unable to keep the panic out of her voice and hating herself for it.

'I have a business trip to Rio; I can't get out of it.'

She nodded, too drained to get into any kind of argument. His shoes now tied, he picked up his jacket and shrugged into it.

'If Mr Mashima goes for the deal, then I stand a great chance of becoming a junior partner. I should be back tomorrow night if all goes well.'

She didn't care and now felt even worse for allowing him back into her life as well as her bed.

'I'll see you tomorrow, you take care.' He said, and without another word, he was gone. She waited for the sound of the door closing and feeling used and alone with her life in tatters, she wept.

## TEN

Jane's funeral was held at Shady Oak's cemetery, with a few family and friends in attendance. Her parents had elected to bury her, and although she was devastated by the loss Terri found that she had no tears left to cry. As the casket was lowered into the ground, Terri couldn't get the image out of her mind of the Jane ghost that now haunted her dreams on the rare occasions she was able to sleep. The one with the put-back-together jigsaw face that although resembling the friend she once knew was somehow off, and not quite lining up how it used to. She had gone through the standard pleasantries at the Wake, making polite Smalltalk with people she didn't know who all wanted the author's opinion, and in one awkward case to ask for juicy details about Bob's accident. As time dragged on, and the childhood stories became too much to bear, she made her excuses and went outside.

The air had taken a cold turn, and great rolling clouds of lead grey threatened to unleash its fury. She pulled her jacket around her, thrusting her hands into her pockets as she walked with her head down. Even though it was supposed to be about her saying goodbye to her oldest friend, all that she could think about was the box. The box with the button that could put everything right in the world. As she approached her car, she was surprised to see a man standing beside it waiting for her. He was dressed in a suit that looked like it cost more than the car itself. She put his age at around sixty, and he had fine white hair that shimmered in the wind. His eyes were pale green and had a hardness to them which she didn't like. His face had the unmistakeable waxiness of too many operations in an attempt to maintain his youth, which had resulted in him looking now like some freakishly embalmed cousin of Tutankhamen. She noticed as she approached that he was leaning on an ornate walking stick and noted that even money couldn't buy a person's health.

'Miss Browning' he said curtly as he held out a black gloved hand.

She shook it wearily.

'Yes. And you are?'

'My name is Sykes. I'm here on behalf of Webster & Fisher Publishing house about your current contract.'

'Mr Sykes, this is hardly the time.'

'I do apologise for the timing, however, due to Roberts unfortunate demise the company is anxious to know if you have finished the manuscript as agreed.'

Careful here Terri.

She didn't like the old man. His eyes were keen and sharp, and he seemed poised like a coiled spring. She wasn't sure if she should lie or tell the truth.

'Bob had the pages. He saw them'

'My apologies Miss Browning. I should be clearer. I'm afraid my reason for being here is to inform you that due to the unacceptable delays and cost to the company caused, as a result, we will not be renewing your contract, and would ask that the remaining pages be turned in within forty eight hours as per the arrangements made at the time of signing the contract.'

He reached into his coat and handed her a copy of the contract she had signed two years before.

'Look, this is unnecessary. Bob saw the pages, he took them with him.'

The old man paused and smiled awkwardly. 'Miss browning, I apologise for my directness, but it is the only way I know. The company feels that there are other writers who they wish to pursue, and as a result, we can no longer afford the hefty costs involved with the irregular flow of your work.'

'But they want the pages, you said so yourself!'

'Indeed, but only so that we might recoup some of the heavy losses that we have accrued.'

'Look, Mr Sykes, I know I'm late in turning in the pages, but I'm having a tough time right now, I can still do this.'

'It isn't my position to say if you can or cannot. My duty was to inform you of the timescale for delivery, which to reiterate is forty eight hours from today.'

'Fine, I'll re-print them and post them later today.'

'We would prefer it if you email them, Miss Browning. We wouldn't want them to 'go astray in transit' now would we?'

There was a condescending tone in his voice which made her furious, but she somehow swallowed her rage. She couldn't handle another confrontation.

'Fine, I'll email them over later today.'

'Very good. I look forward to receiving them.'

He walked past her, leaving a smell of soap and expensive aftershave.

'Miss Browning' he said over his shoulder. 'I would advise you to make haste and deliver these pages promptly. My employers would not have any hesitation in taking legal action for breach of contract.'

He left her standing there, furious and in shock. In her head, she could hear the disembodied ghosts of Jane and Bob from her dream.

Push the button, push the button, push the button…

ELEVEN

She usually enjoyed driving. The Blue Lexus was a place where she used to do a lot of thinking about her books, and many ideas had been born within the cars leather seated confines. Usually, she would be listening to a cd, maybe something by Coldplay or if she were feeling particularly nostalgic, she would whip out Meatloaf's greatest hits and croon along to those epic ballads even though her singing voice was atrocious. Today, however, was different. The radio was off and she travelled in silence. She was on the same stretch of road where Bob had been killed, and her mood was sombre. Despite her best efforts to divert them, her thoughts kept coming back to the Box. Although she couldn't entirely blame it for everything that had happened, certainly things had deteriorated since it found its way to her door. She wondered about its origins, where it came from and more importantly why her. She didn't class herself as a celebrity and although she had enjoyed her five minutes of fame, she had kept her feet on the ground and lived a normal life. Of course, the royalties from her first two books meant that she had the luxury of not having to do a nine to five job, but she was far from rich and enjoyed a reasonably comfortable life of anonymity. She moved the car into the outside lane and noted that she was about to pass the scene of Bob's accident. She didn't want to look but couldn't help herself, and although the wreckage had been removed, the evidence was still on the blacktop. Several sets of tire marks were still visible where the vehicles had tried to stop. She stifled a yawn as she passed the macabre crash site, and although she didn't want to, couldn't help a quick glance in the rear-view mirror as she rolled away from it. The burned image of the Bob from her dream appeared in her mind.

'Why don't you push the button and give me my life back?'

Although she had said it out loud to the empty car, she guessed the words might be fitting coming out of the lipless face of dream Bob, the one who wouldn't stop invading her mind and accusing her, blaming her, pointing his blackened and melted stub of a finger at her. She was overcome with the barren feeling of being alone, and despite the fact that she still hated him, she decided to call Mark. She reached over to the glove compartment and tried to find the Bluetooth headset that she kept in there, but it was elusively hiding amongst the road maps and half-eaten packs of sweets. She couldn't remember the last time she had even used it. Her car journeys were usually quiet times without distractions. Frowning, she picked up her phone and pressed the speed dial for Mark's number, balancing the phone between her ear and shoulder so that she could keep both hands on the wheel. She waited, and was about to hang up when the line connected.

'Hello?'

He sounded distracted, preoccupied.

'Hey it's just me, I needed someone to talk to, I'm just on my way home from Jane's funeral. How did the meeting go?'

'It went pretty well actually, I think I'm close to closing the deal. How are you holding up?'

'Not great if I'm honest, I'm afraid to be alone'

With the box

She had almost added but managed to stop herself. She got the impression that her call wasn't exactly welcome, and the idea popped into her brain that he was with another woman.

'Well, I'll be home tomorrow; we can talk about it then.' He replied irritably.

'Tomorrow? I thought you said it wouldn't take long?'

'I'm sorry baby but I have to look after these clients.'

'What about me? I need you to look after me right now'

She hated how weak she must sound, but was now convinced that he was up to no good, and she could almost see the frown on his face as he tried to cover his tracks.

'This could be a big case for me; it will be worth it in the end if Mr Mashima hires me.'

'I'm struggling here, Mark, I need you, I think I'm losing my mind. When will you be home?'

She was crying now, hating that she sounded so needy and whiny.

'I don't know when I'll be home, I may stay in a hotel tonight and head back tomorrow morning.'

She hated him for this but hated herself more for needing him so much.

'Well, I guess I'll see you tomorrow then.' She said, not

hiding the fact that she was upset. Mark either ignored it or didn't notice her dissatisfaction.

'Ok, baby. Ok, love you, bye.'

Before she could respond the line disconnected, and she tossed her phone onto the passenger seat in disgust. She saw a man on the side of the road just ahead. He had the classic unwashed and weathered appearance of the homeless. A scraggly beard which was mostly grey apart from a few stubborn patches of black. He was holding a crudely made cardboard sign, written in black marker pen. She suspected that his chances of anyone stopping to give him a ride were slim, and she certainly did not intend to do so. She could imagine how he would smell, like body odour and cheap wine. He flashed her a gummy grin as he held one hand out to the road, his filthy thumb poking out of a tattered glove. His sign indicated where he wanted to be. It said:

End of the road.

As she passed him, she felt icy fingers dance up her spine. She thought that the place where the old hobo wanted to go was exactly where she felt she was heading.

Maybe you should have stopped for him and you can go together

She wondered if the destitute old man would push the reset button if he had the chance. She was considering doing so herself.


## TWELVE

Against her better judgement she had picked up another bottle of vodka on her way home, and tried to ignore the shame that she knew she would feel when she drank it later. The rain had rolled in, pounding the windows with its maddening patter. For the last two hours, she had been sitting in the near darkness of the apartment staring at the box. How easy it would be just to reach out, flip open the lid and press the button. Something in her, perhaps pride or determination not to give in forced her not to, and so it was a standoff.

She knew that she should at least try to do some work, but every time she thought about powering up the computer, she remembered the message that she had found and wondered what might be waiting for her this time. Nonetheless, she had work to do. And since the weather outside matched her mood, she supposed this was a good a time as any to get the book finished. She hated how it felt to her. The latest book had initially excited her, and she had thought it might be her best yet, but over the last weeks not only had she begun to hate it, she knew that the writing wasn't her best. If she had the time she would almost certainly rewrite it, but even getting through the pages that were finished had been a chore. She felt like Jacob Marley from a Christmas carol. The book had become her chains, and she had been dragging it around for the last year.

She looked at the two evils on her coffee table, the bottle of vodka and the box, and with a surge of determination reminiscent of the old Terri, decided that she wouldn't allow herself to be beaten, not when it was still in her power to put it right. She stood, crossing the room with determination and plugging the computer back in at the wall socket.

What if there is another message?

She considered this and then decided that the obvious answer was the best. If there was something there, she would delete it and then get on with her work, because that was all she knew how to do. It was all she had ever been good at. Terri Browning who may be unlucky in love, and have a weakness in the willpower department, but she could still tell a good fucking story and no adulterous partners or mysterious wooden box were going to stop her. She pressed the circular power button on the computer's silver tower, expecting the familiar sound of the system growling to life, but instead was met with a strained internal chug. Her heart leapt into her mouth as she looked at the monitor, dismayed at the words on the display.

She thought it had said push the button, push the button, push the button, and was about to scream when she blinked and saw that it read something else. Her trusty computer, although recently neglected, but one that had been with her for the last six years, was obviously sick. And was now displaying a blank screen, with the words:

SATA HARD DISK DRIVE FAILURE. PRESS F1 TO CONTINUE OR F2 TO RUN SETUP UTILITY.

She felt sick to her stomach. Her work, her book, her life. Everything was on the computer. Like a slap in the face, it hit her. You have no backup. No hard copy. Are you fucking stupid? What the hell are you going to do now?

 She wasn't particularly computer savvy. She knew how to use Microsoft word, access her emails and use the internet, but that was the extent of her knowledge. She poised her fingers over the keyboard, licking her suddenly dry lips as she considered how to proceed. She pressed the F1 key, hoping that it may allow her to boot into the desktop and retrieve her files. She waited as the computer struggled to process her request, the screen not giving any idea as the success rate of her request. She was met with a new line of text, equally as to the point as the first in the way computers were.

NO BOOT DEVICE FOUND. F1 TO RETRY OR F2 TO RUN SETUP UTILITY.

She already hated this one-sided binary communication with the computer. She wondered if it were getting its own back for her recent neglect. She could imagine it now, speaking to her, chastising her.
You really fucked up now didn't you girl. I bet all that those weeks neglecting me don't feel like such a good idea now do they? No backup? Who doesn't back their work up, especially in your line of work? I bet Sykes is

laughing his wrinkly old ass off right now and already calling the lawyers. They are gonna take you for everything you have and then some. They will own you until the day you die. Why not just push the fucking button and get it over with?

'Shut up!' she croaked to the empty room. Her voice felt too high, like an over tuned guitar string. She pressed the F1 key again, praying that it would work. Again the computer thought about her request and spat back the same message.

NO BOOT DEVICE FOUND. F1 TO RETRY OR F2 TO RUN SETUP UTILITY.

Ha! You don't listen do you, Terri, that's always been your problem. You and I are similar, fucked up on the inside and not functioning properly. Go ahead, keep pressing retry, and I'll keep throwing you back here. This is all your fault anyway, pulling the plug on me without shutting down the correct way. EVERYONE knows that's a no-no. There is only one-way out of this, but you know what that is don't you?

She was shaking now, her cheeks hot with tears. She didn't care. All she cared about was the computer and somehow retrieving her work. She pressed F2, trying to ignore the imagined computer voice in her head. The rain on the windows sounded very loud, she could hear it singing to her, soothing.

Push the button, push the button, push the button...

'Shut up, all of you just shut up!' she shouted at the empty apartment. She knew how crazy she sounded, how crazy the situation was but sometimes crazy felt right. Sometimes crazy fit like a fucking glove. She waited hunched over in the darkness as she listened to the familiar rhythm of the computer's internal clunking and whirring. The sound was not filling her with hope. The next message didn't even give her any helpful options, nor did it suggest any course of action.

CRITICAL ERROR HARD DISK FAILURE.

She pressed the enter key, then the escape key but the message remained unchanged on the screen. Screaming with rage and blinded by tears, she grabbed the computer tower with both hands and picked it up, ignoring the sounds of the keyboard and mouse clattering to the ground, the sounds of the monitor falling and landing screen first on the wooden floorboards. She struggled to her feet, sobbing and carrying the tower awkwardly across the room, its wires and accessories snaking out behind it. She staggered to the balcony door, pulling against the resistance of the power outlet, which hung stubbornly in the wall.

Oh, go ahead; take it out on me again! It's no coincidence that everyone around you dies is it Terri? First Jane, then Bob. Now me. What did I ever do to you, I was always there, always stood by you, and this is the thanks I get?

'SHUT UP! JUST SHUT UP!' she screamed, hurting her throat as the plug pulled free. Sobbing, she fumbled at the door handle, managing to open it. Wind and rain pounded her face as she staggered out, dragging the computer behind her.

What, you are going to throw me off the seventh floor into the street? That won't help the case for your sanity, and we both know there are more than a few question marks over that as is. They are going to lock you up and throw away the key Terri.

'Shut, up! They won't.' she sobbed, blinking rainwater out of her eyes.

And don't even think you can rely on Mark. He knows he can get away with whatever he wants to. Hell, I bet right now whilst you are out here in the rain talking to a box full of wires and circuits, he's balls deep in some older woman because we both know he likes that don't we?'

'Stop it just stop it!' she pleaded as she heaved the tower over the edge of the balcony. She watched as it fell, its tail of wires, keyboard, mouse and monitor fanning out as it smashed into the floor below. Several passers-by looked up and pointed but she didn't care, she was just happy to be rid of it, rid of its maddening voice. She cackled loudly, pounding the air with her fists. It was liberating

She walked back into the apartment shivering from both cold and the exertion and sat on the edge of the sofa. She opened the bottle of vodka, tossing the lid away and taking a large gulping drink, which burned her throat and caused her to cough. She could hear them knocking at the door now. Muffled voices asking if she were ok, if she needed help. She even heard Mrs Molde, telling someone how something hadn't been right for a while. She ignored them; she knew that their words would soon change. She knew that soon the calls wouldn't be for her concern. Instead, they would be to push the button, push the button, push the button. They were all in on it. How could she not have noticed before?

She thought of Mark and knew in her heart that he was dead. Something inside her just knew it to be true. He would be just like the rest of them, like Jane, like Bob, like her mother and father, like her career. Like her life. She heard snatches of voices at her door, probing, quizzing.

'Threw her computer out of the window...'

'Are you alright Miss Browning?'

'Her agent just died...'

'Always talking to herself…'

'I'm going to break down the door and come in'

'Someone should call the police'

She ignored them. She no longer cared. She stared at the TV. There was some kind of televised magic show on screen taking place from the Great Wall of China. The presenters of the show were speaking to each other, but in her mind, they were telling her to push the button. Taking another long drink of the warming alcohol, this time, the burn not quite as hot on her throat, she smiled to herself.

'You win,' she said as she flipped open the lid of the wooden box.

ERASE ALL

She liked the simplicity of those words. She liked the way they rolled off the tongue. Taking another final drink, she set the bottle down on the table. The pounding on her door was louder now, and more intense. It sounded like they were trying to come in.
 'Don't bother, I know what you are going to say,' she whispered to herself. Reaching forward she picked up the box and set it across her knees. No longer afraid, she ran her fingers lightly across the cool plastic. She closed her eyes, then smiled as she pressed the button and waited to see what would happen.

## THE LAST MAN

*'Magic is the sole science not accepted by scientists, because they do not understand it'*
~ Harry Houdini

The world was empty. He was now certain of that as he walked down the centre of the deserted street. It was the same walk he had done for the last twelve months and during that time he hadn't seen a single living person, animal or other living thing. He had expected it would be some kind of nuclear war or asteroid impact that would be responsible for wiping out the population of the planet, but in the end, it had come down to one man. One man and his greed. One man and his petty desire to get one up on his rival.

That man was him.

Guilt was too weak a word to describe how he felt. He had never intended any of this, none of the hurt, none of the death. He was a simple man at heart with the desire only to entertain by doing what he loved, but as he walked he could hear them, somewhere in the distance and coming closer. Coming for him. He wouldn't let them take him, that much was certain. He would do things his own way and let the higher power (if one existed) to judge him.

He shouldered his way into the building, walking down the empty hallway and bypassing the elevators. There had been no power for weeks now, but it didn't matter. The stairs would serve well enough. He ascended, ignoring the feeling he was being watched. Seven floors, eight, nine. Still, he climbed, breathing heavily, enjoying the exertion. He reached his destination, the twentieth floor penthouse and opened the door. The magnetic locks were no longer functional so he pushed his way inside. The room was large, and priced way above anything that he would ordinarily be able to afford, but money was useless now, and luxury was just a word from a world that didn't exist anymore. He paused to catch his breath, looking around the huge apartment. Deep red carpets, marble walls with gold trim. Someone rich existed here at some point. But for now, it was his. He went to the bathroom, striding past the huge marble tub big enough for five people and looked at himself in the mirror.

Gaunt face, long unwashed hair, heavy beard, Haunted

eyes. Always a man to pride himself on his appearance, at least before the incident, he had let himself go. Suck trivial things didn't matter, not anymore. Reaching into his pocket, he pulled out the small Dictaphone and held it to his lips, before pressing the record button.

'My name is Rick Jones, and I am the last man on earth.'

He hesitated for a moment, licking his lips and then went on.

'It's my fault. Everything that happened is down to me. I interfered with something I didn't understand and couldn't control and...'

He pressed the stop button, overcome with emotion. Tears fall and gather in his beard. He often gets like this. Some days are better than others, but often, the guilt becomes too much to bear. Composing himself, he depressed the record button again.

'I tried to put it right of course I did, and if anyone should happen to find this if anyone is out there, then please know I'm sorry.'

He switched off the recorder and walked to the main room and across to the huge glass fronted wall which leads out onto the balcony. He slid it aside and stepped out, the cold air biting at his body. He looked at the streets below and for a second imagined he could see a thriving hive of activity. Cars honking and jostling for position, people scurrying to and from their places of work. But the illusion lasts a mere split second and although there are cars they are still and silent, husks of dead steel. And of course, there were no people. The wind drops he thinks he can hear them again, that horrible high pitched sound, the sound of his coming death. He hurried back inside, closing the sound out and sitting on the large white sofa. He set the recorder on the table and presses the record button.

'I don't have much time. I want to tell it, to tell it my way how it happened. You might wonder what I am. If I'm a terrorist like Osama Bin laden or some kind of crazed world leader with a vision of a race of super humans. The answer would be no. but I am a murderer. And the scale of my crime dwarfs the combined efforts of both of those evils beasts. Before all of that, before the death, and the guilt I was just like anybody else. A normal man with a gift to entertain. But I lost sight of that. I lost what was important, and because of that, we are here now. I am or was an illusionist, a magician, an entertainer, and I was good. Really good. I don't say it with arrogance or ego, but with honesty. You need to understand, you need to know what happened. This is the story of how the world came to an end.'

## TWO

The stage was hot, and the lights shone into his eyes, too brightly for him to see the audience who he knew waited with bated breath. He flicked his eyes to the right to his rival, then to the show presenter who stood poised with his microphone, indulging in the long overused extended pause. The show was another brainchild of some too wealthy executive who didn't think the public had seen enough reality shows. It was much the same format as other shows of its kind, only this wasn't for singers or variety acts, this one was for illusionists. For the last twelve weeks, Rick and fourteen other hopefuls from the thousands who applied had been whittled down week by week, and now in front of a global audience of millions it had come to this moment, the announcement of the winner. He was confident, his trick, a variation on the great Harry Houdini's famous Chinese Water torture cell had been met with rapturous applause and glowing praise from the judges. He was sure it should be enough to win, but as he cast his eyes to his rival, a young Yorkshire man called Andy Levine, who had a more than a passing resemblance to a huge, prehistoric bird with his gangly arms, long nose, and small mouth. Andy's trick had also been impressive, his own version of the famous Penn & Teller bullet catch trick. It was good, but Rick was certain that his was better. At last the Show presenter was ready to put one of them out of their misery.

Rick lost.

The crowd booed and the judges shook their head but the result stayed the same. Andy Levine won, and catapulted his career to the stratosphere. Rick slipped off the radar. He still worked, he made a decent living playing clubs and pubs, but whenever he saw his gangly bird like rival on the television, he felt a stab of rage and jealousy spike within him. It should have been him. He knew it, and he was sure Andy Levine knew it too. For the next year, their lives grew further apart. Andy became one of those celebrity faces that seem to be on every television program under the sun, Rick, on the other hand, struggled to make ends meet and was close to losing his one bedroom apartment which was far from luxurious as it was. Just when it seemed that he would be forced to give up the keys and be declared homeless, Rick was commissioned to write a serialised newspaper article about the history of magic from its very inception to its modern day. He didn't want to do it, but he was offered enough money to pay the rent for another month and agreed. Although he knew the common history of the business, he was determined to give a full and in depth report, and so it was one warm Saturday morning in June of 2011 that he made his way to the library and set about his research. For the next week, he read, and researched and was beginning to form the basis of an excellent article when he stumbled upon the red leather bound book.

He looked at it on the shelf, pushed back into the corner and covered in a thick layer of dust. Something within him, a quiver of uneasiness made him reluctant to touch it, but he found himself reaching out anyway, taking the huge book and laying it on the table. The binding was a deep maroon colour with faded gold edging. The front read one word embossed in gold.

Heka.

Suddenly hot and uncomfortable and with his heart racing in his chest, he opened the book. That ancient, secret aged paper smell filled his nostrils as he began to look at the words, or more accurately symbols that filled the page from edge to edge, margin to margin.

Some looked like Egyptian hieroglyphs, others ancient Greek or Latin. The words seemed to be a jumble of the three. Part of him realised that any attempt to translate it would take even an expert on languages a lifetime, never mind an ordinary man of average intelligence like him, however, a voice deep within him compelled him to at least try. He looked at the book again, and noticed that it had no library plastic binding, nor did it have the paper index stuck to the inside front page which told the reader who had checked out the book before him it seemed as if it didn't belong there. Rick glanced around the cavernous library, for some reason filled with paranoia and a giddy cocktail of fear and excitement. He decided that he would at least try, and would check it out and study it at home.

Approaching the counter, he placed the leather book on the desk along with a book on ancient Egyptian hieroglyphs, and a second volume about medicinal magic printed in the early nineteenth century. He couldn't take his eyes from the book. The librarian stamped the hieroglyph book and the medicinal magic book. He waited for her to pick up the red book but she paid it no attention, instead setting the two stamped books on top of the red book and pushing them towards him. He thanked her and picked up the three books, feeling like a criminal even though he had made no attempt to hide the book he left the library quickly, anxious to delve into his studies.

THREE

The deadline for his article passed, and even though he had half written a very articulate piece, he barely noticed. Much in the same way that he barely noticed when his telephone line as disconnected and when the final reminders and notice of legal action letters began to fall through his letterbox. He was lost. The main room of his apartment now resembled a huge and impressive research space. Charts of hieroglyphs and ancient symbols were pinned to every wall and the large corner desk which until he had discovered the red book had housed only his telephone was now deep with research. Here was where he spent his days, hunched over the desk, ignoring the unwashed smell of his own sweaty body, and doing his best to ignore the dull headache from the efforts of his research. The first days had seemed like an impossible task, translating the symbols one at a time, trying to put them into some kind of coherent order. Six weeks passed, and then it was twelve, and still he researched, sometimes spending twenty or more hours hunched over the desk. During that time Andy Levine performed what was called the world's greatest illusion when he made the White House vanish. It was televised to a global audience and after it was done (and the presidential property restored) Andy received a personal handshake and thanks from the President himself. Rick paid it no attention.

Five months passed, and Rick's apartment was more like a hovel. Papers and books filled every surface, and flies buzzed and dived around the overfilled waste bins and plates of mouldering, half eaten food. But Rick didn't care as finally, he was beginning to understand. Certain symbols and phrases were beginning to make sense to him. Some passages he could read without referring to his myriad of textbooks and research material. It was only when he began to put the words together that the meaning became clear. Exhausted after ten hours translating the red book, Rick stood and stretched, rubbing his tired eyes. He has become gaunt, and his face now sported an itchy, patchy beard. Moving aside a pile of papers and notes from the armchair, he sat and closed his eyes trying to will the headache away. He is aware that he isn't getting enough sleep, yet it still won't come. His mind is too active. Instead, he stared at the wall, trying to digest the stream of information from the book. Something catches his eye and breaks his concentration. A mouse. It is small and brown, and walking across the back of the room, keeping close to the skirting board as it sniffs at the fleshy remains of a brown, discarded apple core. He smiled to himself for the first time in what feels like an age and watched as the mouse continues to assess the viability of eating the food in front of it. As he watches his eyes begin to feel heavy, his exhaustion catching up to him. He closes his eyes but still imagines he can see the mouse, standing in the endless space of his mind's eye, whiskers twitching as it sniffs at the vast empty void.

The symbols come quickly. They swirl and skitter, duck, and dive and explode into glorious colours, forming new words and symbols which then interlock, and point to other symbols and shapes and phrases. They dance around the mouse, which continues its oblivious sniffing. He begins to read, snatches of the phrases he understands, others he finds he can read even though he doesn't consciously know them. The feeling is of euphoria, of being pulled along by some great, primal force of nature. The words swirl around the mouse, enveloping it and then like switching off a television. His mind's eye goes blank, symbols and mouse alike gone. He wakes with a start, heart thundering in his chest.

The apple core is where it was when he closed his eyes but the mouse had gone. Leaping out of the chair, he flicked his gaze from corner to corner, looking for any possible escape route, but couldn't see one that the mouse could have taken so quickly. He contemplated the enormity of what he may have done but immediately stamped it out. He couldn't be certain. He realised that he could be getting over excited about something that was, in reality, nothing at all but coincidence. Still, he knew a way to be certain. With an enthusiasm that had been absent for some time, he grabbed his coat and headed out of the door.

FOUR

The second mouse was larger than the one that had (or had not) vanished from his room, but he thought it would do the job just fine. Housed in a large plastic enclosure, he was satisfied the mouse would remain contained for the duration of his experiment. He set the enclosure on the table, sat in his chair and took a deep breath, then closed his eyes. This time, the symbols came almost immediately—just as quickly and with the same intensity as before. He concentrated on keeping the mouse in the blank space of his mind's eye, holding it in place as the words ducked, dived, and swirled. Then as before, it went blank.

He kept his eyes closed and counted to five, knowing the next few seconds could define his future. Taking a deep breath, he dared to look.

The plastic enclosure was on the table as he had left it. He took inventory. Circular blue food container, a layer of sawdust in the bottom, water bottle clipped to the side of the cage. All was present apart from the enclosure's resident. He looked around the room, wondering if it had escaped. But the lid of the container was still closed and escape was impossible. Not quite able to believe his own eyes he opened the lid of the container, pushing his fingers around in the sawdust. He knew the mouse wouldn't be able to hide in such a thin layer, but he checked anyway. He needed to be sure.

Satisfied he closed the lid and took a step back. There was no question. The mouse had disappeared. He had always expected that eureka moment to be accompanied by excitement and elation, but for him the enormity of what he had done made his legs feel weak, and he could do no more than flop in his favourite chair by the fireplace. It dawned on him that he had achieved the impossible. Even he didn't believe what he had done, or more importantly know how he had done it. He tried to recall the symbols, the numbers and the words but already they were gone—fading away like the snatches of a dream at the moment of waking. Although he wasn't sure what he had tapped into or how he knew he had somehow blurred the line between possible and impossible. Already he was thinking about how he could use it, and how he could develop the illusion that would get him the recognition he deserved. The mouse reappeared an hour later. Rick had been deep in thought about the enormity of what he had done when he heard it scurrying around in the plastic container. He lunged up and hurried over, lifting the mouse out and almost dropping it due to his hands shaking so much. It appeared to be healthy and although he was no vet, it looked to be showing no ill effects of its disappearance. This time, he did whoop and cheer and placed the mouse back in its container. (He retired it from a life of experimentation and kept it as a pet, naming it Houdini.) Although he was optimistic by the reappearance of the mouse, he was dismayed to find that upon trying to repeat his experiment with a second rodent (third if you counted the initial escapee) this time a black and white one which he christened Herman, he couldn't do it. He closed his eyes and tried to concentrate, to will the words into existence to no avail. Dismayed, he opened his eyes and looked at the container and Herman looked back with his whiskers twitching and his bug eyed rodent stare. The next two weeks were an exercise in frustration, as no matter what he tried to do to replicate the incident he was unable to will the numbers and symbols into existence. He was close to giving up altogether when he made the breakthrough that would change his life forever. Following another failed attempt to make the symbols and words appear, he had wilted into his chair and took a long sip of coffee, then glanced over to Houdini, who had since been upgraded to a much larger enclosure.

'Help me out here Houdini. Tell me what to do.' He

had said to the mouse, which was far too busy cleaning itself in its nest to pay him any attention. He glanced back to Herman who was still on the desk in his enclosure. The mouse looked at him, sniffing at the air and wondering when he too got to retire to a life of luxury like that of his fellow rodent Houdini.

'I'm working on it Herman, I'm working on it.' Rick said in response to the unasked question. He leaned back and closed his eyes allowing his body to sink further the seat. He was close to sleep when they reappeared. The symbols, the words. They flowed slowly at first and from left to right across his closed eyes, then they started to veer off, come in from different angles, words writing on top of words, symbols interlinking and pointing to other words that exploded into kaleidoscopes of colour, which formed their own words and symbols. He began to read, forming sentences, speaking them under his breath. As before he felt more pulled along by some unseen force than in control. The words and symbols built to a crescendo and then stopped. Heart racing, Rick opened his eyes.

Herman was gone.

He leaped from his chair and danced around the room,

the weeks of stress gone.

'Ha-ha! I get it now Houdini! I know how to do it! I was trying too hard! The key is to relax—Relax and Let the mind do the work!'

Ecstatic, he waited for Herman to return and as expected he reappeared an hour later. Rick saw it happen this time. The air in the cage seemed to twist and warp and buckle, and then there he was. It looked like a cheap Hollywood special effect but it was real. With his adventure complete, Herman too was retired to chez Houdini and Rick was left with what to do with his new found gift. The process had become easier the more he did it. Buoyed by the excitement of his antics with the mice, he started to test the method on larger animals. Cats and dogs went and reappeared just as easily and with no ill effects. The process wasn't just limited to living objects as he found he could shift static things too. His television, his chair. Each time he drifted into that strange, pulled along state driven by the symbols and numbers he felt he understood a little more—even though every time he opened his eyes he would always be overcome with that forgetful waking dream feeling. He had even tried to write some of them down, but the half-remembered words and shapes seemed wrong on paper and held neither meaning nor power. He set up two video cameras and began to record his experiments, watching the tapes back in awe as he made various things in his home vanish to wherever it is that they went. Excited, he began to draw out plans for his master illusion, quickly realising that the previous limits no longer applied. As he grew bolder, he began to focus on vanishing increasingly large and more complex objects. First a horse grazing alone in a field, then his beaten old Ford, (which he half hoped wouldn't re appear in the garage once he had made it vanish.) Just like the others he had closed his eyes and pictured the item, imagining it existing in the solid space in his mind's eye and then relaxing, awaiting the words and symbols which would come swirling, ducking and diving, wrapping around the object until it would disappear from his mind's eye and the real world both. In every instance, they would return showing no ill effects of their journey to wherever it was that they went. The word vengeance began to pop into Ricks mind, and over the next days was joined by other words. Retribution. Justice. Revenge. Satisfied with his ability to make anything he set his mind to vanish, he started to think of the best way to apply it in order to showcase his new found skills to the world. He would be bigger than Houdini, More famous than Copperfield. He would show the world he was just as good if not better than Andy Levine. He knew in order to do it, he would need an illusion so spectacular that the world would be left in no doubt. But first, he had to do one more thing. He had to perform the experiment on himself.

FIVE

He wasn't sure what would happen when he put himself on the screen in his mind and willed the symbols to come. He was certain that it wouldn't even work anyway, but sure enough as the intensity and speed of the symbols increased, he began to feel a lightness in his stomach and a tingling of his fingertips. The symbols intensified and as they approached the crescendo he felt his stomach lurch—it was the same sort of feeling as when you drive a car over a dip in the road too quickly, then his ears popped and he knew he had arrived. He wasn't sure what to expect when he opened his eyes, but the reaction wasn't one he had anticipated. He was decidedly underwhelmed.

The world was much the same, although there were

subtle differences. The air had a coppery taste and everything seemed dull and washed out. He had made himself vanish inside his apartment and he guessed that he had arrived in the other world in the exact same place, although the apartment in this world (or dimension if that was what it was) didn't exist. Instead, he arrived on a barren plateau, which dropped away to a thin, dirty river through what would have been the road leading to the centre of town. It reminded him of the way an old house smells that has been closed up for too long, a musky, decayed smell. The breeze ruffled his hair as he stood in a new world which so far as he could tell was empty. He walked, aimlessly but never straying too far away from his starting point. It was twilight and as he looked to the skies he saw constellations that were unknown to him and marvelled as the moon drifted into view from behind the cloud cover, unlike the regular moon of the other earth, this one sported two small moons of its own. He saw no plant life and no sign of anything living. As the hour approached and full darkness came with it, he heard the sound. It was a horrific high pitched noise like fingernails scraping down a chalkboard, or an errant knife scratching against a plate. Unease prickled within him and he glanced over the broken and craggy horizon towards the direction where the sound was coming, and he saw them. Winged things silhouetted against the moon, moving towards him with the undulating motion of a snake. Those sounds again, enough to raise gooseflesh on his arms and sweat to run down his forehead. They were coming towards him as if they could sense him, or smell him. His hour was up, and he waited with clenched fists as his fingers began to tingle and his stomach vaulted. The world grew bright and he closed his eyes, and then he was back, in the world he knew, the one which seemed now so vibrant, so safe. The sound of the winged things stayed with him for many days, and he knew he could never again send anything to that place. Not with those things, even if it did mean that he would never have his revenge, nor his time in the spotlight. But time makes things seem less dangerous, and as days gave way to weeks, he had gone from not ever doing it again, to performing the feat only on an inanimate object during daylight hours. ( he suspected that the winged things were nocturnal) besides, he reasoned to himself that everything he had sent had come back safe, and he would only need to do it once in order to get his well-deserved recognition. He was set, and after shaving and cutting his hair, he called his former manager to make the arrangements. He had something spectacular planned.

SIX

When the press release was issued stating that he was going to make a section of the Great Wall of China disappear the world went crazy. The red tape had been difficult to wade through, but with the help of a hotshot lawyer named Fife and a thoroughly unpleasant broker who managed to swing the insurance called Robinson, contracts were signed and authority given by Horoshimo Mashima, who was the senior president of the Chinese Heritage Management Bureau. Internet forums buzzed with speculation, and Rick was thrust from obscurity back into the limelight, and in high demand for TV interviews and radio appearances. Slowly he released more details. After the section of wall had been vanished, a selection of volunteers chosen at random would be able to walk from one side to the other through the space that the wall once occupied. During the entire media circus Andy's representatives had remained silent, apart from releasing a short statement saying that like the rest of the world, they would be watching with great interest to see what his respected rival was able to accomplish. It was standard public relations stuff of course, and Rick would have bet his life that privately they were furious and with good reason. The day rolled near and the excitement built.

The section of the wall selected was a fifty-foot length in the northern Juyongguan area, and with assistance from the Chinese government, it had been sectioned off by barriers behind which the huge live crowd had gathered. Down at the base of the wall, a temporary scaffold floor had been put in place on both sides of the structure. It was here that the people who would have the opportunity to cross through the empty space once the wall had vanished. The people were chatting amongst themselves as their excitement grew. Although they weren't needed for any reason other than to add to the drama, giant red curtains had been set up and draped over the selected section of wall, covering it completely. Finally, after months of preparation, everything was ready.

Even though nobody knew it at the time, the last day on earth had arrived.

Back in the present from his vantage point high above the city, Rick glanced at the Dictaphone which glared back at him, the red light on its front that confirmed that it was recording casting its accusing eye towards him. He looked to the window and shivered as he realised how late it had become. The last sliver of light was falling below the horizon, and the room was now cast into deep, angular shadows.

 Now with the time to think it over, he was sure he knew what had happened and what had gone wrong. Everything started according to plan. The crowds were hushed, and the television cameras poised as he stood by the base of the wall, eyes closed and arms extended out to the side (for no other reason than to enhance the drama.) a dramatic, orchestral score played as subtly hidden smoke machines covered the stage and wall in its artificial mist. Rick was oblivious to it all. He had the section of wall encased in its red cloth fixed in his mind and was waiting for the words and symbols to dance their unique patterns in his mind's eye. Maybe it was the nerves or the excitement, he wasn't sure. But as the words increased in speed, he found his thoughts drifting, his concentration breaking. He thought about the public, the worldwide reaction to his incredible feat, he thought about how popular and famous he would become. The section of wall in his mind began to warp and shift, and then vanish like a bad TV signal. Instead, he saw himself in the centre of the words in his head, receiving the praise of the world, shaking hands with millions, more popular than the Pope. If he had only been able to stop then, to take a moment to compose himself and try again he might have been able to fix it, but he knew the process didn't work that way. He knew once it began he would be a passenger dragged along to the conclusion. He forced himself to concentrate on the wall and push everything else out of his mind, but he couldn't rid the selfish images of his worldwide fame and the glory of his vindication. He panicked, and instead of letting the words flow naturally, he tried to make them move, to manipulate them to give him time to get himself together. It was an intense struggle as he tried to undo what was happening, the image in his mind shifted repeatedly from the wall to him, to the population of the world, each melting and fading into each other. He shifted symbols, pulling them away when they tried to interconnect, wiping away the colourful explosions. There was a high pitched whine that seemed to come from deep within the centre of his head. It was almost unbearable, and he was on the verge of screaming when his mind's eye went blank, and he knew something had gone wrong.

Silence.

His stomach flipped and he swallowed an acid tasting burp. He didn't want to, he didn't want to see what had happened but he forced himself to open his eyes. The first thing he saw was the wall. It was mostly still in place apart from a large diagonal section which was missing. The red curtains had been sliced through and were hanging loose, fluttering in the gentle breeze. He could see the cross section of the ornate stonework which looked like it had been cut away with laser precision. It was then that his heart sank and he noticed the silence.

SEVEN

Maybe it was because he had tried to mess with the symbols or change something so powerful and already set in motion that he had damaged whatever power was at work, but whatever it was, something had gone wrong and the two thousand people who had been on and around the stage were gone. He waited for an anxious hour that seemed to last a lifetime for them to reappear, and as each moment ticked by, he was unable to shut the image of those winged, flying things out of his mind. The first hour came and went, and then another. It was only when dawn broke the next day and he awoke cold and bleary eyed on the temporary stage floor that he realised that they weren't coming back. He had broken the process and cast two thousand people to some bizarre mirror earth and had no way of bringing them back. Almost a year had passed since that day and he hadn't encountered a single human being since that day. There was nothing left. No bodies, no sign of anyone ever being there at all. It seemed that People had been going about their daily lives one minute, and had been erased from existence the next. He half hoped that it may have just been isolated to those who were present at the site of the illusion, but he had since spent countless weeks knocking on doors, crisscrossing the country and searching for signs of life other than his own and eventually had to concede that it was pointless. There were other signs too, signs that were too awful to consider. Like the day he drove out to the airport and waited for any sign of an incoming flight. On some level, he knew he wouldn't see those tell-tale contrails in the air, or hear the angry sound of tires on asphalt as a 747 came in to land but he still hoped. But hope was only good for so long and he had to accept the fact that he was responsible for the death of—how many? How many people were in the world? His mind boggled as he chewed on the number and tried to put it into a perspective he could comprehend.

Seven billion.

Such an overwhelming number. How can a person live with themselves when they were responsible for the end of the world? He had tried to bring them back, but he had only ever learned to send things. He had no idea where to start when it came to bringing things back. He couldn't even refer to his research, as his books and other notes were thousands of miles away on another continent. For weeks and months, he had tried anyway. But eventually was forced to give up. By disturbing the symbols and moving them around without knowing what he was doing, he thought he must have broken something. Something vital that made the process work. He considered the fact that his initial success was no more than stumbling around in the dark and by chance finding a light switch. Against all odds, his fumbling had found a doorway to something secret, something sacred which he didn't understand. Something that he had then broken and now had no idea how to fix. One thing he knew for certain was that whatever he had broken in the symbols when he sent the seven billion inhabitants of the world to that dry, washed out imitation place, he had left some kind of doorway open to let them, the flying winged things in and although it had taken them a while, they had found him.

He stood and picked up the Dictaphone carrying it with him outside to the balcony. The wind had picked up now and he could definitely hear it, the horrific high pitched screeching. They were close. He held the Dictaphone to his lips, somehow able to stop them trembling.

'And so, that is the story of how the world came to an end. I make no excuses, and no words can ever express my sorrow for what I have done.'

He hooked his leg over the balcony, lowering himself over the other side where he clung to the rail with one hand, clutching the Dictaphone to his face with the other as an immense shadow passed overhead.

'My name is Rick Michael Jones and I truly am sorry. Please, forgive me.'

He depressed the stop button and tossed the Dictaphone through the open balcony door. The screams were loud now, and he can hear the leathery snap of their wings. Rick took a deep breath and stepped out into oblivion. It snatched him out of the air before he has fallen fifty feet.

The last man on earth was dead.

www.ingramcontent.com/pod-product-compliance
Lightning Source LLC
LaVergne TN
LVHW012031070526
838202LV00056B/5463